THE YEAR OF THE
GHOST

ISBN: 979 8 45781 571 1

Cover by Spiffing Covers

Inside pages by Carol Turl Graphic Design

Author photograph by Roddy Paine Photographic Studios

Dedication

To my family, with love and thanks for all those wonderful Welsh holidays together.

Acknowledgements

With very special thanks to Carys Briddon for all her help with the Welsh location and with local and family history; diolch yn fawr.

Thanks also to Lorna Fergusson at Fictionfire for her invaluable insights and to the Irregular Writers Collective for their advice and encouragement.

To the people of West Wales

Sincere apologies for my cheek in wrenching the village of Bont Goch, where my father spent his childhood, from its rightful place and dragging it to a fictional position closer to Llangrannog. Hopefully the upside will be that its true, glorious location remains a well-kept secret.

THE YEAR OF THE
GHOST

SOPHIE KERSEY

CHAPTER ONE

2011 Day 1, Saturday

Wales. It was the best fortnight of the year. Hal had been going every August his whole life, and so had Mum since she was ten. Hal was twelve now so that was a lot of holidays.

That first morning, he thought the only problem would be Imogen going on this blinking Sixth Form Trip instead.

'Hal, don't look at me like that – I can't *not go* to Tanzania,' she said, flying round her room making a drama of last-minute packing. Dad was waiting to take her to her friend Tania's for a lift to the airport.

'I'm sure they can build these school toilets without you,' Hal said, although he thought she probably would be a good builder. Imogen was tall and slim, but awesome at arm wrestling.

'Yeah but *duh*! Then I wouldn't get to see Africa,' she said. Hal remembered her reading the list of trips – she could have gone to Paris or Rome. When she chose Tanzania, Dad gave her a 'that's my girl' high five.

'Aren't you even sorry you're missing Wales?'

She flicked back her crinkly blond hair and looked at her packing list. 'Look, you'll all have a lovely time and… Shit, where's my kagoule?' There was a flurry of searching and swearing until she found it and stuffed it in her rucksack. 'Seriously, can't I do something I haven't done every year since I was *born*?' she said, yanking on the drawstring. 'I need to break out a bit, Hal. I'm seventeen!'

That gave him a strange feeling. You couldn't grow out of Wales, could you? Grand (their grandad) still went and he was seventy-eight.

'Well, suit yourself. You won't be so keen when the massive spiders get you,' he said, but his voice had gone all flat.

'Imogen!' Mum called from the bottom of the stairs. 'Dad's waiting…'

'If you'd let me *think* straight, I might be quicker!' Imogen shouted.

'It's not us… You know Grand. If we don't leave on the dot

there'll be ructions at Membury,' Mum said.

Hal caught Imogen looking at him, her frown softening. 'I am actually sorry I can't come to Wales,' she said.

'Yeah,' Hal said. 'You'll miss the ructions.'

Imogen not going did have an upside: it meant Hal's best friend Josh could go instead. Hal opened the door to him soon after Dad took Imogen. Josh's dark hair looked newly chopped, his Star Wars t-shirt bulging a bit over his belly. 'Hey,' he said, all cool but with excitement in his greenish eyes. He dragged a battered suitcase onto the doorstep and hitched up two backpacks that were falling off his shoulders.

In the car, Mum kept turning round to the boys in the back seat, on a mission to make Josh feel part of things. She told him to call her and Dad 'Carrie and Chris'.

'OK' said Josh. He never actually called them anything.

'The house we stay in is called Noddfa,' Mum explained, blue eyes bright, sunglasses perched on top of her straight brown fringe. 'Hal's Grand – my Dad – was evacuated there during the war.' Mum had just turned forty but she went running and ate health food so she wouldn't get middle-aged. She was wearing a nice top today that showed her arms.

'Is it true the signs are in gobbledygook?' Josh asked.

'Welsh!' Hal shoulder-barged him. 'I can't believe you've never been to Wales!'

'I'm sure Josh has been to lots of other places,' Mum said.

Josh shoved back. 'I have.'

'We go every year,' Hal said. 'Apart from last year.' The memory wafted across the morning like a cloud going over the sun. There had been some murky explanation about Grand's cataract operation. 'This is the first time we've brought someone who isn't family.'

'Not quite,' Mum said. 'One year when I was a teenager, Grand's friend Nick and his wife came.' She chuckled. 'We talk about past years all the time. Don't we, Chris?'

2

Dad nodded. 'We'll drive you mad.' He had his favourite t-shirt on, with a picture of some band he'd liked in the eighties. Dad had short, sandy-coloured curls, a bit thin on top, and a narrow face, usually lit up by his cheeky smile.

'Like the year we found the Secret Beach,' Hal said. He tried to catch Dad's eye in the driving mirror but he was staring ahead.

'Or the year Grand had a row with that man at the café.'

'This'll be The Year Josh Came,' Josh said, dead serious, as though it was the title of an epic film. Hal let out a big belly laugh. Josh looked surprised, but then he started too. Soon they were rocking about on the back seat, helpless.

The first stop was Membury Services, where they always met up with Hal's grandparents. As they reached the top of the escalator, Hal saw them fussing over saving seats with bags and newspapers. Grand had thin grey hair, but his eyebrows were thick and dark. He was in a check shirt and baggy old-person jeans for the journey. Grandma Lisa always said he had stayed 'with-it' because of his years teaching young people. She had had her rounded white hairstyle pouffed up for the holiday and was elegant in trousers and a lacy blouse. Her face creased up in a smile when she saw Hal. He made himself hang back with Josh instead of rushing over to them like when he was little.

'Grand has smuggled in cakes again,' said Grandma Lisa in a theatrical whisper. A tuppaware box of shop scones spread with butter was passed round below the table.

'I'm not paying the prices in here.' Grand glared round at the staff in case they dared to make something of it.

'Thelma was saying they had a Full English here,' said Grandma Lisa when they were all settled down.

'Thelma who?'

'You know – I went to church with her,' she said, nibbling a scone.

Grand rolled his eyes at Hal. 'Your grandmother has started going to church.'

'David, it was just a couple of times…' Grandma Lisa said.

'A load of old claptrap that anyone with an ounce of sense would see through,' Grand finished. People at the next table turned to look. Grandma Lisa brushed crumbs into the tuppaware and looked out the window. 'I think it might be brightening up for us.'

'The opium of the people,' said Grand.

Carrie checked her phone for the umpteenth time as they got back in the car. 'Was she really excited?' she asked Chris.

'Mm?'

'Imogen. Was she excited?'

'You know she was.'

'When you dropped her off, though?'

'Yes. Of course.' She'd been expecting him to do an impression. Usually, he was the silliest of them all on the journey, making a deliberate mess of Welsh place names and singing 'We're all going on a summer holiday' until Imogen shouted at him to stop. As they rejoined the motorway, he was frowning, perhaps at the traffic.

Carrie turned to the boys – what an odd couple they were: Josh plump and wriggly, Hal lean and still with clear hazel eyes. He was tanned already, his mousy hair sun-lightened. 'Make the most of your phones!' she said. 'There's no signal at the house, Josh. And Grand doesn't like it if we go off to find one.'

'Is he in charge, then?' Josh asked.

'He is if we want a peaceful fortnight!' She made a wry face at Chris. He looked blank for a moment, but then smiled.

'It's out in the wilds,' Hal said. 'Miles from anywhere.'

They were crossing the old Severn Bridge: the brown expanse of river stretching below them and the giant cat's cradle of suspension cables above. Just then, the sun broke through, silvering the water and lacing the clouds with brightness.

'What do I tell you?' Carrie said, mimicking her father. 'The sun always comes out for me when I enter Wales.' And in the car up ahead, they saw Grandma Lisa turn round to wave at them, gesturing at the sky.

They stopped as always in Carmarthen for lunch, commandeering a bench in the park while Grand took everyone's sandwich order.

'Bacon and avocado?' he said to Grandma Lisa. 'Why spoil good bacon with something green and slimy?'

'Why ask if he doesn't want to know what I want?' Grandma Lisa said out of the corner of her mouth as Grand and Hal set off down the hill towards the baker's. 'You keep peering at that phone, Carrie – have you heard from Imogen?'

'No, nothing! They'll have taken off, won't they, Chris?'

'Hm? Yes, should have done.' He got up to walk around, perhaps needing to stretch his legs.

After lunch, they set off again in convoy and soon the hills all around them grew greener and higher. The cars wound through towns painted in pastel colours, past Red Lion pubs, farms and churches, and got stuck for ages behind a tractor. Hal hailed the bright lights of Aberystwyth for Josh's sake, pointing out the award-winning toilets, the Vale of Rheidol railway and Grandma Lisa's favourite Matalan. After hours of hedgerows, bunting for agricultural shows, cowpat smells and rutted lanes getting more and more narrow, they arrived at the tiny sign for Bont Gogh.

'Grand's village!' Hal said, 'It means Red Bridge.' And here they were after two whole years, driving past a little row of houses and bungalows. In the middle was a grey-stone building with a small bell tower, its front covered in scaffolding. 'That's the school Grand went to. In the war.'

They gathered speed now – over the bridge and out of the village, and there was the telegraph pole at the turning, where most years you'd see a buzzard perched against the August sky like a holiday emblem. Grand slowed down and sure enough, the hawk sat above them, scanning the fields for a kill.

They made the turn and bumped down the final dusty track, with grass brushing the underside of the cars and fields of cows and sheep on either side. At long last the track took a mini-turn, and there was the house from all their summer dreams: a squat rectangle of grey-brown stone with a slate roof and a newer dormer window looking out over the porch. A pub-style picnic table stood ready on the terrace for sunny mornings and the dark windows gazed down at them with an emptiness waiting to be filled.

'Noddfa,' said Hal.

When Carrie followed her parents in, she caught a musty smell and a chill hush that they would surely chase away with their noise.

'Lovely!' said Grandma Lisa.

There was no Imogen to race Hal to their bedroom. He was showing Josh the way, bumping his case on the stairs. 'You can have the top bunk if you want.'

Carrie was longing to go straight through the hallway and out the back door as she had as a child, but she made herself check there was milk in the fridge, and help the others in with their luggage.

Carrie pulled open the back door and gazed beyond the lush glow of the lawn. Fields of green and straw-yellow rolled towards the sea, the sky, the summer. She sat on the steep steps, inhaling the breezy waft of animals, salt air and hay.

Grand came out and clumped past her. He stood on a lower step, framed in their summer landscape, and she saw that he had got older: his face sinking in on itself in the time away. Beyond him, duck-egg blue arched over a sparkling strip of navy, promising weather she had hardly dared hope for on their first evening here.

'You've got your holiday smile on,' she said.

'There's nowhere like it.'

She was squinting in the light, but thought the smile lifted him and straightened his back, as though the years were falling away to reveal the dark-haired Dad of her childhood, or further back still so that now – any minute – Will and Hilda might call him in for tea.

CHAPTER TWO

2011 Day 1: Saturday

Hal liked having Josh at Noddfa, even if it meant he didn't get the top bunk, which had been his prize every year since he learnt to distract Imogen and make a dash for it. They were just getting settled in when Auntie Ruth's voice came from downstairs. 'That's right, Toby, you stand there gawping while I drag the cases in!'

'Can't a man have a moment to catch his breath?' said Uncle Toby.

'Oh excuse me, I'd forgotten you're completely beyond reproach. Hello, everyone!'

The boys headed downstairs, arriving to laughter and hugging.

Mum's older sister Ruth was bigger all over than her, with much more expensive clothes. She didn't do running or health food – she was too busy being a headteacher. Her brown hair was in a layered do with reddish glints, and her jeans looked way too new to be cool. 'Hello Josh,' she said, when Hal introduced him. 'Welcome to the family holiday. You're very brave joining this lot – I hope you know what you're in for!' Auntie Ruth always said what she was thinking.

'Stop trying to frighten him,' said Uncle Toby, giving Josh one of his public-school handshakes. He came from a posh family but mucked in with the rest of them. He had springy black hair and a tan from golf and was holiday-ready in chinos and a polo shirt.

Hal's cousin Dan, who was sixteen and dressed completely in faded black, said, 'How's it going, Josh,' in his manly growl.

Soon some of them were sitting round the kitchen table while Grand rummaged around looking for the Welsh cakes he'd bought in Carmarthen.

'Toby, where the hell are you?' Auntie Ruth called from upstairs. 'Dan says the attic door won't open.'

Grand had had the attic converted in 1996 when Dan got too big to share with his parents. It was a brilliant room with a sloping ceiling and a view over the track.

'It's locked or something.' Dan's voice came from even further above.

They all followed Grand out into the hallway. 'What do you

mean, it won't open?' he called up the stairs. 'And who would have locked it?'

'It's fine, Toby is sorting it.' Ruth came downstairs raising a 'stop fussing' hand at him. Dan followed behind her.

Soon there were thuds and grunts above. 'It's stuck fast,' called Toby.

'I *told* you,' muttered Dan.

'You'll have to come in with Mummy and Daddy!' said Ruth, chuckling at Dan's horrified face. 'I'll post about it on Facebook!'

'Really helpful,' said Dan from behind his floppy fringe.

'Don't worry, it'll only be for one night,' Carrie told him. 'We'll ask Sue about it in the morning.'

'We might have killed each other by then,' Ruth said. 'Happy holidays, everyone.'

The first evening was sunny and they played cricket in the garden, with Grandma Lisa cheering from the steps. Uncle Toby told everyone that Dan had won his cricket colours at school, but then kept nagging him about his technique. Hal thought Dan was pretty ace already. Mum did her usual – wildly trying to catch the ball and missing or dropping it. Soon even Josh was calling it a 'Mum fumble'. He belted the tennis ball over the fence a gazillion times and kept moaning about going to get it, 'because of the cowpats.' He high-stepped through the grass and went faster past the cows – Hal realised that he was scared of them, but hid his smile. Then Auntie Ruth put the frilly old holiday apron on and made spaghetti bolognese for tea like always.

At bedtime, Hal sneaked up the attic stairs and tried Dan's door again. There was a thick, muffled quiet up there away from the others. He tried to shake the handle, but it wouldn't even wiggle. It felt as though something inside was leaning on it. Or holding it.

He shivered and thudded down to the landing below, where Josh stood in their bedroom doorway in his Pokemon pyjamas.

'Shit! What?!'

'Nothing,' Hal said.

Day 2: Sunday

Josh really liked Grand's cooked breakfast. That was one of Hal's favourite bits of the holiday too, not just eggs and bacon but coming down and finding people in the kitchen: Grandma Lisa really early, then Grand with the frilly apron over his dressing gown ready for his cook-a-thon, and later Mum and the others coming in dribs and drabs. You sat and chatted and told Grand what you wanted, and eventually everyone was there.

Some days Dad and Hal went for a walk first. They liked to be up and out before anyone else. If they met someone out walking, Dad would grin at Hal and say, 'People! They get bloody everywhere!' But usually it was just the two of them. Wales looked brilliant in the early morning and they'd come back starving.

After breakfast on that first full day, the others went out to get petrol and 'a few bits' and Josh and Hal stayed behind. Hal was writing his holiday journal in the living room and Josh was reading *Match*. Grand had said to him earlier, 'Can't we interest you in a book? We've got plenty!' Josh looked like he'd suggested doing maths homework.

He got up now and scooped up Hal's football. 'Kickaround?'

Hal went upstairs to put his notebook away. He could hear the ball bouncing downstairs and was a bit worried for all the family's knick-knacks from past years, which were all over the shelves and bookcases.

When he went down, Josh was in a corner of the living room, wedged behind one of the old armchairs. 'Who are the girls?'

'What?'

Josh pointed into the shadows, where a picture on the wall showed two messy-haired girls in t-shirts and flared jeans, leaning over a low fence. They were feeding lambs with baby bottles. One girl was about Hal's age, with brown hair. She was looking at the camera with an excited smile. The other one was a couple of years younger, fair-haired with loose curls. Her arm was out straight, and she was frowning.

Hal remembered the picture now and pointed. 'That's Mum. And the younger one's Emilia – some cousin I think. She used to

9

come on holiday here. But then her family moved to Dubai or somewhere.'

Josh picked up the football. 'My neighbour went to Dubai. He went jeep racing in the sand dunes. Sounded ace. Hey – you should visit this cousin!'

Hal shrugged. 'I think they lost touch.' It was weird telling family stuff to another person. It all seemed normal to you. He suddenly felt like they should get out in the garden – Grand said the forecast was mixed and you didn't want to miss any sunshine in Wales. The quiet indoors felt stretched tight, like the house holding its breath.

Out of the corner of his eye, he saw a shadow move across the mirror on the wall. He whipped his head round to look.

'What?' said Josh.

'Something moved.'

'That was me, you divvy.'

'No, you're not in the mirror. It was – like a shadow behind me, going over there.'

'Like this..?' Josh held the football in front of him and moved it around.

'No...' Hal waved his arms, but his shadow was nowhere near the flitting grey thing he had seen.

'That – is – weird…' Josh was saying. 'Wait – is this some joke you lot play on other people who come here?'

'No! Something moved from there to there.' Hal wanted the warmth of the sunlight he could see on the lawn. 'Oh, whatever. Let's get outside.' He blundered into the open door to the hallway, banging his knee, then dashed to the back door and hauled it open. Josh's heavy footsteps were close behind him.

They spilled down the steps onto the lawn and stood staring at each other. A seagull shrieked, sailing overhead. Josh's face looked frozen, gawping.

Hal burst out laughing.

'We're freaking out!' Josh cried to the sky.

'I know! I'm scared of a shadow!'

Josh took a deep breath, a hand on his chest. 'It was something paranormal. I get feelings about these things. It's true! Don't you

10

watch *Britain's Most Haunted?* You should, it's epic.' When he looked dead serious like that, Hal usually got the giggles – but not now.

'Noddfa's not haunted. I've been coming since I was born.'

He headed for the far end of the lawn, dribbling the football to take his mind off things. He hooked it into the air and did three counts of keepy-uppy, then trapped it under the sole of his trainer. Josh stood, feet apart, jiggling like a goalie waiting for a penalty. Hal took a run-up and side-footed the ball. Josh went to trap it, but it richocheted off his knee. He stumbled after it and let out a laugh. That was the great thing about Josh: he didn't get cross when he was crap at things.

They carried on booting the ball between them, and soon they heard the car coming along the lane and it was time to go in and find their beach stuff for the first day's outing.

As they walked to the cars, Carrie heard Josh say, 'So what's this place we're going to… Clan Grot Nogg?'

'Llangrannog!' Hal pronounced the Welsh as Grand had taught him. 'It's the best ever seaside town.'

'Town's going a bit far!' Ruth said.

'What? It's got two cafés. And a shop. And two pubs!'

Carrie smiled at Hal's loyalty. 'It seems like a bustling metropolis to us because Noddfa's in the back of beyond. It's a village, really. Isnt' it?' She glanced at Chris, usually such a champion of this place. He gave a half-hearted shrug.

Grand set off in front. When they got to Bont Goch, he drove through it at walking pace, and paused in front of the school's low wrought-iron gates. The playground was full of cracks bristling with long grass. On either side were outdoor toilets marked Boys and Girls. The little tower protruding from the scaffolding looked spindly and brittle with age. The church opposite was squat and grey, with a few headstones creeping round to the front from the graveyard.

'Why've we slowed down?' asked Josh.

'To pay tribute to my father's past,' said Carrie with a chuckle.

Beyond the village, they moved parallel to the coast, pulling into stopping places to let on-coming cars pass, catching glimpses of sparkling water through hedgerows. At last they reached the wider road that led downwards into Llangrannog.

It was crowded at the Patio Café, with a queue already forming in front of the array of ice creams. The usual outdoorsy clientele, with sandy dogs and children in wetsuits, were either enticing wasps on the patio, or inside, choosing from the display cabinet of enormous cakes.

They took a table outside, hoping Grand would approve when he came back from the shop. 'We can always move if he's too hot. Or cold,' said Grandma Lisa.

Grand came and sat down and hung his beige jacket over the chair, fussing over the contents weighing down its pockets. He had bought a *Guardian* for himself and a *Telegraph* for Toby and Ruth. 'Bloody Tory rag!' he commented, adding, 'I'd rather have this any day,' as he put down a *Mirror* for Chris.

'Where *is* Dad? 'Carrie asked Hal.

'He went for a quick look up the left-hand cliff.'

'Before coffee?' She was shaded her eyes to peer over at the cliff path. It was some time before she spotted Chris coming back down the cliff road in his old denim jacket, head bent, phone in hand.

'Look at this bollocks!' said Grand, with his glasses on at last, waving at a picture of a royal visit in *The Telegraph*. 'I mean who honestly gives a shit?'

Josh gazed at him. 'My Nan and Grandad love the royals.'

'Freeloading … bloodsucking… chinless bloody aristocrats!'

'Although your grandparents are entitled to their opinion,' Carrie said.

'Hal has something to tell you,' Josh said over their laughter. 'He saw something freaky in the mirror!'

They all looked up from their papers and cake deliberations.

'Yeah, like a shadow moving across behind me. But it wasn't – I mean, we checked everything that might have caused it.'

'Oh! A shiver down my spine!' Grandma Lisa shook her shoulders and pulled her pale blue cardigan tighter.

'You'll believe anything, you will,' said Grand to her. 'It's just a creaky old place, Hal. Riddled with history. But hey, you could write a ghost story!'

'The world's biggest sceptic, but you love a ghost story!' said Grandma Lisa, giving him a gentle push.

'I teach literature!' he said. 'I love Shakespeare, but that doesn't mean I believe there are fairies in the woods!'

Chris finally stepped up onto the patio and pulled up a chair, his hair wind-rumpled, spots of colour in his cheeks. Carrie had expected an excited account of his walk, but Grand was telling him about the *Mirror*, then blaming Grandma Lisa because it had got lost under all the menus.

The owner came over for a chat. 'David! Lisa! And all the crew... I was worried when you didn't come last year!' He waved a waitress over and there was a clamour for scones and caramel apple granny. They all looked so happy when their order arrived that Carrie got her phone out to take a picture.

Afterwards they set up camp on the beach, finding a good space in the shanty town of picnic rugs, windbreaks and pop-up tents. The tide was out and the stones gave way to slick sand, reflecting the shape of the beach's iconic stacked rock. The stream snaked down to the water, glinting in sunshine, though there was cloud bubbling up inland. On either side of the beach, cliffs rose in sedimentary layers, topped with straw-dry grasses.

'We can do bodyboarding,' Hal told Josh, 'dam the stream or explore the caves. Or climb over those rocks to the second beach, or walk up the cliffs...'

'There's everything here for boys,' Grand said when they had grabbed their bodyboards and were running towards the foaming waves.

Ruth poked Dan, sitting beside her on their picnic rug. 'Are you going to rush to do it all?' Carrie remembered previous years when he was up for any sporty exertion, with Toby always coaching him from the sidelines. Dan had grown his hair longer this year and it hung in curtains, parted on the side, so that his head was always slightly cocked. He lay down and put his headphones on.

'I'm going for a quick walk up the right-hand cliff,' Carrie said.

'Chris?' He was lying down with his head in the *Mirror*, but hauled himself to his feet.

'Did you get any nice photos?' she said as they climbed the stone steps leading to the cliff walk.

'Hm?'

'On your walk up the other cliff.'

'Oh – no. I just went for a look.'

'Dad's happy as Larry,' she said. 'When he's not ranting about the royals. Did you see Josh's face? I don't think he's ever met an old person like it!'

They pressed on up the path and paused at the first promontory to look back at the beach. Carrie squinted, trying to pick out the boys from countless figures silhouetted against the sea dazzle between two red flags. 'He's a funny boy, isn't he? The way he comes out with things. And gets so excited. I can see why Hal likes him.'

'He is a bit quirky.' Carrie lingered to take pictures, but Chris continued upwards. Carrie was aware of the beep of a text coming to his phone as they left the dead zone of the beach and climbed into a signal. She spotted Hal and Josh at last and tried to capture them with the zoom.

When she caught up with Chris, he was frowning at his phone.

'Text?' she said.

'It's nothing.' He strode onwards. She felt a flash of irritation – she was breathless from chasing him. But perhaps he resented the text intruding from the outside world. This was the walk he always said he imagined when he wanted to relax.

She took a few quick strides and walked at his side. 'Hal's always made friends with characters, hasn't he? He's like me. He likes passionate people.'

She took his arm, but after a moment, he turned away and continued up the path. 'Are you all right?' she said to his back.

'Of course, just…'

She cut in, 'You're very quiet.'

'I'm just … unwinding.'

They reached the next viewing spot, where they could see the second beach down to the right, its warm-brown sand mottled with cloud reflections. Chris stared out at the great expanse of bay where they sometimes spotted dolphins. He had been working such long hours, Carrie thought, staying late day after day to get paperwork done. He never seemed to get it finished.

'From teaching, or special needs coordinating?'

'Just… the inspection. And the usual stuff.' He glanced at her. 'What? It's fine. Just things like… those girls I told you about who weren't allowed to go on the school trip…' Carrie had a vague memory of him mentioning it – she'd been distracted by Imogen's packing. 'What was I supposed to tell the parents? Sorry but your kids have to stay behind at school while their friends go on this great trip – because they've got needs we can't cater for?'

They walked along a stony path lined with hawthorn bushes bent, hag-like, away from weather Carrie never witnessed – she had only ever been to Wales in August. She had meant to turn back to rejoin the family – but now Chris was in full flow.

'Then there's Tyrone, the one with Asperger's. He said he was being picked on, and no one listened because he has a history of kicking off.'

That was fine, Carrie thought, if that was all that was worrying him. He had coped with worst things – you did with his job. There had been that boy with anger issues – Chris had stopped him from banging his head on the wall and he'd complained that he'd been groped. Carrie had lain awake at night for weeks. She had urged Chris to contact his union. But it had never gone any further.

The surface of the sea was crisscrossed by the marks of winds and currents; its blues ranging from turquoise to purple. A butterfly flitted over wildflowers at their feet. It was on the tip of her tongue to ask again about that text.

'Sorry,' Chris said. 'I guess one grumpy old bugger is enough for you to cope with.'

She leaned her head on his shoulder. 'And Ruth needling Dan… You wonder if he's going to blow sometimes… Thank goodness for Hal. Nothing gets to him does it? Especially here.'

Later she zoomed into the picture she had taken in the café. Chris was the only one not smiling.

CHAPTER THREE

2011 Day 2: Sunday

Josh dared Hal to go right to the back of the cave on Llangrannog beach where it was dank and dark as if the hill has swallowed you. 'You won't, he said, peering in, 'you never will.'

But Hal didn't get scared that easily. Josh made weird noises, trying to freak him out. Then Dan rushed in from the beach in his heavy metal t-shirt and swimming shorts and roared like a maniac. Josh screamed! The little kids outside the cave all scattered, terrified, and the three boys fell about laughing. It was the most lively Hal had seen Dan for ages – maybe Wales brought out the kid in him.

They had chips from the Beach Hut for lunch, then Josh and Hal dammed the stream and Dan mooched around with them.

'Shame about your room!' Hal said.

'Yeah,' Dan said. 'The roof would have been wicked this year!'

The last time they were at Noddfa, the lock on Dan's attic room window had been loose and Dan had wiggled it until it came off. He told Imogen and Hal and they sneaked up there when all the adults were in the back garden. Right outside the window was a flat bit of roof over the porch, and they climbed out and sat there. It was the coolest thing – you could see right down the track, almost to the village.

A few weeks ago, Dan had said to Hal that the secret roof would be a great place to smoke a spliff. He said it as if Hal had known forever that he smoked drugs, but this was the first he had heard of it. He had to act like it was the most normal thing to do in Wales. It wasn't going to happen now anyway. He wasn't sure if he was sorry or relieved.

Hal came downstairs from writing his journal and Grandma Lisa was doing shepherd's pie and peas, which she always did on the first Sunday. Mum was asking if she could help.

'No, it's all under control,' said Grandma Lisa. 'Although you could see what's up with your father – he's agitating about something.'

'Lisa, where are my spare reading glasses?' called Grand in the living room.

16

'*I* don't know, David. Where did you last have them?'

'Well, if I knew that…' He started turning over the sofa cushions. 'You see, I need to be able to read. I can't even do the *Guardian* crossword without them. Not to mention the pile of books I've saved specially for the holiday!'

Auntie Ruth ducked her head behind her own book, and Dan had his headphones in so probably hadn't heard. Dad was staring at the telly, but when Hal looked, it wasn't even on. Hal made a half-hearted show of looking around him for Grand's glasses.

Mum set about searching in all Grand's usual places. 'Are they your only pair?' she said.

'No, it's the spare ones. I've got the main ones, but if they go too, I'm buggered.'

'I'm sure they'll turn up, David,' Grandma Lisa's worried voice came from the kitchen.

'You sit down – I'll keep looking,' Mum said to Grand.

'I can't find my soap saver either. It's like we've got bloody gremlins!' Grand stalked off into their bedroom, which was off the living room.

'Things going missing – that's poltergeist activity,' Josh hissed to Hal. He was sitting in a big wooden chair with arms, bouncing a rubber ball attached to a ping-pong bat. 'Or a ghost. Has anyone died here?'

'I don't know! Don't bring it up.' Auntie Ruth gave Josh one of her Headteacher looks. She didn't believe in anything weird.

Grand came back in and plonked himself down on the sofa. There was a moody silence and Hal thought of Imogen – she had a way of distracting Grand when he was off on one, by asking for his help with the crossword or wanting to learn phrases in Welsh.

'You'll have to start bringing two of everything, Grand,' said Mum.

'I told you, I *have* brought two pairs!'

'Three then. Four, to be sure?'

Grand shook his head in exasperation but the next minute he gave in to a chuckle, so that meant they could all laugh as well. Hal could see this becoming one of their stories: *When Grand Was Ranting*

About His Glasses.

'So, Grand,' Josh said, swinging the ball on its elastic. 'You must know loads of people from olden times who lived here? And maybe died...'

'Oh my goodness, Josh...' Grand stared into the distance, then pointed to the space around the fireplace. 'That's where Will Evans used to sit of an evening, and Hilda would be there. They were the couple who took me in when I was an evacuee. That's Will's chair you're sitting in now.'

'Blimey.' Josh sat up straighter. Hal sneaked a look at the mirror. No shadows. He caught Josh watching him and looked at the floor.

Grand pointed to another spot near the fireplace. 'More often than not, Barbara Cefn Glas would be sitting there. And sometimes there'd be visitors from the village. Will was a schoolteacher, you see, an educated man. People used to come to him for advice and stay for a chat. He'd tell a story, and then someone else would join in – everyone had a tale to tell. We had no telly, of course – not even a radio. Can you believe, there was no electricity in Bont Goch until 1957. Hilda wrote to tell me when it arrived. She said you'd turn a light on and everyone would jump.'

'Crazy.' It was Josh's turn to shake his head. 'The past and that.'

'That's Will's clock, isn't it?' Hal said. The clock has sat in the middle of the mantelpiece for as long as he could remember. It was old-looking wood, with straight sides rising to a rounded wave shape over the clock face.

'That's right. Will wound it every night. It had a lovely chime... It doesn't work now. We lost the key years ago.'

They all jumped when Grandma Lisa called from the doorway. 'Tea's ready!'

1939

'Cheer up, children. You're going on a lovely holiday!' said David's teacher, Miss Edmonds. She stood at the front of the school hall with some other ladies, all wearing tweed skirts and armbands. Miss Edmonds didn't talk like most people David knew in Bethnal Green. Her hair had hard, shiny curls that looked as if they would break if you touched them and her clothes were clean and buttoned up tight. She always looked ready to get annoyed, even when she was being jolly.

'Hard-faced cow,' Mum muttered. Mum's clothes were a kind of beigy grey and smelled like their house: of cabbage and the *pot* under the bed when it hadn't been emptied. She scratched her elbow now through a hole in her cardigan.

David usually walked to school with his cousin Rodney, who lived down the other end of Pollard Street. Mum always sent David round Rodney's when he was under her feet, so they did most things together.

But today she had made him get up and dressed before it was light. He had a label round his neck and a rough sack to carry. She'd held his hand and pulled him along fast, the loose sole of her shoe slapping the pavement and his gas mask bumping his bum.

When they arrived, the hall was busy. David spotted Auntie Mo in a blouse and skirt and without her housecoat, which usually only happened on Sundays. Rodney stood beside her looking lanky in his raincoat, a duffel bag over his shoulder. He'd had a really short haircut and most of his blond curls had gone. Mum went up to Mo and asked her what they'd missed. She said, 'Shh! I'm trying to listen.'

'What's she saying, Mum?' David said now.

'You're going away for a bit.' Mum's mouth was a hard line like when Dad was up to his tricks at the pub or the bookie's.

'It'll be an adventure, Rodney. Make a man of you,' Auntie Mo said, brushing something off the shoulder of his coat.

Jean Tanner, from David's class, had her arms round her mum's legs. 'You'll love it,' Mrs Tanner said, looking down at her.

David suddenly thought of something. 'Are you coming, Mum?' he said. Mum always told him the truth, not silly stories like Santa Claus that other children believed. She said six was too old for fairy stories.

'No.' Mum pulled his label round to the front and the string scratched his neck. Her eyes were big and dark, and she wouldn't look straight at him. 'I've got to work at the munitions factory, ain't I? I can't go on no holiday'.

David's stomach felt funny. He didn't want to sing 'The Lambeth Walk', which someone was trying to get started. 'Will it be an adventure?' he asked, but the word sounded stupid, like something on the radio that Dad would take the piss out of.

She yanked the belt of his coat tight so he rocked forwards on his feet. It was an old coat of Rodney's and he didn't even need it – the weather was warm like summer. Him and Rodney had only just stopped playing rounders late into the evening with the other kids in the street – and that was because of the war.

The children were getting into a long line, and the front end started to move, with teachers and armband ladies leading the way. David craned his neck and saw children disappearing through the door at the back. It looked like the mums weren't going, they were staying behind in the hall. Mrs Tanner dabbed her eyes with a hankie.

'Come along now, you mothers!' Miss Edmonds said, shaking her curls, which barely moved. 'Let's lead by example and try to keep cheerful.'

'Snooty bitch. It ain't her kids,' Mum said under her breath. Was she going to make one of her scenes, like on the doorstep when Auntie Mo said he'd given Rodney nits?

She got down in front of David. Her hair looked flat and greasy. The black circles in her eyes had swallowed up the blue and she still didn't look right at him, just hitched up the strap of his gas mask case. 'It's only for a while. You're going to the country so you'll be safe from the bombs. I spect by Christmas it'll all be over and I'll come and get you.'

Miss Edmonds was getting Jean to hold her big sister Flo's hand. David could see Rodney in front of them in the queue, his hair so short that the back of his neck looked sore. The children ahead of him were starting to walk away. Should David hold Rodney's hand?

But then he had another thought. 'What about Dad?' he said. Dad worked nights at the docks. 'I haven't said goodbye!'

Mum wiped her nose on her cardigan sleeve. 'He'll be here when you get back. He ain't going nowhere. Do as you're told, David, and don't moan. Or people won't want to look after you.'

Then she did look right at him. Her face crumpled and she made a little gasping noise. She grabbed hold of him and squeezed him so hard he could barely breathe.

'Come along, now,' Miss Edmonds said, pushing in between them and taking David's hand. He caught a whiff of her false, flowery smell. 'Let's see if we can catch up with your friends!' She was walking off with him – he had to twist round to look for Mum.

She was still crouching on the floor. He wished she would make a scene after all, but all she said was, 'Go with your teacher,' in the voice she did for posh people.

'Will you come and get me? Mum?' Other grown-ups were crowding in between them – he had to peer through all their legs and bodies. They were calling out to their children over 'The Lambeth Walk'. It made a jumbled sound like 'London's Burning'. 'Mum! Will you come and get me?'

She had got to her feet, swaying a bit and pulling her holey cardigan tight, her eyes all pink like Rodney's rabbit's. 'Yes. Go on, David! I'll come and get you. I promise.'

Miss Edmonds gave a gentle tug on his arm, and they walked out of the door into the soot-smelling morning, so fast that he was afraid of stumbling and couldn't look back.

CHAPTER FOUR

2011 Day 3: Monday

'Josh.' Hal poked his friend's arm. Josh had thrown off the duvet and his Pokemon pyjama top had ridden up to show a wodge of tummy. He grunted. Hal grasped his shoulder and shook. 'Josh! It's morning. Are you coming?' Josh groaned and curled up tighter, then went still.

Hal crept downstairs, pulling a hoodie on over his t-shirt and jeans. Grandma Lisa was in the kitchen, wearing a floaty dressing gown and clompy slippers, her face pale and unclear without make-up. 'I'm just getting things ready for Grand,' she whispered, opening and closing cupboards. 'You know what he's like if he doesn't have everything to hand. You're up early!'

'Dad said he'd come on a walk if he was awake in time. He said to go without him if he wasn't up by six.' They both looked at the clock. Six-fifteen.

'What about Josh?'

'Unconscious.'

She chuckled. 'He makes me die. *The past and that.*'

Hal was tempted to sit down and chat, but then thought of the fresh morning outside. There was nothing like Wales at this time of day. Once, he and Dad had seen moles trundling around on the cliff-top path; another time they released a sheep that was tangled up in a fence. It was panicking and trying to head-butt them, but they managed to get it free at last. It ran off, bleating and Dad said they were sheep-wranglers. You could see he enjoyed it all as much as Hal. They had rushed home to tell the others.

'I think I'll go anyway,' Hal said. 'Can you ask Grand to do me the full works? I'll be hungry.'

He was hungry already as he pulled the door shut and set off down the track. He heard something behind him and thought Grandma Lisa had come out to tell him something. But he must have made the sound himself – his trainers were scuffing the earth, which was sun-dried in pale clods. As he walked past the parked cars, a shadow passed over him and he heard a plaintive call. He searched the whitish blue above. There! A buzzard – two! – wheeling over the hills past the village.

He walked on in a swift breeze, looking out for the turning where another track took off to the left and joined the lane that led down to the sea.

There were footsteps behind him – Dad had come after all! He turned to point out the buzzards.

There was no one there. He looked right and left. Nothing.

He went on, his stride less certain. The low sun gilded a puff of cloud, then speared through with a golden beam. He reached the narrower track to the left and plunged into shadow between high hedgerows, picking up the pace past wildflowers and leaf shapes.

It was chilly in the shade and he sensed something behind him. His soles pounded towards the lane up ahead, dappled with coppery sunlight.

He arrived, breathless, in the lane. The tarmac was plastered with dried cow-shit and hay. Sunlight filtered between thorny twigs and honeysuckle bobbed in the breeze. He caught a heady sea scent and set off downhill.

Grand would know what all the flowers were, and most of the birds. Sometimes he and Dad pointed and pondered for ages over a lesser-spotted something or a rare type of gull. Auntie Ruth would sigh, 'What does it *matter* what they're called?' But they liked looking it up later in the bird books at Noddfa.

The lane twisted and Hal saw the milky horizon, the sea purple in the shade with golden sparkles. He had the weirdest feeling that someone was watching him. Dad would laugh. He was being silly – this lane came down from the village road, so it wouldn't be that strange to see someone. You just usually didn't.

Halfway down the hill, he turned to look back.

There was a girl standing near the turning. Older than Hal. Watching. She set off towards him, wavy hair bouncing.

Hal hurried seawards, his cheeks burning. 'People! They get everywhere!' It wasn't the same without Dad. Maybe Hal would see a dolphin – then they'd all be clamouring to go with him tomorrow.

The bottom of the lane led to a sea wall, one bench and a tiny bit of beach, with cliffs rising on either side, all craggy and dramatic. Hal took the path up to the left, striding upwards over rocky ground. Sprigs of ragged pink flowers leaned towards the water. Imogen had photographed them last time. A bee droned in the acid-yellow gorse and gulls hovered overhead like kites on strings, then swooped downwards. Hal felt the climb in his leg muscles and breathed in the racing air. He reached up the rocks that were as high as his hips – Dad used to have to give him a leg-up.

He looked behind him. No one. The girl must have gone to the beach, or up the cliff the other side. The last giant step had footholds worn into it. He stuck in the toe of his trainer and hauled himself up. Puffing, he continued as the path went to the left, and soon the bay opened up in front of him. A gull hung in the air at head height. Boats chugged across the water, leaving glittering tracks. To the right, waves licked the feet of cliffs receding into the distance.

He looked left. The girl stood facing the water, hair blowing round her face. Hal's skin chilled. How had she got ahead of him?

He made himself look out at the huge expanse of bay, his eyes raking the water surface for a dorsal fin or a splash. There were only rocks and sea birds. His heart was thudding from the climb.

He looked again – there was no one there. He headed back to the rocky steps, planting his hand and springing downwards. He walked the cliff path with his eyes on his feet, slipping when stones rolled beneath his soles. His trainers made a rubbery slap when he landed at the foot of the last step. He turned up the lane. The hedgerows whipped past him as he hurried back for breakfast.

It was later in the morning and Hal was sitting with the others on plastic chairs in the sunlit back garden. The adults said the forecast wasn't great, but at the moment the sea was all lazy ripples and the horizon was cloudless. Hal was comfortably aware of Grand, glasses on, deep in his book, Dad with the paper in his lap and Mum and Auntie Ruth sipping tea over their novels. A cool whiff of sea stirred their book pages. Grandma Lisa could be heard inside chatting to Dan and getting ready for their second full day.

'I really miss FIFA,' Josh sighed from the steps.

'You need a book!' Grand roared, plonking his down. 'Have a look through the bookshelves. You can't possibly be bored in a house full of literature.'

Josh poked at a pebble with his toe. 'You're book mad, you lot.'

Auntie Ruth raised an eyebrow. 'You're right. It's an illness. I've tried giving them up, but I can't.'

'I miss FIFA too,' Hal said, although at that moment, he didn't.

'*Thank* you!' Josh made X-box controller motions with his thumbs before heading indoors.

Hal went after him, through the house. He found him out the front by the picnic table, waving his phone. 'I can't even get one bar of signal.'

'I know. It's like the dark ages. Sometimes, if you wander a bit along the track…' They set off, retracing Hal's steps from earlier. 'We won't tell Grand! Hey, a weird thing happened on my walk this morning.'

'Oh yeah. Why didn't you wake me up?'

'I tried, you numty! You were like *dead*.' Hal didn't feel spooked now, with the sun warm on his face, and Josh holding his phone above his head like the Statue of Liberty. He told him about the footsteps and the girl.

Josh whirled round to check behind them, but there was no one. 'Could she have got there another way?'

'There is no other way.'

Josh sucked in a breath. 'Was she in old-fashioned dress?'

'No, just trousers and stuff I think.'

'Well, what did she look like?'

'I don't know… wavy hair.'

Josh gave an exaggerated shrug. 'What, blond? Black? Long? Was she see-through?'

'No! Quite long hair. Fairish, I think.' It was hard for Hal to picture her now; he had turned away so quickly.

'We need to look this up! There's this paranormal investigator's website. I'm on it all the time.' Josh gestured at his useless phone as though to make it feel ashamed.

'We might get a signal on the way to Aberaeron.'

'Good! I need to do proper research. Look at similar cases.' Josh stuck the phone in his pocket. 'If I can't get a signal... shit, you know what?'

'What?'

'I'll have to do like your lot keep saying and buy a bloody book!'

Carrie could tell that the rest of the family were not thrilled about visiting Aberaeron. The weather had defied the forecast and remained bright – they must all be yearning for the beach, or for a walk or picnic. But Grand wanted to go to a particular bookshop, and so they had scones and honey ice cream in the Hive on the Quay, where he got irate about the prices. Toby talked about a fellow company director who had shares in a Welsh brewery. He kept trying to see if the Hive had any of their beers. Grand looked grumpy, which amused Ruth. Carrie often wondered if she had brought home a Tory-leaning public-school boy just to aggravate their father.

Afterwards, Carrie wandered around the shops looking at plastic beach toys and Welsh fudge. 'It's like any bloody fudge, but with a red dragon label,' Chris had once joked in a Welsh accent. She spotted the boys in the distance at one point, coming out of W H Smith's.

Grandma Lisa was sitting on a bench by the harbour, her blue cardigan in her lap. She gave Carrie a wave. 'Your father's bookshop has closed down,' she said, looking tired. 'He's gone to sit in the car in disgust.'

Ruth strode over in an apricot linen dress which clung to her bulky middle, clutching a Sale bag from an expensive dress shop. She cocked her head at Carrie, 'A drama? How unusual.' She sat down beside her mother, only to get her phone out and call Toby.

Carrie thought fast. 'I know – I saw leaflets about the Dylan Thomas Trail. I'll go and get one for him.'

Later, as she sat in her father's car enthusing about the leaflet, she could hear the note of strain in her voice. His face retained its despondent look. Eventually he took the leaflet and went to look for a pub with a plaque.

'Please let him calm down so we can enjoy the rest of the day,' Lisa said in her head as she stood up and walked along the harbourside, too restless to keep staring at the boats. 'Look at me, I'm praying!' she thought. Thelma would be proud. She had met her new friend in a café she liked at the bottom of town, which turned out to be run by the local church. They had got talking – about tracing ancestors at first, because Lisa had been reading an article about it – then about anything and everything. One day Thelma was nervous about a talk she was doing at church, so Lisa went along to support her. As it turned out, Thelma had loads of friends there, but they were all very welcoming and seemed excited that Lisa had come. Thelma said praying should be like talking to a friend. 'Lord, if you could fix this for me,' Lisa muttered. 'It can ruin the day for everyone if he's in a mood.'

Perhaps Carrie would have had some luck with the Dylan Thomas thing – she was a dab hand a soothing him. Unlike Ruth, who had sat down with a sarky comment and been no help at all. The girls had always been so different. Lisa remembered when Ruth had got the headteacher's job. 'She can boss everyone about now!' David had laughed. But of course, he was incredibly proud.

Toby had got on his nerves going on about directors and shares and things. Much to Ruth's delight – how she loved to stir things up! If only things would settle down, so they could all get on. David always got pally with Chris over birds and cricket and things. But Chris seemed a bit preoccupied this year. Lisa was beginning to wonder why, when she caught sight of the boys coming out of the sports shop that sold fishing tackle. Hal waved, holding up a carrier bag. Her heart lifted. She headed for the crossing, impatient to hear their news.

⤙

When Carrie got back to the harbour, the boys were lying on their fronts at the water's edge, hauling up crab lines with shouts of excitement, then releasing one scuttling creature after another. She heard Hal's laugh as Josh flapped a hand, a tiny crab hanging from his finger by its claws.

Chris was on the bench, staring at the water. He looked boyish in cut-off denim shorts, his shirt untucked, but grey speckled his tousled hair. Whole days could pass on this holiday when they barely touched base – as if Carrie's family reabsorbed her.

She told him about Grand and the bookshop. 'How can he be so bloody cantankerous? We could have gone to the beach! Imagine how Imogen would be moaning.'

He made a laughing noise, his head turned away. The buildings opposite, with their marshmallow colours, were reflected in the glassy harbour. Boats rolled and yawed with a peaceful tinkling. Carrie got her phone out to take a picture. 'I keep checking for messages from Imogen.'

They'd been to a meeting about the Tanzania trip and chuckled about the fuss some parents were making. One mother wanted the school to ring to say the flight had landed safely. Chris had whispered to Imogen, 'We'll assume you've landed safely if we don't hear about it on the News.' He had always loved her fearlessness and adventurous spirit.

She waited now for his gentle teasing.

'She won't be in touch. Stop expecting it.' His abruptness took her breath away.

'All right!'

'Sorry,' he said, with a pinched expression. He shifted closer and she felt the soothing warmth of his arm. What was it he had been worrying about at school? One of his special needs kids. They'd talked about it at home because Imogen knew the family…

28

'What happened about that boy you mentioned, the one who stopped turning up to sessions. Did he start coming again?'

She saw his ear flush red as he turned to watch the boys.

She remembered now: Tyrone, the sixteen-year-old with Asperger's. He was big and stocky, and people took him for a thug – unfairly, according to Chris, who was working with him. Imogen knew his little brother, Kyle from her work experience at his nursery. The Mum had forgotten to bring in some details the nursery needed and Imogen had handed over her mobile number so she could send them. You weren't meant to give out your own number, but Imogen said the Mum was tearful.

'No, he… went AWOL.'

'What, from school?'

'Yeah. Well, no, that's what we thought but… Turned out he'd cleared off all together.' Chris glanced away, clearing his throat. 'The police got involved but apparently they came to the conclusion he'd just run away.'

'What, just like that? No questions asked?'

'Well what do you want them to ask?'

Carrie put a hand on his arm. 'No, I mean, what made them think he's run away?'

'I don't know! He'd taken stuff. Money – from his Gran's house.'

'So now he's just one of those statistics? Chris, that's awful.'

'I know! But what can *I* do?'

Carrie took away her hand. She was just showing an interest, for goodness sake! But maybe she shouldn't have brought up work – he was finding it hard to relax into the holiday. 'Nothing. I'm just sympathising. I know you were quite involved with him. Is that what that text was about, in Llangrannog. Him going missing?'

'What? No… Someone told me at the end of term.'

A pulse beat in her ears. 'Oh. You didn't mention it.'

'No, well… it was so busy.'

He reached for her hand, his eyes fixed on the jumble of buildings she had been about to photograph. They looked garish now, the colours sickly, clashing. She put her phone away.

Chris's heart was hammering. He'd been sitting on the bench hoping for peace to descend on him. He'd been on a course once – the teachers were asked to think of a favourite place that made them happy. He'd talked about these holidays. Remember that place, the woman said, that cliff walk, that mountaintop – call on those happy memories whenever you feel stressed. Now he was actually bloody here and he couldn't do it.

What did Carrie think he'd done? What *had* he done? It was like hearing that boy Laurie's accusations read out to him in Cowper's office: *groping, humping*. Watching the bastard noting down the fact that he'd sent Amanda away to get help. Them not looking him in the eye – as if they were afraid he'd glimpse their new view of him as something tainted. Wrong. You could bet that was still what Cowper thought about when he saw Chris – however many extra hours he was putting in lately. Though in truth the longer he worked, the more the work seemed to pile up.

He'd gone down another bloody rabbit hole. You scrabbled your way towards the surface, but the sides kept collapsing in on you. He tried to bring himself back to the harbourside, to Carrie's hand in his, and breathed in the sea air with its whiff of crabs and honey. That had all blown over ages ago, the Laurie thing. It seemed to have done, anyway. But now this awful mess with Imogen. And Tyrone. Perhaps he *was* that twisted version of himself now. Perhaps relaxed Chris who loved these holidays had gone.

CHAPTER FIVE

2011 Day 4: Tuesday

Grand was about to reach out to the bedside table for his book and reading glasses to make the most of the early morning sunlight. Thank God for these main ones, the spares still hadn't turned up.

'When you think,' said Lisa through a luxurious yawn, 'how long we've been coming here.' He didn't reply. Perhaps she'd believe he was asleep. 'And you! My God. Seventy-one years! David?'

'It's not seventy-one years! Not every year, anyway.' Damn. He'd blown his cover.

'No. Of course.' She filled his silence with a sigh. 'But over all those years. Extraordinary – the passage of time.'

He had his back to her: she wouldn't see him rolling his eyes at her outpourings.

'It's like that time when Dan was seven and I went to his school to be Living History,' she said. 'I stood among all those little ones and thought, *It's a blink of an eye since I was your age.* Are you getting up to do the breakfast?'

'In a minute.' He had a drifting sensation despite himself. There was no precision or direction to her nattering. He shouldn't let it draw him in.

1939

'David Cole,' said a lady with a clipboard and gold-rimmed spectacles, reading his label. 'Let's check Mother has packed everything.' She stood up very straight in her stiff jacket and skirt. *Poker up her arse,* Dad would say.

They were in the station waiting room after a long, shuffling walk through the streets. The poker lady held out her hand for David's sack, then spoke out of the corner of her mouth to a ginger-haired lady with a biscuit tin: 'A duffel bag or a white cotton bag, they were told.' She held up the sack between her finger and thumb and began to rummage inside. 'Toothbrush? No. Pyjamas? Oh dear.'

She turned her face away and shut her eyes for a minute. 'Plimsolls? No. Spare socks and underclothes...' The pants she pulled out were baggy and grey. She held them out with a long, straight arm.

Colin, a bigger boy from school, said, 'Urgh!' and children giggled. 'Soap? No. Handkerchiefs? No. Comb – yes! Well, thank the Lord Harry for that.' She plonked the sack at David's feet before taking Jean Tanner's kit bag. 'One wonders what they'll think in Aberystwyth.'

David looked down at his stupid, useless sack and wanted to chuck it in the river. Why couldn't he have a white cotton bag? Mum would say it was Dad's fault for spending his wages down the pub.

'Some of them are skin and bone!' whispered the ginger lady, handing David a custard cream. 'And you can see them scratching. The Welsh are going to have to shave their heads.'

The ladies moved on and the biscuit was snatched from David's hand. He turned and saw Colin cramming it in his greedy gob, then spraying crumbs when he laughed.

David looked at Rodney, who was watching with a frown. The two of them could take Colin on, couldn't they?

'He nicked my biscuit!' he said, but Rodney didn't seem to hear and turned away.

They set off across the platform now and all the crowds stood back so the children had an alleyway through. Miss Edmonds got them singing 'Wish Me Luck As You Wave Me Goodbye,' and Colin waved as if he was a film star.

The train carriage was crammed with wriggling children and gas mask boxes. Colin sat next to David and pointed to something on his chest, then bashed him on the chin when he looked.

The city chugged and then whizzed past the window in a cloud of steam, and everyone chattered and pointed at the river and big famous buildings. Later, streets and houses turned into fields and woods, and David gazed out at the incredible expanses of green and wondered if this was what a holiday was like. But it went on and on, and the carriage got hot. It got stinky too because Colin kept lifting up his bum and farting.

Miss Edmonds came in and told them they were going to Wales.

'Welsh ladies are all witches,' Colin said to David when she'd gone. 'They'll boil you in a cauldron and eat you on toast.'

'They'll do it to you too, then!'

'No they won't because I'm strong and I can help and stuff. It's little squirts like you that'll get boiled.'

David was starving by the time Miss Edmonds slid open the carriage door again and said it was time to eat their lunches. There had been no breakfast when he got up, which seemed like days ago. He opened Mum's paper parcel and found a thin white sandwich. He hoped it was jam. Mum didn't spread it to the edges when she was in a hurry but there might be some in the middle. He lifted it to his mouth. It was limp but it smelt bready and his mouth watered.

'Urgh! He's got maggots in his sandwich!'

A sharp nudge from Colin knocked the sandwich onto the dirty floor. Children made horrified noises and pulled away. There weren't any maggots – Colin was a lying bastard – but by the time Miss Edmonds came to see what the commotion was, there was a footprint on the sandwich from Colin's shoe.

'David Cole! What on earth is going on?'

'He dropped his lunch, Miss,' Colin said.

Miss Edmonds made Rodney share with David, but he only gave him a tiny bit of his fish paste sandwich. David tried to catch his eye to do an impression of Miss Edmonds. Rodney had been in her class the year before and this usually made him laugh. But he wouldn't look.

When they arrived at Aberystwyth, David squeezed through the crowd on the platform to get away from Colin.

'Behave yourself, David! Stop pushing!' Miss Edmonds said, and made him wait till last.

They were led into a hall and given a biscuit each, and then they had to stand on a little stage, and grownups came to look at them, yabbering in a funny language, with noises like a frog in your throat. Even when they spoke English, it wavered up and down so you could hardly understand it.

'I'll have the tall boy, that one! Yes you, you're a strong-looking lad!'

'Those two little girls. Oh, look at your lovely curls! Like Shirley

Temple. And your sister looks big and sensible.'

'Wipe your nose, David, and stop scratching, for goodness sake,' Miss Edmonds hissed. He heard Colin's nasty laugh and looked round to see him pointing.

'Don't touch him!' Colin said to Rodney, who was standing next to David. 'You'll get fleas.' Children sniggered.

Rodney thrust his hands in his pockets. He stepped away, his face all red. 'Urgh.'

'You're his cousin, ain't you?' Colin said.

Rodney shrugged. 'I'm not allowed round his house though. Mum says it smells of wee.'

There were groans, and shrieks of laughter. 'Be quiet, children!' Miss Edmonds snapped.

They ended up on a bus going past miles and miles of hedges and fields and lumpy grey buildings. The children who were left had gone quiet and didn't bother to point at the sheep and cows any more. Whenever the bus stopped, more grownups would get on, choose children and take them. Eventually, a man even walked off with Colin, who turned and stuck his tongue out. Now it was just David, Rodney, a fat boy called Roger whose breathing made a noise, and Kitty who had thick glasses and had wet herself on the train.

It was getting dark – in Pollard Street, Mum would be on the doorstep by now, shouting for him to come in. He had messed things up, hadn't he? She had said to do as he was told, but he had got into trouble. The bus stopped in a tunnel of trees, and a load of strange people got on. A man and a lady started talking to Rodney and soon he stood up and walked off with them. He was nearly at the door when he stopped and pointed at David. 'I'm s'posed to look after him.'

'That's very nice,' said the man. 'But we've only room for one. Come on now.' The lady took Rodney's hand and led him off the bus.

David thought of cauldrons and head shaving and his useless sack. He gnawed at the edge of his thumbnail.

There was yabbering, then, 'Speak English, Barbara. They've got enough to cope with!' A shadow fell over him. 'Oh Barbara, *look*.'

A lady was looking down at him, with twinkly eyes behind round glasses and a dimple in her chin. Wispy grey-brown hair escaped from under her hat. Beside her was a younger lady with golden hair and big blue eyes, like a doll David had seen in a shop.

'A quiet older girl, you said, Hilda!' said the doll lady.

He thought of the ruined sandwich and the stolen biscuit; he felt weak and wobbly. What happened to the children who no one chose?

'I don't think that's the point, right now, do you?' Hilda looked into his eyes. 'Well young man, what's your name?'

His chest felt like it would burst and he answered in a stupid, shaky voice, with his nose running.

'David, is it? Well, you're exactly what I'm looking for,' she said, holding out a hand. 'You've had a long journey, haven't you? But it's over now. You're home.'

CHAPTER SIX

Carrie looked up to see that Chris was finally coming, yawning, to join them at the kitchen table, where they sat elbow to elbow. Grand had just put his spatula aside and sat down to eat his own breakfast. He had always been an early riser, and the family fell into line in Wales. When his colleague Nick came that year, he and his wife, Elsa, had had long lie-ins to start with, but they soon got the message.

'I'll get yours, Chris,' Grandma Lisa said, but Grand stood up with a martyred air, flapped a tea towel at her and made a performance of opening the oven and grunting as he took out the foil-covered plate.

'I expect you're missing Imogen, aren't you, Chris?' Grandma Lisa said. He looked put on the spot, staring at a sausage on his fork. 'Ah, of course. It's still lovely though isn't it?'

'The picnic's Hal's favourite day,' Carrie said, and felt her spirits lift at his little fist-pump of agreement. God, he'd be a teenager soon. She looked at Dan in his denim shirt and shorts, his shoulders and neck filling out – you could see Toby's rugby-player genes coming through. What would Hal look like at sixteen?

'So, what's the plan?' Josh asked, looking up from his book, *The Paranormal*. He had bought it in Aberaeron and had been glued to it ever since.

'We don't so much have plans as inviolable rules,' said Ruth, spreading a swathe of butter on her toast.

'God yes,' said Toby. 'Remember when I suggested going to Fishguard?'

Ruth mimicked wide-eyed alarm. 'You poor fool. We do *not* go to Fishguard.'

'Not in our wildest dreams,' Carrie laughed, remembering Grand's resistance to doing something that wasn't rooted in his childhood. 'So Josh, it's coffee in Aber first...'

They all joined in: 'Buy picnic bits in Ypopty...'

'Grandma Lisa has a look round Matalan...'

'Then back to Bont Goch, and drive to the picnic place.'

'Cool,' said Josh, returning to his book. 'Wow,' he said after a moment. 'I so want to have an oobe!'

'A *what*?' said Grand as chuckling erupted.

'An Out Of Body Experience,' Josh said in an hushed tone. 'People are like, lying on the operating table and they float up to the ceiling and look down at their own body. Some people can do it when they want to. Awesome.'

'Oh, well then,' said Ruth. 'I might oobe to Aberystwyth.'

The morning that unfolded was faithful to their description, and as lunchtime approached, they found themselves in the car park in Aberystwyth, waiting for Grandma Lisa, while Grand got furious about the delay.

'She's only been in there five minutes,' Ruth told Carrie out of the corner of her mouth. 'She spent an hour sourcing the perfect bloody sandwich for him.'

'I'd better get her out of there. He's ready to combust.'

'Oh, let them get on with it.' Ruth said. 'What? Oh look, I don't care who's in charge when I'm on holiday, as long as I don't have to be!'

Carrie sighed as Grand raged on. It was all very well to behave as though you were above it all, but they weren't, were they? They were in it. She went into Matalan.

Soon they were in the cars again, with the town far behind them. A red kite hunting on the high winds caught the glint of sun on metal as they wound between hedgerows and fields seething with scuttling life.

At the neighbouring village of Talybont, they got out to stretch their legs while Chris went in the shop to buy water.

'I can't believe there's no shop in Bont Gorr,' said Josh, sticking to his approximation of the name.

'There used to be,' Grand said, picnic-ready in his beige shirt and old brown trousers. 'Jim Siop was Will's best friend. He used to slip me sweets. But Talybont was always bigger. The other evacuees went to school here when I first came.'

'But not you?' asked Carrie.

'No. Hilda got me into the school in Bont Goch, where Hugh had gone.'

'So you'd be near her! How lovely,' said Grandma Lisa.

He frowned, irritated. 'It just meant I could come home for lunch.'

'Oh pardon me for speaking.'

'Anyway,' he went on, 'after that they made special arrangements for the evacuees at Bont Goch school, and we all went there in the afternoons.'

They drove the last few miles to Bont Gogh, and through the village to where the road petered out into a track. Now the boys got out of the cars at intervals to open and shut gates. Sheep panicked at the approach of the cars and blundered along in front of them with despairing cries.

'Lamb chops! Mint sauce!' Josh called in a bleating tone, hanging his head out of the open window. They laughed as the animals finally saw a way out of their ordeal and leaped off the track into the safety of the field.

'More like mutton,' Chris said. 'Too late for lambs.'

Hawthorn bushes crouched over the stream on their left, and Carrie caught flashes of reflected blue among slick rocks. Ahead of them rose the hills of a hundred remembered walks. They parked on lumpy grass, careful not to ground the cars, and lugged camping chairs, rugs and bags to the picnic place, beside a wooden bridge across the stream.

When Carrie was a child, they had always been alone here. Now the ancient track into the hills had been reinvented as a cycle path, signposted for tourists. Grand glowered when lycra-clad cyclists passed, and bemoaned the futuristic wind farm twirling in the distance. But to Carrie, it was as wild and unspoiled as ever. It made her chest ache to see it again.

In the lull between sandwiches and cakes, she walked onto the bridge and sat down, dangling her legs over the water where it fell down a rocky step in a rush of white froth, its noise muffling the family's chatter. Ahead, the stream wound its way more quietly between spongy tussocks. Carrie tried to conjure Imogen, damming the stream in years gone by, but it was Emilia she saw with a jolt:

jeans rolled up to her thighs, rapt and bright-eyed as the two of them mastered the flow of the water with slippery chunks of rock.

And Chris was wrong. You did get lambs in summer.

1983

'They were abandoned by their mother,' the farm lady said. 'You can feed them if you like.'

Carrie was twelve and Ruth seventeen. Their cousin Emilia had come to Wales instead of going abroad with her parents, who were looking at apartments in Abu Dhabi. She'd joined them here several times before, to give Auntie Jill a break. 'A break from her own *daughter*?!' Dad always said.

The lambs were not tiny and fluffy as Carrie had imagined, but muscular and restive, buffeting each other with thick little skulls as they strained towards the lady and their breakfast. She handed two glass baby bottles to the younger girls. Ruth hung back, her arms crossed over her frilled blouse, a bright pink belt at the waist of her jeans.

Carrie and Emilia leaned over the fence in their t-shirts and old jeans, holding the bottles out. Emilia looked excited but nervous, pushing back wind-blown fair hair. The lambs dashed forwards, bumping woolly shoulders. One latched on quickly to the thick brown teat on Carrie's bottle.

'He's really strong!' she cried, surprised by the powerful tug on her arm. She took a moment to get used to the hooves scraping on concrete, the devilish eyes and the smells of poo and greasy wool, but her heart jumped to be giving the young thing its food.

'You've made a friend for life, there,' said the farm lady as the lamb settled into a rhythmical pulling. Carrie heard a sharp intake of breath. Em was holding out her bottle to the other lamb, but flinching away when he tried to grab it.

'Go on, Emilia,' Dad called, a hand in his jeans pocket, dark hair growing over his collar. 'He won't hurt you. He's just hungry.' The lamb gave a loud bleat of complaint, but finally snapped his jaws round the teat and yanked on it. Em's small hand gripped the fence

39

post beside Carrie, her knuckles going pale.

'He's really greedy! He's hurting my arm.'

'Calm down!' Ruth said, tossing her Lady Di haircut. You'll frighten him!'

'It's all right,' Carrie told Emilia. 'They settle down after a bit.' She really hoped Emilia's lamb would settle down so they could both enjoy this.

Carrie's lamb looked peaceful now, his strange eyes closed in the velvety black face. Maybe if she came back tomorrow, he would recognise her and come to the fence. She heard the winding on mechanism of Dad's instamatic camera and turned with a smile.

The shutter clicked. There was a cry of disgust, and Em dropped her bottle.

'Have another try, love,' Dad said.

'I don't want to! He's too hungry!' Em stalked off down the lane, head down.

'Typical,' Ruth muttered. 'Well, she ruins everything!'

The pull on Carrie's bottle relaxed – her lamb had finished and let go.

'Well, you seem to be a natural,' said the farm lady to Carrie. 'Do you want to feed your cousin's lamb as well?'

━✦

2011

Carrie returned to the picnic spot where Grand and Grandma Lisa were sitting on camping chairs. Grand was pointing to the stream, telling the boys, 'You lay on your front on the bank and reached underneath it to where the water was in shadow. The trout would cluster there, and if you tickled their bellies, they got drowsy and you could catch them.'

'Cool,' said Josh, tucking into a bag of crisps. He and the others were all lounging on picnic rugs.

'How did you talk to the village children, David?' Toby asked. 'They must all have been Welsh speakers.'

'Oh I picked up a fair bit.'

40

'Alright, Carrie?' Grandma Lisa said, offering her the greasy paper bag from Ypopty, the baker's.

'I'm fine.' She took a wedge of flapjack.

Her mother patted the camping chair beside her. 'I haven't told you about my new project! I've starting researching my family tree. Thelma did an evening class, so she's helping me. Anyway, it has all got quite exciting.' She pushed back her hair with her sunglasses, her blue eyes bright.

Carrie sat down. 'Really? What have you found out?'

'Well, I've got a few generations back on my father's side. And it turns out my great, great grandfather…' Grand was muttering and huffing and beginning to drown her out. She turned to him. '*What*!?'

'Give me strength!' he burst out.

'Why? What's it to you if I want to look into it?' She shook her head at Carrie. 'He's been like this from the start!'

'Oh come on,' Grand said, crushing his empty crisp packet. 'It's a load of old bollocks. A middle class craze.'

'It sounds really interesting!' Carrie said.

'It's ordinary bog-standard people hoping to find out they're descended from bloody royalty or something.'

'Fat chance with our lot!' Ruth sat with her legs to one side, in over-stretched jeans. 'Although I think Toby's family has its blood-sucking aristocrats.'

Grand stood up, swatting crumbs from his lap. 'I'm going for a walk up the stream.'

Carrie could hardly look at her mother's expression – so eager a moment before. 'What's that all about?' she asked as her father's stiff back receded.

Ruth glared after him. 'It's not all about him, that's what! How could anyone else's family be of any interest?'

Grandma Lisa looked sadly thoughtful. 'I said the wrong thing, that's all. He'll get over it.'

Why did he do this? And why did Mum cover for him? Carrie

could have bellowed – but it would ruin the picnic. They usually set off soon for Hal's favourite walk into the hills. He was on the rug beside Josh, and now got to his feet. 'I'm going to show Josh the tin mine,' he said. 'Coming, Dan?'

'Nah, you're all right,' Dan yawned.

'I'll race you up there!' said Toby. 'Brilliant endurance training!' Dan made a face, and didn't budge.

'Be careful, won't you!' Carrie called as the younger boys walked off, heads together.

Hal turned with a shrug and a smile. 'It's fine, Mum. It's all fenced off now.'

When they had gone, Carrie shot a glance at Chris, who had sat down in Grand's chair. He knew so well how her father got to her. But she couldn't catch his eye.

~

'Please come. I might strangle him,' Carrie said, taking a deep draught of mountain air and willing herself to relax. The boys were back from the tin mine now and they were preparing for the walk. Chris squinted up from the picnic rug, where he had settled down for a snooze. Carrie jerked her head towards Grand, who had set off with the others.

'Oh. Right.' He got up and they followed on, the last in the party.

'Nice day for the picnic,' she said. They had talked longingly of it one dark day in the winter. 'You love this walk. Don't you?'

'Of course.' He took her hand and swung it with a bright expression. Something about it made her look away.

The track that led them up into the hills was of dried earth and whitish stone. Scattered rocks revealed seams of crystal. A puddle with a rich iron hue stretched across their path, and ahead the mountains lured them on.

'Cefn Glas,' Grand said, nodding towards a derelict farmhouse down a track on their right, its collapsed roof exposing a skeleton of timbers. 'It looks more decrepit every year.'

'Did you come up here with your mates?' Hal asked. For a moment, Carrie looked forward to one of his stories. But she thought of his bad temper earlier and fumed all over again.

'Sometimes… Mostly I came with Hilda. She loved the view. *Balm for the soul*, she called it.'

'Was she a Christian, then?' Grandma Lisa asked. Carrie's stomach tightened at the difficult subject.

But Grand looked more peaceful up here. 'She was church and Will was chapel. It didn't stop her swearing like a trooper at times, though! I learned some interesting Welsh.' He passed on the highlights at Josh's request. Grandma Lisa laughed with the others as if the upset earlier had never happened.

'This way!' Hal turned off the path to the right, leading them up the hillside. They heaved themselves upwards over tufty grass full of tiny wildflowers and bilberries, stopping now and then to lean on their knees. Pale stalks fringed outcrops of rock with sheep shelters on their leeward side.

'Don't eat the bilberries,' Hal warned Josh. 'Eh, Dad?' Chris nodded, panting.

'Rabbit shit,' Ruth said through a gasp of exertion.

It grew steeper, and their feet sent the berry-like turds rolling downhill. The view opened out: a farm across the valley; patterns of hedgerows and dry-stone walls giving way to rugged land too high for habitation. An enormous sky dappled everything with light and shadows.

'God, look at it,' Carrie said, and saw Chris pull his gaze up from his trainers.

Higher up, the breeze grew wilder and sweeter, and still they climbed. Hal and Josh were out of sight above them, and Dan, despite himself, was hurrying to catch them up with loping, athletic strides.

Ruth fell behind, her hair sticking to her face. 'I'll catch you up!' she waved them on. 'When my heart gets started again!'

'Don't die on me, darling!' Toby called. 'Who'll share the driving?'

The summit was a flat area of tough, stalky grasses. The main party dragged themselves onto it, puffing and gazing. The view stretched for miles in a full circle around them, pale blue mountains at its far edges, then rough-terrained uplands, forests and gentler hills with sheep dotting the valleys. The stream led the eye westwards to their picnic spot and beyond that in sparkling bursts to the village under its summer canopy. On the horizon glinted the sea.

'Balm for the soul!' said Grandma Lisa. 'Hilda was right.' Carrie braced herself for her father's irritation.

'She said this was Hugh's favourite place.' He was shading his eyes, looking westwards. 'I suppose he came up here with Barbara.'

'Wait, who was Hugh?' Josh said. 'I thought it was Barbara who lived at Nod-fer?'

'Hugh was Hilda and Will's son, who went away to war. Barbara was his sweetheart. She was from Cefyn Glas – that house we passed. Barbara Cefyn Glas, you see.' Grand chuckled at Josh's baffled face. 'It's a Welsh thing, calling people after their house, or their job.'

'Oh! I thought her middle name was Kevin.'

Dan threw his head back and howled with laughter. Hal and Josh stumbled away, whooping, leaving the others to the rush of the breeze.

'Hilda must have missed Hugh terribly,' Grandma Lisa said. 'Perhaps that's why she came up here.'

'She used to say it would do us both good,' said Grand. A briny wind wafted over them, sending ripples through the grasses.

CHAPTER SEVEN

1939

'You'd better get on with your reading, then, if you don't want Miss Edmonds to get even crosser!' It was Will's schoolmaster face that looked down on David after Hilda went out, pulling on her *menig* (gloves) and shutting the door with a bang. There was no sign of his usual after-tea twinkle, which said, *we're going to have some fun now, you and me.* Instead he sat down at the kitchen table and pulled a pile of exercise books towards him, red pen at the ready.

'That was lovely, that was. We should do it at the canteen,' said Barbara. She had come over to see if there was any news of Hugh and had stayed for *swper*. Washing up water ran down her smooth arms as she leaned over the sink in a cloud of steam. 'I'm working at the Bath Street Canteen in Aberystwyth, David! Keeping the soldiers fed. *It'll take your mind off that Hugh*, Mam said.' She pushed a strand of straw-coloured hair out of her eyes. 'It doesn't. But at least I don't feel so useless. What did Hilda call this dish, Will?'

'Goulash.'

'Goulash! There's posh! I'd make it at home, but Mam won't eat anything foreign.'

'Oh we're quite exotic here.' Will's red pen stopped in mid-air, then flicked a tick. He always looked suntanned, even in winter, and the bright blue of his eyes and his thick, black-streaked silver hair gave his face a kind of shine.

'She worries it'd make her sick, with all her problems,' Barbara sighed. David hauled Hugh's old satchel onto his lap and got out the story book from school. His shoulders slumped as he turned to the story he was meant to read. It looked really long and was set out in thick columns – dense clumps of difficult words, with hardly any pictures to give you clues. He leaned on the oilcloth, his cheeks on his hands. It had been a long day: the fight in the playground and having to stand in the corner looking at the pink shapes on the wall map.

Roger had bloody well started it, waving chocolate at David so the smell made his stomach gurgle. 'Mum sent it for me. I'm going home soon! I'll have chocolate every day!'

David made a grab for the bar, but Roger snatched it away, broke off a piece and stuffed it in his mouth. 'Rodney's going home too.' He laughed, his chocolate-filled gob all spitty and disgusting.

'Liar! He's not!'

'He is, he's going back to London and so am I.'

'Good riddance!' shouted David, and shoved him. Why would Rodney be going? He remembered Auntie Mo telling him, 'My Rodney is going to make something of himself'. 'What's he going to make of hisself?' Dad had said with a beery laugh. 'A bleedin' nuisance?'

Roger recovered his balance and that's when the punching started. David ended up with a sore nose and bruised knuckles, but the worst thing had been handing Miss Edmonds' note to Hilda: the disappointed look in her eyes. Then having to explain who he had fought and why, and the muttering when Will got in.

Now he started spelling out the words on the page in front of him, but by the time he got down to the second line, he had forgotten what the first ones said. He tried again from the top, but he kept wondering what Miss Edmonds was saying. Where would David go if Hilda didn't want him any more?

It had been better going to school with the Welsh children. Their teacher was Miss Griffiths, but she was Hilda's best friend, so David held the delicious secret that her real name was Sue. She was not much taller than the oldest children, but she ruled over the classroom with a strong, clear voice and eyes that sparkled when you pleased her. David had been the only evacuee there. On his first day, a girl from the village had said, 'London kids have lice. You have to burn their clothes.'

'Mary Ellis! What kind of a welcome is that?' Miss Griffiths said. She made Mary say 'sorry' in front of everyone. The rest of the lesson was a talk about being kind to strangers, with a Bible story about angels. After that, the village children tried to outdo each other being friendly to David.

But now there was afternoon school for all the evacuees, with Miss Edmonds who'd come with them from London. And David was in trouble.

Will caught David's eye, his gaze softening. 'Hilda will sort it out,' he said.

'She will,' said Barbara, plonking the goulash pan on the wooden drainer. 'Even if you are training to be world heavyweight champion.' She came over, wiping her hands on a tea towel, and ruffled his hair with a tired sigh. 'She must think the world of you, going out on washday.'

Of course – Monday was washday. By the evening Hilda always said her back was killing her and she was ready for her bed. David felt even worse now, and the reading book made no sense at all. Why did Will love books so much? Noddfa was full of them, piled up on tables and beside chairs. Will held them gently and gazed at them, and sometimes he'd read something out.

'Having trouble there?' he said now.

'The writing's too small.'

Will reached over and turned the book round, peering at it down his nose. 'That is small,' he said. 'That's tiny! Running before you can walk, I'd say. Look, try using your finger and do one word at a time. Say it out loud if it helps. We won't mind, will we, Barbara?'

'Sounds brilliant! Save me reading it myself.'

Will pulled his chair back on the flagstones and came to sit beside David. The book he had been marking flapped itself closed.

With Will helping him puzzle through it, a story rose up off the page, and not a bad one either. When David looked back over it afterwards, he could still pick out the words. Will called him a brainbox with a shocked look and they all laughed.

When Hilda got back, the three of them were playing Happy Families on the little card table by the fire. There was a warm, clean smell of washing drying on the rail overhead.

Hilda stood looking at them with far-away eyes, yawning and pulling off her gloves. 'Well, I think Miss Edmonds and I understand each other now. She just needed to know what she was dealing with, really. Be a good boy, David, and hopefully she'll be good to you.' She wiped her hands as she did on baking days when they were covered in flour. 'Oh, Barbara, you've done the washing up! I don't want you slaving here, with all you do at home! Homework all done, David? And you, Will? Well then – can I play?'

CHAPTER EIGHT

In the car on the way back to Noddfa, Mum moaned about Grand having a go at Grandma Lisa when she mentioned the family tree thing. She always got like that about him, but to Hal it was Grand being Grand. 'We had a good time though,' he said, and she seemed to cheer up.

It had been a great day, especially the tin mine, although that had ended a bit weirdly.

He had led Josh up the hill that rose steeply from the picnic place, pushing along sheep tracks through enormous bracken.

'No sign of the weird girl today?' Josh had said, gasping.

'No. Hopefully it's all just... nothing.' Hal stopped to look back at the family, clustered far below on their tartan squares, Grand a tiny beige figure moving away from them along the stream. Across the valley, farms gave way to wilder hillsides. Cloud shadows passed over them in waves, blown by a balmy wind.

'There's a haunting in my book that started with a shadow,' Josh said. Hal turned and set off again, grasping at rocks and undergrowth, hauling himself up the almost vertical slope. 'I wish I had proper surveillance equipment. I could set it up at the cottage,' Josh puffed behind him.

'You wouldn't find anything. I hope not, anyway.'

'Amazing if we did though.'

Hal wheeled round. 'No! It would spoil the holiday!' Josh flinched and tipped backwards, then grabbed at bracken and froze, staring. 'Shit! I thought I was a goner.' He let out a fake scream, and both the boys laughed so loudly that the others heard way down below and looked up.

The hill flattened out and Hal led the way towards a fenced-off square fringed with bracken. In the middle of it, rock was cut away deep into the earth. Next to the fence were the caved-in leftovers of a stone building, overrun with scrubby undergrowth and saplings.

Hal looked around until he found a reasonable-sized stone. 'Watch!' He heaved like a shot-putter and watched it sail over the fence. There was a pause, then a couple of clacking sounds, one more distant than the other. Finally, after a silence, they heard a crash in the bowels of the earth. 'Mineshaft,' Hal said. Josh's awe turned to excitement as he rushed off to find his own stone. He stood by the fence, weighing it in his hand, then lobbed it with a roar.

They went looking for bigger rocks, moving towards the other side of the fenced-off square. Here, a branch from a mountain ash tree leaned out over the shaft. They spent ages naming different types of throw: 'the discus', 'the throw-in' and 'the free-style'. Then they had challenges. Hal thought up the best one: you had to throw a rock straight to the bottom, without it hitting the sides.

Josh moved right up to the barbed wire fence. 'If you lean over and hold onto this tree, you can chuck it right into the middle,' he said. 'I'll time it on my stopwatch – shit, what is that stink?'

'Sheep shit, isn't it?' Hal pushed his way towards him through a sheep track peppered with little dark turds. But closer to the tree, he got a blast of a cheesy stink, like something dreadful rotting. 'Urrgh. No.' His throat heaved. They stared at each other, Josh clutching a rock against his t-shirt. 'Must be a dead sheep,' Hal said. 'Dad and I found one on a walk in Yorkshire. It was really gross.'

Josh threw the rock and clapped his hands over his nose. The smell was all around them now – it filled Hal's lungs and curdled in his guts.

A sound came wafting up from below: the others were calling. Grand was back with them, and they were looking up and waving their arms. 'They're going on the walk,' Hal said. 'Come on.'

They thudded and leapt their way downhill, gravity making them crazily fast. Hal heard Josh behind him, 'Urghhhhh! What a pong!'

Hal slipped and grabbed at bracken to stop himself falling, the death smell clinging to the back of his throat.

When they arrived back at Noddfa that evening, Dad turned the key and they trooped in with their arms full of picnic stuff. There was a tightness in the air like a ringing so high that only dogs can hear it.

Everyone went quiet.

'It stays so cool in here,' Grandma Lisa said at last. 'I'm going to find my cardi.'

It was Mum and Dad's night to make curry, and they were soon clanking around in the kitchen. Hal headed upstairs to write his journal.

'Josh is out there with his nose in that Paranormal book again!' he heard Grandma Lisa say. 'He keeps reading bits out. I don't think Ruth is impressed!'

'Better than nothing, though,' Grand said. 'We'll send him home a reader yet!' They headed outside.

It was still and quiet on the landing. Hal looked back along the dim corridor, past Mum and Dad's room to Ruth and Toby's at the end. Next to the boys' bedroom was the foot of the attic stairs. The door to the room up there was still jammed. Dad and Toby had both tried it again but said they didn't want to wrench it in case the handle came off. Sue was away so they couldn't ask her about it.

Hal's skin prickled. He opened his bedroom door and checked behind it. Nothing, of course.

He sat on the bottom bunk with his back to the wall and wrote quickly in his journal about the picnic and the tin mine and Grand teaching Josh Welsh swearing. The funniest thing was Josh thinking Barbara's middle name was Kevin. Afterwards you just had to say, 'I mean, Barbara Kevin?' with a confused look and they'd be off again.

Hal heard a noise up above. Dan? A see-saw feeling lurched in his chest. He got up and went out on the landing. The attic stairs were quiet; the door at the top was shut. Dan's voice drifted from the garden, gruff in protest over Auntie Ruth's laughter.

Hal was making his way downstairs when he heard Mum's voice in the kitchen. 'I wasn't sure how it would be, our first year back… But I wouldn't miss it for anything, would you? Chris, the chicken! I thought you were watching it!'

Josh appeared, waving his book and gesticulating. He rounded Hal up and pushed him back upstairs. 'I know what we've got to do! When you sense there's a presence, you ask it a question. We could wait till it's dark, or you could ask now.'

'*Me?* Why me?'

'Because you're the one who saw the shadow. And the girl. You have to ask who she is.'

Hal wanted to tell him not to be ridiculous, but he felt jittery looking at the attic stairs and said, 'I thought I heard something up there.'

Josh held his hands out as though to hold everything back while he thought it through. 'We need to go up there,' he said. 'You first.'

Hal started to object, but Josh shushed and pushed him. Hal led the way up the bare wooden stairs, clasping Josh's arm behind him in case he made a run for it.

Soon they stood together, facing the door. 'Try it!' said Josh.

'*You* try it!'

Josh reached out a trembling hand – and then snatched it back as though the doorknob had burnt him.

'*What?*'

Josh grasped the doorknob, making a face. 'It's not budging at all. It's like there's a weight against it.'

There was no sound apart from their breathing. 'Knock,' Josh whispered. 'Ask who's in there.'

Mum's voice and then Dad's sounded muffled way below. Hal longed for the bustle of the kitchen or the evening sun in the garden. He raised his knuckles and rapped, three times. Silence.

'*Ask!*' Josh hissed.

Hal waited for his pulse to settle. 'Is there anyone in there? Who are you?' he said. Sweat broke out under his t-shirt: heat hung thickly under the roof. He did three more raps and rested his fist on the door.

He felt a knock in his knuckles. From inside. He jumped back.

'What?!' said Josh.

'There was a knock.'

'That was you, wasn't it?'

'Maybe… Yeah,' Hal said. It must have been.

'You're shivering!'

'I'm just cold.'

'Shit Hal! That's a sign!'

'It just *is* cold,' Hal said. 'It's Wales!'

They clattered down to their landing, then down again to the hallway and across to the back door, and outside.

'All right, Hal?' Mum said later. They had rescued the curry, although she said the pan would have to be soaked overnight. They were in the living room now, helping Grand with the *Guardian* Quick Crossword while Dad looked through the quiz book for one they hadn't already done.

'Yeah. Fine!' Hal said, rousing himself. 'Does anyone want a chocolate?'

He hurried back from the kitchen with the Celebrations box, not daring to look at the darkness upstairs. He tried to get everyone talking about plans for tomorrow, but the adults were non-committal – the weather forecast wasn't good.

Josh kept reading out bits from his book about cold spots in haunted houses. Auntie Ruth said, 'Oh well that's *proof* then,' and Josh nodded. He tended not to notice sarcasm.

Hal struggled to stay awake once the TV was on, and almost envied Grandma Lisa when she said her goodnights and went off into their bedroom off the living room. Soon Mum headed upstairs, yawning. The late film came on and Dad and Grand agreed it was a classic.

'I might go up,' Hal said.

'Lightweight!' Dan teased, almost horizontal in an armchair with his legs sticking out.

'Well *you're* not tired because you don't do anything,' Auntie Ruth said, poking him.

'I've been up a frigging mountain! Jeez.'

'This does look good,' Josh said, pretending to be interested in the film. Ten minutes later, though, his head was lolling.

'Come on you two,' Dad said, and Hal led the way upstairs, trying to look reluctant.

Usually he loved the soft darkness at Noddfa – it was restful and full of promise. But once in bed, he was grimly alert, the sleepiness he'd been fighting off gone. He heard Dad climb the stairs and go in the bathroom, then a muttered conversation with Mum from their room. There were murmurings from Dan and Auntie Ruth, but then everyone seemed to settle and the house went quiet.

Hal should be tired – they'd done loads that day. He ran over it all – showing Josh Aberystwyth, then the drive to Bont Goch, opening and shutting all the gates, the picnic by the stream. They were climbing up to the mine now – he slipped with a jolt of alarm. His eyes opened to the dark bedroom.

Footsteps up above. There. And there – a clomp! There was a sound like the whine of hinges, or a creak on the attic stairs. A breath outside the door… Hal jerked his head up. Nothing. He lay down to silence and let his eyes close. All quiet, then tiny shufflings – maybe just the duvet brushing against his face.

From the depths of the house came a horrible cry.

'Josh?' Hal sat bolt upright and fumbled on the bedside table for his head torch. He slid the switch and cold light patterned the room, making the darkness blacker. He got up and peered at the top bunk – it was a wind-up, surely! They'd soon be laughing. But he knew Josh's pretending faces. He was asleep, his mouth hanging open.

Hal bumped his way out onto the landing. The attic stairs were in darkness. He began to creep downstairs, the head torch in his hand making mad shadows on the walls.

The door to the living room was closed. He should leave it. But the cry rang in his ears – desperate – urgent. What if something had happened to Grand or Grandma Lisa? He went over and pushed the door.

The living room looked freakish in the torch's glare, and he switched it off, his fingers trembling. He stepped inside. The night closed around him, black and bristling. He shuffled across to the middle of the room. There was no crying now, just a ringing in his ears. He sensed movement in the shadows – something flitting through the darkness. He whipped his head round, but there was nothing.

He began to ache from bracing himself. He turned and made his way towards the exit, blackness and silence pressing at his back.

There was a flutter near his eyes, and something breathed on him.

He blundered out and ran upstairs. He shut the bedroom door and leaped onto the bottom bunk, burrowing under the duvet. Had something chased him? He clutched at the duvet, pulling it tight around him. But it got airless and hot and his lungs were exploding. He stuck his head out and took a great cool breath.

He lifted his head to listen. There was nothing for a beat, a beat, another. His neck muscles began to cramp and he let his head drop. He jumped at an unearthly sound – an animal outside or another cry from the attic room? The house juddered as if someone had kicked it. Then everything went still.

Hal lay there, blood pulsing, clutching fistfuls of duvet. His breath slowed and his fingers relaxed as at last the night was quiet. He was exhausted – limp and spent, like after football and a shower.

Then sunlight patterned the curtains.

CHAPTER NINE

1940

Hilda spoke in a stream of Welsh to David's friend Iwan. David caught *cae bach* – the little field, and *ieir*, which was chickens.

She straightened up from the side oven, her hair all frizzy from the heat. On Tuesdays this oven was the magical producer of black tins swollen with bread and, if he timed it right, a hot crust and a smear of butter for him. Today the kitchen air was so sweet and fat it went straight from your nose to your belly. Hilda looked at him standing with his arms crossed. 'I said, would you go and feed the chickens, you two? I'm getting a special tea ready for Hugh.'

'What, just for Hugh?'

'No, for all of us of course. I want him to feel at home again.' She flapped away steam and took her glasses off to wipe them on her apron. Her face had a glow that was more than the heat of baking. It had been there since a letter came, weeks ago, saying that Hugh was coming home on leave.

'Are you coming?' Feeding the chickens was David's job, but Hilda usually came out to join him.

'Not now, David, I've got too much on. Go on now, you're under my feet.'

He poured a hopper full of feed into the pan, going for noise rather than neatness, and didn't even stoop to pick up the grains that spilt on the stone floor. He expected Hilda's cry to come after him for the mess, but when he and Iwan headed down the hall to the back door, she was singing under her breath.

David led the way to the *cae bach* beyond the garden and the sycamore tree in the corner. There were two metal chairs under its dappled shade, so that David could sit and throw the feed. When Hilda came with him, they talked about rats, eggs, and the chicken's characters, and shared their news, like Miss Edmonds giving him a new reading book or the Pantgwyns' dog having puppies. Iwan took the other chair now and David scattered feed on the crumbly soil. A feathery rumpus rose around him, then calmed into a throaty noise as the chickens began to feed.

Out of the corner of his eye he saw the bright blue of Barbara's dress. He had noticed it when she arrived today. The colour made her eyes look pretty. He'd never seen her in a dress like that before, not even when she was off to work at the Bath Street Canteen. Lately she said she had served soldiers there who had been evacuated from Dunkirk. David pictured them queuing up for their dinner with scratchy labels round their necks.

He waited for Barbara to come over and ask him about the chickens. She liked hearing him call the ones with Welsh names, and Jean and Flo, who he had named himself. But she was doing something to Will's rose bush, the one David was not even allowed to run past, in case he knocked off a flower.

'What are you doing?' he called. Flo leapt up in the air, squawking.

Barbara had a kitchen knife in one hand and a clump of blood-red roses lay in a basket hanging over her arm. 'Don't look so worried! Hilda said to pick them.' She hacked at another stem.

You look after things for me while I'm away, Will said in the mornings when he went off to get the bus to Aber. 'But they're Will's favourites!'

The skirt of Barbara's dress twirled out and settled again over her legs. 'David, you silly, they're for *Hugh*.' She giggled.

He threw grains that kicked up clouds of dust. The chickens jumped back, fluffing up their feathers, then pecked with panicky haste. A blur of blue and red went past. There was talking and a burst of Barbara's laughter from the house, then a door shut.

'Hey! David!' Iwan was nudging him, blond hair messy on top, eyes excited behind smeary glasses. 'Me and my brother saw Hugh and Barbara in the lane by Cefyn Glas. He had his hand right under her cardigan. Feeling her tits!'

This fell into the growing pile of things David didn't want to know about Hugh, like his regiment, the South Lancashires, his training as a radio operator and him being allowed Will's roses. 'Why would he do that?'

'Bryan says it's how you make babies. They were going like this.' Iwan put a hand in front of his face, and pressed his lips against his palm with a slurping noise. 'Mmmm'. He giggled and wiped a spit-covered hand on his school shorts. 'And this!' He turned his back on the metal chair and put both arms round his own chest, hugging and writhing.

'Urgh!'

'I know. They'll end up with babies.'

David leapt to his feet and his chair thudded to the ground. 'Let's look for rats.'

Rats liked to tunnel under the fence and steal eggs from the chicken coop. Once, Will had pointed to a moving lump just under the turf, and had bashed at it with a heavy stick he kept by the back door. There was a muffled squeal, and Will thwacked until the lump went still, then leaned on his knees, puffing. 'I think we got the bugger, David.'

They looked around for good sticks, and then David pointed at various spots in the garden and shouted, 'Rat!' They piled in, swinging and whacking until no tunnelling vermin could have survived. David was breathless and hot he but didn't want to stop. Soon Iwan pretended to spot rats for himself, but it was David's game, so they ended up having a sword-fight with their sticks, and then Hilda was at the back door, calling.

'Iwan! Go home to Mam now, *bach*. And David, go and get Hugh, will you? He's fishing at the waterfall.'

'It's too far to the waterfall,' he said.

'Oh for heaven's sake!' Hilda flapped a tea-towel hard. The boys froze. She didn't often get cross. 'I just want it to be special!' Her face looked tired – the glow had gone. Why did he ruin everything?

'All right,' he said. 'Sorry.'

She sighed. '*Diolch*.' *Diolch* meant thank you. *Cariad* was her kind word for Will, and, it turned out, Hugh as well. *Cariad bach* was David.

The boys swished their sticks at clumps of grass as they walked down the track, then turned them into machine guns and killed soldiers invading over the hedgerows. When they reached the village, Iwan said something about *ysgol* which meant that he would be waiting when David came out of school on Monday.

The waterfall was the only place in Wales that David hated. Most of the stream was brilliant – better for games than Pollard Street, and the village children knew the best places for damming and trout tickling and swinging over on ropes like Tarzan. But here it went down in a dip and the wood was so thick that it was always dark, even on the sunniest day. The children did not go near it, except for dares.

'Best place around for fishing,' Hugh had said that morning at breakfast. Hilda had saved a bit of bacon, but only enough for Hugh. He had caught David looking at him. 'Apart from the eels! The devil to get rid of if you hook one. Slippery and slimy, thrashing about. Shall I bring one home for you?'

David looked at his bread and butter, breathing in the bacon smell with longing in his belly.

'David's doing so well at school!' Hilda had said. 'Miss Edmonds says his reading is getting so good, she's had to find him more difficult books. Da looked out some of your old favourites, Hugh, from the bookshelf in your room. He's enjoying them, aren't you, David?'

'Someone's got his feet right under the table.' Hugh fixed David with a look, chomping on his bacon. 'Must be lovely for you here, eh? After the slums?'

'Oh now, Hugh,' said Hilda. She poured more tea, her head down. Will cleared his throat. 'So what bait have you got, Hugh?'

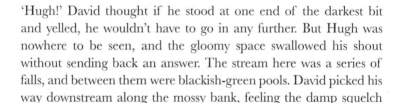

'Hugh!' David thought if he stood at one end of the darkest bit and yelled, he wouldn't have to go in any further. But Hugh was nowhere to be seen, and the gloomy space swallowed his shout without sending back an answer. The stream here was a series of falls, and between them were blackish-green pools. David picked his way downstream along the mossy bank, feeling the damp squelch into his sandals. 'Hugh, where the bloody hell are you?'

In the dimness ahead, he saw a grey-brown hump plop into the water. He shouldn't have chucked away his stick! He turned a corner and an eye-socket stared at him with a bony grin – a sheep's skull lodged among rocks. His sandal slipped and he landed on his bum on the slimy bank, the breath knocked out of him. He scrabbled to his feet. If he fell in, would the water rats come for him? Would the eels?

He saw Hugh's big back in its white shirt and braces, over by the main waterfall. David imagined Barbara squirming like Iwan had, her mouth all spitty.

'Hugh! It's tea time!' The roar of the waterfall buried his cry, and he pushed on, muttering things Hilda said when people were in her way. '*Symud y da dean!*' meant 'move your arse,' and he wasn't supposed to repeat it. Hugh should move his bloody arse – he had taken his bed back and David slept on cushions on the floor in Will and Hilda's room. They shifted in the night and he woke up with his back on the floorboards. *Symud y da dean, Hugh.*

'Oh it's you, is it?'

'It's tea time.'

'Right you are, then.' Hugh reeled in his line and lay his fishing rod down on the bank. Four trout lay in a bucket at his feet, their bellies slashed and bleeding. In the grass was a pile of wiggly guts and dark shining pouches. The carving knife lay bloody and glistening beside it. Did Hilda know Hugh had it?

David backed away, his message delivered.

'Hold on! Can't a man have a fag?' Hugh reached into his pocket for his tobacco tin, then sat on a rock and licked the edge of a cigarette paper. David watched this grown-up marvel, the shuffling of hairy brown tobacco into a line, then the rolling and fastening of a perfect fag. He pictured doing it himself while the village children watched.

'I saw *dwrgi* earlier,' Hugh said, tipping his head upstream, his eyes dark in the gloom. David had heard people say there were *dwrgi* here. It sounded so ghoulish that he never dared ask for the English. 'Sit down, will you? You'll put down roots and grow. Although that wouldn't do you any harm, little squirt like you!'

As David sat on the rock, he felt how wet his shorts had got when he fell. Hugh would laugh if he saw.

A flame flared with a rasping sound in the cup of Hugh's hand. Out of the corner of his eye, David studied the pursed lips, the bluish smoke wisping out. He breathed in deeply.

'That's where the eels come,' Hugh called over the water's noise, waving the fag towards the waterfall. 'Dead sheep get washed downstream and trapped under the cascade. The eels come to eat their brains.' His cackle echoed in the dark space, the roar of the waterfall cutting them off from the world. David saw again the eye socket, the toothy jaw.

'Mam keeps on about you in her letters. So does Babs.' David had a strange rush of sensation. Perhaps the smoke was going to his brain. If they made friends, would Hugh teach David how to roll a fag? 'I hope you appreciate all they're doing for you,' Hugh said. He chuckled and let smoke out of the corner of his mouth. 'A slum kid no one wants.'

David stood up, a pressure in his nose and throat. What if he shoved Hugh into the water? The *dwrgi* would get him. The eels would eat his brains.

'It's you no one wants!' he said, and ran from the thought of the rock-heavy splash, the eels thrashing and feasting. He stumbled over rocks and sank in boggy ground, but struggled on, his legs aching, until he ran out into daylight.

CHAPTER TEN

'What the bloody hell..?'

Grand glared down to see what he had stubbed his toe on and saw a lump of sparkling quartz that Carrie had brought back years ago from a walk to the tin mine.

'What?' Lisa was calling from their bedroom. 'David? What?'

The living room floor was littered with bits and pieces gathered over the years: pastel-coloured pebbles, a plush red dragon of Emilia's that made a chuckling noise if you tipped it up, a snow globe from Aberystwyth and a framed photograph of Lisa with Hal as a toddler, paddling at Llangrannog. When Grand tried to picture what might have happened, he saw a slow-motion movie explosion of knick-knacks flying from the walls.

'Good grief.' Lisa was at his elbow, tying her dressing gown. 'It looks as though there's been an earthquake.'

'An earthquake? In Wales?!' They stood staring.

'Well, I don't know. Caused by fracking or something.'

'Fracking?! What are you on about?'

'It causes little earthquakes!'

'Well, it's a right fracking mess, that's for sure!'

They tried to stifle their laughter because the others were still asleep, but that only made it funnier. When they finally subsided, Lisa bent down to start tidying, 'Someone must have come down for something in the night, and blundered around in the dark.' He had come to the same conclusion. 'Maybe Josh had an oobe,' he whispered, and they were off again, chuckling.

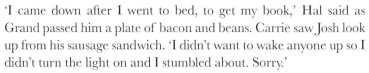

'I came down after I went to bed, to get my book,' Hal said as Grand passed him a plate of bacon and beans. Carrie saw Josh look up from his sausage sandwich. 'I didn't want to wake anyone up so I didn't turn the light on and I stumbled about. Sorry.'

'Don't be sorry!' said Grandma Lisa. 'Nothing wakes me up here,

I sleep so heavily! It's all the fresh air and exercise.'

'Not much chance of that in this poxy weather,' Grand said. The hopeful brightness first thing had been swept away by gusting rain.

'We'll make the best of it,' Grandma Lisa soothed.

'Make the best of it? It's pissing it down!'

Carrie had lain awake last night, brooding about his outburst at the picnic, before slipping into an exhausted sleep. Now Hal was poking at his breakfast instead of eating it.

'Definitely not a day for the seaside.' Chris stood at the rain-spattered window, cradling a mug against his chest.

'Aren't you going to sit down?' Carrie snapped, suddenly unable to bear his morose form, looming there. 'All right, Hal?' she said, and winced to see, fleetingly, that it took him an effort to look bright for her. Perhaps he was coming down with something?

He had been so even-tempered since babyhood. She had taken him for his first injections, anticipating the screams of outrage she remembered from Imogen. But he had just let out a cry as the needle went in, and stopped, mid-yell when it came out. No fury, no *How could you do this to me?* Just a shocked look and then peace, as if the world was good again. She could almost feel his tiny limbs calming in her embrace. His peacefulness had seemed a miracle, the downy skin of his cheek against her lips a stolen pleasure.

'Come on, people, we can do this,' said Toby, rubbing his hands together. 'Who's got a good rainy day game. Dan?'

'We did some great ones at Greg's party…' Dan started.

'Not *drinking* games!' Ruth cut in.

Josh suggested something they had played at his house, and Hal laughed as they remembered. Carrie felt the muscles loosen in her shoulders when she saw him start to eat his bacon. 'Isn't Sue back from the Eisteddfod today?' she said. 'She'll be expecting a visit. Should we go later, as the weather's rubbish?'

'We could,' Grand said. 'Prepare yourself, Josh for a hundred years of village gossip. And a catalogue of who has died.'

'But there's always cake,' said Hal.

'We can ask about the attic room,' said Ruth. 'Toby's going to do himself an injury trying to force it. And Dan's trainers are stinking our room out. Well they *are*, Dan! It smells like something's died in there.'

Dan looked at the ceiling.

'What? It's my job to embarrass you.' Ruth winked at Carrie.

Hal was willing the drizzle to stop as they set off on foot, in kagoules. The sea was invisible in a veil of grey and fat, leathery slugs sprawled across the track.

'I can't believe I missed a haunting,' said Josh, his kagoule hood pulled tight. He had set himself the task of kicking a stone all the way to the village. 'Wake me up next time. And promise you'll tell me if you see the girl again.'

Hal glanced around him. The memory of the night had lingered over breakfast, but then the holiday had enveloped him in the meaty warmth of the kitchen. Even Josh's enthusiasm for hauntings was a comfort, somehow; in daylight it felt more like a game. There was nothing remotely ghostly in the rain-soaked track, just the family in their waterproofs, nattering.

Josh's stone tumbled over Hal's trainer and he side-footed it and set off after it. He hoped Dan would join in, but he didn't. Hal and Josh had a tussle over the stone, then took turns in kicking while Dan plodded after them, shoulders hunched.

By the time they reached the village, the rain had stopped and the sun was appearing in snatches. Steam rose in wreaths from the wet tarmac, and swallows swooped over the hedgerows.

Sue's bungalow looked sparkling white; the lawn velvety and level like a bowling green. The lace curtains in the enormous windows hung in symmetrical waves. Sue stood on the whitewashed doorstep between pots of geraniums, holding a broom.

She was a tiny old woman, thin but lively, not frail-looking. Her hair was arranged in curls so white and thin that you could see the blue veins and freckles of her scalp. She was wearing a white cardigan over a blouse and skirt, with tights and slippers.

Josh and Hal had reached the bungalow first, and Mum hurried to catch up with them. 'Sue, you're back!' It's Carrie! David's daughter.'

For a moment Sue just stared, her blue eyes pale around the pupils, as though she couldn't see them – or was seeing something else. 'Oh!' she said at last. 'Carrie, is it? And David with you?'

'Yes, he's just coming.'

'Oh! Dew dew, yes. David back. And Carrie and…'

'Hal,' he said, smiling to show he didn't mind. He had been visiting her since he was a baby. 'And this is my friend, Josh.'

'And this great brute is Dan, grown enormous,' said Auntie Ruth. 'I'm going to stop feeding him!' Dan shot her a look, but smiled for Sue.

'Oh, dew dew. You've all come! And look at me – in my slippers!'

Grand and Grandma Lisa came up the path, puffing slightly, and the rest of the family stepped aside so Sue could see them. Her face crinkled into an enormous smile, her eyes little blue chips of brightness. She darted forwards to fling her arms around Grand's chest.

'David! Dew, dew, look at you!' She stared upwards as though he'd grown, and he smiled, embarrassed.

'You must come in. Fair play, you must come in.'

They all trooped in after Sue, Mum pointing to the perfect carpet and making 'take your shoes off' motions. Tidy houses made her panicky – theirs was comfortably messy.

Sue shuffled into the kitchen, scoffing when Grandma Lisa said that she mustn't wait on them. They sat in her light, airy living room, admiring the view she had of her neighbours and anyone passing. Pot plants sat on doilies over polished wood. Tiny shelves held china thimbles, brass bells and miniature photographs. The chinking noises from the kitchen got louder and Mum went to help. She came back carrying a tray of tea and two types of shop-bought cake.

They ate on tiny china plates, with cake forks. Grandma Lisa asked Sue where the National Eisteddfod had been that year, but she couldn't remember, even though she had just got back.

'Well, I hope Noddfa is nice for you?' she asked, beaming from her armchair. 'I went with Dewi, my grandson, and Elin, his wife, to make sure they made a proper job of it. I hope you've been warm enough? It felt chilly to me.'

'No, no, it's lovely!' Mum said.

'But we haven't been able to get into the attic room,' Auntie Ruth said. 'The door seems to be locked – or jammed?'

'Locked, you say? Well that's peculiar. Elin definitely went up and cleaned it. Oh now, we did hear a door slam as we were leaving! I said *Shouldn't we go and check, Elin – maybe a window's open and the wind's blown it shut?* But she didn't want to go up there again. And Dewi wanted to get off for some match or other… I'm so sorry, I should have gone to look. Oh, you're a bedroom down – what must you think of us?'

'Oh, it's fine!' Mum said. 'Dan's OK in with his Mum and Dad, aren't you? It's all perfect, as always. This cake is lovely!'

'Well, that's all right then.' Sue's eyes twinkled and her gaze strayed to Grand. 'Sugar sandwiches, I used to give you when you came to visit!'

'That's right!' said Grand, as if she didn't say this every year.

'Sue knew Grand in the war,' Hal said to Josh. He tried to nod with interest while pushing an upright slice of cake into his mouth.

'Oh, yes yes. I taught at the school here. Miss Griffiths, I was, before I got married. And I was good friends with the Evanses, so I kept up with David. He came on something marvellous at Will and Hilda's. A fine time you had of it, didn't you? Running riot in the woods with the village children, playing in the stream, catching trout…' She tailed off, shaking her head.

'It always sounds so idyllic,' said Grandma Lisa, with a bright nod at Grand, who looked irritated. Cups and saucers clinked in a moment of quiet.

'Well I'm afraid I have bad news for you, and on your holiday too,' Sue said. Hal left his fork hovering over the bit of cake he was saving till last. 'I'm sorry to have to tell you that it's Barbara Cefn Glas.'

There was a general *Oh!*

'I wrote to you that she was having tests for her bad chest, didn't I, David? Well, it was lung cancer. Dewi took me to see her at Bronglais Hospital. That was the fourteenth of June. Six weeks later, she was gone. Yes. Dew dew. It was terrible. Just like that. So quick.'

Hal saw Josh giving him a big-eyed look. His fork clacked onto his plate.

Sue dabbed at her eyes with a tiny cotton hankie from her cardigan sleeve. Apart from her, Grand was the only one who had really known Barbara. He sat with a small frown, like when he was trying to work out a crossword clue, while the rest of them made sad noises.

'How old was she, Sue?' Grandma Lisa asked.

'She was eighty-eight. Yes, yes. Six years younger than me.'

Carrie had always had a soft spot for Sue. She was ten when they first visited Wales, and Dad hadn't been there for years before that. After a thrilling but endless journey along winding roads, he had finally led the family though this village – the place of family legend – and knocked on the bungalow door. Carrie's memory was like a home movie viewed over and over: how he had stepped back off the doorstep and stood waiting; how this sprightly old lady had appeared and given him a long, haunted stare. Dad – his hair dark and thick then – had said, 'Hello, Sue'. She had put a hand to her heart and cried, 'David! David bach!' and leapt off the step to embrace him. Dad had looked awkward but happy as she held him tight. 'Oh, David, you'll never guess who's visiting me today!' she had cried, calling, 'Barbara!' and then a bit in Welsh.

A lady with grey-blond hair had come to the door and taken Dad in her arms. 'If only Will could have seen you before he died!' Barbara had said, tears streaming. 'But you'll visit Hilda, won't you, in the home in Bow Street? Oh, David, it'll mean everything to her.'

Carrie and Ruth had stood watching, shocked that such a fierce love was felt for their father.

'Poor Barbara,' Grand said now. 'We were just talking about her!' Thank goodness Sue didn't know they had been laughing about Josh thinking her middle name was Kevin!

'Were you? Well well! That's nice, really, fair play.' Sue gave a final sniff and stuffed her hankie up her sleeve. 'Well, I don't want to spoil your holiday.' She sat forward a little, clasping her hands and smiling at Hal, her eyes still wet. You could still see the love of children that had led her into teaching. 'What have you boys been up to?'

Josh was off, counting things off on his fingers as though she needed an exhaustive list. Hal interjected with the things they still had to accomplish, like seeing a dolphin. Even Dan showed a glimmer of his old enthusiasm for Sue's sake.

Grandma Lisa began to ask about families in the village, and Sue strayed into a level of detail that left most of them behind. Carrie recalled childhood hours spent sitting on the arms of chairs while adults talked and dusk fell, but no one put the light on. That one visit to the old people's home in Bow Street: the wizened, weeping old lady who kept apologising for not being able to welcome them at Noddfa. 'So that's the famous Hilda!' Mum had said afterwards. Dad had had one of his awful moods.

Seeing the boys looking restless, she nudged Chris beside her, and before long he patted his knees and said that they had better get back to find out the cricket scores. They began the process of extricating themselves from Sue's tenacious kindness.

As they made their way back through the village, Grandma Lisa and Grand began pondering what they would have for tea.

'I don't know how they can bear to think about eating,' Ruth said.

Carrie chuckled. 'It *has* been ten minutes since the cake.'

A cloud passed and sunlight gilded the edges of Hal and Josh's hair as they walked ahead. She quickened her steps, wanting to tell them that in the midst of the sad news, she'd had to stifle a laugh about Barbara Kevin.

'It's her!' she heard Josh say. 'It has to be, don't you see? She's just died!'

CHAPTER ELEVEN

Hal was on the sofa with Grandma Lisa when she got up to get the chocolates. They were sitting in the living room so Grand could let his tea go down while deciding for or against the evening walk. 'You're very engrossed in that book, Josh,' she said, rooting through the unpopular flavours at the bottom while peering over Josh's shoulder. '*Calling up the souls of the departed?* I don't think you should be doing that! Thelma says the Bible calls it *despicable practices.*'

'The Bible? Since when do we kowtow to the bleeding Bible?' Grand raged.

She plonked down beside Hal, unwrapping a miniature Bounty. 'I was just *saying*. It's best for the boys to steer clear, or they could give themselves a fright. You don't want that on your holiday, do you Hal?' She reached out and patted his knee.

Auntie Ruth made a face. 'You're not seriously suggesting the souls of the departed could *actually* be unleashed?'

This gave Hal a little shiver, but he felt quite grateful for the way she said it. It must be great to be so sure.

'Do you remember that girl in the sixth form?' Josh said, wide-eyed, holding out a hand as though to calm down an excited crowd. 'She and a load of other kids were in this remote cottage overnight with no parents. And they had a go on a Ouija board. This girl got so freaked out that they had to call an ambulance. She ended up raving mad in hospital, and no one knows what happened because none of the kids will talk about it...'

The story had gone round school, getting more gripping with every telling. The girl had been frothing at the mouth. The other kids had been struck dumb by terror. It was exciting at first, but then Hal noticed that no one seemed to agree on the girl's name or form.

He didn't want to make Josh look stupid, though, so he nodded with a shrug. 'That's what people said.'

Auntie Ruth shook her head. 'Oh well then, that's concrete evidence!'

'No, but it goes to show,' said Grandma Lisa, 'it's all best left alone!'

Mum peered at the pile of board games in the shelves of the TV stand. 'We haven't got a Ouija board anyway. I'm not sure you can raise the dead with Trivial Pursuit.'

Grand laughed, perking up after his rest. 'Right, who's for the evening walk? Josh, I'll tell you the village ghost story!'

'Coming, Chris?' said Mum. Hal thought Dad was going to say 'no' for a minute, but he always went on the evening walk, and he hauled himself out of his armchair.

Auntie Ruth stood up and put on her Enid Blyton voice. 'Terror after tea! Where's Dan?'

'In your room,' Hal said.

'Oh! How unusual.' She pulled a navy sweater over her head.

Josh looked confused. 'But… he is quite often up there.' He went off to call Dan.

'Josh doesn't really get sarcasm,' Hal said.

Auntie Ruth flicked her hair free of the sweater neck and laughed. 'Oh Hal, you're priceless. Don't ever change!'

The sun was shining as they set off, but without much warmth in it. Swallows swooped in the fields on either side of the track. Sheep bleated in an amber glow. Josh hopped about, waiting for the story, but Grand didn't start until they reached the village, where lights were beginning to come on.

'You know the mineshaft you two went up to at the picnic? Well, the villagers used to tell strange stories about it… I heard them first at the Siop.' He stopped walking and Hal realised where they were: right in front of them was the old Siop: a dilapidated brick structure with a corrugated iron roof. It had looked derelict for years, but Sue said that an eccentric man lived there. 'In squalor,' she'd said with a shake of her head. Ivy crawled over the crumbling brickwork, and brambles and bracken grew as high as your hips. Hal and Josh peered through the letter box: grass was growing through the floor of the hallway. The sun had gone below the hedgerows and Hal pulled his hoodie sleeves over his hands.

David arrived at the Siop to see a cart on the verge opposite, the horses reaching out their heavy necks and tearing off clumps of grass. He headed past the Lyons Tea sign to the side of the building with its wavy metal roof. As he went in, the door jingled over the murmur of concealed Welsh voices.

'All right, David?' said Jim, heaving a sack of flour onto a pile on a trolley. Jim had sticking out ears and a wispy brown moustache with long, sharp points. He wore a shirt with rolled-up sleeves, a tie and a long apron. 'I've got Geraint Bwlchrosser down today. You can go in and wait with the others. But first…' He tapped the side of his nose and turned to take a toffee from a jar. He pressed it into David's hand. 'That's between ourselves, mind. What's Hilda after, now?'

David handed over Hilda's list. There was warm laughter from the living room, and he peered inside. Geraint came down from his Bwlchrosser hill farm once a month for supplies. He sat in an armchair, cradling a cup and saucer in both hands, his eyes like chips of slate in a leathery, wrinkled face. All the hill farmers looked craggy and windswept to David, like the landscape. Across from Geraint sat Elfred from the Post Office in a tweedy jacket, smoking his pipe. Avarina Siop, Jim's wife, perched on the arm of a chair with a white apron over her dress.

'*Sut dych chi, David?*' said Elfred.

'*Da iawn, diolch.*' He was fine.

'Well, listen to you. You've gone native!' said Elfred, switching to English. There was chuckling. David began to chew on the toffee, which soon stuck his teeth together.

'Geraint was just telling us, one of his sheep went down an old mineshaft,' Avarina told David.

Geraint shook his head. 'Young sheepdog, one of Ceri's pups. Scatty thing! Must have chased her. They don't usually go near.'

'Remember the story, Elfred,' called Jim from the doorway, 'about the old tin mine on the hill?'

There was a drawing in of breath in the crowded parlour. David released the toffee with his tongue and a burnished taste swirled out in a rush of sweetness. 'What story?'

The listeners settled in, leaning forwards in anticipation and making the old armchairs creak. 'Well in the old days, you see,' said Elfred, holding the bowl of his pipe, 'it was a busy mine, and Cefyn Glas was a pub for the workers. Now the publican's daughter was very beautiful, and had a lovely voice. She used to win prizes at the eisteddfod at Bethesda Chapel, Tynant. Well, when she was sixteen, she fell in love with one of the miners. Her father was furious, but she adored this chap. He said he'd come for her at closing time one night and take her away to the South. He'd find work in the coal mines, he said, and they'd get married. Well the night came, and she waited and waited, but he never turned up. He'd gone, you see, back to his wife in Brynamman. And the next night, this beautiful girl went out for a walk and she never came back. They found her at the bottom of the mineshaft, her back broken. Dead.'

'Ohhh!' Avarina pressed a hand to her neck.

'But that wasn't the end of it!' called Jim from the shop, over the sound of something rattling into his big metal scales. 'Was it, Elfred?'

'No it was not!' Elfred pointed the end of his pipe at David. 'The miners walking home from the pub used to see a beautiful woman, walking up to the tin mine. And long after that mine closed, there were still stories of strange happenings. Geraint, your father had one, didn't he?'

Geraint nodded, rattling his teacup, and Avarina stood up to take it from him. He took a moment of silent head-shaking, until David couldn't wait for him to start. 'Young man from the village came to visit my father at the farm. That evening, he was walking back to the village when he saw a girl on the path in front of him, wearing a white dress. She turned and smiled, and she was beautiful. When she walked on, she started singing. A lovely sound, it was, and he followed her down to the stream and then up the hill. It got dark and all he could see was the white of her dress – but he could hear her singing. She made her way up to the disused mineshaft and something made him follow her. When he got to the edge, he couldn't see her any more, but the singing sounded nearer than ever.

Suddenly he felt two cold hands on his back, giving him a great big shove! He'd have fallen to his death, but he caught hold of a tree branch. Well he ran down that hill like the devil was after him. They found him in the village, white as a sheet. He was never the same again. His family were so frightened, they moved away from Bont Goch and never came back.'

2011

'Woah!' said Josh. 'Are there loads of stories like that about Bont Gorr?'

'One or two,' Grand said with a grin. 'No truth in them, of course. Just winter's tales, to help pass the long, dark evenings.'

Grand began the walk back and they all followed. Hal stuck close to the centre of the group, peering into the dusk. It was cold as they reached the turning and set off down the track to Noddfa in thickening darkness. *Her back broken. Dead.* Bats were flitting about under the black trees overhead.

'Was that a bat?' said Uncle Toby, in a silly scary voice. 'Or a ghost?'

Something swooped at the boys and Hal felt a panicked flap whizz past his face. He and Josh ducked and ran, shrieking – only half as a joke.

They ran the rest of the way and didn't stop, panting, until they were outside the house.

'That smell at the tin mine!' Hal said when he'd got his breath back. 'I thought it was a sheep...'

'Oh my God! A ghostly stink...' Josh clutched his arm. 'This could be Britain's Most Haunted Village!'

Dan loomed out of the darkness, making them both jump. 'Chill, you two!' he said. 'It was a *bat*!'

CHAPTER TWELVE

1940

David heard a shriek and whirled round. He had been playing on the hillside behind Iwan's house. He was the only evacuee who was allowed to be an Indian with the Welsh kids. If you were an Indian, you leaped out of a thorny hideaway and hurtled down the slope, screaming a war-cry. When you got to the bottom, you might get to kill one of the cowboys (evacuees). It was only shouting *You're dead* but the whooping celebrations with the other Indians made you want to climb right back up the hill and do it again. The shadows were deepening as David hurried along the track to Noddfa. He felt the shriek right in his heart.

'David!' Barbara was hunched, sobbing, her hands flailing through her hair. 'A bat!'

He waved his arms around her head. 'It's all right! Barbara! It's gone.'

She slumped to the ground and sat on the sun-dried earth. 'Oh David! What am I going to do?'

When David went out to play earlier, Barbara had been laughing too loudly in the kitchen at Noddfa, and Hugh had been looking even more full of himself than usual. Will and Hilda had whirled round, hugging everyone. 'You'll help me plan the wedding, won't you?' Barbara had said, clutching Hilda's hands. So why was she sitting there now, all upset?

Barbara was usually so cheerful with her jokes and bits of news from the Bath Street Canteen. Her voice went all high with admiration when Hilda told her about David's reading and his Welsh, and how strong his arms were getting from helping knead the bread in the old tin bathtub every Tuesday.

David remembered what Hilda always did when the other evacuees got parcels from home. He crouched down next to Barbara and put his arms around her. He could feel her warm softness shaking.

'It's Mam,' Barbara said, a sob in her voice. 'She won't hear of us getting married. Says it's not respectable in such a hurry, and we should wait till the war's over and Hugh's settled. And he's furious and says we should go ahead anyway – it's what everyone's doing. But Mam's so delicate, David. What if it made her really ill?'

Will and Hilda called Maggie Cefyn Glas *a perpetual invalid*. There didn't seem to be a word for her illness, apart from *bedridden*, but Barbara was always fretting about it and rushing home. 'Oh, Maggie's always on the brink of death,' Hilda would say when she'd gone. 'Especially when it suits her.'

'Where's Hugh?' David asked.

'Probably at the White Lion in Talybont. And now I've got to tell Will and Hilda. What on earth are they going to think of us Maddochs? I mean, who wouldn't want Hugh in their family?'

David was glad of the deepening darkness to hide his face. It was getting colder and his legs were stiff from crouching.

'We've got such plans,' said Barbara. 'Hugh's going to set up a shop in town, selling transistor kits and radios. Imagine us, in a flat above a shop in Aber, David. You could come and visit!' Perhaps he would, David thought, but only when Hugh was out. Barbara sniffed. 'Well, looks like that dream's over.'

David scrambled up and pulled her hand to haul her to her feet. 'Will and Hilda will know what to do.' He led the way down the track and round the bend where patches of warm light spilled from the house.

⤛

Later, David crept to the top of the stairs. He had been sent up to bed, but his guts were all tight in case there was a row like in Pollard Street. But the talk from below was Welsh and muffled – Will's low rumble and Hilda's exclamations, and Barbara's *Oh Hildas* and *Oh Wills*. It lapsed into silence and then started again. No smashes, though – no bellows or screams.

His head was lolling against the wood of the banister when he heard the front door close. Will and Barbara's voices drifted off into the night. He must be walking her home.

David's bare feet made no noise on the stairs. Through the living room doorway, Hilda sat in her armchair, darning a sock in the circle of light from the oil lamp.

'David *bach*, what are you doing up?' He was afraid she'd send him back upstairs. But she put the sock down and he ran and climbed onto her lap. 'Couldn't you sleep?' He shook his head, leaning into the yielding warmth of her front.

'That bloody woman will have Barbara in that house till she's old and grey, if she has her way. Waiting on her hand and foot. She does all the cooking and housework, you know. Maggie makes her rub the flagstones with a dock leaf to make patterns! It's no life for a young girl. But Barbara's afraid to go against her.'

'She should listen to you,' he said through a yawn. 'Not the bloody woman.'

She went still and stared at the fire, barely aglow now in the grate. 'Maybe she will, in time. Yes! We should go ahead and plan this wedding. I could run up a nice outfit for Barbara, and we could think about a spread afterwards at the school. Keep her happy and hopeful. Then by the time Hugh gets leave again, she'll have plucked up the courage.' Hilda's eyes were bright, reflecting the last of the firelight. 'Now up to bed, young man!'

He woke later still to pitch blackness, lying on his cushions on the floor. Someone was crashing around below. Will and Hilda were out of bed, muttering and fumbling to light the lamp. He followed them downstairs.

Hugh was slumped at the kitchen table, his eyes half closed. There was a waft of beer, like when Dad was up to his tricks. David's tummy felt shaky.

'Hugh, you silly bugger,' said Hilda, adding some fruity Welsh. 'Let Dad get you up the stairs. It's going to be all right.'

'I love her, Mam,' said Hugh with a babyish noise.

'You might want to tell her then, instead of going to the pub!'

'All right now,' Will said. 'We'll talk in the morning.' He leaned down, got his arm round his son's back and hoisted him upright. Hugh flopped where he stood like a great beer-stinking Guy on bonfire night.

Hilda looked tired. As the two men thumped and dragged up the stairs, a London memory came to David. 'I'll get the bucket,' he said, 'in case!'

Footsteps up above. A slither and a clomp. Hal stared into the blackness, a vice round his heart. There was someone up there in the attic room. It went quiet again. He'd dreamt it, surely.

Then a squeal of hinges. He held his breath. Was that his own blood, pulsing in his ears? It beat on until he breathed again, but then came a creaking, closer.

It might be Mum or Dad – perhaps he should open the door. No! His ears strained. A faint rattle from the top bunk was Josh snoring.

Knock knock. Gentle but real.

'Yes?' he yelped. The silence stretched out. When he was little, Dad said that old houses made all kinds of noises, settling in the night. It had always calmed him down if he was jittery. His pulse began to slow.

Knock, knock, knock.

'Josh!' he hissed, bashing the slats of the bunk above. He clambered out of bed and reached up to poke him. 'Someone knocked at the door!'

He sat up. 'Shit. Really?'

'Listen!' They froze, Hal gripping Josh's arm. 'It's stopped,' he whispered. He grabbed the head torch from the bedside table and switched it on. Josh's face was white, with shadows in the eye sockets. You could hear him breathing.

'Should we look?' Josh said finally. 'Or try to get to sleep?'

Hal was tired of being screwed up tight, afraid of being afraid. Maybe he should get back into bed. But Josh would fall asleep first – he always did – and Hal would be alone. 'What does your book say?'

There was a shuffling as he changed position on the top bunk. 'I've left it downstairs. But you should ask if it's Barbara. Go to the door.'

'No way, Josh, shit!'

'I don't mean open it. Just ask. Ghosts are trying to get your attention. Sometimes if you find out who it is, they go away.'

'If I'm going to the door, you're coming with me.'

'All right. Chill out,' Josh said. The creaky frame shook as he climbed down the ladder. Hal whispered, *Now* and they both took a step towards the door. The shadows swung with the head torch in Hal's hand.

'Who are you? Is it Barbara?' Hal said. They waited. Did the silence feel different now? With less of a sense of *someone*? It went on, unchanged.

Josh nudged him. 'What if it's the girl from the mineshaft? Was there singing?'

'No! Just knocking.' It seemed silly now, standing there asking questions, like in the daytime when it was all more like a game.

Hal backed up and sat on his bunk. His head felt heavy. Soon he swung his legs up and lay down. Josh climbed up to the top bunk, his weight wobbling the frame with a reassuring noise.

'Josh?' Hal said. 'Would you stay awake for a bit? Keep watch? Things seem to happen when it's just me.'

'Of course. I've got it all covered. You go to sleep.'

Carrie woke with a jolt of fear. Had there been a noise? A nightmare? Her dream unfurled before her – she and Emilia in a pen with lambs pushing all around them. Em was a little girl, drinking from a baby bottle, and then suddenly a teenager, shouting about something, furious. The lambs were bleating, frightened by her noise.

But this hectic heat, this racing in her chest! Her mind ranged bleakly over everything that might have caused it. The bookshop? No, she was on holiday. She had texted the owner, Rhoda, earlier, to check everything was OK. Dad? Or Chris? Nothing rushed to engulf her. And yet she daren't even move to look at the clock, or push the duvet off her. Imogen, in Africa? *Oh Chris, wake up and be with me.* But he slept on, a still, dark shape. The sweat went cold on her skin and chilled her through.

CHAPTER THIRTEEN

Carrie woke in a milky dawn and lay exhausted, longing to slip back under the cover of sleep, but her mind was whirring, alert for trouble. She reached through a fog of befuddlement. It was the first Thursday. They were going to see the seals. There had been no fallings out – in fact they had made the most of a rainy day yesterday and she had enjoyed the evening walk.

Maybe she should go out for a walk now to shake off this mood. She had always liked to be alone with her thoughts in the quiet of early morning, in a landscape both ancient and fresh, reborn with each new day. Sometimes she and Chris snatched this time together before they were swallowed up by the family. But she knew in a dark instant that she didn't want him to come today.

Memories crept in between sleep and full wakefulness. Sandaled feet on powdery earth; pink mist on the horizon and a shivery breeze…

1981

Hungry for sea-kissed air, Carrie had got out of her bunk without waking Ruth, then stepped carefully round Emilia's camp bed. She was tiptoeing to the front door when a creak sounded behind her.

'Where are you going?' said Emilia, on the stairs in her orange and white gingham nightdress.

'Shhhh!' Carrie pointed to the door.

'Can I come?'

The walk would be spoilt if something upset Emilia, and she could get upset about *anything*: a bee flying near her, a taste she didn't like, something she ate that made her lips or her throat hurt. There had been a furore over a roll yesterday lunchtime – she had wailed like a toddler, mouth wide, spewing half-chewed mush into Mum's tissue. 'You're eight years old, for God's sake!' Ruth had hissed. Carrie was sent to ask for water and walked through a barrage of stares, her face hot with shame. Then Dad had snapped at her for taking too long. The water seemed to make things worse, so Mum took Emilia to the loo, while Ruth said, quite audibly, 'Why does she even have to *come*?'

Em stood there now, fair hair a messy mop, limbs still gently rounded like the toddler Carrie used to comfort with a cuddle. Maybe a walk together now would make her easier to cope with for the rest of the day. Carrie nodded.

They stepped outside to sun blushing through mist, leaves dancing. A summer day was holding its breath before unfurling. Tiny birds swooped over the track with joyful chirrups. They had barely gone two steps when Emilia stopped with a sharp intake of breath. *Already?* thought Carrie.

'Oh! Mum's right. I *am* a disaster area!'

'What? Why?'

'I forgot to put knickers on.' Her face was so stricken that Carrie burst out giggling, and then Em was laughing too, clamping a hand over her mouth and another over her gingham-covered bum as she turned to go back inside. 'What if Ruth wakes up?'

Carrie shrugged. Ruth was fifteen, five years older than Carrie, and acted above everything she liked doing. 'She won't want to come.'

Emilia returned quickly and they made their way down the track. 'A knicker disaster,' Carrie chuckled, and that set them off again. Some way along, Emilia picked a stalk of dry grass and ran a finger and thumb up the seed head, her face quiet, enraptured. A beam of sunlight turned the flying seeds to gold dust. She walked ahead, smooth brown legs between her nightie hem and sandals. She didn't ask where they were going, and Carrie didn't know. Just out, into the day.

A cow gave a sudden moo from the other side of a hedge, and Emilia froze, startled, but her face relaxed as Carrie giggled. 'You went like *this*,' she said. Em laughed and did it again. No telling off from Dad about teasing with just the two of them. No lip-trembling or falling out.

Carrie was chilly even with a cardigan on, and Emilia had nothing over her nightie. But she walked on at a dreaming pace, without complaint, her small feet and sandals soon coated in dust.

As they turned round a curve, she stopped.

On the grass beneath the hedgerow was a cluster of rabbits, nibbling and loping about, noses twitching, eyes dark and beautiful. And there were little ones. Carrie's heart ached to hold their soft brown sides in her arms.

Em's whisper was husky: 'Oh Carrie, look! Babies!'

They froze like in 'musical statues' and the rabbits ignored them, as if they were part of the landscape like the trees.

The spell was broken by another loud moo and cow-heavy crashing beyond of the hedge. The rabbits looked up. Tails flashed white as they scattered with their fluid, tumbling run.

The girls didn't speak of it. No one said, 'Well, wasn't that lovely,' or 'I'm so glad we came.' They just turned and headed back to Noddfa in companionable silence, their sandals scuffing up the dust.

2011

Carrie tensed, hearing muttering down below: Grandma Lisa's surprise and Grand's bass mumble. But the voices sounded peaceful enough amid the grunts and shuffles. She had a sudden urge to be with them.

'Hello darling!' her mother said. 'We've had shenanigans again! Look – all the chocolate wrappers –they were all in that bowl, but we've just found them all over the room. I mean everywhere, as if a wind had swept through. Or some magical force.'

'Some joker more like,' said Grand, tying his dressing gown. 'Must think we were born yesterday. You don't know anything about it, do you, Carrie?'

She gave an outraged laugh, anticipating Ruth's reaction when she told her. 'No! I went up before you did. They were still in the bowl then.'

'Probably just boys being boys,' Grandma Lisa said as they made their way into the kitchen.

Carrie made a pot of tea and she and her mother sat sipping; easygoing chat breaking out in snatches. Grand put the apron on and started banging about with frying pans and laying packets of sausages on the worktop. He swore when he couldn't find something, but waved Grandma Lisa away crossly when she tried to help. Gradually the noise and the bacon smells brought the others down one by one.

'Ah, I love it when we're all together!' Grandma Lisa said as Dan finally took his place, yawning behind his floppy fringe. Grand gave the sausage pan a vigorous shake, as if to shush her. She put a hand on Hal's shoulder and he smiled. 'When you think of the memories in this place! The people who've been through it. And some of them no longer with us...'

Did Carrie imagine that her father froze, hunched over his pan? She wanted to cut Mum off – talk about the day ahead, the seals, anything – but her throat tightened. She waited for Ruth to issue one of her retorts, but she was staring at her cereal and silence had descended like a shroud.

'Barbara, I mean,' Grandma Lisa said, with a little cough. Scraping and frying sounds started up again. 'I wonder what Imogen's up to in darkest Africa? I keep trying to picture her.'

'I bet it's *amaze-balls* and *awesome*,' said Hal. 'Do your impression, Dad! What were they like when you dropped her off at Tania's? Was Holly there? Was there loads of squealing?'

They all turned to Chris, and for a moment even Carrie expected one his skits – he was a brilliant mimic with his teacher's ear for teenage affectations. He just shrugged. She had a strange wave of missing him, as if he wasn't here.

'Oh my God,' said Hal, with a Facebook pout. 'I'm like, *so* in Tanzania, I can't *believe* it.'

Chris's eyes were blank and distant in the laughter that followed. Carrie hoped desperately that Hal hadn't seen. Was Chris missing Imogen that much? Or worrying about her?

Grand put the final breakfast in his own place with a flourish. 'Today, Josh, it's the Thursday, so that means Cardigan Island Coastal Farm Park – or as we call it *The Seals*.'

'I'm there, Grand,' Josh said, and they were laughing again as though the day could be lifted and everything healed.

'I mean who the hell wants brie and cranberry?' Grand said later to Carrie. They had stopped at Tesco's for sandwiches. 'And what's a chicken and chorizo wrap when it's at home?'

'An abomination!' said Ruth, snatching one up and plonking it in her basket. Carrie pointed out other options to him, and eventually he resigned himself to tuna mayo, but only if it was on white.

But it was a beautiful day as they walked out of the modern barn that housed the ticket office and café for the Farm Park. There were puffs of fair-weather cloud on the horizon, but deep blue arched over the cliffs undulating into the distance.

Carrie thought the boys might be too old to buy animal feed for the petting farm, but Hal, Josh and then even Dan joined the queue. Ruth opened her mouth as if about to tease him, but her face softened as she watched him telling Josh about the place. She shared a look with Carrie, a hand on her heart.

And there was still plenty to entertain them: emus and a wallaby among the donkeys and pigs. A goat head-butted Josh's feed bag out of his hand and gobbled up the spoils.

Once they were through the farm, the walk began in earnest. Grassy hills cut away in dramatic rock faces to the waves below. At every turn of the cliff edge, they stopped and peered out.

'Seal!' Hal yelled, his arm outstretched. To their right was an inlet of greenish water, lapping gently against rock, and yes! A slick head bobbed up and a whiskered face looked at them. The seal dived and came up closer – doe-eyed, putting on a show. Moments later another emerged. Hal's shout had attracted a little crowd, who gathered around, exclaiming.

Ruth nudged Carrie, who was snapping away with her phone, and pointed out Dan, peering at the seals, hands thrust in pockets. 'I don't think he knows whether to be excited or mortified. God, remember those teenage agonies?'

Carrie smiled, remembering Ruth's scornful teenage years, when the age gap between them had seemed bigger than ever. They hadn't really been close until Ruth had Dan a year after she had Imogen.

Grandma Lisa clapped her hands together, gazing at the seals. 'I just love to see life in the wild! So much nicer than sea life centres and circuses.' She said this every time they came. Grand stood like an old bull seal basking in the sunshine, jacket over his arm, and let everyone have a go with his binoculars.

'I've taken three hundred rubbish pictures!' Carrie said to Chris, still holding up her phone.

'Well I for one can't wait to see them,' laughed Ruth when Chris didn't react.

The seals headed seawards now, dark shapes gliding through turquoise water until the waves further out concealed them. The family continued in buoyant spirits.

Their destination was the gate with a notice saying you ventured beyond it at your own risk. Grandma Lisa always sat nearby while the others embraced the danger.

'Your seat's free!' Carrie said, and walked her to the usual bench.

'There you go,' said Grand as he pushed open the gate for the others. 'Scaredy-cats need not apply.'

Grandma Lisa tutted, but looked serene, sitting back and admiring the bay. 'I just love it here! And the children do too, don't they?' A little frown deepened the wrinkles in her brow. 'Although, do you remember when Imogen got that awful vertigo? We couldn't work out why she was in such a terrible mood, and it turned out the cliff edge was making her feel sick! She had to sit here with me.'

Carrie turned her face away at the mistake. Imogen always made a point of going through the gate. Last time she had had a craze for photography and had scared them all with her forays towards the sheer drop, wielding her digital SLR. It was Emilia, years ago, who had been afraid of the edge. How could Mum confuse her and all her fuss with Carrie's brave, sturdy girl?

'See you in a bit, then,' she managed to say, standing up to go and push through the gate.

Beyond the boundary were dry, spongy grasses and rocks crusted with yellow lichen. There were no fences to interrupt the view, and the others sat looking down at the shore where seals came to bask in the sun.

Dan got up to peer over the edge and Toby called, 'Don't come running to me if you dash your brains out!'

Carrie sat close to Chris. Talking seemed too much effort, and they watched a seal gliding towards the rocks. She recalled Chris's steadying comfort last year, his knack of knowing exactly when she needed him, his hand closing round hers. But when she glanced down, half thinking she'd felt it, his hand was limp in his lap.

The seal had hoisted itself up and was slapping and dragging across the rocks, robbed of its watery grace.

'I'm going over the other side,' Carrie said, scrambling up.

Across the promontory, blackish rocks covered in barnacles led in rugged steps towards the sea. She imagined the cuts if you fell.

Chris had got the hint and followed her, and as they came to a stop and stood looking out, she told him about what her mother had said. 'I mean, she's always a bit vague but… I could have screamed.' A glance at his face showed only bafflement. 'It was Emilia who was scared of the edge,' she said, 'not Imogen. God Chris, are you with me at all?'

He made a half-hearted gesture at his standing presence. A joke too feeble to count.

She wanted to shout, but there were people around. 'I might as well be alone.'

Chris's foot scuffed the rock. 'All your family's here.'

'That's why I need you! I thought after all that's happened, you'd have some fucking clue…' She had thought tears were coming but instead this nasty voice – and now his stricken face.

'Sorry. Carrie?!'

She had whipped round, she was storming off, stumbling on scrubby grasses. As the gate slammed behind her, she looked up at the bench. Somehow she managed a fake smile at her mother, so she wouldn't know they were rowing.

Chris needed to get where no one could see him. Carrie had stormed off and left him standing there, exposed. The rocks that stepped down seawards were strewn with black pools. The sea roared as he thudded to the next level, sick with the danger of falling. The next step was deeper. He hung off the edge by his hands and dropped, grazing his palms on barnacles. His foot slipped as he landed and he ended up on his arse in a wet patch, winded, staring at foam bursting from the rocks below.

There was no relief after all in being alone. He had seen the look on Carrie's face: he was useless to her. Worse than useless, if she knew the truth.

Imogen in the car on the way to Tania's house, gabbling about what they were going to do in Tanzania: not only bricklaying for the new building, but teaching a lesson at the makeshift school. Visiting a craft centre for the disabled. Shopping in the market. The more she talked, the more his heart burned. Almost as if she were goading him.

'We will miss you in Wales,' he said.

She gave a tinkling laugh and flicked her hair. 'Oh I know you will. I am lovely, after all. But I've got bigger fish to fry this year, Dad. Africa!'

He should have been thrilled – he'd wanted this for her. But everything had taken such an ugly turn. She had no sense of the dangers pressing in on her; the shadow this was throwing over the holiday, which he needed like a lifeline. He wanted to stop the car and make her see – wipe that lip-glossed smile off her face.

And then her bloody phone beeped: a text message. KYLE'S MUM. Tyrone's Mum too. Why was she texting Imogen? He flushed hot, then went clammy and cold, his pulse revving faster.

And now on the black rock, he sweated with shame. Because he had done it, he had stopped the car.

Carrie rounded a corner in the cliff edge, not knowing where she was going. It was all churning over in her gut. She headed uphill towards a bushy stretch of fence. She wasn't even sure what had really upset her. That no one talked about it? She didn't herself. Did she want them to? No, it was Chris's weird mood… it felt like a desertion. A tightness mounted her spine and gripped the back of her head.

Her phone beeped – she must have walked into a signal. She fumbled in her bag in her haste to get it out. It was a text from Rhoda. *Hope you're enjoying your annual pilgrimage! Was at the shop this morning, everything's fine. Amanda came in. Said Chris texted her from Wales, about a student! You both need to forget about work. That's an order from me! xx*

She approached the wooden fence and leaned on it. Amanda, a Teaching Assistant from Chris's team. That must be who the text was from, the one he wouldn't talk about. A reply to a text from him about a student. The bay stretched ahead of her: peaceful water criss-crossed by boat trails. Sea birds bobbed and dived. A bee buzzed past.

What am I really worried about? Chris. Tyrone. Imogen. Worst case scenarios stirred up her belly. There was still no news from Tanzania. She had a signal – a chance to put her mind at rest. She could carry on then, despite everything.

Carrie had swapped numbers with Eileen, mother of Imogen's friend, Holly, at the Tanzania meeting. She tapped fast with her thumbs. *Have you heard from Holly? I know they said we wouldn't hear but am stupidly on tenterhooks!*

She sent it. It was done. Could she calm down and go back to the others? No, not until she heard.

People were approaching, pointing at the water. Their exclamations drifted over on the breeze: excitement from a more innocent age. Carrie stared out but saw nothing.

When her phone beeped, she started, and it leaped from her hand and fell on the far side of the fence.

'Shit. Shit!' She leaned over, feeling around, and found the hard shape in the undergrowth. She tapped in her pass code, wrong first, then again. A text from Holly's mum.

Yes she managed to get a message out through Facebook. She's fine – a bit overwhelmed at first but enjoying it now. I thought Imogen went to Wales with you instead?

CHAPTER FOURTEEN

1941

David huddled in Will's armchair in the living room, reading. It was Tuesday, but there had been no Welsh cakes, hot off the griddle, when he got home from school. There was no yeasty fug of baking to keep him warm now. Some kind of sewing fuss was going on in the kitchen.

He heard Hilda say his name and '*A Christmas Carol* – Dickens, Barbara!' then in Welsh, 'He's not even nine. We're so proud of him.'

David had asked so many questions about the tin mine story that Will had said, 'I know just the book if it's ghosts you're after. I'm sure we've got one in the school library that would do for you. Oh, I know you're not grammar school age yet, but you're a reader. You need feeding!'

'David, *bach*, come and help, will you?' Hilda called.

'You should get him reading in Welsh,' Barbara said.

Hilda muttered something David couldn't quite hear. He put the open book face down in the seat of the armchair and went into the kitchen.

'Excuse my state of undress,' said Barbara.

She was wearing a silky slip, her hair a loose blond rope hanging over one shoulder. The wintry light from the window made her face and chest look bluish, while the yellow glow of the oil lamp lit up her back. On her bottom half was the skirt of the wedding suit that Hilda had made her; dove-grey, they called it. The jacket lay on the table with pins in its sides. The suit was kept in the wardrobe upstairs, but every now and then, the wedding talk started again and Hilda got Barbara to try it on.

Hilda was on her knees on the flagstones in her green wool dress with her thickest brown cardigan on top. She took two pins from between her lips, stuck them in a pincushion and handed it to David. 'Hold this for me, *bach*.' She put two fingers inside the waistband of the skirt and said to Barbara, 'This rotten bloody rationing! You've lost another inch off your waist.'

'I think it's that letter from Hugh. I mean, I missed him when he was at Formby, but I could sort of imagine him there. And York. Even that place in the Orkneys… you got the gist of it from his letters, didn't you? But people keep saying it could be India he's going to…'

Hilda tweaked the skirt and looked up, but Barbara's head was turned towards the window where a cold, damp afternoon was fading into evening. David thought of the deep snow that had piled on the sills last winter. One day they had had to dig their way out of the front door with shovels. 'Another Christmas in Wales, is it, David?' Roslyn Post Office had said recently with her staring eyes and frizzy black and grey hair. 'Still, it's lovely for Hilda and Will.' He shivered, wondering when Hilda would get the fire going.

'There,' she said. 'I'll start sewing tomorrow when the light's better. Then why don't you take it home, Ba? Show Mam and Dad?'

'I wish I had the courage… I saw Sue Griffiths at the Siop today. She's all giddy. Her Bryan arrives in Aber tomorrow. I said of course I'd be at the wedding – but I'm not looking forward to it, Hilda! People keep asking about Hugh and me… And now this posting…'

Hilda patted the skirt down and sat back on her heels, looking up at Barbara. 'All the more reason,' she said.

'I know. You are right. I know that.'

'Well then. Help an old lady up, David!' Hilda leaned on his shoulder and groaned, getting to her feet. 'Have a word this evening, Ba. Kind but firm, like we said. We can have everything fixed for his next leave.'

'Yes. Damn it, I will.' Barbara seemed to forget David was there. She took the skirt off with a faraway look, revealing a confusion of white skin and dark belt contraptions before stepping into her old one.

When Barbara had left, Hilda riddled the fire and put another log on, then hoisted a pot of soup on the range to warm. 'We just have to pray.'

'What for?' said David. He was laying the table in the hope of hurrying up tea.

'For Hugh and Barbara's future.' Hilda stirred the *cawl* with her eyes closed for a moment, then looked at David. 'And that the old witch doesn't have one of her emergencies.'

Hal watched Grand walk off after the others. 'So what do you think?' Josh said, the minute he had gone. He had a way of starting conversations in the middle.

Hal knew in a second what he was asking, though he had forgotten for a bit, what with seeing the seals. 'I think there's something in the attic room. And … I think it comes downstairs.' Just saying it aloud made his back go all shivery.

Josh looked solemn. 'But do we still think it's Barbara?'

'I don't know. It makes sense, because she's just died. And there's never been anything weird at Noddfa before. But…'

'What?'

'Well, Barbara was *old*. Chucking chocolate wrappers around seems like something a kid would do.'

Josh tapped at his top lip, deep in thought. 'But she might have come back to haunt Grand, because he knew her.'

Hal felt a little spark of hope. 'Yeah! It was Grand who found the mess that first time. And then the chocolate wrappers.'

'But he doesn't seem to have heard the knocking last night…' Josh said.

'No, but he often doesn't hear stuff.' Hal picked off a chunk of moss with his fingernails and scraped the rock beneath. Who was he trying to convince that Grand was the target of all the weirdness – Josh, or himself? 'Didn't you feel anything, last night?'

'*Duh*, of course I did. It was spooky as shit.'

'Right. Cos I'm not making it up.'

'Course not. Why would you?' His honest shrug released a pressure in Hal's belly. Snide digs were not Josh's thing.

'Doesn't he ever strike you as a bit of a div?' Ethan had said in those first weeks of Year 7 when they were sitting on their usual tree stump. Josh and Hal had paired up early on, but Ethan was from a cooler crowd – clever boys with good haircuts who made witty comments and did impressions of people. Something Hal said had got Ethan's attention and he invited him to go with them to the out-of-bounds woods at lunchtime. It was good to be in a crowd if you were heading for the woods, because on the way, the Year 8s pelted you with acorns and tried to snatch your bag. Hal wouldn't have gone without Josh but he noticed the others giving him funny looks when he got excited, or couldn't stop laughing, or made open, Josh-style comments, like, 'Oh yeah, my Mum does that.'

As Hal watched, Josh was humming and shuffling his feet through piles of dry Autumn leaves. He saw the others looking – like wolves prowling.

'Josh? A div? No way,' Hal said. And he meant it. You could be yourself with Josh, and somehow the wound-up feeling you got at school – from always having to be impressive – let go so you could relax. 'He's just 100% Josh.' He looked at Ethan's tanned, regular features, blue eyes and dark brows that had all the girls after him. 'He doesn't care.'

Ethan looked back for a minute, then shrugged and nodded.

After a bit, most of the Year 7s found their feet – and their people. Hal didn't hang out with that crowd so much, but they acted like they thought he was all right, and so was Josh if he was with him.

'I wouldn't make something like this up,' Hal said now. 'I don't want to spoil the holiday.'

'It's not spoiling it,' Josh said. 'It's awesome. Where's your Dad?'

They found him climbing up from the rocks below. He looked all sort of white and sweaty, like when he and Hal had flu together the previous winter. They had a sofa each and huddled up under their duvets, watching daytime TV. They would take turns making Lemsip and dropping off to sleep. Dad pretended they were zombies. In a weird way it was nice.

Perhaps he was hot and breathless from the climb. He said it was time to head back. Mum had gone for a walk. They went back through the gate and she was coming down the hill, waving her phone.

'Chris? What's going on? Eileen thought Imogen came to Wales with us!'

Dad stood hunched over, hands on hips. 'She must have got the wrong end of the stick.'

'But she's heard from Holly,' Mum said. 'So why would she think

Imogen's not there? I mean, God, Chris – she did go, didn't she?'

That gave Hal a really jumpy feeling. It was such a weird thing to say. Where would Imogen have gone, if not to Tanzania?

'Of course she did!' Dad said.

'But she hasn't been in touch! It's so unlike her,' Mum said. 'The school said…'

'But Holly's been in touch!' Mum's voice was shaky. She wouldn't catch Hal's eye. 'Did you see her in?' she asked Dad. 'Did you talk to Tania's parents?'

Dad was usually really good at reassuring anyone who got upset. He'd say something funny to make it OK. But he just stood there as if he was trying to catch his breath. 'I – no,' he said at last. Then when Mum looked panicky, 'I mean, yes, Tania let her in.'

'Oh.' Mum calmed down a bit. 'But you definitely saw her go in?'

Dad nodded, looking miserable.

Hal thought fast. 'Maybe Imogen just *talked* about not going, because of Wales, and Holly's Mum thought she actually didn't go. You know what those girls are like, Mum – it's hard to tell what they're on about half the time.'

Mum nodded and smiled but there were tears in her eyes. 'I'm sorry,' she said. 'It has given me a fright.'

Hal asked how Holly got in touch. Mum thought it was Facebook or Messenger.

'We can look her up!' said Josh.

'Yeah,' Hal said. 'We'll find a café with wifi.' Mum nodded and thanked them. Hal was thinking aloud. 'There's no way Imogen wouldn't have gone, the way she was going on about it. She's probably just really busy. I bet Holly got homesick and some teacher helped her get in touch. She's always upset about something.'

'Eileen did say she was a bit overwhelmed,' Mum said. She turned to Dad. 'Oh! They gave us that number at the meeting… to ring if we had any issues about the trip.' He looked a bit blank. 'You saved it, didn't you, on your phone? God, Chris, tell me you did!'

'No, I… I thought you did.' Poor Dad got his phone out and scrolled through the numbers, shaking his head.

Then Grand, Auntie Ruth and Grandma Lisa were coming

over from the bench, and Uncle Toby and Dan joined them. Mum blinked, wiped her eyes and turned to them with a smile. Hal suggested going to the café near the ticket office, but Grand wanted to get back to Noddfa. And there was no way you could tell him what they were worried about, so that was that.

They stopped on the way home for pizzas from the petrol station shop, and Uncle Toby heated them up for tea because Auntie Ruth said it was his turn to cook. He made quite a production of it and she said, 'Oh yes, you're a martyr to the kitchen!'

Later Mum came into the living room and spoke quietly to Dad. 'I'm going to go out to find a signal so I can call and ask Eileen for that number, then I can call the school in the morning.' She nodded towards the next room, where Grand and Grandma Lisa were resting. 'I'll say I have to call Rhoda about the bookshop.'

Dad didn't look very happy. Mum found her phone in her bag. 'Shit!' she said. 'My battery's flat.' She caught Hal's eye and gave him a faint smile. 'I'll call in the morning. It's too late to call a school number now anyway. I'm sure it's nothing. Just a Mum fuss. Don't worry.'

Grand came out waving his paper. 'I've gone as far as I can on this crossword,' he said. 'I'm opening it up to the rest of you.'

By the time they'd finished, it was late. Hal was really hoping for a quiet night.

CHAPTER FIFTEEN

2011 Day 6: Thursday night

The roof of Noddfa was broken and the wind blasted in, moaning; the walls were dark with decay, the furniture covered in cobwebs. A growl rose to a roar, ending in a crash. Ringing in Hal's ears. Real. He was awake, head up, staring into grey.

There was a moment of suspense and then a thud shook the ceiling.

'Josh!' Hal bashed at the slats above him. 'Josh!' He stepped up on to the bottom bunk and shook his arm. Josh stirred and went still again. There was a slither and a thump. There it was again, and again, like something being dragged downstairs.

'Josh! You've got to hear this!' Josh pulled himself up, eyes rolling back in their sockets. Hal took hold of his hair and yanked his head upright, making him yelp. 'There's something coming down from the attic! Listen!'

There was a muffled sound – something outside the door, or the blood roaring in his ears. It sounded again, getting quieter. 'Can you hear anything?'

Josh shook his head, wild-eyed. 'Can you?'

'I *swear*… It's gone downstairs now. Come on!' Hal stepped down off his bunk.

'All *right*!' Josh said. They stood on the floor together, Josh holding a fistful of Hal's pyjama top, Hal holding his arm. 'Are you sure about this, Hal..?'

Hal lunged towards the door and pulled it open. No one – just a silvery light. 'Come on!' They stumbled down the stairs, still holding each other, breathing in gasps.

There was a chill in the downstairs hallway. Something creaked and Hal whirled round. 'Did you see that? I thought the living room door moved!'

Josh nodded, open-mouthed. Relief surged through Hal. It wasn't just him! He pushed the door open. Something flashed across the room, hair flying. There was a bump and a collapsing sound. Fingernails gouged his arm. He followed Josh's gaze to the front door. It was open, and a figure stood in a slice of moonlight.

'Fuck! Oh bloody fuck.' Hal's legs went weak.

'Boys?' It was Dad, in pyjama bottoms and a t-shirt, staring.

'Oh my God!' Josh Chinese-burned Hal's arm, then let go.

'Dad? What are you doing?' Hal's heart was still hammering.

Dad rubbed at his cheeks. 'I – came down for a drink of water and saw the moonlight. I stepped outside for a minute.' He seemed caught out. Wrong-footed. He hadn't even asked what they were doing up.

Hal thought of all the noises. 'Did you go up to the attic?'

'Of course not.' Dad stepped inside and pulled the front door shut, running a hand through his hair.

'You gave us a fright.' Hal had the childish feeling of wanting his Dad. Stupid! He was standing right there.

'I almost pooed my pants,' said Josh.

'Sorry boys. I didn't mean to cause... all this.'

And he did look sorry. He looked so miserable that Hal turned away, towards the living room. 'I thought I saw something in there.'

Had he really, though? The living room mirror showed nothing but darkness now. The sense of a presence had scattered in the shock of seeing Dad.

Hal went and peered inside, Josh behind him. It was dark, but as his eyes adjusted, everything looked normal.

'No chocolate wrappers,' Josh whispered.

'Wait! Look!' Books lay in a jumble around the small bookshelf, as though something had shaken them free. 'That wasn't us,' Hal said. 'Have you been in there, Dad?'

Dad stood looking in. 'No but... there was a bang. Maybe the wind slammed this door when I went outside.'

Josh looked from the books to Hal. 'Or maybe it was Grand in a rage. Desperate for a read.' His chuckle turned into a yawn.

Dad yawned too, then. 'Let's get back to bed, boys.'

They trooped upstairs together. 'You never got your water, Dad,' said Hal.

Carrie walked fast up the track. It would be OK to call Eileen at
nine. When a signal made her phone beep, she dialled – but the call
went to voicemail. Should she leave a message? No, she needed an
answer now. She scrolled to find the main number for the school
– there would surely be someone there. She clenched her fist as
she waited, and then the secretary answered. Carrie found herself
gabbling, barely drawing breath.

'And, your daughter's name is..? 'How stupid, she hadn't said
it! 'Oh, I know Imogen! So, sorry, you took her to Tania Green's
house…'

'Yes. Well, my husband did.'

'And… you're worried that she didn't go with the Greens to the
airport?'

'Well I don't know. I don't know what to think.'

'Hmm… I haven't heard that anyone dropped out of the trip at
the last minute. And I'm sure if they had, the parents would have
been called immediately.' There was a pause and a clicking of keys.
'I can try to get through to the trip leader, Mr Rylance. I'm sure he'll
be able to reassure you. I do have to warn you, though – contact is
sporadic at best on these trips, so you may have a bit of a wait. But
I'll do my best. Does that sound OK?'

'Yes. Oh yes, thank you.'

She must have sounded completely neurotic, Carrie thought,
walking back down the track. Of course they'd have been in touch
if Imogen hadn't arrived at the airport. Maybe Eileen had just got
confused.

She saw Hal and Josh bouncing a tennis ball near the house and
told them about her call, which she said had been really reassuring.
'Is everyone ready for New Quay?' she asked.

Hal shrugged. 'We all got ready, but then Grand sat down for a read.'

Sure enough, when she arrived back, Grand was sitting in a
plastic chair on the front terrace, reading his book in the dappled
sunshine. The others sat around with their bags at their feet, reading
or fiddling with phones. Dan came out in a black t-shirt with a
picture of a wild-looking guitarist, but then he saw how the land lay

and went back upstairs.

Carrie slid in beside Chris on the picnic table bench and lowered her voice to let him know about her phone call. He raised his eyebrows and nodded, then drifted into contemplation of the view.

Grand looked up from his book and enthused to Carrie about the drama section of a bookshop he loved in Bath. It was far from the first time he'd mentioned it. 'Do you have a drama section?' he asked.

'No.' *He knows I don't.* It was no use pointing out that Bath was a university city – the demand was different.

Carrie had got the job at the bookshop in the High Street soon after Hal started school. She had been excited to tell her parents. There were a couple of tables where coffee and cake were served, and Grand was suspicious, as if this meant she was a waitress. But it was definitely a bookshop, and a few years later when the owner, Rhoda, moved on to open another branch, Carrie took over as manager. She finally felt she had something to say when Ruth and their father talked about work.

'Oh,' Grand said now, 'so what are you selling at the moment?'

'Holiday reads, mostly.'

'I don't know what you mean by that.'

She meant undemanding page-turners for the mums who came in after the school run. They would grab a book off the shelves if it had a Richard and Judy sticker and the cover blurb appealed. They had no time to browse, with restive toddlers in pushchairs blocking the aisles.

'No, but then you've brought *Crime and Punishment* on holiday,' said Ruth to her father.

Even Chris raised a smile, though it didn't quite reach his eyes.

'They want chick lit these days, don't they, Carrie?' Toby said with a wink.

'Have I spent my entire career teaching English literature, to have girls end up reading bloody chick lit?'

'Is that books for chicks to read,' Josh pondered, 'or books written by chicks?'

Carrie roused herself to joke, 'Chicks like Jane Austen wrote some really good lit!'

Grand muttered, 'You don't even sell Jane Austen, last time I looked.'

Carrie felt very tired suddenly and thought longingly of her bed. Through the open front door, she saw Dan coming downstairs. His feet paused on a middle stair – he was checking for something in his bag – and a memory stirred from her own teenage years.

1989

Nick and Elsa came to Noddfa that year. They were much younger than Carrie's Mum and Dad. Nick taught at Dad's college. There were not many people that Dad considered clever, but Nick was one of them. He was a brilliant drama teacher and an original thinker, Dad said. Carrie liked his witty take on things, earthy and outrageous, as well as his dark hair and poetic brown eyes. Elsa, his wife, wore long, ethnic skirts with Doc Martens and seemed happy to let Nick do the talking. They would sit around at home while Dad and Nick took the mickey out of fellow teachers or discussed books, plays and politics. Carrie loved their family visits to the couple's flat with its polished floorboards, Indian rugs and health food smells. Nick would try to include Carrie by asking her questions, which always made her blush.

That summer in Wales, Ruth had finished her first year of teaching, and regaled them with the quirks of children and colleagues. Carrie had just done her A levels. She had spent the past year holed up in Dad's freezing study (the bedroom vacated by Ruth, who had moved into Toby's flat). She had worked away on essays and revision while evening snack smells and TV laughter drifted up the stairs. However much she exhausted herself, teachers would still tell the sixth formers that more effort was needed. When she finally stopped work at night, her mind was so crammed that she couldn't sleep, but lay panicking that she wouldn't have the energy for school. Every day was vital at this point, the teachers said.

'You don't need to listen to them,' Mum said. 'Everyone says you're tipped for success.'

On parents' evening, Miss Talbot, her English teacher, had said, 'Carrie has a gift for empathy that shines through in her work'.

Carrie's periods stopped and Mum sent her to the doctor. She had to explain to ancient Dr Hughes that she had never had what he called 'intercourse,' so couldn't be pregnant.

'In that case, I won't give you an internal examination.' He looked down his specs at her as her face went hot. 'Your hormones are probably disrupted by too much work and worry.'

When results day came in the second week of the holiday, Carrie walked to Sue's bungalow to phone the school. The secretary read her grades out one by one: 'English: A. French: A. History: A. Well done!'

'Your father will be so proud!' Sue said, tears in her eyes.

Even Ruth was pleased at the party they had at Noddfa afterwards. 'Well done, young Caroline!' she said, raising a glass of Lambrusco. But Emilia, still waiting for GCSE results, was glum. 'I'm dreading it,' she confided, her hair hanging in limp, mousy curtains, hiding most of her face. 'The exams were a disaster.'

'I'm sure it'll be fine,' Carrie said with a sigh, her cousin's miserable face dragging at her party mood. It probably wouldn't be fine. According to Auntie Jill, Emilia had been 'tramping around' and hadn't done any work. Em kept hinting to Carrie about dark secrets involving older boys, but wouldn't elaborate. 'You wouldn't understand,' she said.

The morning after the party, Carrie woke up and heard the adults in the kitchen. She got out of the bottom bunk without waking the others and pulled a dressing gown on over her over-sized t-shirt. There was still a fluttering inside her from yesterday's celebrations. Three As! It was the proper start of her holiday.

As her bare foot found the second stair, she heard Nick say 'gifted,' with a rising inflection. She stood there unseen and smiled.

'Carrie's a worker, all right,' Dad said, as if debating a point. 'Not as brainy as Ruth, but she puts the hours in. But you know, Emilia is the gifted one, if we could only get her to focus.'

Carrie stepped silently back to the bedroom and stood there for a while, then dived at her bunk and stuck her head under the pillow.

Her shoulders began to shake, making the bunk beds creak. Her stomach hurt as though someone had kicked her. What about her three As, her gift for empathy? They were nothing, it turned out. Who cared what Miss Talbot thought? Her gasps made a squelching noise, muffled by the bedding.

CHAPTER SIXTEEN

2011 Day 7: Friday

When the boys had got back to the bedroom after seeing Dad, Hal had tripped on a bag and kicked it across the floor.

Josh said, 'What's up with you?'

'What, apart from a ghost picking on me and my Dad acting like a nut job?'

Hal pretended to be asleep when Josh went down to breakfast. The weird thing was, by the time he went down himself, he was already feeling better and looking forward to New Quay. All that horrible stuff seemed to be gone in the daylight and it was just Wales again.

'You got over your strop then?' Josh said later. They were kicking a tennis ball down the track.

'Yeah. Sorry.'

'No big deal.' Josh did a sly grin and went in for a tackle. 'You're not usually Mr Angry.' He got the ball off Hal and did a lap of honour with his t-shirt pulled over his head.

'I think it's the ghost who's angry,' Hal said. 'All that banging about, and the books everywhere. And I thought I saw that girl again, before Dad freaked us out. She sort of whizzed across the doorway.'

'Shit, this is escalating!'

'I know. It's like someone's furious.'

'Why would Barbara be furious?' Josh said. 'If it is Barbara.' He bounced the ball and caught it before Hal could grab it off him. 'You know what, throwing things is a poltergeist thing. But poltergeists are usually caused by kids. Or teenagers. Hey, what if it's Dan? Is he, like, troubled?'

'Dan? I don't think so!' Hal remembered Dan on previous holidays, mucking about all the time like him and Josh. Then last time they came, he'd started gelling his hair and worrying about showing himself up. This year he seemed a bit stuck inside his own head. 'I mean, he does look pissed off sometimes... Like when Auntie Ruth goes on at him...'

'Yeah!' said Josh, holding the ball behind his back. 'I've noticed that! He could be causing a paranormal disturbance.'

'Or he's just moody, like Imogen.'

Josh stared ahead and forgot about hiding the ball. 'Sometimes people seem OK on the outside but inside they're like murderously angry. What? I saw a programme about it! Shit, I should be writing all this down.'

'Why don't you make a note on your phone?' Hal said. Josh fumbled in his back pocket and Hal snatched the ball and ran off towards the house. Behind him, Josh's roar of outrage turned to laughter.

Dan was coming down the track towards them, hands in pockets. You couldn't really tell anything from glancing at his face. The others were getting up from their chairs on the terrace. They must be heading off at last.

Carrie got out of the car in the car park at New Quay.

'There are bound to be cafés with wifi here,' Hal said. 'We can friend Holly on Facebook and get her to tell Imogen to contact you.'

'Thank you, Hal.' Carrie fought the urge to hug him in front of Josh.

'We've had a brainwave,' Grandma Lisa called, coming over from their car, beaming. 'Remember last time you wanted to go out on the dolphin boat, but Grand wasn't sure about the weather? We thought we'd go this morning!' She lifted her sunglasses to see their delight.

'Great!' said Hal, and he and Josh shared a high-five. Then Hal shot a glance at Carrie. 'Oh... after coffee, maybe?'

'I thought I'd treat everyone to cakes from the bakery to eat on the boat,' Grand said. 'Their Welsh cakes are not bad if I remember rightly. Better than the sorry imitations you get in England anyway.'

It was impossible to say no. Perhaps it was wiser, anyway, to rely on a call to Mr Rylance rather than on and teenagers and technology.

'Remember how Imogen loved the shell shop?' Grandma Lisa said as they walked downhill towards it. 'We couldn't get her out of there.'

Ruth caught Carrie's eye with a *What is she on about?* face. Carrie sighed. It was Emilia, years ago, who had spent ages in the shell shop, unable to decide between crystal-encrusted stones and tatty shell souvenirs. Imogen had laughed at the 'new-agey vibe' of its posters about the power of crystals. When they reached the shop with its outdoor stands of postcards, shell wind chimes and plastic beach toys, Carrie yearned to go inside – perhaps out of nostalgia, although she wasn't sure who for. But Grand was fussing with Grandma Lisa over a canvas bag to put cakes in. Then he pushed on downhill, and she didn't have the energy to stop him.

She reached out for Chris's hand, then saw his sombre look. 'All right?'

'Fine,' he said, jiggling his car keys. But he didn't have to be dancing for joy, did he? Far better to be honest.

They hung back from the others. At the bottom of the picturesque street, the sea sparkled. 'I know you're stressed about work,' she said. 'And I've been making a fuss about Imogen. It's been a tough year. But the holiday will help. It always does.' She felt more confident as she said it. She could be the reassuring one. 'So tell me about Tyrone. You'd been working with him, hadn't you?' He ducked his head – a kind of nod. 'You said he wasn't the tough nut everyone thought. It must have been horrible for you when he went missing.'

He squeezed her hand. They'd both be relieved when they heard from Imogen. The boys could go in a café after the boat trip. It might be quicker than the school calling. She'd be more use to Chris if she could get some news. And she owed him that.

They had been together since university. They had known each other for two terms and then she surprised herself by sleeping with him: she hadn't thought of him in that way before. She half expected him to blame the booze and retreat into an awkward friendship. But as they lay squashed together in her single bed, he confessed he'd been mad about her from the start.

It was their island-hopping holiday in Greece that decided it. They would arrive at some new island past midnight, to be met in balmy darkness by locals offering rooms. They moved so often that Carrie would awake in the morning disoriented and say, 'Where are we?' He would mutter the name of the island.

One bleary morning, he said, 'I can't think. Where *are* we? We're totally lost!'

But what did it matter, as his arms went round her? He kissed her hair and then grasped it so her scalp tingled. The sheets tangled as they clutched each other and rolled over. They couldn't even keep their noise down for the old Greek couple who had led them from the quayside, and so they stifled laughter throughout their yoghurt and honey breakfast and hurried out into a golden morning.

They announced their plan to get married not long after graduation. Mum and Dad looked dumbfounded, but then rallied. Mum found a bottle of leftover Christmas sherry in the sideboard and they drank a toast. Carrie could still have a career, Dad pointed out, as if someone had doubted it. She was writing for a local Arts magazine, which he always said he supposed was a start.

They talked about dates and venues in a haze of sherry and novelty: she felt like a fiancé in a play. Then Emilia turned up.

She had stayed with them during her A level courses two years before – her parents had moved to Dubai for Uncle Rod's work. But Emilia had crashed out of the sixth form, saying she wanted to be an actress. Uncle Rod had barely concealed his disappointment – with her and with Mum and Dad's guardianship. Em began a life of bar jobs and fruitless auditions followed by fury and tears. Auntie Jill had come to take her back to Dubai, 'to keep a proper eye on her'.

Now she was back, in moth-eaten, hippyish clothes, her hair and skin greasy. She couldn't stand Dubai or her parents. She wanted to go to drama school, and that meant doing A levels after all. 'I need somewhere to crash,' she said. 'I can stay here, can't I?'

'Of course!' Dad said. They explained what they were celebrating and she raised and gulped a sherry, but she barely looked at Chris, and soon slouched upstairs for a bath.

Dad paced the living room, throwing out ideas. Emilia could go to his college. She could do drama with Nick! He was good with artistic temperaments. With a couple of other subjects, she'd get in to do a teaching degree, so she could go on to teach drama! She'd be brilliant.

But when Emilia came down with wet hair, she said, 'Teaching?

I told you, I want to be an actress. I mean *do* it, not talk about it. Don't you think I'm good enough? You're as bad as Mum and Dad!'

'Why does Dad think she'd be such a brilliant drama teacher anyway?' Carrie said on the drive home to their flat.

'Well,' Chris said, 'she does love a drama.'

Laughter eased through Carrie, releasing the knots inside her. 'Oh God! I've still got to tell Ruth we're engaged. She'll come out with some *quip*.'

'She can quip all she likes,' he said, with a cheerful shrug. It was her and Chris now, Carrie realised with a pulse of joy.

Lisa carried David's jacket to the gathering point for the boat trip, while he held the canvas bag, now heavy with cakes. 'We've got a selection,' he said when they met the others. 'You'll have to take pot luck!'

The boys looked so happy. Lisa had felt awful, that time before when the kids were keen on a boat trip, and David had vetoed it in favour of a tea shop. But today he'd agreed to her suggestion when she came up with the bakery idea.

Welsh cakes – a masterstroke! She'd made them for him once when they were first married, fretting over Hilda's recipe. They browned so quickly on the hot, dry pan – how could you be sure they were done inside? They were and he declared them 'not bad', but she'd seen the look on his face. She never made them again.

Small sailing boats and motor craft bobbed in the harbour as they were led along the quay, passing stacked windsurfing boards and a jumble of lobster pots made from turquoise rope.

They stepped onto their boat and arranged themselves on the wooden seating. A lacework of puffy white cloud had covered the sky all morning, but as they set off in a burst of spray and noise, the sun peeped through and the sea was a lustrous green. Lisa leaned back on the rail, looking at rows of toy houses cresting short, grass-topped cliffs. The boat slowed to a chugging pace, moving parallel to the shore, and the waves lapped the bows.

David started nagging about the cakes, so she passed round the first of the baker's bags. Ruth took the millionaire's shortbread, then Carrie peered at the flapjack and cream slice. Oh, it was Emilia who liked those, wasn't it? Lisa could see her now, biting into the pink icing and dense pastry, and shrieking when the cream squirted out. She'd be mortified if it went on her clothes, and then it was all Lisa could do to reassure her that no one minded. Carrie would never eat a cream slice – well, you couldn't kid yourself that they were healthy! And yet she pondered for a moment before lifting out the flapjack.

With the cakes distributed, David shaded his eyes and looked out, his hair, so thin and grey now, flapping in the breeze. 'First one to see a dolphin is the winner!' They twisted round to look seawards.

The cloud dispersed, leaving a great dome of blue. The cliffs got higher and wilder as they chugged southwards, passing sandy little beaches that surely only boats could reach. Seagulls bobbed on the glassy surface like ducks on a pond.

When she had finished the cream slice – without any squirting disasters! – the motion of the boat lulled Lisa into a reverie. She'd got mixed up earlier about the shell shop, hadn't she? Mixed up and wistful, with no Imogen and, well, everything else. Carrie must have noticed, was she too kind to say anything? 'So many memories,' she sighed, gazing at the cliffs.

'Memories?' said David. 'What are you moping about, woman? We have literally never done this before.'

Ruth hooted with laughter. For all their bickering, she had always shared David's sense of humour, especially when it came to Lisa's vagueness. Good thing I don't mind, she thought. Nothing wrong with being relaxed and intuitive, not sharp as a tack, like them.

'It is sad about Barbara though,' Hal said. Lisa turned to him in surprise – he wasn't one to dwell on sadness. Then she saw him nudge Josh. Did they still have their heads full of this paranormal business?

'Barbara?' she said a little sharply. She wrapped the paper round the remaining wedge of bread pudding and dropped it into the canvas bag with a thud.

'Yeah, what was she like, Grand?' Hal said.

David wiped the corner of his mouth with a napkin. 'Oh, she was lively in those days. Full of dreams and plans. Completely held back by her invalid mother.'

'So,' Josh jumped in, 'was she angry about that?'

'Angry? Not really. She went quite peculiar though, after Hugh died.'

'Hugh *died*?!' They all turned to see Josh's shocked face as the boat reared up, missed a wave and smacked down.

'Well, yeah. In the war,' Hal said.

'You never told me! How can you not say that someone *died*?'

Lisa looked down at her lap. What a mess she had made. She brushed off flakes of pastry with a sigh.

'It was 1942, Josh!' David said. 'Ages ago. And lots of people were dying…'

Josh finally closed his mouth. 'I just – Hugh *dead*?!'

'And never called you Joshua,' Ruth intoned. 'In other news, Queen Anne – also dead!' And then they were all laughing.

Chris had choked down a chocolate shortbread and the taste was rising in his gullet as the boat chugged on and on, rolling and yawing in the swell. They were laughing to the left of him, their words fogged, distorted. Carrie had cut right through to him earlier. *A fuss about Imogen. Tell me about Tyrone.* As if she knew, or suspected. Except she then said all that stuff about him caring.

They should chuck him in the sea. Sit him on this rail and tip him backwards. His head plunging in through deep, cold water, never to think again. Sinking slowly upside down. Serve him right. The farce of him as a caring man – as a Dad, a husband, a teacher – cut short as the water crushed his lungs. Best thing that could happen to him – disposed of over the side.

Imogen beside him in the car. He thought his chest would explode – but you couldn't leave a boat trip, you were trapped until you docked. They were pointing to Ynys Lochtyn, the little chunk of island just off-shore. He saw the long slope snaking seawards from the cliff path. His favourite walk. The third beach, slick in sunshine. The boat plunged on. The second beach, licked by foam. The tide was out, Hal said, then something to Chris about walking round. Sweet Hal. Unbearable.

'Llangrannog!' they were calling, waving to the lifeguards on their towers. He looked at the stacked rock but saw the big hunched shape of Tyrone, hoodie-shrouded, walking away from a crowd. Chris staring from his car.

He had seen the boys from the estate hanging around Costcutters, cat-calling. He saw the pace of Tyrone's walk and sped up to pass him, then took his eyes off the road and twisted to look back. The clenched fists were adult-sized but Tyrone's mouth was turned down like a toddler about to cry. Chris slowed down, his hand hovering over the indicator. Guidelines and boundaries hammered in his head. He thought of that time with Laurie. Was this a chance he should take? Or madness? Had anyone seen him there?

Now a muffled quiet closed over him as though some noisy thing had died. The others had stood up and were moving round the deck. Llangrannog was way behind them. They were a long way from the shore.

'We've stopped to look for dolphins,' Carrie said.

He managed a nod but saw her flicker of anguish. He got to his feet, his legs like jelly. He wasn't sure he could even walk. He didn't know what normal was any more, or how to act at all. And the question wouldn't go away: should he have stopped the car? Or shouldn't he?

CHAPTER SEVENTEEN

Day 8: Saturday

Hal stared at the curtains in the half light. Something had woken him: there was an echo in the air like a ripple of shock. His gut tightened. He was half afraid to look at his watch, as if movement would give him away. When he did look, it was five o'clock. The second Saturday, a week since they came.

He heard a whisper, or perhaps just the rustle of the duvet. He flushed hot, straining to listen, then got up to look at the top bunk. Josh's mouth hung open, dribbling a bit – he couldn't be faking that.

There was a breathy noise, like a hiss or a sigh. Hal stepped across to the door. There was no one on the landing, just the early dimness. He went to the stairs and started down, his palm damp on the banister. That might be voices he heard, muffled by white noise – sea sounds, breeze, the hum of the fridge.

They had looked in Josh's book the night before, the bit about poltergeists. It said they were often trying to tell you something. But what?

A screech – no, something creaking. The staircase… or a door?

His heart pounded. When it slowed down, he went on downstairs and across the hall, then opened the door to the living room. He stood and made himself breathe. Then he stepped into the dark inside.

'What do you want?' he said, to no one. His eyes were adjusting to shapes in the dimness when one rose from the floor. The bookcase! It hung a foot in the air, then thudded down. Books flew out, flapping. Hal let out a cry as the bookcase tipped forwards and lay on its front.

Pages riffled over and stilled in a ringing hush. Hal stood frozen, his guts falling. Nothing was moving now. He forced himself to move.

Books were strewn all around the bookcase. Most were leather-bound or faded like the ones in Grand's second-hand shops. Then there were newer ones: quiz books, novels and biographies. Nearest to Hal was a big black one with no markings – perhaps some kind of album. He crouched and reached his hand towards it, half afraid it would fly up and hit him. It lay still. Dust prickled Hal's nostrils as he picked it up.

'Hal?' He flinched and dropped the book. Grand was in his

bedroom doorway in baggy striped pyjamas. 'Everything alright?'

He stood up, dizzy. 'Yes – just – this has happened again.'

'For crying out loud!' Grand pulled on his dressing gown and came over, frowning at the mess.

Shit. It must look like Hal had done it. He'd even been holding a book.

Grand was looking at him now. 'Come on. Let's get a cuppa.' He shuffled towards the kitchen, tying his dressing gown cord.

Hal looked down. A sweaty handprint marked the black book cover. The day felt ruined and it hadn't even started. He followed Grand into the kitchen with a quick glance backwards.

Grand fiddled around with the kettle and got out two mugs, humming. Hal sat down and crossed his legs tightly, still seeing that rising shape, those books flying at him. His hands were trembling. He stuffed them between his thighs, but then his shoulders shook. How could he tell Grand what he'd seen?

'There.' Grand put a mug of hot chocolate in front of him. It was that luxury one that Grandma Lisa bought specially because one year, Hal said he liked it. He wrapped his hands round it and the warmth seeped into him.

'Thanks.' The chocolate was strong and silky with a zap of sweetness.

Grand pulled up a chair. 'We're the early crew. I used to say that when you were a baby and you stayed with us. We'd be up at the crack of dawn, just you and me.'

'Where were Mum and Dad?'

Grand shook his head and took a sip of tea. 'Oh some trip, I think. I didn't mind you being an earlybird. I'm one too, within reason. Four o'clock, you can bloody keep. I get the horrors if I wake up at four. But once the dawn comes, I'm ready for the day.'

Sure enough the grey outside was getting silvery and a thin sound of birdsong was piercing through the quiet. Was it all gone, the night stuff? It felt like just the two of them.

'The horrors. Huh. Maybe that's what I've been having…' Hal's pulse began to pound but Grand just raised an eyebrow. 'A few times this holiday I've heard a noise, or felt something weird…

And then we've found stuff in the morning, like the books today. The bookcase…' He stopped. What if Grand thought he was lying? 'Have you ever been spooked here?'

Grand sat back. 'Spooked? Not for years… But Will had all kinds of stories. You're in good company.'

Hal managed a sort of laughing noise. 'I thought I was a nutcase.'

'Oh no, of course not. Not our Hal! You're the sanest of us all.'

Birds were cheeping louder now. Sunlight dappled the table and leaf shadows bobbed.

Grand leaned forwards and lowered his voice. 'Of course, Barbara was the one for hauntings, after Hugh died. She was so desperate to hear from him. She went to see a spiritualist medium.'

'Really?' Hal's heart was going again. 'And did she? Hear from him?'

'She never said…' Grand peered into the distance through the steam from his tea. 'But then Hilda didn't like that kind of talk, so maybe Barbara kept quiet.'

'Didn't Hilda want to hear from Hugh?'

Grand shook his head. 'She said it made her head spin, the way Barbara talked about it. Her church friends certainly wouldn't have approved. Hilda kept saying, *I've got to try and face the fact that he's gone.*'

Hal spoke quietly too. 'Josh is really into the whole haunting thing. With his book and that.'

Grand smiled. 'Well, it does fascinate people, that kind of thing. Everyone loves a ghost story.'

Hal slurped the chocolatey sludge at the bottom of his mug. 'So did *you* want to hear from Hugh?'

'Oh, God no!' Grand looked as though he'd surprised himself with this outburst. He got up, scraping back his chair, and looked in the breadbin. 'Shall we sneak some toast in before the others come?'

'Go on then.'

'Oh, we've got Welsh cakes! I'll warm a couple up and we'll pretend they're freshly made…' He stood over the toaster as it whirred into life. Hal got the butter and plates. 'To be honest,' Grand said as they began to eat, 'I didn't like Hugh much. He used to tease me. I don't think he liked me having his room and everything.'

The Welsh cake crumbled in Hal's mouth, all warm spice and

melting butter.

'Talking ill of the dead!' Grand said. 'I'll have the spirits after me.'

They were still chuckling when Mum came down, looking groggy. 'I'm off out for a walk,' she said. 'I didn't think anyone would be up.'

'We're the early crew,' Hal said.

Carrie rushed along the track, phone in hand. She had woken up with chaos inside her and couldn't pinpoint the cause. Unless it was Chris on that boat trip. She'd tried so hard to calm herself so she could reach him in whatever underworld he was stuck in. Talking was better than not talking, wasn't it? But on the boat, far out in the bay, she'd caught his expression. She couldn't have felt more desperate if he had fallen over the side.

And Imogen. With no call from the school yet, she was banking on the Facebook idea. But why bother with a café stop, Grand had said after they docked yesterday? He fancied a sit on the beach before heading homewards. The quay had rocked beneath her feet like the sea swell they'd left behind – and Hal, lovely Hal, had said he'd pop up to the café. But a wasp had got up Grand's trouser leg, causing a drama of leg-slapping and swearing that had entertained half the beach. And there was no calming him afterwards: there were more of the bastards round the bin – why couldn't the bloody council empty it? Grandma Lisa looked fretful, and then Ruth made him worse with some jibe about him having a go at the workers. So they'd trailed up the hill to the cars, Carrie's hope wasting away. The wasp hadn't even stung him.

But now she'd come across him and Hal laughing together. She thought suddenly of what Em had said about living in London: that it was awful and wonderful all at the same time. But how could Wales be awful?

Chris's mood had got to her so much – she could scream. He'd seen how painful it was when they couldn't come last year. She longed for it, every year, as soon as the sun had any warmth in it.

The slightest whiff of suntan cream or sun-warmed grass and she'd say, 'It makes you think of Wales.' And yet it was hard being back too and he wasn't there to turn to.

Her phone beeped and she stopped to look – a spam text. No other messages. She walked on, looking, but nothing came. She looked up – she had come too far – she'd meant to turn off the track and head seawards, but she had almost reached that field near the village. Needing the movement, she strode on anyway, her sandals stirring up a cloud of dust. There was bleating beyond a hedge laced with honeysuckle. A sea-scented breeze sent a chill down her neck.

Round a bend in the track she started – a figure! But then the dust dispersed and it was Sue, gazing up at seagulls sailing on the wind.

She called out and Sue turned. She was wearing a pink housecoat and slippers. Carrie saw that unsettling pale blue gaze, the black pinpricks for pupils. 'Sue, it's Carrie! Are you coming to see us? How lovely!'

'Oh! Carrie. I remembered something. At least I think I did… I was just coming to check. Yes, yes! I saw her here, see.' Sue looked past Carrie's shoulder, her confident expression fading. 'It's a worry…'

'Who's that, Sue? Who did you see?'

'The girl… oh dew, I'm no good with names now. And yet you know, when I was teaching, I knew every child's name by the first day of term.'

'Which girl?'

'You know, your girl! There was an M in it…'

'Imogen?' Goosebumps prickled Carrie's arms.

'Is that it? Well, yes, I saw her.' Sue looked triumphant.

Carrie's stomach swooped. 'That can't have been this year, Sue. She's not with us.'

Sue shook her head thoughtfully. 'She was right out here.'

'Out here near Noddfa?'

'No… out here.' The rope-veined hands made a full-bellied gesture.

'Pregnant?' Carrie's jitters subsided. 'Definitely not Imogen, Sue. She's away on a school trip.'

Sue didn't seem to hear her but pointed a finger as if to pinpoint something. 'She looked happy that first day. She went *Shhh* and smiled at me. But when I came up the next day, she passed by me in a car. Tears running down her face. Oh dew, as if her heart was broken. I called out, but she didn't stop.' Sue's frown softened into sadness as though on the edge of tears herself.

A rumble sounded down the track, and they turned as a car approached from the village. Carrie almost expected the tear-stained girl from Sue's story – surely some recollection from the distant past – but it was Dewi, her grandson. Carrie still thought of him as a teenager, but he must be nearly thirty: olive-skinned and dark-haired, with Sue's blue eyes. He got out of the car, a new beer belly pushing against his polo shirt.

'Mamsen? What are you up to? I came to pick you up – you've got the doctor's, remember?'

'Of course.' Sue looked down. 'Why've I got my slippers on?'

'Good question.' Dewi smiled at Carrie, with a weary look. 'We're having a few issues with memory, aren't we, Mamsen? That's why we're going to the doctor's. Don't worry, we'll stop at home for your shoes.'

'Bye, Sue. See you later, Dewi,' Carrie said as Dewi helped his grandmother into the car.

Before he could shut the door, Sue stuck her head out, 'Did you get that attic room door open? Perhaps Dewi can help you? Erin was so scared when she heard that bang.' She'd had no problem remembering that, then?

'Don't worry, Sue, we're fine. You get to the doctors!'

Sue shook her head. 'I don't know what I was thinking. Silly old fool!' She gave a quick smile but Carrie saw her haunted look as they passed her, tyres scrabbling on the stones.

Hal was keen to be first in the shower after breakfast, because otherwise you ended up in a queue. As he got up from the table, Auntie Ruth and Uncle Toby were arguing about their South of

France holiday, which was after Wales.

'You always book the Dijon stop!' Uncle Toby said.

'But *you* were going to this year because I've been so busy… and why should I always do it?'

This sort of thing happened most years. Dad had once said on the quiet that it was funny how two high fliers couldn't organize a holiday.

Hal had left them to it, and now hot water was easing away the last of the stressy feeling from the bookcase thing. He had just put a handful of shampoo on his head when he heard a violent rattling from above.

He grabbed the shower head to wash the suds out of his hair, then turned the shower off and stepped out. He pulled clothes on stupidly fast so they rolled up and tangled.

Clammy and cold, he rushed into the bedroom. Josh was sitting on the bottom bunk in his shark t-shirt, reading his book as if nothing was happening, even though there was still a racket coming from upstairs.

'What the hell..?' Hal gestured at the ceiling.

'Oh – it's Dan. Ruth moaned that his trainers were stinking out their room. She went on about teenagers and smells and that, and he stormed off…' Josh saw Hal's face. 'Why? Oh, did you think..?'

Hal let out his breath and sat on the bunk. 'For a minute, maybe.' More thumps overhead – Dan must be kicking the attic room door.

Josh leaned in. 'Bet he wants to smoke a doobie in there.' Hal almost laughed despite everything, but then swearing erupted above. 'Shit,' Josh said, 'he is *maaaaaad*!'

'Dan! What are you doing?' called Auntie Ruth, stomping past their door in her long white shirt and jeans.

'Trying to get into my own room.' Dan's voice was ragged and shrieky.

She was on the attic stairs now, calling up. 'For God's sake, stop it, you'll break something!'

'I don't give a shit! You don't get it, do you? You're fucking poisonous!'

'How *dare* you, you little bastard?' Her voice was tight and vicious.

'Why do you have to put everyone down just to feel good about yourself? I mean, just exactly how fucked up *are* you? No – get away

114

from me!'

There was clattering on the attic stairs.

'Where are you going?' Auntie Ruth snapped.

Dan appeared in their doorway in a grey hoodie. He turned to bellow, face distorted, spit flying. 'I don't care. Away from you!' He ran downstairs. The whole house shook as the front door slammed. Auntie Ruth stomped after him, muttering under her breath.

'Well, that was *definitely* enough to cause some paranormal shit,' said Josh.

Maybe he was right. The house felt fraught with rage. The boys went downstairs where the others were sitting around in the living room, looking miserable.

'Where's Auntie Ruth?' Hal asked.

'Gone after Dan,' Mum sighed.

There was nothing to do then but hang around. Later, bored of waiting, Josh and Hal walked up the track to see what they could see.

As they got near to the shaded lane, Hal heard Dan's deep voice. He moved onto the verge, out of sight. Not to eavesdrop – he just felt awkward. Josh gawped at him for a minute, then twigged and joined him.

'I just said that to wind you up,' said Dan.

Then Auntie Ruth's voice: 'You did. You're good.'

'Well, I learnt from the master.'

'Mistress, if you don't mind.'

'*Really?* We're doing grammar?'

There was a huff of laughter. They came out of the lane and Auntie Ruth stopped and turned to Dan. 'No. We're actually doing *sorry I was a cow, please forgive me* and...' She opened her arms, and the next thing Hal knew, Dan was letting her hug him.

The boys stood still, Josh pulling in his chin as though this made him invisible. Auntie Ruth moved off, smiling, the tail of her white shirt fluttering. Dan was chatting with her, hands in his hoodie pockets.

'Hey,' Hal called.

'Oh, hi you two,' Auntie Ruth said, shading her eyes. 'We'll go soon, shall we? Patio scones won't eat themselves!' She and Dan walked off towards the house.

'Your face when you heard him banging…' Josh said. He did an impression.

'Yeah all right. I was spooked. Especially after… what I told you, about the bookcase.'

'Shit, yeah… Hey, Hal! Maybe the disturbed teen isn't Dan. What if it's you?!'

'What?! I'm not disturbed!' Hal tried to sound calm.

Josh examined his face. 'No… You don't seem all that poltergeisty.'

'Duh! Thanks!'

'So if it's not a poltergeist,' Josh said, 'it has to be a haunting. The book says, *Hauntings come from a spirit source…* ' They had reached the front door and he stopped, peering inside. 'So. We're dealing with a dead person.'

CHAPTER EIGHTEEN

Day 8: Saturday

Hal and Josh were the first to reach the Patio Café on Llangrannog Beach and they bagsied a table outdoors.

'We don't want to sit outside with this wind blowing,' Grand said when the others caught up with them.

'Don't we? Have we voted on it?' Auntie Ruth said, rolling up her shirt sleeves to get the sun on her arms. But Grand was already heading inside.

'It is rather a lovely day,' Grandma Lisa said, looking smart as always in a purply blue shirt and trousers. 'But I suppose Grand's right. I don't want the top to blow off my cappuccino.' Hal turned with her to look at the glistening sand stretching out towards the rolling foam of the sea.

'Surf's up!' Josh said and did a little jump, with balancing motions of his hands. A man coming into the café had to wait to get past him and the boys were still cracking up about it when the waitress brought their order to their table.

It was hot indoors and Mum took off her hoodie, got a scrunchie from her backpack and pulled her hair into a ponytail. 'I keep thinking about Sue,' she said as Hal's teeth sank into the buttery chocolate of his brownie.

'What's happened with Sue?' he asked. He must have missed something when he had his shower.

'I met her on the track, in her slippers,' Mum said. 'It was all very confused, like some absurdist drama that Grand would like. She reckoned she'd seen this mysterious girl.'

Hal saw Josh's tongue stop still, an inch from his ice cream. 'What girl?' he said.

'Well, she thought it was Imogen.'

Hal glanced at Dad and saw his grim expression. The bite mark in Hal's brownie showed the squishy shine of the inside.

'Imogen?' Josh said, shooting him one of his significant looks.

'Yes but she was rambling. Something about the girl crying. And being out here.' Mum gestured. 'Shocking, really. She has always been so quick and bright.'

Josh kicked Hal under the table, but he wouldn't look. He did it again and Hal frowned at him. Josh's ice cream was starting to drip.

Through the big picture window, between the lifeguards' red and yellow flags, body boarders were riding in towards the sand. A surfer leapt onto her board, stood upright for a moment, then crashed into an exploding wave.

If only there was a signal here. Hal thought of Imogen with her massive rucksack on her back, almost over-balancing as she gave him a quick hug and air kisses. 'Mwah. Mwah. Say hi to Wales for me!' It seemed like ages ago.

~~

They set off from the pebbly bit at the back of the beach, climbing the steep steps to the cliff path that led to Ynys Lochtyn. Grandma Lisa huffed and puffed. 'Don't feel you have to stay with me, Hal. I take forever!'

Josh was forging on ahead but kept looking back with a stupid pantomime of gestures and faces. Hal fell into step with Mum and Dad, who were walking in silence, Mum's hoodie tied round her waist, Dad's denim jacket over his shoulder. Up ahead, Uncle Toby in his beige chinos was shading his eyes and shouting something at Auntie Ruth. She shouted back, but then let out a shriek of laughter. Dan walked behind them, taking no notice. The sea was all ruffled and turquoise on their left.

They stopped at the viewing place to look back at the main beach. Body boarders were dark shapes in the surf. To their right was the second beach where frothing waves sucked at the sand. A black dog rushed in and out, barking.

They continued past thorn bushes and peered down at the empty third beach. Someone had written HELP in huge letters in the sand. Josh got excited about calling the coast guard, but they persuaded him it was just a joke.

There was a climb next through a steep, scrubby field that led up towards the top path. Gorse bushes were wreathed in spider webs, strung with twinkling beads of dew.

'It's like Halloween!' Josh called back. 'Hal? It's like Halloween!'

They pushed through the heavy wooden gate and trooped through to join the top path of pale dried earth. There was an almost vertical hill on the right, and Grand stopped to speculate with Dad and Uncle Toby about a hawk riding the wind way above it. Ahead was the holiday home that looked like an Australian sheep station, with a verandah all round and beach towels fluttering on a washing line. Sheep were everywhere, filling the air with their bleating.

Dan vaulted over the five-bar gate that Hal used to swing on and raised his arms as if crowds were cheering. Josh tried to do the same but collapsed, laughing, and pushed it open for the others instead. Hal turned towards the sea through the field full of rabbit holes. *Bunny heaven*, the family used to call it, and when Hal's pet rabbits died, he had pictured them there. Now he hardly noticed the rabbits until Mum pointed them out, and then he felt stupidly guilty.

Josh beckoned wildly, but Hal waited for Grandma Lisa to catch up with him. 'Oh Hal,' she puffed. 'You are a darling.'

Soon they had the sea on their left and were heading towards the place where the land plunged seawards like a giant's arm, with Ynys Lochtyn, the broken-off island, just beyond its reach. Far ahead, the path divided. The higher route led along the hillside, and a sheep track went steeply down to their favourite place, where you stood on the edge of the low cliffs and looked at the whole of Cardigan Bay.

Josh had stopped by the bench at the top of the slope. 'He doesn't know the way,' Mum said. 'Go and show him, Hal!'

'Thank God,' said Josh when Hal finally reached him. 'I've been wanting to tell you. That girl you saw, and all the haunting. What if it's Imogen?'

There was a ringing pressure in Hal's ears. *Imogen!?* Of course it's not!'

'But it might be! Think about it! She's your sister, that's why she's haunting you. And Sue said she saw her!'

'But Imogen's not dead!'

'But no one has heard from her... What if...'

'She is *not dead*,' Hal said as to an idiot. 'She's in Tanzania.'

'All right! All right.' He shut up for a minute, but then his face lit up again. 'What if it's telepathy, then? Like she's in some kind of trouble and she's trying to let you know?'

'Telepathy? What are you talking about?'

'There's a whole chapter about it in the book. And she's your sister. You might be psychic!'

Hal leaned close to his podgy face. 'Do you believe everything in that stupid book of yours? Shit. Ethan was right. You are a dipstick.'

Josh's pupils sprang into great black holes and a shove landed hard on Hal's chest. 'Sod you, then. Sod you! I bet you're making it all up anyway. Funny how no one sees anything except you!'

Carrie followed the others downhill, scanning the vast, wind-flurried sea. It was probably too rough for dolphins, but you couldn't help looking. Ahead, her parents picked their way down, followed by Ruth, Toby and Dan. Chris stumped behind them in his short-sleeved tartan shirt, head bowed. Sheep crossed their path at a panicky trot. She saw Grand pointing to the cliff to the left. A great cleft had opened up parallel to the edge, almost severing a grassy land chunk they had stood on last time they came.

They had nearly reached the broken stretch of dry-stone wall when Carrie stopped to look back for Hal and Josh – they'd be excited about the cliff breaking away. But Hal was coming down alone, a slim figure in his t-shirt and jeans, his gaze on his feet.

'Where's Josh?'

'We had a bit of a fight. It's nothing.' His hazel eyes looked bleak.

'But – where is he?'

Hal shrugged. 'He stormed off along the top.' They both looked up at the path curving round the hillside, fringed in dark green with pink flowers. 'He'll come back. He's being a divvy.' Hal continued loping downwards, his footsteps heavy.

Carrie walked beside him in silence. The bay opened up on either side of them and the land revealed its rocky edges, seamed with minerals and crusted with yellow lichen. The sea slapped below them and sea birds soared out from roosting places in the shelter of the rock. 'What did you fight about?' she asked.

'Just… stupid stuff. It's all right, Mum.'

But it wasn't all right. Carrie turned and searched the slope they had come down, the hillside path way above. 'I am a bit concerned though. Where is he?' Hal searched with her, looking miserable. 'I don't want to make a fuss, Hal, but he's not my son. And it's a cliff edge.'

Hal chewed a fingernail, the wind flattening his brown hair, showing the white of his scalp. She had never known him to fall out with Josh.

'Chris!' she called, but the wind took her cry. The others were way below, fanning out towards the land's edge on the left. A second shout made Chris turn and look. She gestured and he shook his head, but began to climb slowly, clutching his denim jacket – wasting so much time. She thudded downwards, stones rolling beneath her deck shoes.

When she finally reached him, he stood fiddling with a jacket button, looking weary and worried while she ranted. 'Oh. Right… Do you want me to go after him?'

'No. I'm going.' She turned and strode uphill and Hal came with her.

Carrie thought she was fit from running, but the hill made her lungs ache and her legs weak with effort. They had to stop, gasping, several times. By the time they reached the top, Josh could have gone miles.

They hardly paused at the bench where they usually sat recovering. Carrie swept along the track, Hal making long strides to keep up with her.

'I'm sure he's OK,' she said, panting. 'I just want to make sure. It's a Mum thing.'

They whipped past ferns and pink-flowered thistles. Acid-yellow blooms zinged out against the sea. An enormous skyscape was scribbled with clouds.

They paused at the place where you could take another path and double back up to the hilltop observatory.

'He doesn't know that way,' Hal said. 'He'll have gone on.'

Carrie pushed on with him, a cool wind drying the sweat on her face. 'All right?' she asked. Hal nodded at his shoes.

The path wound onwards, narrowing in places, with nothing much to stop you plunging down an almost vertical slope. Time was hurtling away, and no Josh appeared. Her stomach clenched at the thought of his parents. If he was upset, he'd be careless.

They passed the top of the dry ski slope at the back of the outdoor pursuit centre. The others would be worrying, but they couldn't go back without Josh. Had he doubled back after all – was he lost?

The path turned inland and took on an official look, with litter bins and sturdy fences. Carrie had never come this far, not even on walks with Chris. Signposts in raw-looking wood announced the Cardigan Coastal Path. They turned a corner and stopped, staring. A notice showed a map of the area with pictures of flora and fauna. Behind it was a café.

'Hal?'

He had darted forwards to pull open a thick glass door and was heading inside. She followed. Underneath the café's name in orange, it said: *Free wifi.*

Only a few tables were occupied. Families dressed in the traditional black of orthodox Jews sat at two of them. Carrie had often seen similar groups in Aberystwyth, where they had a summer conference. As the door thudded shut, a small boy with close-cropped hair and two long, dark ringlets stared at her, until his mother tugged his sleeve.

Josh sat hunched over a table. Carrie was about to call out when he clenched his fists, 'Yes!'

'Josh?'

They rushed over and he gazed up at them, phone in hand. 'I friend requested Holly. She's just accepted!'

He held out his phone and Carrie watched him negotiating the Facebook site with stabs and swipes of his finger. A glamorous picture of Holly came up. They all leaned over the phone as Josh scrolled through her latest posts, then clicked.

A selfie appeared of Holly and three other girls with an airport departure lounge behind them. Next a group of teenagers stood in a dusty yard in front of an African guesthouse. Picture after picture rolled by: there were girls and boys from the sixth form, and Tania, and Holly, and teachers, and Tanzanian children at rows of desks in a dim, low-ceilinged classroom. But no sign of Imogen.

Josh came out of the post and clicked on a more recent one; but it buffered, struggling to load. At last new pictures began to roll under his finger. Carrie searched, her heart in freefall.

'Go back!' Hal yelped. 'There!'

And there was Imogen: hair scraped back in an African print scarf, face shiny with heat, smiling. Blond waves tumbled over tanned shoulders.

'Yes!' The boys were face to face, wide-eyed, triumphant.

Carrie sank into a chair.

'And here's another one. She's bricklaying! And... look, she's eating with a bunch of them. And at a market. Are you all right, Mum?'

She nodded, tears pricking as she devoured the pictures. 'Oh, thank you, Josh. Thank you.'

'Yeah,' said Hal. 'Thanks. And... sorry.'

Josh looked sulky for a moment, but soon gave up. 'S'all right. We found her!' He high-fived Hal, who pulled a chair round to continue looking.

'Send Holly a message,' he said. 'Tell her to tell Imogen to get in touch.'

Josh typed in a quick burst with his thumbs, sent the message and continued scrolling. 'Does Ethan really say I'm a dipstick?'

'Who cares what Ethan thinks? Ethan's a dipstick.'

Josh sniggered. 'He does think he's really cool, doesn't he?'

Hal shrugged as though it was obvious. 'Yeah. And thinking you're cool just makes you a dipstick. It should be in the definition.'

'Yeah! On Wikipedia. *Dipstick. A Year Seven who thinks he's cool.*'

The view was gorgeous on the way back to Lochtyn.

'I don't know what I've been thinking,' Carrie said. 'I've had all kinds of stupid worries.'

'We all think weird stuff sometimes,' Josh said with an understanding nod.

'We found Josh! And we've seen pictures of Imogen!' Carrie called out as they rounded the hillside and saw the others gathered round the bench.

'We thought you'd fallen off the cliff,' Grand said. Carrie noted her parents' sagging posture on the backless bench and forgave his irritable tone. Chris, beside them, looked almost as tired.

Hal explained about the café and the Facebook post as they made their way back towards Llangrannog. His grandparents' faces brightened.

'Cool,' Dan said. 'Like digital detective work.'

'Yes, well done, boys, cracking effort!' Toby said, to the evident embarrassment of all three.

'She looked happy,' Carrie said, taking Chris's hand. 'Doing all sorts. Bricklaying and talking to nursery children and shopping in the market. It looks brilliant!'

He gripped her hand – a loving squeeze? A plea?

She slackened her pace so that the others were out of earshot. 'Were you worried, then? You kept saying I shouldn't be.'

He stopped and shook his head, his long face drawn, eyes dull. *As if he can't speak*, she thought.

'It looked great, didn't it?' Hal said, approaching, grinning. 'I mean, not as good as Wales, but not bad, considering!'

Chris cleared his throat. 'You'll have to show me.' He gave her hand another squeeze and let go.

'It took a while to find the pictures, didn't it?' Carrie fell into step with the boys.

'Yeah. You were like, breathing down my neck,' said Josh.

'Well, I kept thinking, where is she? She wasn't in any of the early ones.'

'Maybe they'd had a falling out?' Hal said. 'You know what they're like, Mum.'

'I suppose,' Carrie said. 'Although it's usually the others. Imogen and Holly seem much more stable.' The sea sparkled above a tangle of bloomy blue sloes, gorse and wild roses. 'I think Imogen's a good friend.'

'Maybe she banned pictures!' Hal said. 'Like when she's got a spot. Or a bad hair day.'

Carrie laughed, blinking away tears, heady with a rollercoaster energy. The oversized statue of Saint Crannog came into sight on the cliff across the beach, raising his staff in welcome. 'Shall we get chips at the Beach Hut?' she said.

Hal, Josh – even Dan tumbled down the last few steps, shouting their approval, and crunched across the pebbles to join the outdoor queue for the fish and chip bar. Carrie settled her parents in the shelter facing the sea and they saved seats for everyone.

'Savloy with extra chips for you Carrie?' Ruth teased.

'How very dare you! I'll track down some quinoa.' She headed for the café.

They ate watching children damming the stream. The tide seeped inwards and the boys made plans for the afternoon.

'Alright with you, Grand?' said Grandma Lisa.

He twisted round, pointing to the sky over the land: a white puff or two from earlier had swollen and darkened into looming towers of cloud. 'That's rain coming. Let's get back to Noddfa.'

The boys looked crestfallen. 'That's that, then,' said Ruth.

Grandma Lisa patted Grand's knee. 'He always wants to get back there. It's his refuge!'

'Well that's what Noddfa means,' Grand said. 'It's Welsh for *the refuge*.'

CHAPTER NINETEEN

1942

The evacuees were lining up in the playground ready for afternoon school. Sue was having her usual chat with the new afternoon teacher, Miss Haines. David had to remember to call Sue 'Mrs Davies' since her wedding, not 'Miss Griffiths' any more, but at Noddfa she was still just Sue. Miss Edmonds had gone back to London suddenly a few weeks before. Her Dad had been driving an ambulance that was hit in an air raid on the docks, according to Roslyn Post Office. The other children got all breathless and chatty, passing round the news, but it gave David a tight feeling in his chest.

He had been down the docks once with Dad. He'd wanted to run and look at the giant ship and the cranes and the men heaving sacks, but they had walked slowly because of Dad's limp from polio. They had gone to the pub afterwards. Everyone there was Dad's friend.

There was a picture in Will's newspaper of the docks smashed up, burning. Hilda drew in her breath when she saw David looking. 'We don't want that at the tea table!' she said and whipped the paper away.

Now Miss Haines called for quiet. David was trying to persuade Keith to swap a Gary Cooper cigarette card for one of his two Mickey Rooneys. He waved Mickey Rooney and made an encouraging face. Keith shook his head, but then reached out and tried to snatch the card.

'Telegram boy!' Sue said to Miss Haines as something sped past the wrought-iron gates. Sue went and looked. You could hear the ticking, whirring of a bicycle fading through the village. 'I'd better go, Miss Haines.' She glanced at David. 'Goodbye, children. Have a good afternoon.' The look on her face didn't match the jolly voice.

Iwan was at the gate when school finished, shirt untucked, one sock down, hands in the pockets of his shorts.

'Let's look for moss!' David said. 'Will says the chickens like it to line their nests.' They walked to the bank opposite the Post Office, where moss grew a bright, luscious green in the shade of the trees. Iwan pushed his glasses up his nose and poked at the moss with a stick. David reached into the undergrowth to pick off a lump. Something moved under his fingers, and a snake shot out and over his shoulder. He screamed, turning to see it thrash and coil on the road before zipping away.

'*Cach!*' Iwan's shout (which meant 'shit') turned to helpless laughter.

'I'd better get home,' David said.

'Why? You scared?' Iwan danced round, screwing up his nose, making hissing noises.

'No. Hilda's making a cake.' She wasn't really, and anyway, his stomach felt funny.

'Cake? On Monday?' Iwan called after him. 'Wait! I didn't mean to laugh! It was the shock!' David waved without looking and set off down the track to Noddfa.

He was half-way home when he heard a rumbling. Not a car, surely? They were so rare in the village that if they heard one, the children ran out to look. The sound rose to a chugging roar and a familiar cattle truck rounded the corner.

David stepped back onto the grass verge. It was Will's brother, Uncle Jack, at the wheel, in braces and shirtsleeves. He was bigger than Will, with a broad back and thick, dark hair, and he was always full of jokes and tricks. David waved for him to stop and let him get up in the cab as he usually did. Iwan would be jealous. But as the truck came alongside, Uncle Jack's gaze passed over David and he drove on.

The front door was open and people were milling about inside. Faces turned towards David as he went in – Mrs Knock, the English vicar's wife in a green flowery dress, Roslyn Post Office, bulky in a tight jacket, and Avarina Siop who must have come in a hurry – she had forgotten to take off her apron.

The kitchen was full, with a hush and a clinking of tea-cups.

'Where's Hilda?' he said. They were trampling mud from the track over her clean floor – and how would she get his tea in this crowd? Roslyn shook her head, starey-eyed.

He went back into the hall. The living room door was open but the curtains were closed. People were muttering in the half-dark. Someone touched his shoulder.

'David, *bach*.' It was Sue. 'I'm so sorry. There's been terrible news.' A strange noise rang in David's head. A tear slid down the side of Sue's nose and her voice went husky. 'Hugh has been killed in action.'

Bodies shifted in the dimness of the living room and David saw Hilda's slippered feet in front of her armchair. The strange noise was a howling, like that time in Pollard Street when a car hit a dog. But it was coming from Hilda. He went to run to her, but a hand held him back.

A whispering spread from the hall. 'It's David. Wanting Hilda.'

'No, David, leave Hilda alone.'

'Has someone told Will?'

'Jack's gone to Aber. And Barbara! Oh dew, Barbara. Jack will have to tell her too.'

Bodies shifted in the room, and David glimpsed Hilda's crumpled face. Why wouldn't they let him go to her?

Then suddenly he knew. He'd been glad it was only Hugh. He had wanted the eels to eat his brains.

The whispers shushed over him like the rush of the waterfall. 'He might be a comfort…'

'Or a reminder! Best keep him away.'

'Poor Hugh. Such a fine boy.'

'This is a fine boy too!' Sue's voice rang out, and she folded David's hand to her chest. Everyone went quiet, like when she spoke to the class.

Hilda's gaze was watery and pale. Did wishing for things make them happen? Could she see what he'd done?

'David!' She reached out, her hankie in her hand.

They released him, and he ran. She pulled him onto her lap, and held him tight, rocking backwards and forwards, pressing kisses into his hair. 'My boy,' she said. 'My boy.'

Grand was right, of course – dirty great clouds crowded out the sun and fat drops were falling by the time they got inside. He put the kettle on and Lisa said with a huge yawn that she'd just have a quick sit down. Then the sugar was nowhere to be seen, and when he went to ask what she'd done with it, she was asleep on the sofa, mouth agape.

Carrie found the sugar for him – hidden unaccountably in the left-hand cupboard. Then she and Chris headed for Tesco's, as it was their turn to cook.

Christ, how long had he been up? The early start was deadening his brain. He sat at the kitchen table slurping too-hot tea while the boys went to look for Scrabble.

He thought of sitting here with Hal in the early hours after that funny book business. He had a creative mind, that boy. Dan had never had a flair for English, for all his private education (Toby's influence, of course). But Hal had loved wordplay and stories ever since he was tiny. Liked a ghost story, too, like his Grand. Had he tried him with M. R. James?

It wasn't like Hal to be troubled. Grand remembered him as a two-year-old, splashing in the paddling pool on their back lawn. It was the first time he'd looked after him on his own, and he'd worried about entertaining him. He had stepped away to dead-head some roses, and the next thing he knew, a wet little Hal was at his side. They had finished the bush together, petals sticking all over Hal and making him cackle until he got hiccups. Extraordinary, really, the way that child had turned out.

All this talk about hauntings must be Josh's influence. No doubt it was him scattering things. It wouldn't take a genius to do it when no one was looking – and they'd never had such shenanigans when it was just the family here. As it always had been. Apart from the time Nick and Elsa came.

He had been surprised when this charismatic younger teacher had made a beeline across the staffroom towards him, but Nick grinned with delight at his political comments, his rants about Tories, incompetence and ignorance. They'd laughed a lot that holiday, with in-jokes and running themes. They fed on each other's enthusiasm, talking about books, films, plays, TV programmes... Ruth joined in their teacher talk. Once or twice he had seen Carrie and Emilia's eyes flicking between him and Nick, following what they were saying.

But later Nick had left the college without warning and the couple had moved to Yorkshire. David had been told by the bloody head of department. And yet in ten years of friendship, they'd shared confidences, hadn't they? Nick had even talked about Elsa being desperate to have children. David hadn't quite known what to say, but he'd felt trusted with the news. The thought came to him in a great slump of tiredness that Nick had been his closest friend, before everything ended so suddenly.

'I'm not sure my brain's up to Scrabble,' he said, when Hal and Josh came in with the box. 'Our early start's catching up with me!'

'Me too,' said Hal. He and Josh sat up at the table, flicking a screwed-up chocolate wrapper between them.

'I heard about the bookcase,' said Josh. 'We wondered before if it was Barbara doing all this haunting. We're not sure now.'

Grand was going to scoff, but then he recalled Hal's talk of the horrors and bit his tongue.

'Is it true she was into seances?' Josh asked. 'Because that might explain it. I mean, if you believed in that stuff when you were alive, you'd come back to prove it, wouldn't you, and leave signs and that?'

Hal put on a wavering, ghostly voice: '*I told you it was true!*'

Josh flicked the bright foil ball at him and they were off, giggling.

Grand gazed at Hilda's old kitchen table. Sleep pressed at him muffling the boys' noise. He should go for a read on the bed.

1942

David was in bed with chicken pox, the blackout curtains only half pulled across, letting in the light of a drowsy summer morning.

He was not even very ill, just itchy and tired, but he couldn't go to chapel with Hilda or to church with Will because he might be contagious. He didn't want to, anyway – people might stare. It was all right at school, or out playing with his friends. Children carried on as normal. At home, Hilda still got up to make *brecwast* and came out to feed the chickens. She got him lunch and his tea after school. But she was grey like a shadow and hardly ate herself.

Silver hairs had spread over Will's head, and his face had a sunken look. He didn't say much to David except to help him with his homework. David didn't really need help these days, but sometimes he asked for it anyway.

When the letter came from Hugh's commanding officer, Noddfa filled up again. People drank tea and spoke Welsh with a moaning sound like the wind around the house in winter.

'At least we know what happened now,' Hilda said, pressing her hankie to her face.

Barbara gave her a haunted stare. 'Does that help you Hilda? I'm not sure it does me.'

The only time Will's face got a tiny bit brighter was when he was talking to David. So when everyone else had gone, he asked about the letter, and Will got it out and read it to him. The South Lancashires had been on a joint mission with the East Lancashires to recapture Madagascar from the Vichy French. Hugh had been killed as they advanced on the French naval base. Will's voice got wavery. His face wasn't bright at all. David asked where Madagascar was and Will got the Atlas out.

'There. That's where he is,' he said. His finger trembled on the map.

There was no body for a funeral, so they had a memorial at the church. Afterwards, everyone came for plates of ham and *bara brith*, Hilda's fruit bread. They opened the curtains for the first time since the telegram. It was strange to see the house light again, and full of talk. Reverend Knock had been on excellent form, people said. It was a good memorial, with not a dry eye in the house. And a lovely spread, because, rationing or not, ham and sugar could be got in Bont Gogh in memory of Hugh.

The voices got louder as the afternoon went on. The women said it would have been quick – Hugh wouldn't have suffered. The men talked about how the war was going. Below all this was a quieter sound. David had an ear for whispers – he followed them, weaving among the crowd.

'She said to put the coats in David's room.' Roslyn said. 'Not Hugh's room, you notice!'

'When you think… He's all she's got now.'

'But you worry for her.' This was Mrs Knock. 'They'll all be going back to their parents. He'll be off too.'

'I'm not so sure about that, the way things stand.'

David's chicken pox spots were pulsing now in the heat. He shoved the bedclothes away to scratch the skin round a big one on his tummy. There was a sound downstairs – perhaps the back door banging in the wind. He was in his old room again. Hugh would never get it back now. David thought of him in the earth in Madagascar, dirt in his eyes and up his nose. Footsteps sounded, slow and heavy, coming up the stairs.

There was a screech as the bedroom door swung open.

'David?' It was Barbara, with a shopping bag. 'Did I wake you up?'

'*Cach!* You gave me a fright!' He slumped back on the pillows.

'Sorry.' She sat on the bed. Her face was a waxy yellow as if all the pink had gone, her blue eyes dull, with dark shadows beneath them. 'I said I'd drop in on you. *Sut dych chi?*'

He made scratching motions, his teeth gritted. 'Itchy.'

'You didn't miss anything at church. People don't know what to say to me. I'm not even a proper widow.' The words seemed to tire her out. She slumped, hugging the shopping bag. Her blond hair was hanging loose, not done in a style like before. 'I can talk to you, though, can't I?'

He shrugged. He had always liked talking to Barbara.

'I don't want to make Hilda and Will any sadder. And at home, well, it's hopeless. I still take Mam's meals up, but I can't look at her. She said the other day, *It's not my fault, Barbara.*'

She pulled a tress of hair over her shoulder and ran her hands over it.

'What's in the bag?' David asked.

She looked down at it. 'I want you to help me with something. Will you?'

He nodded.

'Hilda says she keeps hearing his voice. Here at Noddfa. In the *cae bach*. Walking in the hills. I don't, David. I don't hear his voice.' She faltered. 'There's an old lady at the canteen called Mrs Rees. She goes to a special church where they talk to the spirits.'

She took out a wooden board with letters and numbers on it and put it on the bed between them. David saw the words *Yes* and *No*, and a smaller piece of wood in the shape of a raindrop. He had seen something like it in a film he and Rodney had sneaked into in London. He'd only seen a bit before the usherette caught them, but it had given him nightmares.

A strange excitement made Barbara's eyes brighter. She got up and went over to the window, where she tugged the blackout curtains together, leaving just a slice of daylight. She sat beside him again. 'Promise you won't tell Will and Hilda?'

He nodded. He didn't want that dull look to come back.

Her voice sank to a whisper. 'It's for communicating with the spirits of the dead. We put our fingers on this thing – it's called a planchette. Like this. Go on, you too. That's right. Mrs Rees showed me in the back room at Bath Street. She called for Hugh's spirit to come.'

'And did it?' Blood thumped in David's head.

'No, but she said it might work better in his home. In here should be best of all. His bedroom!'

David's spots were flaming. His fingers felt sweaty on the planchette thing but a draught was chilling his neck. He pushed his back against the pillow in case someone was behind him. 'Barbara,' he said, 'I have to sleep in here.'

'Please David.' She whipped her head round and her hair brushed his cheek. 'I need to hear from him. Do you understand? He can't just be gone.'

'All right!'

'Thank you.' She swallowed. 'First we move the planchette round the board, to warm it up. That's it. That's how it moves. But from now on, we don't move it. It rests there, on the letter G. Only a spirit can move it. Mrs Rees did this next bit.' Her voice got louder, startling him. 'We call upon the spirit world. We call Hugh. Are you there, Hugh?'

He stared at the board. All their fingers were crowded on the fat part of the raindrop shape. Its sharp bit pointed at the letters of the alphabet set out in two curving rows.

'Speak to us if you're there. Hugh, are you there?'

David stared at the *Yes* in the bottom left-hand corner. His legs were hot, crossed under the blanket, but his top half was shivery. *I'm sorry*, he thought in the thunder of the waterfall. An eel, slick and muscular, slipped out of an eye socket. Did something move in the bedroom shadows? He squeezed his eyes shut.

'Are you there? Hugh, love? It's Barbara. Are you there?'

David heard a gasp and cried out, his eyes springing open. Barbara was hunched over, sobbing.

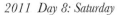

2011 Day 8: Saturday
The front door banged and Grand started, thinking that Will and Hilda were home. Then Lisa slurred a sleepy welcome. The world lurched – it was years and years later. Carrie and Chris were back from Tesco's.

Grand got up off the bed and went through into the living room, where Lisa was sitting up on the sofa, her hair sticking up on one side and flat on the other. 'I went for a read,' he said. 'Must have dropped off.'

Ruth smiled, 'Dostoevsky will do that.'

Lisa fluffed up her hair and went to put some face powder on, then rolled up her blouse sleeves and made a pot of tea. Carrie and Chris unpacked their shopping and Grand asked Ruth how she was getting on with the book he had lent her. He listened to her witty summary, pulling himself out of a pit of tiredness – his blood sugar got low if he slept during the day. He remembered there were Welsh cakes and sneaked one from the breadbin. Could he butter and eat it without them fussing that he'd spoil his tea? Lisa could pull a meal together in no time, but with Carrie and Chris, it might be ages.

'Where are the boys?' Carrie asked.

'Hal went for a sleep and Josh said he had some reading to do,' he said, swallowing the last of the Welsh cake.

Lisa lowered her voice. 'That was quite a row they had earlier!'

'They'll be angry young men before you know it!' he said, sitting down beside her.

'How come it's only the men who get to be angry?' said Ruth.

Had the girls been angry as teenagers? Ruth had been sulky for several years, but without too many fireworks. Carrie had been so self-contained. If she was angry, she kept it to herself. It was Emilia's fractious teenage years that came to mind. They had looked after her a lot, with Rod working all over the place and Jill going out to join him. Em had veered between heady excitement, fury and despair.

'Were you angry, darling? At Hal's age?' Lisa asked. 'That's when you went back to England, wasn't it, at the end of the war?'

'Those were different times. No one asked what the young thought about anything.'

'That's true,' Lisa said. 'It wasn't considered relevant.' Why couldn't she resist poking about in these cans of worms? And now Carrie was looking round, all sympathetic.

'There was no navel-gazing, no *counselling*,' he said. 'You just got on with it. Auntie Mo did her duty and I – well no one cared how I felt about it.' That had come out all wrong. He'd meant to put a stop to the hand-wringing.

'I did. I cared how you felt.' Lisa's expression was clear and earnest. She sat with her arms crossed, her long fingers, manicured for the holiday, resting on sun-freckled skin.

'Well yes. *You* did.'

He subsided, the fight all gone out of him. When Lisa came along, everything had been different. She leaned on his shoulder and he let her kiss his cheek.

CHAPTER TWENTY

2011 Day 8: Saturday

Mum and Dad came back from Tesco's with a spit-roast chicken. Mum was going to do it cold with potato salad, but Grand wanted it hot with gravy because of the 'wintry' weather! Everyone was cheerful because of the Imogen pictures. What had they been thinking, Hal thought? Well, he knew what Josh had been thinking but that was Josh for you.

Hal hadn't slept after all when he went up to the bedroom, because Josh came up to read his book, so they got chatting, sitting on the bottom bunk. Hal told Josh what Grand had said about Hugh being angry with him for taking his room.

'Oh my God!' said Josh. 'It's not Barbara haunting us, it's Hugh! He's come after Grand!'

Hal was trying to think of an objection, but then he remembered something. 'Actually, this was Grand's bedroom during the war…'

Josh's gaze swept around them. 'That's why he's been waking you up, then!'

'But Hugh died years ago, and it's never felt weird before.'

Josh looked stumped. 'Yeah, and you saw a *girl*.' But after a bit, he got excited again, 'Maybe Barbara's the girl, and Hugh's come looking for her because she's recently… *passed over to the other side.*'

He whispered the last bit and it would have been funny, except that Hal knew he would have to lie here every night for another week, thinking of Hugh wanting his room back.

Later as they sat eating the chicken and gravy, he had a funny feeling that there was someone missing. Josh was mashing chicken and gravy into his potatoes and Grand and Grandma Lisa were watching, amused but a bit disgusted. 'Will you stop sniffing!' Auntie Ruth said to Dan, who said he had hay fever. 'Well have it quietly!' she said, and Mum got up to get Dan a tissue. Dad and Uncle Toby were just eating – so all nine of them were there.

Hal felt Mum touch his shoulder – but when he looked up, she was back in her seat. He twisted round – no one there. Maybe the 'touch' was just a muscle jumping, but he shivered.

He was exhausted when it was finally time for bed. If anything weird happened, he slept through it.

~~

Day 9: Sunday
They played cricket in the morning, but then fat drops of rain began to fall and they had to go in. Grand grumbled because it was leftovers for lunch. He said, 'It's like the bloody war all over again!'

Much later, Hal opened the back door and found evening sunshine making jewels of the raindrops in the lawn. Low clouds were racing away, leaving wispy white trails and blue over the water. The sea had got its vivid colours back and a salty flavour wafted on the breeze.

'Does anyone fancy a walk?' he called.

They wandered along the track, Grand wearing his kagoule just in case, then took the shaded route to the lane that led down to the sea. The warmth of the sun released damp hay and hedgerow smells.

Josh took off ahead of the group and turned to throw a frisbee. It swung in a weird curve and Hal rose up, snatched it from the air and landed on his rubber soles. He jerked the frisbee as if to throw it, and Josh did a mad leap to one side, his Iron Man t-shirt riding up to show his belly. Hal flicked his wrist again and this time let go.

'Arggghhh!' Josh cried as the frisbee crashed into long roadside grass. Hal ran downhill and Josh raced him. They fought for the frisbee, laughing.

The group turned a bend. The sky over the sea was turning gold with purple clouds.

Josh pretended to throw the frisbee downhill, but then turned to hurl it back the way they had come. It narrowly missed Dan's head and hurtled beyond him round the bend.

Hal ran in big strides up the hill past the others. He heard Josh calling, 'Sorry!' and turned, breathless, to see their backs as they walked seawards, two groups of four and one in the middle with bouncing fair hair.

Wait – nine of them? He grabbed the frisbee from the wet tarmac.

He ran back round the bend, breathing hard. His parents and grandparents on one side, and Auntie Ruth with Uncle Toby, Dan and Josh, all ambling down the lane, the sunset lighting up the edges of their hair. Eight of them, of course.

Would she get a signal, Carrie thought, if they went up on the cliffs? Would Imogen have sent her a text? She'd need wifi for Messenger. It was probably too soon after Josh sent that plea.

Hal appeared round the bend with the frisbee, a knot in his brow. He saw her looking and shook off the frown.

They continued down to the beach and stopped to skim stones, Grand unzipping his kagoule for the exertion, the boys carefree in their t-shirts and jeans. She clutched Chris's hand, holding onto the brighter outlook of their shopping trip and cooking. Flat pebbles skipped across the sunset sheen of the surface then plunked through and were gone.

They opted for the right-hand cliff path and set off up the slope, calves straining, the three boys striding ahead. The air filled with ululating cries. At the brow of the hill, only a hedgerow stood between them and the drop to the rocks and water.

At a break in the hedge, they stopped to look down. Canoes tracked across a little bay, ploughing Vs into the surface shine. Could they do that with the boys one day? They might discover beaches that were only visible from the sea. But it wasn't on Grand's usual itinerary, and he would fuss about waiting for them if they went without him.

When Carrie looked up, the boys were out of sight. She set off up the muddy path at a trot. Hal and Dan had been walking these ways all their lives: they knew to keep away from the drop. But the land's raw edge, receding in waves, set off an echo in her head as if time had folded inwards.

Imogen was six and Dan five that summer at Noddfa when Hal was a baby. The family had agreed to share the 'baby-wrangling' as Ruth called it. But Emilia held back, saying she was hopeless with Hal. She was all over the place that holiday: positive one minute, then sombre, then angry and tearful. Grand kept trying to persuade her to go back to college.

'Nick always said you had a talent,' he said when they were sitting in the living room one day. Em looked thin, sitting on the sofa in a hippyish skirt and black vest top, her over-dyed hair dry and tangled. She kept her arms tightly folded as Grand went on. 'They tell me the new drama woman's good. You could pick up where you left off!'

Hal's little grumblings sounded behind them: Ruth was walking up and down, jiggling him in her arms. Em chewed the edge of her fingernail; Carrie saw blood smear her lip.

'That's my turn done!' Ruth said, plonking Hal on Emilia's lap. At nine months, he had only downy hair: you could see the lovely shape of his head. They photographed him constantly to capture his delighted smile. But now he rubbed his big hazel eyes and began to whine. Em put her arms around him, but his bottom lip stuck out in a comical pout.

'It's all right,' Em said, bouncing her leg just a little too much. Carrie saw him draw in his breath and knew what was coming. Soon his little back had gone rigid and the air was full of wailing.

'I can't do this – I can't!' Emilia let out. Hal jerked in alarm, his face stricken.

Carrie couldn't help herself. '*What* can't you do?!'

'Happy bloody families, that's what! You take him!' Emilia drew back from Hal and turned her face away.

Carrie gathered Hal to her chest and carried him up to the bedroom. She stood rocking from hip to hip, singing a breathy song. *Row, row, row your boat.* Downstairs, Em railed, 'Well it makes me feel like shit! It's like I can't do anything right!'

Voices spilled into the garden – Chris was taking the children outside. 'What's wrong with Auntie Em?' came Imogen's voice.

'She's in a mood!' Chris said. 'About food. That she's chewed. And then – she pooed! How rude!'

Imogen giggled. Chris was brilliant with her, and with Hal as well. But when he needed to sleep, only Carrie had the power to soothe him. 'It's the Magic Mummy thing, like with Imogen,' Chris said.

'We can't all be Earth Mothers,' Ruth said downstairs, and the back door banged. Grandma Lisa's voice and then Grand's sounded, gentle and consoling. Gradually Em's protests subsided. Hal's eyelids drooped. Carrie shifted him to horizontal and rocked him, her fingers tapping his back in time to the song. He started once or twice, and his eyes opened, but then the long, thick lashes fell again. She felt his head go heavy as he surrendered to the afternoon peace.

She lay him on the bed, surrounded by pillows, and snuggled beside him to read while he slept.

He stirred half an hour later. Imogen as a baby had been grumpy after a nap, but Hal always woke up sunny and raring to go. Carrie lifted him onto her lap and kissed his white-blond hair, gossamer soft against her lips. He smelt of warm baby, with an undertone of wee.

'Here he is!' said Grandma Lisa, clasping her hands when Carrie brought him down. The family were sitting round the kitchen table having tea and chocolate cake. Emilia, pink-eyed, gave Hal a hopeful smile. He wriggled his legs joyfully. 'Ah! He's happy to see you,' Grandma Lisa said, and Emilia held out her arms.

'I think his nappy needs changing,' Carrie said.

'Oh, that can wait, surely?' said Grand in a brittle, upbeat tone.

'Come for a walk, little boy,' Emilia cooed, her eyebrows raised in appeal.

'He's quite wet…' Carrie said.

Em's face clouded. 'We'll only be a minute.' She smiled again for Hal. 'Shall we go round and round the garden? Shall we?'

Carrie's throat caught, despite herself, at the effort in her voice. Maybe if Emilia had some fun with Hal, she'd relax and feel better, and there'd be peace. She stepped over to Emilia and shifted Hal's soft weight into her arms.

He jiggled with cheerful energy, and Em headed towards the front door.

'Do you want the changing bag?' Carrie called.

'Let her *go*,' muttered Ruth.

Carrie had a stupid urge to run out after them.

'Come and have a cuppa, love – give her a moment,' her mother said. 'I think it's hard for her, seeing you with the children. She feels inadequate.'

Carrie sipped at her tea without tasting it, craning to look out of the window. Ruth was making a shopping list while Imogen, blond hair sticking to her chocolate-smudged face, chanted nonsense rhymes. 'Chicken, licken, bag of salad, wine, pine, something for pud...'

Had Emilia said that Carrie made her feel inadequate? She only ever meant to help her... but perhaps she was making it worse. And was Carrie the target of Ruth's Earth Mother jibe? It was ridiculous to call her that. She'd had Imogen – an accident – at twenty-three. Her carefree life with Chris and her career hopes had stumbled to a halt, and now there was Hal.

She got up and went through to the front room to peer out. There was no one in the garden. She went to the back door.

'Emilia?!'

No answer. She ran down the steps and past the sycamore tree, then round the side of the house. Em would be sitting at the picnic table on the terrace. Carrie could go over and make a fuss of how well she was doing. She emerged, panting. There was no one there.

The front door opened. They had heard her calling. 'They're not in the garden,' she said.

How long had it been? Twenty minutes – more?

'She did say she was going for a walk.' Grand peered down the track, shading his eyes. 'I'm sure it's fine.'

But Carrie's heart was thumping. 'Round the garden, she said!'

'She can't have gone far.' Toby's hearty assurance.

Chris ran to her side – thank God for Chris – and they set off jogging up the track. How would it look if Em came round the bend now with a smiling Hal? Like a search party, chasing her. Carrie slowed to a walk. Perhaps things were going well and Emilia was relishing it. Perhaps she should just butt out.

141

Row, row, row your boat. Her feet thudded to the rhythm. The turning was coming up – they'd see Hal soon, in Emilia's arms.

But when they turned, the lane was empty.

'Oh shit, Chris, where is she?'

'We'll find her.' He squeezed her arm, then pointed, 'You go that way, to the beach. I'll head towards the village.'

Carrie ran down the shaded path. She thought of her parents, getting alarmed by now. *Merrily, merrily, merrily, merrily. It's not bloody fine.* She crashed towards the downwards lane, her lungs beginning to ache.

She emerged on the wider slope and stood panting, her gaze sweeping up and down. She set off downhill in big strides, glad of a puff of breeze.

Thump, thump, *row your boat.* Could they really have come this far? You couldn't walk fast with a baby. You had to keep things gentle and peaceful. *Happy bloody families,* she thought, fingernails gouging her palms.

A roar started up ahead, and a tractor turned into the lane. She pressed herself back into the spiky hedge and watched it lumber uphill. The noise rumbled through her; it would frighten a baby. The driver, with mousy curls and a baggy orange t-shirt, raised a hand as the tractor heaved past. Thorns poked into her back and cloud of straw-dust filled the air, catching in her hair and nostrils.

The view widened as she ran on downhill, wiping at bits stuck to her face.

She hit the beach with a crashing sound. Waves seethed up empty pebbles. Her legs went weak. Was this a real panic – or a fuss about nothing?

Chris might have found them, coming back from the village. They could all be in the kitchen now, awaiting her return. *Life is but a dream.* A longing rose at the back of her throat for the feeling of Hal in her arms again.

She blinked tears and saw the wind ruffling grasses on the clifftop. A gust dried the sweat on her face and brought the distant sound of birds crying.

Wait, *was* that birds?

She ran across the beach, sending pebbles crackling and flying. The stones gave under her, sucking the strength from her legs, but she plunged on, gasping, and made for the right-hand path. She hauled at the handrail to heave herself upwards.

A turn in the path brought the sound of crying. She struggled on and up, her legs nightmare-heavy. Sound sharpened as she staggered higher. A shrill scream, then a sobbing breath.

Her knees almost gave under her as the slope evened out. Waves crashed, way beneath, screened by a hedge on her left. Cliff edges stretched away, the rock cut raw like a wound.

Carrie's chest was exploding. She rounded a curve, her vision swimming.

Emilia stood facing the sea, Hal grasped in her arms, arching his back, shrieking.

Weakness fled in an instant of clarity. Carrie took the distance between them in powerful strides. Em didn't see her until she was right beside her, then she started, eyes wide, flashing guilt or alarm. Carrie reached out and took Hal, finding no resistance. She held him to her side.

'All right,' she panted. 'All right, baby, all right now.' She was drenched and trembling, but she kissed his head; she made shushing sounds and felt her own heart slowing.

Hal's breath was snotty, his throat rasping, but his crying was subsiding. He was soft as a newborn against the skin of her arm.

She could have kicked Emilia to the cliff edge and shoved her off. 'What were you doing?'

Em's eyes sank away. She looked tearful like a troubled child. 'Just walking. I like it here. I was showing Hal…'

'He was hysterical.'

'I – I was going to come back with him.'

Hal shuddered and Carrie pulled him closer. He leaned in, his forehead hot against her sternum. His sobbing breaths were slowing; he had cried himself to exhaustion.

'Carrie!' Emilia's call rose, pleading, complaining, but Carrie had turned her back and left it behind. If there was another cry, it was lost among the gulls' squawks.

I've left her on the cliff edge, alone, she thought on the path down to the beach. But she didn't care. She had Hal now. A door had slammed in her heart.

2011

'All right, Mum?' Hal was waiting now on the path ahead.

'Just having a Mum fuss about the cliff edge.'

He grinned, rolling his eyes. His jaw was taking on a solid look; there was a muscled hint of adolescence around his shoulders and arms.

It had turned out OK, hadn't it, in the end?

Then the ending rushed to meet her and she cursed herself for the thought.

CHAPTER 21

Carrie woke in a gentle dawn. Nothing rushed at her; nothing tightened round her heart. She drifted in memories of the previous evening. On the way back from their cliff walk, she had fallen into step with her father. They had marvelled at the hedgerows, the variety of colours and leaf shapes riotously beautiful, like a gentle jungle.

'What's that?' she asked, prodding a little purple flower with blue-green fronds.

'Vetch,' Grand said, 'and that yellow one's a wild snapdragon. But this I don't know.' He peered at a tiny violet-shaped flower. 'I should note down a description.'

'I'll photograph it, Dad.' She snapped a close-up with her phone.

'Oh well, yes. I suppose you could!' He admired the result. 'With your finger in it for scale! I'll look it up when we get back.'

'There are so many wildflowers I only see here.'

'Yes. Hilda used to press them and send them to me.'

Carrie had squirreled away this nugget that she had never heard before as they walked side by side on the cliff path. 'I suppose she thought you missed it all, in darkest Kent?'

There was a rush of sea sound, then a hush when they passed a hump of undergrowth.

'I suppose so. Huh! Darkest Kent. You're not wrong there.'

The bedroom was getting lighter now. Before bed last night, Hal had asked Chris to go for an early morning walk with him. If he didn't wake soon, she would nudge him. It warmed her to think of them out together, Chris hopefully returning to his brighter self.

He was curled towards her, his face in repose, his upper arm reaching forwards. She turned to press her back into the shelter of his front – the safest of havens; her favourite way to sleep.

He had been brilliant, that summer with Emilia. After the incident with Hal on the clifftop, they had all gone for fish and chips at Llangrannog. Em had barely eaten, and afterwards she had disappeared into to the Ship for a drink. Chris had had to go in and

145

get her so they could go back to Noddfa and put Hal to bed.

Later, he and Carrie had lain in this bed, whispering.

'Thank God you got her out of there. I don't think she'd have come for me.'

'Pub experience. I'm a natural.'

'Of course. All your drunks.' Chris was doing shifts in their local to help make ends meet. He made her laugh, talking about the punchy drunks, the funny ones, the philosophers and the bores. 'What type of drunk is Emilia?'

'A sad one,' he said.

She groaned. 'I don't think Hal's safe with her, Chris. We can't let her look after him any more, can we?'

'Of course not.'

'She'll despise me.'

He smoothed her hair. 'But you're right. He has to come first. And it's not just what happened yesterday, is it? Things have been getting worse for a while.'

His quiet confidence had given her the courage she needed.

'Chris!' she whispered now. 'Are you getting up?' He twitched, but then went still again. 'For your walk, with Hal?' She twisted round in his arms and saw his brow tense.

He rolled away and lay on his front, his arms up round his head. 'Sorry,' he said. But he didn't get up.

Carrie stared out of the passenger window and willed herself to recapture her early morning tranquillity. Chris had been last down to breakfast; she had waited through Grand's simmering fuss over keeping his portion hot, and Ruth's irritation with Grand. Hal, bless him, hadn't said anything about a walk. Perhaps he'd slept too late as well.

Josh had his paranormal book open in the back of the car and kept whispering to Hal as they set off for Newcastle Emlyn.

'Was she like that one, then, the girl with the hair? Scarier? No?

What then?'

After a while, he seemed to give up asking, and now he was laughing at a bilingual Hidden Dip sign. '*Pant Cud*! Welsh is hilarious.'

They passed a community hall and a neat grey cemetery, then a caravan park flying a Welsh flag. Bluish-pink hydrangeas flashed by, then pebble-dashed houses in pastel colours. Chris was bent over the steering wheel with a washed-out look – perhaps because of the muddy-brown shirt he was wearing, one she had never liked. He was often run down at the end of term. Perhaps he had a virus?

An old chapel had a sign advertising beds and carpets. Over a dry-stone wall, the land stretched away in a palette of different greens. A house huddled against a hill with dark trees around its shoulders.

At Newcastle Emlyn, they parked near the dragon-crested archway which looked like the entrance to a Chinatown but led to a new dragon-based outdoor experience. Sue had told Grand about it weeks ago after Dewi and Elin discovered it. She said a regeneration grant had paid for it and it was all over the local news. Grand was sceptical about its roots. 'Welsh folklore and hippy bollocks all scrambled together,' he said. Chris had laughed when he found an online article that pointed out the phallic shape of the dragon egg sculpture.

'Grand will want coffee and cake. Never mind that we've just had breakfast,' Carrie said as Chris came back with a pay and display ticket. 'Hal, you'll have to show Josh the dragon sculpture later.' She smiled at Chris as she got out of the car. 'Wales's most phallic visitor attraction.'

'What?' Chris said.

A weight fell on her chest. 'The dragon,' she said in a dead voice, and slammed her door.

Hal exhaled, turned on his heel and headed off after the others. They looked after him and a moment later, Josh followed. Hal's head was down, his arms rigid at his sides.

Pressure rushed to her head. 'I knew he'd be upset. You didn't get up for your walk.'

Chris looked stung and hung back as she swept off. Was it really

Chris, or her snapping, that had upset Hal? 'Alright?' she said, reaching him.

'What's up with Dad? Has he got flu or something?'

She had a childish urge to throw fuel on the fire. 'No, I think he's just tired. I'm sorry he didn't get up for a walk this morning. Did you?' He nodded and she ached for him. 'I'm sure he'll come another day. It's only the second Monday.' She could hear the shuffle of Chris following, but didn't look back. 'Don't worry, love.'

Hal managed a smile.

They went in the first café on the High Street, because Grand was reluctant to search any further. As they found seats, Carrie saw a notice explaining the ordering system and Ruth came back from the toilet full of the officious signs about washing your hands.

'Like a police state!' she said. 'It's what Toby thinks Britain will be like if Labour have their way.'

'Bloody right,' he grinned.

The staff were friendly as Carrie placed everyone's order and most of it was brought quickly to their table.

'Where's my millionaire's shortbread?' muttered Grand as the waitress went back to the counter.

'I'm sure it won't be long,' she said. 'Did you look up that wildflower – the violet one?'

'No, you must show me again.' He frowned towards the counter as Carrie searched through her phone.

'We were talking about the pressed flowers Hilda used to send,' she said, to distract him.

'Oh yes!' Grandma Lisa put a hand on Grand's arm. 'When we were first married, letters would arrive on beautiful notepaper, and inside you'd find these flowers. You kept them, didn't you, darling?'

'I'm sure I didn't,' Grand frowned.

'I think you did. I'll have a look for them. She started years before, didn't she, when you first left Wales?'

Grand's cake arrived at last and he bit into the chocolate crust. Perhaps they'd be cheerful after all.

'Must have been weird being back in London after Wales,' Hal said, turning to Grand. 'Was it all war-torn?'

'Like that film we had at school!' Josh said. 'Kids playing on bombsites. And having guns and that. It looked cool.'

'I went to Kent, not London,' Grand said.

Hal looked confused. 'I thought your Mum was in London…'

Grandma Lisa put her head on one side with a sigh. 'You went where you were sent in those days. We were just saying, weren't we, darling?'

Grand took a fierce bite.

'The hedgerows are so lovely here,' Carrie tried. 'I suppose Hilda wanted to send a little touch of Wales.'

'I must show you her letters, Carrie,' her mother said. 'They have me in tears.'

Grand scraped back his chair. 'I'm going to the toilet!' he muttered and pushed his way out.

'Make sure you wash your hands!' Ruth called after him.

Why had Carrie brought up the letters and the wildflowers? She'd had a nice moment with Dad – now he seemed angry with her for sharing it. Carrie was a child again at the top of the stairs, listening to his raised voice below and trying to tell if she was to blame. Back to overhearing, on one of these holidays, 'Oh, no one cares what I want!'

But they did care – they had to. She spent the whole fortnight pussyfooting round him, with this same bloody inevitable ending. And Ruth said what she liked, stoking the fires for fun. Why did Carrie forget, every year, and keep on coming? She was forty, for God's sake. She seemed to shed her adult self somewhere on the journey.

'So – lunch,' said Grandma Lisa after a while, picking the last cake crumb off her plate. 'Shall we each go and buy what we fancy? I'm going to have a potter down the High Street. Then we can meet up at those benches for a picnic. Perhaps you boys could bagsy them for us.'

By the time Grand came back, a liveliness had returned, with Dan building up the mystical attractions of the dragon and Josh, oblivious to his irony, very keen to see it. Carrie asked her father what time they should meet for the picnic, and he decreed twelve thirty as if nothing had happened.

She and Chris headed through the castle ruins with Hal and Josh. 'There you are, boys, that must be the mythical beast!' she said, a heaviness on her heart.

A bulbous wooden sculpture rose from a paved area, suggesting a dragon emerging from a giant egg. There was no denying its phallic shape, but she didn't feel like laughing. The surrounding mosaics and story boards merged genuine history with a dragon legend that looked dreamed up for tourists.

Carrie took photographs of the boys and then Josh pored over the story boards. 'What's all this about the dragon egg hatching and that?'

'It's made up!' Hal said.

Dan shook his head, 'Your face!'

'Doh! Course it is. I knew that.'

The river glinted between a screen of trees, and Carrie made herself look at Chris. 'Walk?'

He nodded, tired-eyed. They set off on the downward path towards the river, hearing Josh's laughter behind them as he read out bits of the story.

The park was tranquil and dappled with sunlight. When they reached that place with the waterfalls, they would talk things through under the noise of the water. She reached out a hand, but Chris didn't notice.

A bend in the path revealed slabs of grey rock at the river's edge. Further out, a series of waterfalls broke up glassy calm expanses. Chris was walking on, head down, and looked startled when she pointed out the place. He sat down on the rocks as usual.

'Sorry I snapped,' she said. He shook his head. 'That was classic Josh,' she said, 'believing the dragon thing.'

He was frowning – not following. She might as well be alone.

'Chris! What's wrong?'

'Nothing. I just – nothing.'

'It's not nothing! Tell me!'

He stared at her, brow twisted, sweat beading on his top lip. When had he ever been lost for words? She slapped hard at the rock beneath her, pain jarring through her palms.

'Don't!' he cried.

'Tell me then. Is it Imogen? I thought you'd be OK when we saw the photographs, but you're not, are you? Oh God, I can't do this.' She went to scramble to her feet, but he put out an arm to stop her.

'Carrie!' He looked tormented. She sat down again, trembling. 'When I was taking her to Tania's… I stopped the car on the way.'

The river raged past them, churned into an ugly brown. 'What?'

'I was… stupidly worried. I had this feeling of dread. That she'd never come back.'

It was like something out of Josh's book: *A premonition. A feeling of doom.* 'But Chris, why?'

'I don't know. I couldn't take her there. I was literally shaking. I stopped the car and – you'll hate me.'

She was trembling now. 'What?!'

'I begged her not to go. I said, *Come to Wales with us. Please. I can't bear it, if you go.* She just looked at me. She'd gone white. She said, *Drive me to Tania's.* So I did, but when she got out of the car, she wouldn't speak to me. I saw Tania open the door, all excited, and then her face fell. I called out to Imogen, and I heard her burst into tears. And then they went in.'

Carrie's palms throbbed. She fought a rising tide inside her. But it explained something, didn't it? His mood about Imogen. And she would have been angry and upset – frightened, even; she'd have refused to have her photo taken – hence her absence from the Facebook posts. Perhaps after the first few days, her friends had talked her round. That at least made some sense.

'But why were you so worried? What is it you're not telling me?'

Voices cut through the river's noise. The boys were coming down the path, Josh expounding some theory about dragons. She managed an ordinary Mum smile and Hal raised a hand. She watched their backs, one wide, one slim, retreating through the deep shade of the trees and wanted to run after them into the sunlight beyond.

'Chris? Is it stress? All the extra hours at work? This thing with Tyrone?' She saw his expression darken like a shutter coming down. 'Chris?' There was no flicker of response.

She pushed up from the rock, her hands stinging. 'I'm going for a

151

walk.' She walked off towards the castle ruins without looking back.

She went back through the dragon archway and downriver, on and on. What would it be like to just keep going? She barely knew where she was heading, but her feet thudded on. Later she turned and headed back towards the high street, where she went in one tasteful gift shop after another, staring at things. She came to the deli where she was usually tempted by every treat. She went in and ordered a wrap, but then couldn't imagine eating it.

Stepping out onto the street, she bumped into her mother, her blue cardigan tied round her shoulders, putting a gift shop parcel into her canvas bag.

'Oh there you are! I've just seen the boys. They've bought some disgraceful ready-made burger things you really won't approve of. They've bagsied the benches, though. Ruth's bought some ethnic jewellery, and Toby's calling her an Old Hippy. Alright, love?'

'Yes. Just – miles away.'

Their picnic benches had a view of the water through a haze of purple snapdragons. Chris was at the far end, peeling the cellophane off a sandwich. He glanced up, his smile wan. Beside him, Grand, in his holiday jeans, was tucking into a sausage roll.

'Well, this is nice,' said Grandma Lisa. 'Do you remember last year, Imogen had us playing charades?'

'We didn't come last year,' said Hal.

'Last time, I mean. She was hilarious.'

'She is hilariously rubbish at charades,' Dan agreed, tossing aside his floppy fringe so he could attack his burger.

'Wait,' Josh said. 'I've got one!'

And then he was on his feet, miming, and they were calling out film names as his actions got more frantic. Was Carrie's father even talking to her? Hal had got up to put his burger wrapper in the bin, and looked a bit subdued, despite Josh's antics. Chris chewed slowly with that shut-down expression. Hadn't anyone else noticed?

She nibbled at the end of her goats' cheese wrap, but her stomach felt closed. No one could guess Josh's film. When they gave in and he told them, he'd got the title wrong.

'It's like Imogen's here!' said Ruth, and Grand laughed with her, apparently happy now.

Carrie got to her feet. 'I want to show you that thing, Chris. In the gift shop.'

He looked baffled, but cottoned on and when she walked off, he followed. She stopped out of sight of the others, round a bend in the riverside path. Something fluttered in her belly, maybe hope, maybe dread. The river was a glassy deep-green, with yellow flowers acid-sharp against its darkness.

'It it something to do with Tyrone?'

Chris made a sound between a breath and a sigh. He nodded at the ground, his face contorting. But she made herself wait, his expression cutting through her. Then at last he began to talk.

CHAPTER 22

July 2011

Chris and Amanda met with the rest of the Special Needs team on Fridays for coffee and cake, but today their sticky-fingered review of the week was hijacked by a call from Cowper, the Deputy Head. He asked Chris to come to his office, and when Chris said they were in their meeting, he said, 'Yes, I'm aware of that.'

The kids called him *Cowpat* – so did some of the staff. He could only have been in his forties but made them all feel like feckless youths. Chris headed for his office, an ache tightening his skull. What was so urgent that it couldn't wait until after the meeting? He had a queasy feeling it might be about Tyrone. He hadn't come to their sessions that week – Amanda suspected he was off school again. Chris had been about to talk to the team about it.

Chris and Tyrone had been meeting every Tuesday and Thursday lunchtime in the team's cubby-hole of an office. The muscular, tough-looking sixteen-year-old had been agitated when they first met, answering every utterance with, 'Why do I even have to come here?' He knew it was because he had shoved Ben Ridgeley, a popular Year 10 footballer, who had fallen and injured his ankle. Chris knew better than to confront him with this at the start. Usually with angry students he could rely on his own natural air of calm to de-escalate things, but he sensed that wasn't going to work with Tyrone. Instead he subtly mirrored the boy's posture, sitting back, legs crossed and pulled to the side, arms clasped round his chest. With some teens, you didn't want to be the most positive person in the room.

After a while, Chris reached for his biro. As ever, with a pen in his hand, he began to doodle, and caught Tyrone watching, his big eyes rain-cloud grey, as a jagged, cross-hatched decoration spread over the paper. The charged atmosphere in the small room eased.

'I like drawing. Just not fuckin' art lessons,' Tyrone snapped, as though they had been having a heated argument on the subject. Chris looked him in the eye for the first time that session. He'd be good-looking if he weren't for the almost constant frown. His Mum

154

had put up a punchbag in the garage so he could thump it when he was agitated. Apparently this was often, because he'd built up the kind of upper body that teenagers usually admired. His upper arms bulged through his school blazer, which was worn to a shine. Chris tore off a blank notebook page and handed it over with a biro. When he looked up again, Tyrone was filling his paper with a graphic-novel square, all dramatic angles and exaggerated perspective. Soon it showed a hooded figure in a boxing stance, surrounded by leering oafs.

'That's brilliant, Tyrone. Who is it?'

Tyrone seemed irritated by the question. 'Just some character.'

Over the following weeks, they doodled and drew through sessions and Tyrone let slip random confidences. His mum 'went mad, crying,' when he got into trouble. If that or his little brother Kyle's noise 'did his head in', he went to Gran's. He used to go to his cousin's, but he'd gone off somewhere. Chris's enquiry about his Dad led to a similar shrug. Chris recalled a social worker's report about the father breaking into the family home in defiance of a restraining order. Later a figure in a raincoat appeared on the paper, his face in inky darkness.

Chris began to work in an unobtrusive way through some anger management material. The biro moved fiercely if he brought up Tyrone's outbursts at schoolmates. 'It's not me. It's them. They make me mad.' But at least during their sessions, his aggression was channelled into the drawings. In their last meeting, he had produced a graphic novel-style series showing the hooded figure flattening his enemies and marching off into the distance, a muscled colossus, towering over the street scene he was leaving. 'He don't have to take it no more,' said Tyrone. Chris hesitated to move on to the next topic in his material: forgiveness. He picked up the drawings instead.

'These are good, Tyrone. I mean, really good.' Tyrone raised an indifferent eyebrow. 'Maybe you could get something in the Art Show this year, if you can commit to working on your anger? Use some of the techniques we've talked about?' Chris saw his head tilt. With a calmer, more open look – like the one flitting over his features now – he was handsome in a conventional, boy-band way.

Tyrone gave a shrug of assent. Could this turn into a breakthrough? As Tyrone headed towards the door at the end of the session, Chris had risked putting a hand on his shoulder. He'd been struck by the jump of muscle, firm under his palm.

But this week, no Tyrone.

When Chris arrived, Cowper was fidgeting around his office, his bald pate, ginger-edged, shining in the neon light. He pointed to the chair facing his desk and sat down, sweeping at a speck on his suit jacket sleeve. His eyes, turned on Chris, were a blue so pale they were almost colourless.

A memory juddered Chris's heart – of Laurie losing it in the Special Needs office. While Amanda ran for help, Chris had had to stop him from hurting himself – smothering the thrashing boy with his own adult body. It had been described to him later across this very desk as 'humping'. Had Amanda's protests that of *course* she believed him been a touch too earnest? Cowper's response had been textbook but cold. A slimy heat broke out under Chris's shirt collar.

'So,' Cowper said, 'we've had a tip-off.' He lifted his palms at Chris's silence, as though his meaning were obvious. 'Ofsted. Inspectors in from Monday. Just about as close to the end of term as they can get.' Chris's heart eased, but then Cowper added, 'You need to contact the parents of your Special Needs cases. Tell them not to come in until Wednesday.'

'What, none of them?' Chris felt winded. *Cases*, were they – not students like everyone else?

'The severe cases, definitely.'

He gave a humourless chuckle. 'Define severe…'

'Oh come on, Chris. You know what I mean.' Cowper straightened a pile of papers by knocking the edges on his desk. 'We've put two years' hard graft into getting an Outstanding. We don't want that jeopardised by kids climbing the walls.' He placed the papers into a tray and gave a nod of dismissal.

Chris thought of his beleaguered team: the hours they crammed in around the normal teaching and planning and marking, Amanda for barely more than a cleaner's wage; the late nights, the meetings, the endless paperwork that seemed to be taking him longer and longer lately – all from sheer bloody commitment to the students. Kids who were an embarrassment, to be airbrushed out for the inspection. His ears were hot and ringing.

'Well, if there's nothing else,' Cowper said. 'Lots to do.'

And Chris walked out without so much as a murmur. He was too busy thinking what he could say to all those parents – he'd always told them their children's needs were paramount. It was his *job* to make them paramount.

He smashed a hand down on his steering wheel as he drove down the gravel drive. What use was he to anyone lately? He emerged onto drizzled streets.

Halfway down the High Street, a flurry of motion caught his eye. Tyrone. His heart flipped. He hadn't had time to ask Amanda if he was confirmed absent. He'd meant to get an update from the social worker in case there were issues at home. But he hadn't followed it up, had he? Hadn't even done the bloody basics.

Jeering sounded over the traffic noise. Tyrone was outside Costcutters, surrounded by a group of boys. They were the ones from the estate, he saw now, always loitering outside the shop, hoodies over their school shirts. Imogen called them *the Costcutter Massive*. Chris slowed down and missed his turn-off. As he drew level, he saw faces snarling, others laughing. He knew most of them from school. Shit, Ben Ridgeley was among them, in a designer hoodie. Chris hadn't thought of him as part of this group. But there he was, pointing and mocking, his face twisted with spite.

Chris drove at a crawling pace. Tyrone turned on his heel and stalked off, hunched over, hood up, fists at his side. The traffic moved off and Chris sped up with it, then craned to look back. Tyrone's stance threatened violence, but his face was a child's, crumpled with despair. Chris faced front again, his hand on the indicator, sweat trickling in his underarms.

Tyrone had tried to tell them he was being bullied – but the story didn't fit the school's narrative: big, scary Tyrone, always lashing out. And Chris was no better than the other teachers. He'd wanted to be Tyrone's hero, putting those drawings in a bloody art display – instead of addressing what they were telling him. But he got it now, he understood. His whole body tingled with the urge to let Tyrone know.

What was he thinking? Tyrone lashed out when he was upset, he might make a scene. And how would Chris explain why he was hanging around Costcutters with schoolboys after hours? A man glanced at him from the pavement. Shit, he was virtually kerb-crawling. Had the kids seen him? Had anyone? He should pull over now, he had to get to Tyrone – but he was dragged along with the traffic in the steady flow homeward.

He looked in the mirror. Tyrone was lost in the evening crowd. He could go back and find him… Chris gazed at the back of the car in front but remembered the boy's tear-stained face.

~

August 2011 Day 10: Monday

'I just drove past and left him to it. Then we heard that he'd gone missing.' Chris was trembling, a hand to his mouth.

'But Chris – you're not responsible.' Carrie tried to take his hand but he held tightly to his face.

'I am! I am responsible. I was working with him. I saw what was happening to him.'

'But – the inspection was on. I don't suppose anyone was listening.'

He hung his head. 'I didn't tell them.'

'Oh.'

'How could I let them know what a mess I'd made?'

'But it wasn't your fault!' She clutched his hand in both of hers as though her strength could quell his shaking.

'Yes it was. I've ruined everything. For Imogen. Hal. You...' His deep voice broke to a squeak.

'Chris! You've just got yourself into a state. You've been working so hard. All those extra hours you've put in! You've done too much, darling, not too little. Look at me.'

His face was greyish-white against the darkness of the river. He wasn't seeing the world she saw, but some horrible distortion. 'Chris, don't worry. As soon as we get home, we'll get you help. You're not well. It's an illness.' Her heart felt bruised as though he'd kicked it.

'OK.' She held him tight, his breaths heaving against her chest. She would help him through this week. Keep things calm for him. If they could just make it to Saturday, he could go to the doctor at home. She thought of people who'd know about counselling services. He'd be OK. He'd get better.

They stood clinging together until his shaking subsided.

'All right?' she said, looking up at his face.

Chris pulled his mouth into a dreadful smile, and nodded.

CHAPTER TWENTY-THREE

2011 Day 10: Monday

Hal reflected that evening that it had been an OK day after all, even though Mum and Dad had some kind of row. It was so funny when Josh thought the dragon thing was true, and after that he kept doing his dodgy Welsh accent and going, 'I don't know what's real any more! I think I've been enchanted!'

Mum and Dad went to bed early, and then Auntie Ruth made a big thing of Uncle Toby snoring on the sofa and after some sleepy banter, they went up too. Josh and Hal stayed up with Dan and Grand, doing the Guardian crossword. Grand started watching a French film about a boy, with subtitles. Josh did a huge yawn.

'Not your sort of thing, Josh?' said Grand.

'I don't know what's going on, I really don't!' said Josh, all Welsh again. He and Hal were still laughing when they went upstairs.

Then on the landing, Hal felt it. A dark, dank feeling like when the sun goes in.

Josh pushed past into the bedroom. 'Brr! Parky up here.'

'You felt that?'

'What? Oh, you mean..? Yeah – it went cold!' Josh got his jeans off quickly and scrambled up into the top bunk, rocking the whole bed. 'A cold spot!' he whispered. 'It's a classic sign.'

Hal switched the lamp off, weirdly relieved he wasn't the only one to have felt it.

'Is it pissing you off, all the haunting stuff?' Josh said in a low voice.

'I just don't want it to spoil the holiday,' Hal said. 'But when it happens – like when I've seen the girl – I sort of want to go after her. Even though it's scary.'

'Shit. Do you feel like that now?'

Did he? He had the feeling of someone hidden, watching – but he made himself snap out of that. 'No. I can just hear Grand's film.'

Josh's head hit his pillow. 'Well that'll get us off to sleep in no time. Most boring film EVER.'

160

Day 11: Tuesday

Carrie saw the heaviness of Hal's eyelids when he came down to breakfast.

'Did you sleep all right?' Grandma Lisa asked him.

'Eventually.' He shrugged and gave her a little smile.

Josh had an entire cooked breakfast squashed between two slices of bread. He chomped down, dislodging a slice of sausage and a jet of ketchup. 'We got a bit spooked,' he said through his mouthful. Carrie caught Hal flicking him a glance.

'I'm not surprised!' Grandma Lisa shivered in her light cotton dressing gown. 'I was looking at that book of yours. Talk about creepy. It should have a health warning.'

'Everything's got a bloody health warning these days!' Grand burst out, stabbing a sausage with his fork.

'*May Contain Nuts,*' Toby laughed. 'On a bag of nuts!'

'And every other TV programme has helplines at the end,' Grand said. 'As if you need help because of something on the telly! And the slightest thing happens, and everyone's offered counselling! I mean, how bloody fragile do they think we are?'

Chris was sitting at the head of the table with the morning sunlight behind him, making it hard to see his face. Carrie had encouraged him to get up with her rather than lying there, stewing in anguish. She hadn't put it like that, of course.

'They think navel-gazing's the answer to everything,' said Toby, sinking his teeth into a bacon sandwich.

For once, Grand agreed with him. 'We had none of that malarkey in our day. No support groups, no getting in touch with your inner what-not. You either got on with things or went to the nuthouse.'

Ruth let out a sharp hoot of laughter. 'And men were real men, and women were grateful.'

'There's nothing wrong with counselling,' Carrie said. The sun went in and revealed Chris's long, drawn face. No wonder Hal had thought he had flu.

'No but it does get a bit over the top,' Grandma Lisa said.

Carrie couldn't muster an answer. It had felt like a breakthrough yesterday after the shock of Chris's outburst, as if knowing the truth was half the battle. She'd fallen straight to sleep for the first time this holiday. But then she'd woken up in the early hours, going over it all in her head.

Grand slapped his knees. 'The forecast is great, boys. What do you say we do a cliff walk near Cwmtydu?'

'I'm in,' Dan said.

'We could show Josh the Secret Beach!' Hal said. 'Do you remember, Dad, when we found it?'

The silence stretched out. 'Chris?' said Carrie. She heard Hal's quiet patience when he had to repeat what he'd said.

Carrie volunteered to drive to the Londis at the petrol garage to buy a picnic.

'We'll come to help you choose,' Hal said.

'Yeah,' Josh said, fastening his seatbelt. 'Mums just buy salad and stuff.'

She smiled and felt lighter as they set off up the track away from the house. There was a stillness in the air that promised heat later; sunlit straw glinted in the hedgerows; the greens were lush against a deepening blue. Chris would be all right with the others.

'What's all this about you two being spooked?' Glancing in the driving mirror, she saw Josh rocked by a nudge.

'There was this presence,' Josh said. 'We both felt it! But we don't know if it's Barbara because she didn't live at Noddfa, did she? Didn't anyone die there?'

'Not that I know of. Will died in hospital in the early eighties and Hilda went into an old people's home in Bow Street. Barbara lived in Bow Street too, after she got married.'

'She got *married*? After Hugh died?'

Carrie marvelled again that Josh seemed so involved in their tired old family stories. But they did feel more vivid here, as if they had left some kind of echo. 'Yes, years later. Hilda didn't like the husband, according to Grand. She called him *that miserable bugger* in her letters. And they never had children, which Hilda thought was

162

a terrible shame.'

'Maybe Barbara's angry about the miserable bugger. Or about not having children…' Josh said. 'Or maybe just about being dead?'

Hal left a little silence, then said, 'Well, that would be annoying.'

Josh let out a hoot and Hal joined in. When they turned into the village, Carrie was rocking in her seat, stomach muscles cramping. 'I don't know why it's funny,' she gasped, but then Hal repeated, 'Well, that would be annoying,' and she was helpless again.

'There's Sue!' Hal called. Carrie spotted the upright little figure walking along the side of the road with her pink housecoat over a blouse and skirt. There were matching furry-edged slippers on her feet.

She drew to a halt, climbed out of the car and approached the little old lady, feeling as always that she towered over her. Would she have to explain who they were?

'Oh, hello!' Sue said, bright-eyed. 'I've just been to see Elin with a recipe. And where are you off to?' She beamed at the boys as they got out of the back seat.

'Londis, for picnic things,' Carrie said. Sue's mind seemed clear today.

'You'll come in, though? I'll make tea!'

'That's sweet of you, but the others will be waiting. We did enjoy our visit the other day!'

'Josh specially liked the cake,' Hal said.

'And the stuff about Grand and the war and that,' Josh said, elbowing him.

'Dad's been showing the boys his old haunts,' Carrie said.

'Oh dew yes. He did love it here.' Sue's gaze twinkled over the boys' faces. 'Although it wasn't all fun and laughter. Well, with the war on. There were boys who never came back, you see. Hugh Evans. Jim Owen. Oh dew. And I always thought, Carrie, how awful for your father.'

Carrie noted the change of mood, the confusion. 'Being evacuated, you mean?' she said.

'Well no, he loved the Evanses. *He's like our own, Sue,* Hilda used to say. Well, she left Noddfa to him, fair play, doesn't that show what she thought of him?' Carrie gave little nods. She had heard all this before. 'The way she took to that boy was something to see. I always hoped it made up for it, you know.'

'Made up for what?'

'That his mother was never in touch!' Sue said, as though it were obvious.

'Dad's mother? Wasn't she?' The sun was warming Carrie's back, but the rest of her felt chilly.

Sue went on in a confiding tone. 'Hilda kept it quiet around the village. She didn't want gossip. She told me of course – well, I was her friend, and David's teacher. His mother dropped him off for evacuation in London and he never heard from her again. The boy we had, Kenneth, he got a letter every week. His mother came to visit. Sent him presents all the time. But poor David – not a thing. Not even birthdays and Christmas.'

Hal and Josh, who had been play fighting, had fallen still.

'Terrible. But there you are,' Sue said.

Carrie chinked the car keys in her hand. 'Well, it's lovely to see you. Come on, boys, we'd better get on. We'll see you again, Sue. Take care!'

Sue had a faraway look, standing on the grass verge as they got back in the car, but when they passed her, she gave a lively wave.

Carrie put her foot down, heading uphill towards the petrol station. The roaring power of the car beneath her was a reminder of today and their plans.

'What was that about Grand's Mum?' Hal said above the noise of air whipping in the open windows.

'Oh, I think Sue's getting confused. His Dad was killed during the Blitz. But his Mum was alive until the end of the war. I'm sure she kept in touch. Or he'd have *said*, wouldn't he?'

'She didn't seem confused.'

'No... She was brighter today... Perhaps it comes and goes. Don't let me forget to get Grand's pork pie, or I'll never hear the last of it.'

'How can it be secret?' Josh said as they parked beside Grand's car at Cwmtydu and joined the others to walk along the coastal path. The sea was a deep, still blue, dappled with purple and green, and the sun was hot on their faces.

'There's only one place on land you can see it from,' Grand said. 'Walking back this way from New Quay. And even there you can't see how big it is.'

'We could show you,' Hal said. 'But we'd have to kill you, wouldn't we, Dad?'

Chris gave him a little smile. Carrie remembered him and Hal when they discovered the Secret Beach: they had gone to see what the views were like off the northern edge of the promontory. They came back much later, wide-eyed and sweaty, finishing each other's sentences. Imogen had been so jealous.

'Alright, love?' Grandma Lisa said, and she nodded.

When they reached the promontory, Grand got out his binoculars and headed out to look at the bay. Grandma Lisa shook out the picnic rug that was as old as Ruth, and settled on its faded tartan, her face tipped up to the sun.

The others set off towards the northern edge, Hal glancing round making sure no other walkers had seen them. 'Coming, Mum?' he said, and she joined him.

'You're walking me off a cliff edge!' Josh protested as the land sloped downwards.

'It looks like a sheer drop, doesn't it? Hal said. 'That's what we always thought.'

Now the grassy soil was dropping away, cut through with rocks and scree. Soon they needed hands as well as feet to keep them upright.

'There!' Hal said. They had reached the rocky natural steps and Carrie glimpsed wet sand in deep shade below them. Stones slipped underfoot and she clung on to grass tufts, her head ringing with the boys' cries. They all scrambled over black rock, crusted with barnacles. An old rope hung in tatters from a shallow cliff, and one by one they grasped it and walked themselves downwards. She saw Hal, Dan, Ruth, Toby and then Chris turn and leap to the unseen place beneath.

'I can't do it!' Josh said. 'It's madness! I'll be smashed to smithereens! OK, I'm going! Aaaaaaagh!' There was a loud thud, and laughter.

Carrie's knees felt scuffed, her hands rope-burned when she finally landed in damp sand. They walked out together onto a wild, deserted beach. The rocks clawing out from the cliff edge were striated and piled in chunks, like the leftovers of an eruption. Most of the sand was in deep shade, but the sun sparkled on soft-lapping water with barely a lick of foam.

They walked with the cliff on their right, deep grey swirled with iron stains, verdigris and white. Crevices and caves cut into the cliff face and piles of stones suggested recent rock falls. Carrie picked up a chip and it crumbled, the green coming off on her hands. Was the rock face so unstable? You'd think it had stood here forever, unchanged.

There were pools of brackish water, but seaweed and crab shells were the only litter, and they made the first footprints in perfect sand.

Ruth squinted in the light. 'It's a relief not to be in a café.'

'Ha! You never turn down a scone,' said Toby.

'Keep your nose out of my scones, and I won't count your beers.'

Josh was shouting and pointing at a clear jellyfish the size of a dinner plate. They gathered round, Hal wobbling it with the toe of his deck shoe and Josh swearing it was alive.

'Good, here isn't it?' Hal said.

'Epic.'

'We don't think anyone else comes here. Except maybe by boat.'

Chris was staring down at the dead thing. Watching him was giving her an ache like a physical strain. She thought of the tartan rug back up on the clifftop and longed to lie down and sleep.

They were heading towards a stretch of rock that was sharp and tricky to scramble over. On the other side lay a great hidden vista of beach.

'I'm going to head back and help Grandma Lisa get the picnic ready,' Carrie said. 'You lot go on exploring.' Ruth gave her a funny look, but she waved them off and turned back alone. In a crevice she hadn't spotted before, she noticed the remnants of a bonfire.

Grandma Lisa sat up with a sleepy smile, her long bobbed hairstyle ruffled, when Carrie plonked down beside her.

The sea breeze was gentle and balmy; the gulls' cries melodic. Her mother was peering at her, shading her eyes.

Carrie began rooting through the Londis bag. 'I got Dad a pork pie. And all sorts of rubbish the boys chose. Oh, and melon pieces...'

'Lovely. Is Chris all right?'

Carrie stared at the plastic fruit container in her hand. What if she said, 'No' and everything spilled out? The bright cliff top, the sparkling water might fold in on itself and collapse. 'Chris?' she said. 'Yes.'

A wave slapped and boomed against the rocks deep below. What was she doing, carrying on like this? Chris was desperate. She must stop it all now and take him home. Hal could stay here with the family. She just had to explain. But here was her father, making his way back towards them, pausing with his binoculars raised to search the bay for dolphins.

Carrie cleared her voice, unsure she could trust it. 'He's been a bit stressed about work. The inspection and everything.'

'Ah, of course,' her mother said, patting her hand. 'They take a while to wind down after term ends, don't they? Your father was always like a bear with a sore head to start with.'

'Who was a bear with a what?' Grand loomed over them, hands on hips, puffing.

'You were! I was just saying we thought Chris had been quiet. He's had a stressful time with the inspection.'

'Well, it's this bloody regime. Schools are run by managers, not teachers. It's all box ticking exercises and sodding league tables. Listen to Ruth sometimes, it's like she's running a business. And she says to me, *I am running a business*, as though that's what it's all about! Good holiday's what Chris needs, Carrie!' He glanced in her direction – did he see the tears that welled in her eyes? – then turned towards the horizon. 'This is the perfect antidote. And it's dolphin spotting weather!'

He strode off again towards the northern edge, binoculars at the ready. Grandma Lisa lay down, folding her hands over her middle.

So they were concerned about Chris – Dad's political rant was his weird way of showing it. Had Carrie really been about to say that she was breaking up the holiday? She imagined the looks on their faces and her insides turned over.

It was too early to get the picnic out. She dropped things back in the bag and lay down, the familiar scratch of wool against her bare calves and elbows. The sun glowed orange through her eyelids.

'It's your Dad's religion, this place. His spiritual home.' Her mother's voice was sleepy.

'Oh, I forgot to say – we saw Sue,' Carrie said. 'Saying peculiar things again. She said that Dad's Mum dropped him off in London and he never heard from her again. That's not right, is it?'

She had expected a laugh or a protest, but none came. Her mother's lids were squeezed shut, her brow knitted.

'Is it?'

Carrie's mother sat up and scanned the area. Dad was in the distance with his back to them. 'You know what your father's like. He didn't want to talk about it.'

'About what?'

'When we were at Rod's – you know, last year – he mentioned a folder Dad might like in a box of Auntie Mo's things. Dad had never shown any interest before, certainly not when Mo died. There were a couple of photos of Dad as a boy, and his ration book, that kind of thing. And then this postcard from Canada, with just the address and a signature, *Beryl*.'

'Beryl? That was his Mum's name, wasn't it?'

'Yes. And it was dated 1960.'

'But I thought she died just after the war?'

'So did we. There were diaries of Mo's too, and your Dad asked to see them. Rod thought they were just appointment diaries. But Mo had written proper entries, and in the 1945 one...' She stopped and turned to check behind her. Carrie could see her father making his way towards them. They sat up.

'What?' he said when he reached them, levering himself down onto the rug.

'Mum was saying... about *your* Mum... And Auntie Mo's diaries?'

He glared at her mother.

'Sue told Carrie,' she said.

'Oh. *Did* she.'

'Yes. Why don't you tell her about your investigations?'

He looked weary. 'I did a bit of detective work, that's all. Stella helped me – you remember, from college? She's into all this internet research. Archives and so on. She found things in the records that confirmed what Auntie Mo had written.'

'What *had* she written?'

'My mother took up with some Canadian after Dad was killed. She went off to Canada and had a family with him.' He half-raised his eyebrows as though only mildly interested.

'She didn't just leave you behind?!'

'The Canadian bloke insisted, according to Mo. It was just the two of them, or the deal was off. So.' He shrugged. 'She died in Toronto. In 1975.'

Carrie stared at the thin, tanned wrist emerging from his shirt sleeve as he leaned back on one hand, gazing out to sea. She managed to keep her tone neutral, betraying only surprise. 'Sue just said she never wrote to you …'

Carrie's mother filled a silence. 'Well, that's another thing. We think Beryl was illiterate.'

He looked irritated. 'Mo didn't have a good word to say about her in the diaries. She was *that useless cow* or *that filthy bitch*. She said: *She can't even read and write because Mum could never get her to school.*'

'Mo sounds horrible,' Carrie said. How would it feel to hear that about your mother?

'Yes. But it makes sense, what she said. I never remember any books at Pollard Street.'

'So she couldn't write to you… And then your Dad died and she left… so that's why Mo took you in?'

'It's like I said, you went where you were sent.' He took a deep breath and slapped his knees. 'Did you get me that pork pie, love? Ah! Thank you. Where are the others? I'm starting to get peckish.'

She gazed at him from behind her sunglasses. She had absolutely no idea what went on in his head.

CHAPTER TWENTY-FOUR

July 1945

'It makes you talk posh, honest,' said Ceinwen, whose eyes were the same blue as her cotton summer uniform dress. She shook aside her long, dark pigtails and popped the plum in her mouth. *'We interrupt this broadcast to bring you some important information.'*

She made her voice posh like people on the radio, but it was muffled by the plum. Her face was dead straight, but her eyes sparkled. Iwan and David bent over in the village road, laughing. *'Be sure to tell your friends and neighbours,'* said Ceinwen, but then a guffaw of her own made the plum shoot out between those pursed pink lips. She threw out a hand and caught it like a fielder.

'That's not posh!' David said, his stomach aching from laughing, 'that's completely… *jargled.*'

'Jargled?' Iwan said, pushing his glasses up his nose, his hair sticking up in sweaty blond spikes. 'What's that when it's at home?'

David shrugged, heady with the joy of invention. 'What she said! It was completely and utterly jargled by a plum.'

Ceinwen wiped the plum on her school cardigan. 'Who's next then, since you're so clever?'

'Eugh, no,' said Iwan. 'It's got your gob on it.'

'I'll have a go!' David held out his hand.

'Disgusting boy!' boomed Iwan in a pretty good impression of his Da.

Usually spit was disgusting, but Ceinwen made you carefree and bold.

'Oh it's my Three Musketeers, is it, making all that racket?' Sue came up behind them carrying her wicker basket, her tartan flask nestling among exercise books. 'Isn't your Mam waiting, Iwan? She said you were going to your Auntie's after school.'

Iwan's eyes popped like the cat's in *Tom and Jerry*. 'Auntie's!' he said, and raced off, waving his hands above his head. All for Ceinwen's benefit of course. She rolled her eyes with a vague smile, the plum nestling in her hand.

'Boys,' sighed Sue. She was David's teacher again, now that evacuee school had finished. It was great being the oldest, you could muck around a bit and not get into trouble. The three of them had passed the Eleven Plus and got places at Ardwyn Grammar School.

'Sue says you're all getting boisterous!' Hilda had said the other night. But she wasn't really cross.

'Big fish in a little pond,' Will had said with a wink. 'They're ready for bigger things.'

'Don't you two keep your mams waiting either,' said Sue, setting off towards her bungalow. You could see it made her happy to look at them.

Usually, Iwan wouldn't go home before Ceinwen. He'd hang around doing things to impress her. Sometimes he'd say to David, 'Aren't you late for your tea?'

Ceinwen grinned now and turned her hand over, plopping the plum into David's hot palm. It lay there, warm and firm in its purple-black skin. He brought it to his mouth and held it, teasing, just beyond his lips. The summer fields were bleached in the sun. He jerked his head forward and took a great bite. The plum was gashed open, showing juicy, yellow flesh, the stone peeping out in a flourish of pink.

'Boys! So greedy!' Ceinwen said. 'That was my tea, that was!'

He held out the other half and she took it and bit in so juice ran down her chin.

They strolled through the village, Ceinwen humming a wandering tune. 'It'll be great, won't it, in September? We'll all be getting the bus together. Or will you sit at the front, with Will?'

'No! They'd all call me *teacher's pet*.' They were approaching the Post Office, which was really just a cottage with the front room converted. The postmistress was standing among towering foxgloves in the garden, the light making a halo of her grey frizz. 'Look out!' David said.

Ceinwen giggled. 'What have you got against Roslyn?'

Roslyn often stopping talking when David went in the Post Office. She'd shake her head: no letters for him. Her sad, worried face and staring eyes had a hint of relish, like when she told you someone's bad news.

He set off running as they passed her, Ceinwen right behind.

'Witch,' he hissed with a mad little caper on the cow-shit-crusted tarmac. 'Witchy, witchy *bitch*!'

'You're bonkers, you are!' they heard Rosyln call as Ceinwen overtook him.

Better to be bonkers with Ceinwen than lying awake in the darkness, wondering or hoping or dreading.

He raced after her, their school sandals slapping, satchels bouncing. Her socks had fallen down, showing the brown curve of her calves.

She stopped at the turning to Noddfa with a sigh of subsiding laughter. 'Come to tea at mine. Mam won't mind. Dilys can't eat – she's got toothache.'

'I'll have to ask Hilda.'

'Run, then! I'll wait here.' She pulled her satchel off her shoulder and dropped it on the wayside grass, then sat on it, cross-legged, pulling a stalk to chew on. She looked up at him with her blue gaze. 'What? Don't you want to come?'

'Yes!' Hilda would have baked, probably Welsh cakes. But she always smiled if he mentioned Ceinwen. 'I'll be three minutes – a hundred and eighty seconds! Count!'

He set off, full-pelt down the track, scattering stones. He heard her shout 'One' and a giggle burst like a bubble in his throat. He'd race in, explain and be out again in no time.

The front door opened before he got there. 'David, you've got a visitor,' said Hilda from the shadows. Her face had a sunken look, the apron over her dark-green dress was coming untied.

Even then, not knowing, the joy of the run left him like a dream on waking.

'What?' he said. 'Who?' As if questions could stop it, the walk through the shaded hall, the door opening onto the kitchen, the thin lady at the table, black-eyed, pinched-looking.

Was it? His chest thumped. He'd never told anyone that he couldn't remember her face. He tried so hard, going over and over that day in the school hall, her crouching on the floor as they led him away.

'Is this him?' the woman barked, frowning.

172

'Yes,' Hilda whispered, her grey eyes wide.

The lady sounded irritated as though he'd done something to upset her. 'It's me, your Auntie Mo.'

Mum's sister. Her house, only a few doors up Pollard Street, was another world, clean-smelling and tidy. If he hung round at the right times, he might get bread and dripping with Rodney, but they'd both get a slap round the head if they disturbed Uncle Pete after a night shift.

'Sit down, *bach*. I'll get your tea,' Hilda said, her hand warm on his shoulder. 'We've got lots to tell you.' She fumbled and burnt herself dishing up the Welsh cakes, her apron now hanging untied from her neck. David's Welsh cake lay on his plate, steaming up the china. He thought of Ceinwen giving up on him and walking home alone.

'Well, are you going to tell him?' Auntie Mo said. Her face and her grey-brown hair looked old and dry.

Hilda's chair bumped the flagstones as she sat beside him. 'You remember we told you a long time ago that we were trying to get in touch with your mother?' He nodded, but couldn't look at her. 'We went to all the authorities we could think of,' said Hilda. 'We told you about your father, didn't we, but there was no record of your mother… We kept trying, especially in March when the last children went back to London.' She looked across at Auntie Mo, who shrugged and crossed her arms. 'The thing is, *cariad*, the thing your Auntie has come to tell you…'

Auntie Mo gave an impatient *tut* and burst out: 'She's dead.'

Hilda's hand crept across the oilcloth and lay firm on top of his. 'I'm so sorry, David.'

Well that was that then. No more London. He saw his Ardwyn Grammar School blazer over the back of Will's chair. Hilda had sewn his name tag inside the collar. His *gwisg ysgol* for September.

'Thank you.' He heard his own voice and then didn't know why he'd said it.

'That's right, you should be grateful,' said Auntie Mo. 'There's lots died. My Pete too, I was telling Mrs Evans. That's when me and Rodney moved to Kent.'

Hilda fished out the hankie she kept up her cardigan sleeve. 'Do you have any questions, *cariad*?'

'Did she die … with Dad in the Blitz?'

Hilda shook her head, sad-eyed. 'We think it was more recently.'

Auntie Mo snorted. 'And it wasn't the Blitz that killed him. He was run over by a car in the blackout – probably staggering home from the pub, whatever Beryl said.'

Hilda's hand curled round David's.

'But Mum..?' he looked at Auntie Mo's mouth. *Like a cat's arse*, Dad used to say. He saw her at their door on Pollard Street, saying David had taught her Rodney a bad word. The neighbours gawping from their doorsteps. Mum bellowing from inside, *Don't you look down on me, you snooty cow!*

'All I heard is she died,' said Auntie Mo. 'Like I said, we'd moved to Kent. We'd lost touch.'

The Welsh cakes had cooled down. They might as well be stones.

'I'm so sorry,' said Hilda, her hand moving over his. He thought of Will stroking the white cat who was afraid of the chickens: *It's all right, scaredy-cat, I won't let them get you.*

Hilda stood up, her chair screeching on the stone floor. 'There's been a mix-up,' she said, pouring tea. 'The authorities located your Auntie Mo at last and gave her our address. But we didn't get the message to say she was coming. Or we'd have told you.' Her voice went up and down as if she was telling a story. She put a cup down in front of him, and went to get sugar.

'Yes, well, there's nothing else for it. You need to pack your things.' David wasn't sure he had heard right. He was more used to Welsh now than Auntie Mo's Cockney.

'Oh but, you'll give us a few days to get him ready?' said Hilda, breathless.

'Oh no. That's out of the question.'

'But – it's so sudden!'

'I can't help that,' Auntie Mo said, straightening her back. Her accent got posher like Mum's used to when she was talking to the rent man. 'I've left my Rodney at the hotel in Aberystwyth. I need to get back tonight. We're getting the train in the morning.'

'Tomorrow?' Hilda's voice was a whisper.

'Look, Mrs Evans, this is not what anyone wanted. I'm a widow. I've got Rodney. But I won't have people saying I didn't do my duty.'

And there was talk and then more talk, the lilt of Wales and the clatter of London colliding in the kitchen, talking of packing and a journey and a place called Tunbridge Wells. And Will wasn't home yet. They hadn't had their tea.

David slipped the Welsh cakes into his pocket. He might be hungry later.

CHAPTER TWENTY-FIVE

Carrie pulled the car door shut. 'You were right, Hal. What Sue said was true.' She felt a sour sense of release as though the words had been stewing inside her.

'What? That Grand's Mum didn't write to him?'

'Yes. She dropped him off in London and he never heard from her again.' Through Hal's window she saw her parents fussing: Grand, as ever, battling with his seatbelt.

'But you said she was alive at the end of the war…'

Grand got his car started and led the way, up past the little tea shop with the unreliable opening times that annoyed him so much and into the narrow tree-shaded lane that wound steeply uphill.

'Turns out she went to Canada and was alive until 1975!'

'*What?*' Even Chris exclaimed.

Carrie told the story, the words heavy in her mouth. The roads inland from Cymtydu were a labyrinth of tunnels through dense foliage, under mossy low branches. They turned a corner in convoy between Grand and Ruth and found the next stretch narrower and steeper. The engine sputtered as Chris changed into first.

'But how did you *not know* this?' Hal said.

'They only found out last summer, when Rod was over from Bahrain.'

'Shocker for your Dad,' Chris said.

'But why's he been so secretive?' Her voice wavered and rose. 'He never even told me about his mother not contacting him. And now it turns out she'd buggered off to Canada – and they've known since last summer!'

What was wrong with her, ranting – and with Chris in his state? She gazed out at the green dimness where sunlight barely filtered.

'There was a lot going on then,' Chris said with a sigh.

'Like what?' Hal said.

'Oh you know – Grand and his cataract op,' Carrie said. Had they lost their way in the network of tree tunnels? It seemed to be going on for ever. 'I just don't think you should have secrets like that in families.'

She turned and caught Chris's look.

'Well that was lovely, wasn't it?' said Lisa, settling back in the passenger seat. Grand set off after Chris and didn't think to answer. 'Are you all right?' she said, lifting her sunglasses.

'Of course I'm all right, why wouldn't I be?'

'I'm just so glad we've had picnic weather,' she said with her usual determined cheeriness. 'And Hal got to show Josh the Secret Beach.'

'I was bloody starving by the time we got the food out.'

'Chris lost track of time,' she said, with a fading chuckle. 'At least we know now, why he's been quiet.'

'It's this fucking Tory government.' Grand put his foot down to power up the hill. He didn't want Toby pulling out to overtake so Ruth could do her queenly wave. He was always bragging about their four-by-four's superior engine. Cars had been a rarity, Grand mused, when he lived here as a boy. He once asked if they were a London thing and hadn't really come to Wales. Will chuckled and explained about petrol rationing and the ban on private vehicles.

Kent had seemed so busy afterwards. Auntie Mo would nag him for dawdling across roads. 'You'll end up under a bus! Why can't you keep up with Rodney?' David couldn't keep up with Rodney's chess club and his maths prizes either – he was 'bettering himself' Mo said. Soaking up the poshness of Royal Tunbridge Wells. David was *a Taffy; a bookworm; in a world of his own.* And these were bad things – irritations. He blinked away the memories.

'Yes. The pressure is ridiculous. Poor Carrie,' Lisa said. 'Fancy Sue coming out and telling her!'

Shit! That was the turning – he'd nearly missed it! He braked hard, the seatbelt grazing his collar bone, and only then thought of the cars behind. He twisted round, hurting his neck. Luckily they had stopped in time. Ruth was waving her arms, pointing out the turning.

'For Christ's sake! I know where I'm going.'

'Of course you do.' He made the turn and drove on. Lisa patted his leg. 'Back to Noddfa, eh Grand? For a cuppa? I think there are cookies left. Those ones you like, with the chocolate lumps.'

When they emerged from the warren of lanes, sunlight slanted in and warmth filled the car. He squirted screenwash and put the wipers on to clear the polleny dust, then opened all windows a crack with a poke of his finger. A sense of control returned.

'I can see clearly now…' Lisa sang, and he had to smile.

Cloudless blue arched over them as he turned into Bont Goch. The sea glittered through a gap in the hedge. Lisa was yawning – she'd crash out when they got back. He might have a read on the back step. Perhaps cricket with the boys after one of those cookies.

'I hope Carrie isn't cross,' Lisa said.

'Cross? What's there to be cross about?'

She started as if he'd shouted, which he hadn't. 'Oh, just…You know.' She mouthed, '*Secrets.*'

This was Lisa all over, looking for trouble. And now she had him wondering. He sought a stinging riposte. 'She can bloody talk!'

'Oh look, I'm sure she's fine.' He didn't answer, and after a moment, she sighed. 'It's going to be a beautiful evening.'

They were chattering on the doorstep in the sunshine when Mum put the key in the door, but when Hal stepped in to Noddfa after her, everyone went quiet.

There was someone there. Hal could sense it. It was like that morning at home, when he came downstairs and stood frozen in the living room, feeling that he wasn't alone. Then a great fat frog flobbered out from under a chair. The cat, Muffin, must have brought it in when it was lively in the daytime warmth but lost interest when it cooled down and stopped jumping around.

'That empty house feeling.' Grandma Lisa shivered.

There was a tight, still moment before Mum stepped into the

kitchen – why did she peer behind the door? Dad glanced upstairs.

Grand cleared his throat with a fruity noise. 'Empty house, with our racket? No chance.' They all pushed into the kitchen and started searching for cookies.

Hal had meant to go up and write his journal, but he stayed in the kitchen. Mum was pondering if there was time to make lasagne, and Grand and Grandma scrapped over the last cookie, then saw Hal looking and insisted he should have it.

'Do you think it's really a secret?' Hal said. Everyone turned and looked at him. 'The Secret Beach, I mean.'

'Oh!' Mum said. She'd been rummaging for cooking things but stopped. 'You do wonder, don't you? We always thought only boats could get there.'

'It did look like someone had had a fire,' Dan said.

She gave him a rueful smile. 'Maybe we've been wilfully ignoring the signs.'

'Well, things don't stay secret forever,' said Grandma Lisa, her yawn swelling into a sort of wail.

Mum plonked a pottery dish on the table. 'I will do lasagne, if everyone can bear to wait.'

'We'll get out of your way,' said Grand.

'Ooh yes,' said Auntie Ruth, 'call us when it's too late to help.'

Something touched Hal's head. He flinched away with a gasp.

'It's a fly, you numty!' said Josh. He stood up. 'I'm going upstairs to look in my book. Coming?'

A finger of cold ran down Hal's back. 'Nah. Let's play Scrabble.'

Grand and Grandma Lisa went to their room and the others went out to the garden to catch the last of the sun. Hal followed Dad into the living room, dragged up a side table and set up the board.

Josh came and sat opposite, making 'I need to talk to you!' faces, but Hal ignored him. Dad hunched over the newspaper, frowning.

Josh plunged his hand in the bag of Scrabble tiles and leaned closer. 'I've been thinking. What if it's Grand's Mum?'

Hal pulled the bag onto his lap and raked through the tiles, the cookie taste rising in his throat. Dad was still staring at the *Mirror*, oblivious. 'She died ages ago, though.'

'But maybe Grand finding out about it has caused a rumpus in the spirit world.'

'A rumpus?' Hal tried to laugh but he felt jumpy, like with the fly.

'Yes. A disturbance. What if her spirit feels guilty and she's come back for him at last?' Having to keep his voice down gave Josh a manic look.

'I don't know.' Hal's hand hadn't moved in the Scrabble bag, but the tiles shifted beneath his fingers with a plastic rattle. He dropped the bag. Stupid! As if a board game could be haunted...

'Chris!' called Mum from the kitchen. Dad hauled himself out of the armchair and went out. 'Can you stir the cheese sauce, while I sort out the mince?' Hal heard her say. 'Do what I do. If it won't go smooth, I squint at it to blur out the lumps.'

Hal laid his tiles out – a jumble of letters, making no sense.

'Who do you think it is, then? Hal?'

He shrugged. *Not Imogen.* Barbara, then, just dead? Or Grand's Mum after all this time? 'You go first,' he said, his pulse racing.

'What? Oh.'

They started the game.

Lisa had said the house felt empty, but she wondered now if it did. It had a jittery quality she couldn't remember here before. David was sitting on top of the duvet, deep in his Dostoevsky, and she dared to disturb him by climbing underneath.

'You can't possibly be cold?' he said, exaggerating the effect of her burrowing tipping him sideways.

'It is Wales!' she said.

'It's been 26 degrees!'

'Oh well. Not cold then. Just tired.' She usually fell blissfully asleep when they got home from an outing, but there was a disturbance inside her now – perhaps from eating those cookies when she wasn't really hungry.

Or just from the day. Carrie's face when she asked about Chris:

the sense of a shadow looming over the holiday. Then David having to talk about his mother. She found herself searching for a jaunty phrase to make light of it. Stupid! She didn't have to now. She wasn't out with the family, but here in bed.

She reached for her heavy hardback book and tried to read it, but she could barely decipher the words. Memories crowded in like clouds over the mountains. Jill round to visit when Emilia was two. The sweetest face, that little girl had, and a mop of silky blond curls.

Lisa crouched down to her eye level and helped her off with her coat. 'Hello, poppet, have you come to play with my girls?' You forgot how soft-edged and delicious they were at that age.

'But we were playing my game!' Ruth said, hands on hips. She was nine, and used to Carrie doing her bidding. Her frown cleared. 'I know! She can be in the game. But only if she does what I say.'

Emilia backed into her mother's legs and reached up to grasp her hand, but Jill shook her off and launched herself into an armchair. 'Go and *play*, Emilia. Mummy needs to think straight.' Emilia's face contorted, ready to cry, her eyes flashing alarm.

'I know!' Carrie spoke softly. 'We can go up to my room and play dollies!' Emilia blinked, her expression clearing. 'You can choose whichever dolly you want,' Carrie added. 'Or a teddy if you like them best.'

'Oh yes, that's a lovely idea!' said Lisa. 'Go on poppet, you and Carrie will have all sorts of fun!'

Jill watched, hunched in her chair, arms crossed. You never heard her doing mummy talk – perhaps she thought it was soppy.

Carrie led Emilia towards the door with the bright chatter she used with her dolls. Four years old, and she had pretty much saved the day. Lisa felt a melting hunger and sneaked a kiss of her daughter's neck as she passed. They even heard a little giggle from Emilia as the two of them went upstairs.

'They're too silly for my game anyway!' Ruth said, and went off to her room.

'How do you do it?' Jill burst out when she and Lisa were alone.
'What..?'

'Emilia's so bloody difficult. Nothing I do seems to work with her.

You know what, Lisa, I just don't think I get on with her. There, I've said it. But that's terrible, isn't it?'

'Oh but... two's a difficult age. It gets easier,' Lisa said.

'I suppose so.' Jill looked at the floor with deadened eyes. Lisa moved the talk onto other topics. Jill never brought it up again.

And God knows, Emilia could be difficult. Lisa remembered her, years later when she'd come to Wales with them, moaning and scratching midge bites from the previous evening's walk. Her girls had been eaten alive too and were gamely rubbing on bite cream – but Emilia wailed that cream made it worse.

David was looking forward to a day out in Aberystwyth – he wanted to find the building in Bath Street where Barbara used to work. They were all keyed up for the search, Lisa hoping to God he'd find it.

Emilia complained for the entire car journey. You reminded yourself that she was sensitive and had allergies – but it was draining, keeping her spirits up. For all Lisa's instinct with her own two, there was something in Emilia that she couldn't seem to soothe. Sometimes she was tempted to say *No* to having her, but David wouldn't hear of it. He had nothing but contempt for Rodney and Jill and their puffed-up ways – but Emilia captivated him. He said these holidays were the only time she got what a child needed.

When they arrived in the car park in Aberystwyth, Lisa opened the rear door for the girls. Emilia sat frozen, hunched in her seat.

'Get out, Emilia, love, the sea air will do you good,' said David, but Lisa heard the strain in his voice.

'I can't! It hurts!' said Emilia with a shuddering breath. There were livid pink bumps on the pale thighs pressed against the car seat. 'I'm sorry,' she wailed, 'I just can't. I'm useless!'

'Do something, Lisa!' David said... but his voice was a booming echo, and Emilia was a baby now, writhing in her car seat with a high-pitched scream. Lisa sat down beside her, undid her bra and hoiked out her breast. She pressed the baby's face to her nipple and it clamped on and sucked. The crying had stopped and Lisa looked down in relief at the peaceful infant. But her breast ached, caught in its grip, and the pain grew sharper – the little face was ugly now as it sucked harder and harder. Then Emilia was a full-sized child again and milk frothed from the corner of her lips, tinged pink with Lisa's blood. Lisa tried to push this child thing off but it clung on to her nipple with an agonizing grip. She shoved at it and flailed until its soft-fleshed limbs began to disintegrate, bones giving way like rotten wood as her own girls cried out in fear –

She woke with a gasp and flung out a hand, a wail echoing around her. Her book slid off her chest and thudded to the floor.

David just looked at her. 'All right?' he said.

Overhead, a seagull cried.

CHAPTER TWENTY-SIX

A hard shake of Hal's shoulder dragged him from a troubled sleep. What the hell was Josh doing? He must be crouching there in the darkness. Wind was rushing through the house. No – whispering. And thudding downstairs.

'*What?*' There was a panicked shout from the bunk above.

'Nothing. What do you mean?'

'You shook me!' Josh complained.

'No. You…' Hal's mouth was dry. He sat up, straining to hear. 'What's that?' The rushing had stopped. There was a tinkling – or a crackling? A familiar sound, but he couldn't place it. 'Can you hear that?'

The bunkbeds creaked. 'Yeah.'

'It's not a fire, is it?'

'I don't know.' Josh sounded scared.

Hal got up and blundered to the light switch, dreading what he'd see. But there was just Josh gawping from the top bunk, his hair sticking up. 'We should go down and check.'

Josh shook his head. 'I don't know…'

'Well, I'm going.'

'I'm not staying in here on my own!' Josh scrambled down.

Hal's shoulder felt faintly bruised from the shaking. Josh's hot breath was on the back of his neck. If he opened the door, would something pounce? He gritted his teeth and pulled the handle.

The landing was a murky grey. Hal stepped across and gripped the banister rail ready to go downstairs. Silence. Something made him glance up the attic staircase.

Shit! Was the door open up there? Was that black rectangle the darkness inside?

'Look!' he whispered.

'What?!' Josh crashed into him. Hal almost fell, but caught his breath and pulled himself upright. When he looked, the attic door was shut.

'I thought… Nothing. Come on.'

Josh grabbed a handful of Hal's t-shirt and they crept downstairs like in a three-legged race. They stopped at the bottom. There was a pressure in the house like something ready to erupt.

'What?' hissed Josh.

'Wait.'

Something was coming. Hal could feel it. There was a gasp, like a breath sucked in. Then a groaning, a creak and a rush in the air. The door to the living room shook on its hinges and something clattered against it from inside. There was a thud, and then that tinkling sound again.

They gripped each other. Hal struggled to step forwards, slapped at the hall light switch and turned, blinded by the glare.

The living room door swung inwards. Bits flew out, hit the wall behind them and scattered on the floor of the hall.

There was a moaning sigh, then everything went still.

Josh's fist released Hal's t-shirt. His eyes were black in the electric light.

'Scrabble. We left it out,' Hal said. Tiles were scattered round their feet.

Nothing was moving now. They crept into the living room and Hal turned on the lamp. The Scrabble board lay near the door and tiles were all over the carpet. The bookshelf had fallen over, scattering books across the floor. Hal prodded one with his bare toe. It felt cold. The pressure he had felt before had disappeared. There was a sad but peaceful emptiness.

'It's gone,' he said.

'How do you know?'

Hal shrugged. He picked up the big black book he'd held that time before and sank onto the sofa.

'Wait, do they spell anything?' Josh began to go round the room, peering at tiles. After a while he plumped down beside Hal. 'Nothing. Unless it's Welsh. What Welsh do you know?'

'Just that long place name. *Llanfairpwllgwyngyll* and that.'

'Oh.' Josh rested his cheeks on his hands and sighed. A moment later he whispered, 'Can you imagine, if the ghost had spelt out Lan-fair-McWhatchamacallit?'

Hal could even smile now. 'We'd be like, *What the hell are we meant to make of that?'*

He opened the book – an old photo album. There was a little girl in one picture – oh it was Mum, damming a stream with her cousin and Auntie Ruth.

Josh yawned. 'D'you think it'll be all right in our room?'

'I think so. We'll go up in a minute.'

Hal turned a chunk of pages and saw the three girls again, eating ice cream in Aberystwyth with Grand and Grandma Lisa. Grand looked weird with his hair black instead of grey. Then there were Mum and the cousin as teenagers – their jeans a strange high-waisted style that Imogen would call *retro*. Only it wasn't retro then, it was fashion, Hal supposed. He yawned and his jaw cracked. Had he seen this album before? He flipped to near the end, sleep beginning to swamp him. Mum and Emilia were grown-ups now, on a picnic rug with a smiling baby. Five-year-old Imogen was leaning on Mum's side. Auntie Ruth was with a little boy in tiny swimming trunks – Dan, of course. It was funny to see him so small and skinny. Then Hal looked back at the baby. That must be him!

A wheezy snore from next door was a comforting sound. Josh sniggered, but then looked thoughtful. 'I'm sure the ghost is Grand's mother,' he whispered. 'Grand's angry because she went and left him, and she's felt it from the other side. Unfinished business! That often causes hauntings.'

'I'm not sure Grand's angry, is he?' Hal said.

Josh looked at the mess around them. 'Someone is.'

Carrie was about to face some horrible nightmare trial when she was woken by groaning. The cool light through the curtains said it was early.

'Chris?' she said. He made a sound like a tiny sob. 'What is it? Chris, talk to me!'

'I just…' he rolled onto his back, his fists to his temples.

Was he in agony? Was this a brain tumour? Her mind raced with her heart. She might even prefer a tumour – something physical they could take out of him – not like this darkness, this horror. Oh but what was she wishing on Chris? She looked at him beside her, stuck mid-sentence, grey-faced.

She sat up. 'Is it a headache?' He shook his head. 'What then?' Another head-shake, a gasp for breath. 'Anxiety?' He nodded and rolled away, onto his side. 'You seem worse first thing.' She reached out to his shoulder – it was hard as a clenched fist. 'Could you get up with me? We could go for a walk. Talk if you want to.'

Bleakness enveloped her at the thought. In any case, he was shaking his head. 'Chris, we'll sort this out. We'll get you help. It's Wednesday today, there's not long to go.'

Could she keep him going for three whole days? She rubbed his shoulder, then got up on her knees. 'Lie on your front. Chris? That's it.' She massaged the knotted muscles around his shoulders, then probed with her fingers up into his hair. Her own back clenched with the effort, but at least she was doing something that might help. 'Is that better?'

A tiny nod. Carrie sat back against her pillow. 'Do you think you should get up? Staying in bed doesn't seem to help.'

'Sorry, Carrie.'

He sighed, peacefully she hoped, as if she'd held back a tide. Maybe he'd get some sleep now and come down feeling better. Someone was shuffling around downstairs. She longed to be with them.

'Oh, hello darling,' said Grandma Lisa, holding her head away from the steam as she filled the teapot. 'I hope I didn't wake you up?'

'You woke *me* up.' Ruth was sitting at the table in green silk pyjamas, her hair a mess.

'I was awake already.' Carrie got mugs and sat down.

Her mother glanced round at her. 'Chris all right?'

'Hopefully.'

'Teaching is not for the faint-hearted these days,' said Ruth, fiddling with her phone.

What was she implying? Chris had never been faint-hearted! He worked every hour God sent and fought for the kids in his care.

Their mother mashed the teabags in the pot. 'It wasn't in my day, either. Thirty children, all with their own needs, and only one of you. And the parents to deal with! The pressure at eleven plus time…'

Ruth snorted, 'That was *aeons* ago!'

'Well yes, I gave it up to look after you girls.'

'To look after *Carrie*, you mean. You worked when I was little.'

'You went to a lovely nursery. You loved it.'

'Oh, that's all right, then.'

Their mother looked at her, then turned to Carrie. 'He'll be fine, love. You'll look back and wonder what all the fuss was about.'

It was like one of the jolly stories she used to tell them to chase away nightmares. And she had just glossed over this ancient resentment which Ruth had never voiced before! Carrie thought of her cheese sauce trick, squinting to make the sauce look smoother. Perhaps that was how Mum got through life – blurring out the lumps.

'I hear Dad had some revelations,' Ruth said, putting her phone down at last. 'Carrie filled me in.'

'Yes.' Grandma Lisa sat down, bumping the teapot on the table. Carrie noticed dark bags under her eyes. 'I'd have told you as soon as it came out. But you know your father. He doesn't like a fuss.' Ruth snorted and made a face at Carrie. 'Oh, you know what I mean,' their mother said with a weary laugh. Steam twirled from the kettle's spout in a low shaft of sunshine. 'He's talking about Cardigan today.'

'Is that the drill on the second Wednesday?' Carrie said. She had been hoping to lie on the beach and just read.

'Apparently…' Grandma Lisa poured three mugs of tea and they all sat sipping.

'As long as we keep Toby occupied,' Ruth said. 'He keeps going up the track to ring the bloody office.'

'Men, eh?' said their mother. 'At least our Hal's OK. And Dan,' she added hastily.

They sat for a time in comfortable quiet. Grandma Lisa yawned and put her palms flat on the table. 'I suppose I should get ready for the breakfast palaver. Save your father fussing later.'

'Oh my goodness,' Carrie said. 'Look who's up!'

Hal had come in, his t-shirt crumpled, hair tousled. 'Whassup.' He clattered into a chair, teenage style, but Carrie longed to squeeze him like a child. 'I might have one of those hot chocolates.' Grandma Lisa leapt up to make it for him. 'More spooky stuff last night,' he said when the mug was in his hands.

Carrie's heart sank. Could they not have some peace?

'Josh and I heard noises. I thought he'd woken me up and he thought I'd shaken him. And then I thought there was a fire…'

'Oh, it's the heat!' said Grandma Lisa with a hand to her chest. 'It always gives me nightmares. And last night… I can't tell you! I thought I'd slept right through, but this morning I'm exhausted.'

'It wasn't a nightmare,' Hal muttered into his lap. Nerve-pain stabbed through Carrie's forehead. 'We came downstairs. And there was like… an explosion. We saw the Scrabble tiles fly out of the living room, and the bookcase had fallen over again and… there was mess everywhere.'

'Wait – not a real explosion?' Carrie said, thinking of gas.

He looked up at her. 'No but… tiles flying, right in front of us. And there was no one there.'

Not gas then. Not anything, surely?

'It looks fine this morning.' Grandma Lisa was slapping breakfast things on the counter top.

'We tidied it up,' Hal said.

'Well if you ask me, darling, Josh should leave that book alone.' Carrie was surprised by her mother's tone. Usually Hal was beyond reproach. He looked taken aback, but then sipped his chocolate with a shrug. 'All that *business*,' Grandma Lisa went on. 'It isn't – well, normal.'

'That's the paranormal for you,' Ruth said.

'There! We're ready for anything. Or bacon and eggs in any case.' Grandma Lisa sat down. 'We thought Cardigan today, Hal.'

Grand always got excited, Hal thought, when something from this part of Wales got famous, and now he had read that you could visit Cardigan Castle while it was being renovated. It had been on a competition on the telly.

'It's not bloody butter, I'm telling you. It's marge,' Grand said now, at a table in Sylvia's Café in Cardigan.

'But it *says* scone and butter.' Grandma Lisa waved the menu.

'Maybe it's I Can't Believe it's Not Butter!' Josh said.

'I can bloody believe it! It's catering margarine!'

Auntie Ruth raised her eyes. 'It's like Groundhog Day. We say this every year.'

'I'm looking forward to seeing what they're doing to the Castle, though!' Mum said.

Their cakes and drinks arrived. Whatever the spread on Hal's scone was, it tasted fine with jam. 'I know what I meant to ask,' he said. 'Who's Emilia exactly?' They all looked at him. 'I mean I know she's some cousin of Mum's… I saw photos in this album in the living room. I didn't know she came to Wales when I was here.'

Grandma Lisa glanced round, then wiped her mouth with a paper napkin. 'Well, you know Rodney is Grand's cousin. Rodney's Mum was Grand's Mum's sister, Auntie Mo.'

Grand nodded, swallowing a bit of scone. 'They lived up the road from us in Bethnal Green. Then my Uncle Pete died in the war and Mo and Rodney moved to Kent. Rodney grew up and married Jill, and they had Emilia a couple of years after we had your Mum.'

Mum poured tea and blew on it, narrowing her eyes in the steam.

'Emilia came to Wales with us a lot,' said Grandma Lisa.

'Sweet little thing.' Grand swiped his hands together to get the crumbs off them.

'But complex…' said Grandma Lisa.

'All those allergies…' Auntie Ruth said, shaking her head.

'Yes! Jill reckoned it was just her fussing… she didn't believe in allergies like people do now. But the poor thing did seem to suffer…' Grandma Lisa looked into the distance, then gave Grand a faint smile. 'You could never say no to bringing her on holiday, could you? Your sense of duty!'

'It was nothing to do with *duty*! Poor kid didn't fit into that family from the minute she was born. And then Rodney started chasing money around the Middle East and Jill went with him, lapping up the expat lifestyle. They treated the child like an inconvenience. We were all she had.'

'I know. I know. And she was lovely. But hard work,' Grandma Lisa caught Grand's look. 'She was!'

'All right!' said Grand. It wasn't often he was the one who got snapped at.

'So, that's who she was, Hal,' Mum said with a smile. 'Not our actual cousin, but the daughter of Grand's cousin.'

You could hear the tinkle of teaspoons, and other people's conversations.

'Right,' said Grand. 'Who's for the Castle?'

Mum made Hal go with her to buy school shoes in the shop near Sylvia's where they got them every year. She went on as usual about missing the queues at home. As they were coming out with the shoes, Auntie Ruth was heading inside with Dan. 'Yes we *are* getting them here,' she was saying, 'and no, you are *not* having DMs. Don't even bother arguing.'

'All right, my love?' Mum said outside, ruffling Hal's hair, which was a bit over-affectionate for the High Street.

'Yeah. I'm going to find Josh. He went in one of those crystal shops.'

'All right then. I'll catch up with the others. Don't let Josh get anything paranormal!'

The crystal shop was draped in black velvet and hung with dreamcatchers and leather-thonged pendants. A girl with dirty-blond dreadlocks and black lipstick was pricing wooden boxes with brass hinges. Dan had shown Hal a similar box hidden at the back of his wardrobe. 'For my stash. Weed and rizlas and stuff.'

Hal dodged round a stand of fantasy-themed posters and another of pentangles on silver chains. There was a thick smell of patchouli and a tinkling of wind chimes.

Josh was in the far corner where faint spotlights barely reached. Behind the counter was a very fat twenty-something bloke wearing a black t-shirt with a sword and dragon design. He had a babyish face with a shiny forehead and streaks of green in his hair. On shelves behind him were glass globes with pipes coming out. Hal knew from Dan that they were bongs. He wondered if Josh had twigged all this and was keen to get him out of there and tell him. But he looked deep in discussion.

'People always think it's poltergeist activity when things get thrown,' the man was saying with a strong Welsh accent. 'But spirits can get angry and move things too.' He saw Hal and stood upright, gathering big cards with weird pictures up from the counter.

'Oh, it's my mate,' said Josh, looking flushed and excited. He seemed to have picked up a Welsh lilt. 'It's his family's place that's haunted. This is Iestyn, Hal.'

Iestyn gave Hal a tiny nod, as though he was too cool to move much.

'Iestyn thinks it could be a haunting,' said Josh. 'From the spirit world. Not a poltergeist.'

Iestyn fanned the cards through his hands, then plopped them in a box. His gaze passed over the rest of the shop but kept coming to rest on Hal.

'You coming?' Hal said to Josh. He noticed he was holding a black plastic bag with a witchy face design.

'OK.'

Iestyn flipped the card box shut with his thumbs. 'Remember, they're usually trying to communicate with you.' He looked right at Hal. 'Be careful, all right?'

'What a div,' Hal said when they got outside, shaking off the creepy feeling of the shop.

'He knows a lot of stuff, though,' Josh said. 'Look, I'm stuck out here without a signal, Hal, I've got to get information where I can.' He pushed Hal into a narrow alley leading off the High Street. He wouldn't stop until they were half-way down, where it was edged with bin bags and stank of wee.

Josh opened the witch bag. 'Last night was insane. We've got to find out who's haunting Noddfa. And why.'

He pulled out a box. Hal saw the letters 'OUI and JA'.

'It's a Ouija board,' said Josh.

CHAPTER TWENTY-SEVEN

The plan was to do it in the living room when everyone else was asleep.

'The book says go where the spirit activity is strongest,' Josh said. 'And it started in the living room, didn't it? And that's where things get chucked about.'

That evening, Grand was watching a documentary about a writer. It seemed to go on forever. Everyone else went to bed, but Josh and Hal stuck it out for a bit longer. When they couldn't stand it any more, they said their goodnights. They went up and sat on Hal's bunk with the light off, trying to play games on their phones.

'The blue light will keep us awake,' said Josh. 'It messes with your brain.' But when Hal next looked up at him, his head was drooping.

'Josh!' He shoved him, panic surging as if something would grab him the minute he was alone.

'What? I wasn't asleep!'

There was movement downstairs. They froze – but then heard familiar plodding footsteps, the chinking sounds of glass and china and water running in the sink.

'Grand,' they said together. The light showing round the bedroom door clicked to a fainter glow, then went out. Grand's footsteps receded – he was off to bed.

The boys waited some more, then Josh got the box out from its hiding place at the bottom of his suitcase. 'You ready?'

'Wait. I don't know. That freaked me out last night.'

'But this is how we fix it, by finding out what it's all about. Iestyn said so.'

Iestyn saw you coming, Auntie Ruth would say. The Ouija board had a fake look, with letters in curling brown script, like some spooky kids' game. Well, if there was no real power in it, how could it do any harm? But Hal thought of that story at school, and of what Grandma Lisa had said.

'What if it makes things worse?'

'We've been through this,' Josh said. 'I like it here. I wouldn't do anything to spoil it. Whoever this is, if they want to tell us something, this'll help them, and then they'll leave us alone.' His face was lit from below by his phone screen, his eye sockets cavernous. The screen timed out and the room went dark.

'OK. Let's get it over with,' Hal said.

On the landing, he thought he heard a creak and looked up towards the attic room.

'What?' said Josh.

Hal strained his eyes. 'I keep thinking it's open.'

'It's not. Come on.'

They crept downstairs, Hal bracing himself for chaos like the previous night. But their footsteps were the only sound. The living room was tidy and still. A wheezy rumble from the next-door bedroom told them Grand was already asleep.

There was a waiting feeling, a creeping tension. Hal clicked on the lamp.

Josh sat on the sofa opposite Hal's chair and they set the board up on the side table. 'Just do what I say. Iestyn showed me.'

The lamplight didn't reach far – shadows pressed in from the corners. Hal was thinking of the Scrabble game – even that had got weird. There was a crawling feeling at the back of his neck, as if something were behind him. He fixed his eyes on the stupid board.

'OK.' Josh's eyes darted round. 'We put both our hands on this. It's called a planchette. Move it round a bit. Then let it rest in the middle. And then ask.' His voice was husky, with a Welsh lilt on the word *planchette*. Channelling Iestyn, Hal thought. It should be funny – but nothing was. 'Is there a spirit here?' Josh said.

The planchette was motionless, pointing to the 'G'. Hal realised he was leaning on it and tried to relax his shoulders. Josh's pupils were huge. 'Have you recently passed over?' Again that super-taut tension. 'Are… you… Barbara?' Josh put weight on each syllable, as if spirits were hard of hearing. He caught Hal's look. 'You say something, then!'

Hal's fingers were sweaty on the planchette, but he stifled a shiver. 'I saw a girl,' he said. 'Was that you? Are you Barbara?'

The planchette was stock-still under their fingers. If someone was trying to tell them something, it wasn't getting through.

Hal thought of the girl again; the flash of hair in the mirror. He focused on it, on how real it had been, and could almost imagine that something opened up inside him, like a willingness to know. But to know what? What might a spirit want to say to him? 'You're not Imogen, are you?' he blurted.

The tension tightened. His ribcage hurt.

Josh's gaze flickered around. 'Nothing. That's good,' he whispered. 'Is there a spirit here? Are you Will?'

Hal's shoulders were cramping. 'I can't do this much longer.'

'Wait. We just need the right question.' Josh heaved in a breath and let it out. 'Are you Hugh? Have you come home from the war?' Nothing.

Hal's nerves tingled with the sense of a silent presence. 'Are you Hilda?' he said. Nothing moved or spoke. *We're trying half the village now*, Hal thought, his focus slipping. He'd got worked up over nothing. They should go back to bed.

There was a huff of impatience. Had Hal made it – or Josh? Something flew off the sofa with a papery shuffle. Hal felt a bolt of fear as it landed at his feet. 'Grand's *Guardian*,' he breathed. As if that made it OK.

'Are you Grand's Mum?' Josh said, eyes wild. 'Have you come back for him?'

A wind rushed by like an angry sigh and they both whipped their hands off the planchette. Something thumped the back of Hal's head. The photo album! It had landed on top of a pile of other books. And now a prickling feeling crawled over his scalp.

'Hal, your hair!' cried Josh.

'What?!'

'It's moving!'

Hal leapt up and the table went flying, the planchette and board clattering to the floor. Something was raking through his hair. A force tightened round his chest, pushing him towards the door. His feet took two tottering steps – he couldn't stop them. There was a pressure round his fingers and his arm lifted from his side.

'Hal! What are you doing? Come back!' A shriek. Things flew

from the shelves. The lamp flashed and fizzled out – the living room door crashed open.

Something soft hit Hal's back with a dreadful inhuman chuckling.

'What's all this racket?' said Grand in his bedroom doorway.

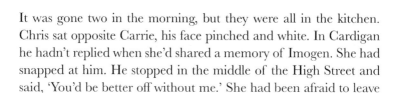

It was gone two in the morning, but they were all in the kitchen. Chris sat opposite Carrie, his face pinched and white. In Cardigan he hadn't replied when she'd shared a memory of Imogen. She had snapped at him. He stopped in the middle of the High Street and said, 'You'd be better off without me.' She had been afraid to leave his side ever since.

Then tonight, when that scream awoke her – she could barely admit to herself the fear that had gripped her; her relief when Chris sat up.

'We didn't mean to scare you,' Josh said in a shaky whine. 'We were trying to fix it!'

'By meddling with all this *darkness*?' Grandma Lisa said.

'It's meddling with us,' said Hal. He looked like his younger self, awoken from a nightmare. 'Didn't you notice the weird feeling when we got back from the Secret Beach?'

Grandma Lisa pulled her dressing gown around her. 'There was a chill… And I did have a horrible nightmare.'

'For Christ's sake, Noddfa's draughty – not *haunted*!' Grand said, in his pyjamas, plonking a plush red toy on the table. 'Who would want to haunt us?'

'That's what we were trying to find out!' Josh muttered.

'But all you've done is frighten yourselves,' Grandma Lisa sighed.

'Takes more than this to scare me.' Ruth picked up the toy. 'Remember this? Emilia's Welsh dragon!'

'I used to play with that when I was a kid,' said Dan. 'I didn't know it was hers.'

'I woke up to screams, and that bloody thing chuckling,' Grand said. 'I was on my feet before I knew it. Didn't know my arse from my elbow!'

They managed to laugh. He turned the dragon over, but the noise had stopped working.

'Completely non-spooky tourist tat,' Ruth yawned.

And then they were all talking – an exhausting clamour. Carrie retreated from the effort of trying to work out what had happened.

'Mum!' Hal nudged her. 'I didn't make it up. Do you believe me?'

His face, tanned but pale, had a yellowish look of appeal. 'Of course. I just want us to calm down so we can go back to sleep.' He nodded, his head on his hand as though he couldn't hold it up. 'Why don't you boys go up to bed? We'll sit up for a bit. So you won't need to worry.' She caught his look and lowered her voice. 'Hal, I wouldn't let anything hurt you.'

Dan stood up, his chair noisy on the stone floor. 'Yeah, c'mon guys. Let's crash.'

The boys shuffled off, yawning – perhaps to persuade themselves they could sleep again.

Grand went over to the kettle. 'I don't know about anyone else, but I'm up for a cuppa.'

'Nightcap, more like,' said Toby.

'Ooh yes,' said Grandma Lisa. 'There's Baileys in the cupboard.'

'Go up if you like,' Carrie said to Chris's fixed stare.

'I think I will.' He went out, heavy-footed, and creaked his way upstairs.

Grand passed out tumblers, each with a generous measure of creamy liqueur.

'I don't know what to think now,' said Grandma Lisa. 'You said things were flying about?!'

Grand shook his head. 'No, the boys said that…'

Grandma Lisa was insistent. 'But you did too! You said when you opened the door, you saw things flying…'

'Well, the boys were crashing about in there…'

Ruth made an exasperated noise. 'Exactly! Big, real boys trying to scare themselves. It's typical of their age.'

Grandma Lisa looked only partly reassured. 'But we've had funny things all week, haven't we? What do you think, Carrie?'

'I don't know. I can't think straight.' She had to get Chris home. She had a mental glimpse of his poor face, then Hal's, and took a gulp of her drink. Tears prickled her eyes as the sickly sweetness coated her throat.

'You've changed your tune,' her mother was nudging her father. 'Because this doesn't fit in with your sceptical beliefs!'

'It's not that. Place could be full of spirits. I'm not sure I'd mind.' Grand picked up the dragon. Carrie remembered it now, the wobbly eyes, white teeth and claws and the fat pointed tail.

Emilia had come out of that gift shop in Aberystwyth with it under her cardigan and thrust it at Carrie as she rushed along the street.

'*Emilia!* No. You stole it!'

'I took it for you! As a souvenir of our holiday.'

Carrie at fourteen had never dreamed of stealing anything. But Emilia had already taken eye shadow and pick 'n' mix sweets from Woolworths this week. She would have a bold thrill in her eyes as she went in, but once the rush of swiping things was over, she would try to offload them on Carrie. Carrie pushed the dragon back at her. It fell to the pavement with its babyish chuckling. She felt hot, imagining her parents' reaction if they were caught – it wasn't fury she feared but shock and disappointment.

What if she told them now in the night-time kitchen that Emilia had stolen the dragon? She hadn't wanted to take it home, so they had kept it at Noddfa all these years.

'I think I'll go up,' Carrie said.

'Right you are, love.' Grand slurped his Baileys.

CHAPTER TWENTY-EIGHT

'All right?' Hal said when they got back to their room.

'Yes. Are you?'

Hal nodded. 'I just want to sleep.'

And that was true, but he also had the weirdest feeling, like when you're watching something on TV, and you're just about to find out the answer to everything – and the episode ends.

Josh was really staring at him. Hal said. 'What? *I'm* not the ghost!' He even managed a laugh, and Josh sort of did one back.

When Hal woke up, he thought it must be halfway through the morning. It was only nine o'clock, but that was really late for Wales. He wondered if everyone was annoyed with them and thought they'd been faking.

He went down to the kitchen, but everything was quiet. It was sunny and a cow mooed, like a normal holiday morning, except it was just him. In a funny way though, he didn't feel alone.

He made a bit of noise, opening cupboards, half hoping someone would hear, but no one came. Eventually he made himself a hot chocolate. There was still no one stirring so he went back upstairs.

Josh was sitting up on the top bunk. He jumped when Hal went in. The Paranormal book was in his hands and he clamped it shut, trapping his finger. 'I might phone the crystal shop,' he said, a bit breathless. 'See if Iestyn knows an exorcist. I think that's what we need.'

'What?! My lot are never going to agree to that! Look how they freaked out about the Ouija board.'

'We could ask at the church, then! Get the vicar to do it.'

'That's mental!'

'Well last night was mental…' Josh said. 'Your hair was moving on its own! Like some kind of spirit *shitstorm!*'

'I know… But if Grand hadn't turned up, we might have got an answer.'

'What do you mean?' Josh's eyes were popping. 'Do you think you know who it is?'

'No…' Hal shrugged, not sure what he thought. 'I just felt closer to knowing last night.' He took a step towards the bunk beds. Josh flinched. Hal didn't know how to react so he grabbed for the book and Josh tugged it away. Suddenly it was like a serious tug of war. Josh's knuckle hit the side of the bunk bed and he winced and let go.

Hal could see the bit he'd been reading. It said, 'Possession by demons.'

It was a beautiful day and the sun was well up. Carrie stood in a patch of warmth from the kitchen window, trying to soak in its solace like a cat. The interrupted sleep had left her raw and exposed, as if walking barefoot on something broken. She stared at the patio table outside and glimpsed long bare legs crossed tight, hair morning-tousled. Imogen! So clear that she gasped. Then leaf shadows bobbed and shifted and of course there was no one there. The sixth formers were flying back tomorrow. She would be with them, of course she would.

'Carrie!' Her mother had appeared in the kitchen doorway.

'Oh God! You scared me.'

'I'm not surprised you're jumpy after last night's shenanigans.' Grandma Lisa came in, dressed already in navy slacks and a long-sleeved lilac top. She put a hand on the teapot, with a little shrug of pleasure at finding it warm. 'It all seems ridiculous in the daylight, though, doesn't it? All right, love?'

'I was just thinking about Imogen.' She was going to go on, but what could she say? Her parents didn't know about Chris begging Imogen not to go on the trip, did they? Or about Carrie's peculiar fears. In fact she was too frazzled to keep track of who knew what – she might blurt out the wrong thing and it would all unravel.

Carrie's Dad shuffled in. 'I assume I'm doing breakfast?' He was dressed too, in worn olive-green trousers and a brown checked shirt.

'Well, we must keep up appearances,' Mum said, with a wink. She started recalling bits of a programme they used to watch, chuckling as if nothing had happened.

Carrie sat down and let their chatter wash over her. Was it fragile – a fraud even, this cheerful morning scene? But then Hal appeared in the doorway, and she was glad of it. She saw his dulled expression perk up, though perhaps just for her benefit.

'I'm glad you caught up on your sleep, darling,' she said. 'It's a lovely day. What do you fancy doing?'

He sat down, looking at the bright window as if seeing something else.

'It's too late to fit a coffee in now.' Grand banged a drawer shut and opened another. 'We've missed half the day.'

'Well, never mind,' Carrie said. 'We needed the sleep. What about staying around Bont Goch this morning?' Hal nodded, rubbing his eyes. 'The fridge is full of bits and bobs, I could do a leftovers picnic. Then we could do something in the afternoon. Whatever everyone fancies.'

'I fancied Llangrannog,' her father said. 'But we'll never get parked now. You have to get there early.'

'We can park at the free place at the top and walk down.'

'With all the beach stuff?' said Grandma Lisa.

'Well, we can all pitch in.' Did they have to be so difficult? Carrie wished she were lying on the beach now, sunlight on her eyelids, everything bleached and muffled as she drifted back to sleep.

'Sounds good, Mum,' said Hal.

'Right you are,' Grand grinned, Hal's words a charm. 'Bacon, Hal? A sausage or two?'

Hal was full of breakfast, and calmer, when they parked in the village for a 'wander' with Grand before driving on to the picnic place. As they got out of the cars, Grand was talking about a waterfall at a scary part of the stream. 'Right up your street, Josh, with all your hauntings and whatnot.'

'Spare us,' said Auntie Ruth.

Hal tried to catch Josh's eye, but couldn't.

Grand stopped at the turning, where a lane led downhill past a field of horses. Dan went to call them over with a fistful of long grass.

'Do you know what,' Mum said, 'I fancy a walk to the picnic

place now. You show the others, Grand.'

This was weird. Usually everyone went if Grand was going to show them something.

Josh said, 'Actually, I'm going to go and have a look at the church.' They all looked at him. 'The graves and that. What can I tell you? I think I'm becoming a goth.'

Dad looked uncertain, as if he thought he should go with Mum, but she waved him away. 'No, go and see the stream, it's brilliant.'

A horrible suspicion came to Hal about why Josh was going to the church. He wanted to shout at him to stop being such a dick, or worse – tears pressed at his eyes. 'I'll come with you, Mum.'

'Oh. Does Josh want to come? You could go up to the tin mine.'

'No, you're all right,' Josh muttered. Hal followed Mum as she walked through the village. It was bathed in sunshine, cloud shadows passing over but barely troubling the warmth.

When they got to the old school, they peered through the wrought-iron gates. The playground was a crazy pattern of cracks, sprouting foot-high weeds and grass. Through the scaffolding, you could still see doors either side marked 'Girls' and 'Boys', and a little turret on top where Grand said there used to be a bell.

'You can just picture Grand, can't you?' Mum said. 'Up to mischief with his mates.'

Hal tried to imagine it. 'It's weird that he never told you about his Mum, isn't it? I mean, it's sad and all that, but why should it be a secret?'

'I don't know. Families, eh?'

They walked past Sue's bungalow – there was no sign of her at her lookout in the window – and on to the end of the village and the first gate in the lane.

'You and Josh all right?' Mum asked with a sideways glance.

Hal knew of course that he shouldn't say – it would worry her. But as they were climbing over the gate, he suddenly felt sick of all the secrecy. 'He thinks I'm possessed by demons', he said, thudding down, dust flying around his feet.

She stared. 'Why would he think that?'

'I don't know. Because of all this haunting business. Especially last night. He said my hair was moving on its own.'

'What?' She looked gutted. Did it show on his face, the sick memory of that pressure in his hair and round his chest? '*Was* it?'

'Sort of. I don't know! It did feel funny… But not like demons.' Shit, what if something *had* taken him over, and Josh and Mum could tell? Maybe Grand had turned up just in time.

'Oh love, of course not!' Mum reached a hand round his back and pulled him to her side so their hips bumped. When she let go, they walked on together. 'What on earth has got into Josh? Is it that book, do you think?'

'Yeah. And some bloke in that crystal shop in Cardigan. It was him that sold Josh the Ouija board. I thought all along it was stupid.' He had a dark stab of pleasure at dobbing Josh in. 'Now he's gone looking for a vicar to do an exorcism on me.'

Mum made a scoffing noise, but it wasn't a real laugh. Sheep came out from the shade of a thorny hedge, leapt across a gulley and scattered in panic. A ram with gnarled horns stopped and stared at them with devil's eyes.

Shadows rippled over the hills and valleys. A hawk wheeled high up in the blue and Hal pointed, but Mum barely looked, her forehead pinched. 'I'm sorry,' Hal said, 'I didn't mean to worry you…'

'Oh! No.' Mum smiled. 'I'm glad you told me. It's like we said, no secrets…'

They walked on and climbed over another gate, the sun hot on the top of Hal's head. The stream was on their left now, irony water shaded by crouching trees. Its rush and tinkle made a soothing backdrop.

'So beautiful,' Mum said. 'You don't see it from the car.' They continued in silence. The land sloped gently up to their right, the grass scrubby, nibbled to its roots. Tatters of sheep's wool were caught on thistles. Hal side-footed a sheep's turd and it exploded, flying everywhere. Josh would be laughing.

'Talking of secrets,' Mum said, 'there's no reason I shouldn't tell you.' She took a deep breath. 'You know last year, when we didn't come?'

I knew it. I knew there was something. Hal had a sudden feeling that he didn't want to know.

'Well, Grand had his cataract op, that was true. But the actual reason was that last summer… well… we heard that Emilia had died.'

'Emilia?' The stream was a white noise, roaring.

'Yes.'

Not emigrated, then. Dead! 'Why didn't you tell me?'

Mum shook her head. 'There was such a lot going on. You were changing schools… we didn't want to upset you.'

Hal thought of Imogen. 'Upset *them*, more like!' she'd say. 'I am not some delicate *child*!' she said when they wouldn't let her watch something on telly. And they were being silly, thinking he'd have been upset. Emilia. No wonder they'd been funny about it in the café in Cardigan.

'Look, since I'm being honest,' Mum said, 'we thought it might have been suicide.' They had reached the place where they usually parked the cars; the bridge was right there, beyond the stream. The hill loomed beside them, leading up to the tin mine. 'Shall we sit on the bridge?' said Mum.

Hal shook his head and kept walking to the water's edge. They'd had a talk about suicide in PSHE at school. It was mostly about how important it was, if you were upset, to have someone to talk to. They'd been asked to think of someone they could confide in and he'd said Mum or Dad of course. 'Why did you think that?'

'She was troubled,' Mum said. They began to walk upstream, climbing over grassy tussocks and taking long strides over cracks in the bank. Hal ducked under a low-hanging tree and a rough branch raked his back. 'She'd had a love affair that didn't work out and never really got over it. She started drinking a lot. The last time she came here with us, she was all over the place, really.'

'Was that when I was a baby?'

The branch must have got Mum too because she sucked in her breath. 'Yes. She went to London after that. I think she was sleeping on people's sofas. She'd be in touch every now and then, but then nothing for ages. Once we had a call from a hospital. She'd taken an overdose, but when we got there, she said it was an accident.' Mum glanced over at Hal, perhaps checking to see if he was upset. 'We didn't hear anything for ages. Years. Eventually we found out she'd gone off travelling. Then this terrible news, she'd been found in a hotel room in Tonbridge...'

They had come out into an open place and Hal turned to watch the stream's downhill progress: glassy blue-green stretches and bubbling falls. His favourite place in the world. You could never feel really bad here.

'Shit. Sorry, Mum. Your cousin.'

'Yes.' She gave him a sad but reassuring smile. 'Although we hadn't been in touch for a long time.'

They started walking back downstream. 'It might not have been suicide,' she said. 'Someone at the funeral seemed to think not... That's why we couldn't come to Wales, you see, the funeral.' They were skirting the hunched trees at the water's edge, Hal's deck shoes thumping in long downhill strides. 'I'm so sorry we didn't tell you.'

He didn't want to give her a hard time, like Imogen did. 'It's OK, I get it. And I'm older now, it's fine.'

Wait, Emilia died last year. This was their first time back.

Something glinted in the distance: Grand's car and Auntie Ruth's behind it. Hal saw Josh getting out to open the final gate. He wanted to bound across the valley to tell him the news.

They ploughed through bracken up to Hal's waist, Mum going ahead and pushing it aside. They reached the grass at the bottom of the hill just as the cars crunched onto the parking place.

CHAPTER TWENTY-NINE

Josh had a shifty look when Hal got near him. He made a big show of staying close to the family. They headed for the bridge, lugging picnic things. 'How did it go at the church?' Hal said.

'I just had a look round.'

'And a talk to the vicar?'

Josh shrugged. 'No one there.'

'Huh! You'd think they'd always be waiting. In case someone needs an exorcism.' Josh gave him a warning look, indicating the others. 'Come with me,' Hal said. Josh didn't move, so Hal stepped closer. 'I think I know who it is!'

He turned and splashed into the stream. Water soaked through his deck shoes with a shock of cold. A big stone in the stream-bed tipped up and he staggered and banged his ankle. He righted himself just in time and heard Josh sloshing behind him.

On the other side they stooped under low branches into green shade with a carpet of moss. The bridge and the family seemed miles away, their sounds muffled by the water's rush.

Hal led the way to the central tree with its knotted trunk, where he, Imogen and Dan had once tied Dad up for a game. 'Mum just told me why we didn't come last year. It was Emilia – she died.'

'Shit! The batty cousin?!' His face was greenish in the gloom.

'Yeah. So it makes sense that the haunting's started this year. It's our first time back.'

'Did she die at Noddfa?' Josh asked.

'No, some hotel room in Tonbridge. But she came here a lot.'

Josh paced up and down, his trainers squelching. 'And she was stressy, wasn't she? The sort of spirit who'd throw things!'

'And Mum thought it might be suicide.'

Josh wheeled back towards him. 'That could definitely cause paranormal activity!'

There was a deliberate edge in Hal's voice. 'So it's a ghost then, a haunting? I'm not like, possessed or something?'

'No. Shit, I dunno why I thought that. I didn't know about Emilia then, did I? And last night really freaked me out.'

'Yeah well, me too.' Hal leaned against the knobbly bark. He was sick of falling out. 'I half thought you were right.'

Josh clapped a hand on his shoulder. 'No, it's definitely a haunting. Trust me, it's classic! You're just sensitive to it. You should be an investigator, really. You'd be better at it than me, even.' He turned towards the bridge, where they could just make out the family through breaks in the foliage. 'The others have felt it too now, haven't they? Hey, remember that night when we found your Dad outside?' Hal nodded. He'd pushed it to the back of his mind. 'Maybe he's seen scary things and doesn't want to worry everyone.'

Dad had been acting strangely that night. 'Maybe,' Hal said. 'He is quiet.'

'Boys! The picnic's ready!' Auntie Ruth's Headteacher voice pierced the hushed green space.

As they ducked back under the canopy, Josh said, 'Now we know it's Emilia, we can ask her things. Like why she's haunting us. What she wants.'

And then Hal had that feeling again, of being close to knowing... or close to something horrible, like falling off an edge. 'We could just ask her to leave us alone,' he said. They splashed out into the sunlight.

~

Carrie, Ruth and their mother sat on the picnic rug, while Grand and Chris stood on the bridge, eating chicken legs. 'All that fuss about not wanting leftovers,' said Grandma Lisa, 'and look at him tucking in! Where have those boys got to?'

'Dan went up to look at the tin mine and Toby went after him.' Ruth twisted round to look at the bracken-shrouded hill, where two distant figures were nearing the top. Now Toby stopped and stood still. 'I bet he's actually calling the bloody office!' Ruth scrambled up and headed off to follow them.

When she'd gone, Carrie said, 'I told Hal why we didn't come last year.'

Grandma Lisa looked startled. 'Oh! Not…'

'Just that she died.'

'My goodness. Well, I suppose he asked about her at Sylvia's, didn't he? I'm sure you know best, darling.' She touched Carrie's knee… 'You're doing such a great job.'

Carrie meant to thank her, but the words caught in her throat.

August 2010

When Chris asked her how the funeral had been, Carrie said, 'Angry.'

From the first phone call to her father, Uncle Rod had sounded exasperated. 'For years I've barely been told what country she was in,' he said. 'And then this. In the middle of a conference. Did *you* know about any of it, David?'

'Maybe it's shock talking,' Carrie's mum said in the passenger seat on the way to the crematorium. 'It can't have sunk in.'

'Don't *you* stand up for him,' he spat. Carrie winced as he turned to her mother, his eyes off the road. 'This tells you everything you need to know about Rod as a father. And then he asks what I knew, as though it's my fault for not telling him!'

'But we didn't know anything. How could it be your fault?' Mum soothed.

'Tell that to him!'

The anteroom to the chapel was all steel and windows, like a 1970s classroom. It was stifling on a warm August day. Auntie Jill and Uncle Rod were putting on a bitter show of co-hosting, while Jill's new husband, a Swiss banker, tried to smooth things over with suave politeness, which only made things worse. Carrie kept wondering what Ruth would have said. She was at Toby's family villa, and so couldn't make the journey, though it was only in the South of France.

Dad refused to join the mourners gathering round to mutter condolences, so it was Mum who stepped up and said, 'Hello Jill,

I'm so sorry.' Carrie saw Auntie Jill pause in her fitted navy suit, her gaze elsewhere, then turn away without answering. She clasped her mother's arm through the sleeve of her jacket.

Uncle Rod leaned over, a tall, stocky man, older and greyer than Carrie remembered, the deep black of his suit absorbing any light. 'Some boyfriend has come out of the woodwork.' He shook his head as though it was another outrage. It took Carrie a moment to realise he meant Emilia's boyfriend, not Auntie Jill's.

Talk faded to breathy whispers, the air bristling with body spray and hostility. Carrie hardly recognised anyone: she had rarely seen Emilia with her own family.

Had Carrie's family been any good for her? Had anyone here? Not according to the bleak finale in the Travelodge room. Some of the mourners were in their thirties and might be friends from Emilia's travels: a man in a suit with tanned feet in flip-flops; a woman with blonde hair in cornrows and a skirt fringed with beads. There was barely any whispering now, as though they were all weighed down by their collective failure.

Maybe Carrie had been the worst – the reason behind all this.

Through the wall of windows, men in black hats and tailcoats moved in formation. Carrie glimpsed white gloves and a stomping and shouldering. There was a muttered announcement. Everyone shuffled across the anteroom and trooped after Uncle Rod and Auntie Jill.

Emilia was in a box. Sleek and black with silver handles, with Emilia in it. A box.

Carrie sat between her parents, aware of her father's stiff-backed silence when the hymn was sung. Why a religious service, for Emilia? It was just the thing to annoy him.

They played a song that was apparently Emilia's favourite. Carrie had not known that she liked it. Why would she? The two of them had once sung Wham's 'Wake Me Up Before You Go Go' in the car on the way to Wales, over and over until Ruth had shouted. But that was so many years ago.

The order of service said someone called Paul was going to do a tribute. The man Carrie had noticed got up, the slapping of his flip-flops the only sound as he walked to the microphone. He looked tanned in a weather-beaten way, with dark hair beginning to recede. He stood in front of the coffin, gripping the lined page of a notebook, and spoke in a wavering voice.

'I had only known Emilia for one short year but she changed my life.' He paused and looked out at the small crowd. Was he staking his claim over any of theirs? 'We met in Thailand where I was running a bar. We worked side by side and her quirky, beautiful spirit captivated my heart. Emilia loved the life there. She taught English to the bar girls and they helped her to run a dance class for tourists. Everyone loved her. But her plan was always to go back to England. She had unfinished business. She said that our relationship gave her the strength she needed to sort herself out. It was time to go home for a new start, together. She went on ahead to get things ready. Then in that hotel room, the allergies she had suffered her whole life finally caught up with her.'

Carrie gulped down a rising in her throat. Allergies? She felt her parents shift on either side at her.

'I will never forget her, or stop missing her,' Paul said, his voice shaking. 'She was my soulmate.'

There was an odd murmur among the mourners as he slip-slapped back to his seat. Did he glance at Carrie as he passed? *Unfinished business. A new start.* The Travelodge was only a few miles away from home. Was Emilia coming to them? Was it an allergy that stopped her, not despair?

'Paul says it was anaphylactic shock,' Mum said in the dark, low-ceilinged pub where sandwiches were laid out on tinfoil platters.

Carrie stared. 'Oh! From what?'

Her mother looked uncertain. 'They don't know. Maybe sesame seeds… He said she'd never had an allergy test but she'd had reactions before.'

'God,' said Carrie. 'Do you remember, she used to say things made her throat hurt? We just thought she was being fussy. But we didn't know about allergies then, did we?'

'No.' Her mother lowered her voice. 'And Rod's saying maybe Paul just *wants* people to think it was allergies. So…' She shook her head and took a tea from the rows lined up in sludge-green cups and saucers. 'David, Rod wants you to go over to Auntie Mo's. He says he'll have a chat with you later.'

Carrie's father wriggled as though his dark suit was chafing him. 'I'm not staying.'

'Really? Have a sandwich at least. There's smoked salmon.'

'Oh well, Rod has pushed the boat out.' Carrie followed her Dad's sardonic gaze at the stained carpet, frayed beer mats and ring-marked pub tables. It was the nearest pub to the crematorium. 'Mr executive. Flew over business class. Come on, I've had enough.'

It all felt raw and unfinished. But Carrie had come in his car, so would have to go too. She could see his fuss escalating, a black mood on its heels. 'Can I just go to the loo?'

In the dingy corridor on the way back from the Ladies, she bumped into someone. 'Paul?' she said. 'I'm Carrie. Emilia's cousin.' Close-up, she saw the lived-in look of a reformed party animal.

'Oh yes.' He clasped her hand, kindness in his pink-tinged brown eyes. 'More like sisters, Emilia said.'

She nodded, her throat tight. 'Sorry,' she said as someone pushed past them.

They moved over to the wall. He ran a hand through thinning dark hair. 'It's all a bit fucked up. I don't think her Dad had ever heard of me.'

'No but he's been out of the picture. Your talk was lovely. It was so nice to hear that she had you. That she was… well, better.'

'We'd both been round the block a few times. But she was determined to move forwards. Put things right, you know?' He'd been staring at his flip-flops, but looked up at her. 'It was all going to change. I can't believe this has happened.'

In his eyes, Carrie glimpsed the horror-film fear of it: someone you wanted to spend your life with, turned into a thing that rots.

'Oh there you are!' It was the cornrow woman, carrying two pints, her skirt swirling round her ankles. She was a friend of Paul's, over from Thailand for moral support. Through the introductions, Carrie could see her mother in the crowd, craning her neck, looking for her.

212

'Well, it was nice to meet you, Carrie,' Paul said. 'I'd heard a lot about you.' He was moving away, pint in hand.

'You too,' she said. 'And I'm sorry. Take care.'

Carrie sat through her father's foul mood on the journey home, her only consolation the thought of telling it all to Chris. He hadn't been able to get time off school.

'Well obviously, on a day like this, it's all about him,' he said later.

'It's not just that. What if she hadn't died and she'd turned up here? And I was thinking this at her *funeral*, Chris. I'm a terrible person.' She felt choked with the threat of tears.

'You're not, you're absolutely not.' He rocked her, like Imogen when her rabbit died. She sank into the comfort of it: his warm, calm body, her head against his chest. Her throat went on aching, but tears never came.

CHAPTER THIRTY

During the picnic, the clouds cleared altogether. They pulled off hoodies and cardigans and sat enveloped in warmth. It would have been blazing hot, Carrie thought, without the breeze wafting from the mountain heights.

'Well this is rather perfect,' said Grand from his camping chair. They were all in sleepy agreement, their faces tipped to the sun.

Hal and Josh were friends again and had climbed over the stile to walk downstream with Dan, cheerfully assuring Carrie that their shoes were soaked already.

She lay back on the picnic rug between Chris and her parents. The day was surreal and soft-focused, perhaps from the lack of sleep. She felt drained from the heart-rush of telling Hal. But he seemed OK, didn't he? Tomorrow, surely, she'd get to talk to Imogen. Sunlight soothed through her; melting tight knots inside. Just one more day of keeping things under. She reached out her hand to Chris and felt him take it.

She was drifting into the clear blue when splashing and laughter awoke her. The boys were coming back over the stile, wet legs flashing in the sunlight.

'It's deeper than you think,' said Josh, leaping to the ground, rivulets pouring from his shorts.

'Especially if you fall in!' said Hal.

'I didn't fall! I was wading through the rapids.'

'Yeah,' said Dan. 'White water walking!'

'Listen, what about Llangrannog?' said Grand, throwing a peach stone into the long grass.

'I thought we weren't allowed,' said Ruth. 'You said it was too late.'

'Ah but I've got a plan. The beach. A cuppa and a cake in the Patio Café, to make up for missing coffee. Then the evening walk. And that will make room for a meal at the Beach Hut. On Grandma and me. Our treat.'

The day's heat had intensified into a sticky, dream-bright evening as Carrie strolled with the family along the cliff-top path towards Ynys Lochtyn. At some point in the sun's decline, the light appeared to have flipped at the horizon: now it shone pink and golden from the sea. Everything had a trance-like air of significance.

They walked some way down the final spur of land and stopped near the land's edge to gaze. The sea was oil-smooth and barely rippling in the enormous bay; the sky suffused with a coppery haze.

'What a blessing,' Grandma Lisa breathed. Carrie was too awed even to flinch in case her father scoffed. In any case, he was walking away from them along the edge, binoculars at the ready.

'What's that?' said Hal. A criss-cross pattern disturbed a patch of the sea's surface, flipping, splashing, getting choppier all the time.

'It's mackerel!' called Grand. 'A great school of them, jumping!' Carrie saw Toby, Ruth and the boys run to join him, even Dan quickening his pace.

'Look!' shouted Hal. 'Dolphins!'

And there they were at last – one, two, three slick backs surging through the water. They leaped through the thrashing surface, then curved over to plunge again. Gulls wheeled overhead with a chorus of cries.

'All creation praising God,' Grandma Lisa said. 'That's what Thelma would say! *Even the stones cry out...*'

'Do you think that?' Carrie asked as the dolphins leaped again.

'Me?' her mother raised her eyes. 'Ha! What would your father say if I really got religion?'

'No but... if you believe, you believe, don't you? No one can tell you not to.'

The air ululated with the gulls' calls as they swooped towards the fish.

Grandma Lisa sighed, looking across at Grand. 'I've been to church with Thelma a couple of times. And it's nice. I don't mean just nice – it feels meaningful. I could get pulled in, I suppose, but I don't think it's worth the aggro.'

'But why won't he let you believe, just because he doesn't?'

'It's not that he doesn't *let* me, darling.' She saw Carrie's doubtful look. 'I think he just wants me beside him at his barricades.'

'Barricades? Fighting what?'

'Oh, you know your father. He's always battling something.'

They looked over at him, standing hands on hips near the cliff edge, his face gilded by the fiery light. Carrie found that she was smiling.

At least Carrie wasn't looking, Chris thought, though she had turned back before to check that he was following. They had held hands earlier at the picnic place and he had dropped off to sleep. It was easier to sink into himself when she wasn't searching his face with her hopeful smile. Or saying 'Alright?' for the umpteenth time.

He hung back now on a grassy outcrop – was there solid rock below him, or just earth jutting out over a heart-stopping drop? He could see the whole family ahead of him, glowing in the strange light, gazing at the dolphins. The first they'd seen this year. And here he was, joyless, staring – the spectre at the feast. There'd be hope for him if he could love seeing the dolphins. He refocused his eyes to search where they had been leaping, but the water was empty, shivering in the breeze.

Excited chatter drifted from the others. His gaze shifted to the dark water in the shadow of the overhang. It slapped at the rock and made a cavernous booming. They'd had a talk at school about the danger of cold water in hot weather. If you fall in and go under, the freezing shock makes you gasp. Your lungs fill up in an instant, and that's how you drown.

Grand had never seen anything like it in all these years. Incredible how the place could still surprise him. It lived so vividly in his mind all winter, the very definition of longing. His own promised land, bright now like some new creation. Like that first time he came back after moving away to Kent.

It was 1950: five years after he left so suddenly. Five winters with no snow, no Christmas in the meaty-sweet warmth of Noddfa;

five summers without the people he'd known, the stream and the mountains, these cliffs, this sea. Just Hilda's letters with the village news and Will's passed-on messages. And all those dried flowers that he rubbed between his fingers, searching for their faint scent of here.

He'd surprised them, that first time. Saved up all year from his paper round to get the train. He could almost feel it now, the excitement in his belly on that lumbering bus from Aberystwyth, and Hilda's hug on the doorstep – shocked but fervent, as if she'd never let him go. The strangeness of being taller than her, of being held. Mo barely touched him except to hand him something, even when he was a child.

When Will got home, Hilda made David step out from behind the kitchen door. Will stood, hat in hand, his face older, blue eyes gazing. He made a big show of scolding about the surprise, but then grabbed David and held him tight. For all his manly back-slapping, David could feel him trembling.

When Barbara heard, she came running round and appeared breathless in the doorway, a worn-looking version of her previous self, with duller lips and hair, but as chatty as ever. Later that evening, he walked her home. Even under cover of darkness, they met half the village, and each time David was hailed and hugged and had to promise he'd visit properly tomorrow.

'You're like one of our own in Bont Goch. We don't say that about just anybody,' said Barbara as they walked down the lane towards Cefyn Glas, trailing cigarette smoke between the hedgerows. He'd just started smoking, as you did in those days, behind the bike sheds at Skinners School – but it was bizarre to be doing it with her. 'I haven't seen Will and Hilda so happy since – well, since before you left.' David had let the cigarette hang from his lips, Bogart style. He plucked it out, glad of something to do with his hands. 'They were devastated, when you were taken away. You know what Hilda said to me? David?' She stopped walking as the house came in sight. David handed her the cigarette and she drew on it, little lines cracking her lipstick. 'She said, *God forgive me, Barbara, I miss him as much as Hugh.*'

He hadn't said anything. Well you didn't, did you? Life wasn't all outpourings like in women's magazines. Barbara gazed into the darkness with shining eyes. Then a light came on in an upstairs window.

'There's mother. She'll be mad I've been gone so long.'

Then the summer was over. A few weeks later in Tunbridge Wells, he went to that party at the Vale Royal Methodist Church Hall. His friends from Skinners had found out there would be girls there from Bennett Memorial. Rumour had it they were easier than the Grammar School girls, so they all went to find out, absurdly agitated at the thought. That's where he first saw Lisa, laughing with her school-friends in a trim-waisted turquoise dress, her hair up in a pony-tail, slim arms bare.

'I've never seen anything like it,' Grand said now as Hal and Josh joined him.

'Yeah, it's cool.' Josh raised his eyebrows and reappraised. 'Really cool.'

'Don't go overboard, Josh. You're getting poetic.' Grand glanced at Hal, his face aglow with the sunset. 'How's it been this year, Hal? Not spoilt by all this ghostly business?'

'Oh no.' Hal thrust his hands in his jeans pocket and hunched his shoulders, looking out at the bay where seabirds bobbed on the glowing surface. Grand remembered what Lisa had said, that Carrie had told him about last summer. Hal shifted, chewing the edge of his thumbnail. 'Weird, though.'

'Bloody weird!' Josh agreed. 'Don't you believe any of it, Grand? I mean not even a sort of echo of a person, hanging round where they lived?'

Ruth had wandered over and he was about to laugh, but then he saw Hal's face. He wouldn't ridicule him for the world. 'Well, no one's ever managed to prove anything, however much they believe in it all…'

'That's not true!' Josh said. 'There's loads of stuff on Youtube!'

'Youtube?' said Ruth. 'That proves it, then.'

'I think people believe it because they want to,' Grand said. 'They can't bear for death to be an ending.'

Hal scuffed the rough grass with his deck shoe. 'That's not me though, Grand! I'd rather it *was* an ending.' In this rare, clear light, Grand caught his look of appeal.

He remembered Barbara's desperation for Hugh to come; the

thought of him, weeks dead, his tread mud-heavy on the stairs. He could almost catch the sickroom whiff of calamine lotion and fever. 'Well no – you're like me. Maybe that's why I don't believe in it. I don't want to!'

'Have you ever felt anything at Noddfa, though? Like a presence – Will or Hilda maybe?'

A little chuckle escaped him but he turned it into a cough. 'I don't know. I think of them there, because it's where I knew them… But that doesn't mean they're still around!' Standing there with the boys, he was too content to put up much of an argument. 'I suppose if anyone was going to haunt the place, I'd like it to be Will and Hilda. They always made everyone welcome.'

There was silence, then Josh let out a ghostly wail. 'We-e-e-lcome! You are we-e-e-elcome!'

Lisa, Carrie and Chris had come downhill to reach the group. 'What's all this, Grand?' said Lisa, her smile crinkled. Christ, she was older now than Hilda had been that summer! He had a weird sense of vertigo like falling through a hole in time.

'Ghost talk,' said Josh, pulling his cheeks down in an attempt at a spooky look. 'Will you haunt the place, Grand, when you're gone?'

'I think I will!' he said. 'One day, another family will be sitting in that kitchen and there'll be a strange smell of bacon that no one can explain.'

'And Grand will shuffle in,' said Ruth, 'looking for his spatula.'

Laughter made light work of the steep climb back uphill. By the time they reached the top, deep purple was crowding the light from the sky, and a delicious heaviness filled his limbs.

'Scampi and chips for me!' said Lisa as the lights of Llangrannog twinkled in the distance.

'Don't worry, Carrie, we'll find you some mung beans,' said Ruth and they all began to plan their orders at the Beach Hut. Grand stopped to get his breath back and looked out at the water where the mackerel had been. And dolphins – there had been dolphins at last! He thought of people who were missing all this and wished they could be here.

CHAPTER THIRTY-ONE

Hal felt a sleepy peace from the hot day, the walk and the scampi and chips with sticky sauces.

'Last day tomorrow!' said Grandma Lisa as they piled out of the cars and trooped towards Noddfa. 'I don't even want to think about packing!'

The house looked dead-eyed in the darkness – they hadn't left a light on. Mum got the door open and hunched her shoulders as they stepped inside. 'I didn't think I'd ever feel cold today!'

Hal had been looking forward to the evening and then the comfort of his bunk bed, like on every other holiday, but now he was peering from shadow to shadow. The others dispersed to the kitchen and living room. He lingered in the chill of the hallway, his skin crawling.

Could he just go up to bed, Chris wondered? Call the day over and get a break from it all in the dead time of sleep? He dropped into an armchair and tried to think through a pall of tiredness. They were all gathered around him in the lamplit living room. What would Chris From Before have done? Carrie's Chris. Dolphin-loving Chris. Hal and Imogen's Dad. His pulse lurched and raced. Imogen was due back tomorrow. It was all going to come out. About Tyrone as well. *We'll get home and find help,* Carrie kept saying. She wouldn't want to help him when she knew.

'Alright?' Her cheery look now was a plea for him to be better. He couldn't go to bed – Toby would call him a lightweight and Ruth would laugh and Carrie's heart would sink. He had to sit here, guts in turmoil, a great blot on their holiday brightness.

Grandma Lisa gasped, a hand to her throat.

'Calm down, woman, it's me!' Grand had poked her with the Guardian. 'It's your turn. The *crossword*!'

Ruth laughed, 'He's haunting the place already!'

Grandma Lisa poked him back. 'It's those ghost stories of yours – they've made us all jumpy. That one about the miner and the girl. I keep thinking about her ending up down the tin mine…'

'It's just a story,' Carrie cut in, louder than she'd intended, and they looked at her, taken aback. No one was laughing now.

He had ruined everything. The chattering, the crossword – it was a trap closing in. Panic fizzed in his chest. He had to get out. But how, when? In the morning, before Carrie got up? He could set his watch alarm to vibrate and be out of there before anyone missed him. He let his breath out and slumped in the armchair.

There was a way after all. His heartrate was settling. He hardly recognised the feeling of relaxing, like a choke-hold releasing.

'Tea, Chris? Last night lacers?' Grand was heading for the kitchen.

'Go on then, why not?' he said. He even managed a smile.

Hal was little again. Imogen had borrowed Mum's hair things: scrunchy bands for pony tails and clips that pinched. She was practising on him. Her tongue peeped out at the corner of her mouth, her eyes round, eyebrows raised as she twisted a band round a clump of his fringe. Sometimes his scalp pulled and stung, but then her fingers would move through his hair, making him feel dreamy.

'We saw dolphins, Imogen! And mackerel!' he said. 'You missed it.'

Her face darkened. 'The dolphins were killing the mackerel. They were *eating* them.' She always thought she knew better than him.

'How would you know?' he said.

She leaned closer and hissed, '*I was there. I've been there all along.*'

He woke up in the dark bedroom. A figure was leaning over him. He tried to scream, but he couldn't. He couldn't even move. And now something was pressing on him, crushing the air from his chest.

A signal reverberated in the dark house on a frequency only Carrie was tuned into. It had started in Hal's babyhood, the sixth-sense alarm call that made her eyes spring open, followed by crying that was audible to all. When he was older, he rarely cried, but she could sense his wakefulness, sharing the night air with her; a comfort, a relief in a way. She hadn't thought, after Imogen, that she could be so close to another child.

It hadn't happened for a long time, though. She strained to listen, blood thrumming in her ears.

Grand hauled himself up from the sofa. He must have dropped off – it was late. Time to tidy up and get to bed. He was stiff after all that walking, and winced, bending to gather glasses and mugs. He had a couple of inches of tea left, with 'lacers' as Lisa called it. A tot of brandy in a cuppa, her family's treat for Christmas and holidays. More bloody fun than his lot, he thought, walking to the kitchen. Mo didn't hold with treats.

A shame to chuck good booze down the sink, so he popped his mug in the microwave, pressing the door shut slowly so as not to wake the others. He caught sight of an article on the table that he'd started reading earlier, and soon he was sitting down, fighting sleep, only half-aware of the microwave's ping.

What was that faint smell, tantalising, delicious? Surely not just tea and brandy? No – a warmer, ancient aroma was filling the kitchen. Bread baking in the side oven! If he narrowed his eyes against the electric brightness, he could almost believe in its yeasty promise. And was that Hilda humming as she cut a pat of butter, and Will's throaty murmer, asking about David's day? If he turned and looked, were they there? A gentle sound echoed, calling him, each note teasing, just beyond reach.

'Aaaghr! Hal!' Josh's yell ripped through the bedroom.

Hal could move suddenly. He sat up and pulled his legs up, shrinking from the darkness. 'What?!'

Josh was panting. 'Oh! Sorry. I thought I saw someone.'

'*I* saw someone! Standing over me! I couldn't move!'

Above them, a door closed.

'Shit! Hal!'

The bunk beds creaked and shook. There were three big thumps, and the light came on. Josh stood by the door, staring, black-eyed. There was no one else there.

They stared at each other. Something scraped the attic room floor above them. And then a thudding, closer now.

'What the..?' said Josh. There were footsteps outside their door.

'Boys?' Hal scrambled upright as Josh opened the door. Mum stood in her nightie, her hair sticking up. 'All right? What's going on?'

'We heard something.' They walked out onto the landing with her. Hal looked up, but the attic door was shut. There was a scrape from below, then a clatter. 'Oh, it's Grand!' He appeared at the foot of the stairs, staring up at them in the light from the kitchen.

'But what's *that?*' said Mum. A weird sound was ringing through the house. Grand tipped an ear towards the living room.

Hal stepped onto the stairs, his skin tingling. His chest still ached from the crushing feeling. And that figure, when he couldn't move! But surely nothing could get to him with the family all around? He crept down close to Mum, and Josh followed behind them.

From the living room came a chiming. Grand stood looking in wonder. Hal went towards the sound and pushed open the door.

They looked round the room in dim yellow lamplight.

'Will's clock!' said Grand, gazing at the mantelpiece. The sound stopped abruptly, a chime fading in the air.

'I thought you'd lost the key?' said Josh.

'We did,' said Grand. 'Years ago! I suppose we must have shaken it with all our bumping around.'

But they hadn't seen what Hal had seen as the door swung wide: the hands of the clock spinning, a reflection of long fair hair whipping across the glass.

CHAPTER THIRTY-TWO

2011 Day 14: Friday

'That was mental.' Josh's first words the next morning were mangled by a loud yawn.

Hal was glad to hear his voice. It felt really early, but he had been lying awake for half an hour. 'I know. Two nights running. What the hell.'

'How can Grand and them still think it's nothing? That clock thing was freaky!'

'That's not all, Josh. When I woke up, someone was standing over me and I couldn't move, or shout, or anything.'

'Wait! I think that's an actual thing,' said Josh. There was a creaking and a fluttering of pages.

Last night tonight. Hal usually hated the thought of leaving. But that figure! And the weight on his chest… He had a cold, queasy feeling remembering.

'That's it!' Josh said. '*Sleep paral-ysis*. When you can feel someone in the room and you can't move. Wow, it happens all over the world. The Chinese call it *a ghost pressing down on you*. And in Mexican it's something like *sub-ears al muerto*.'

'What's that mean?'

Josh read for a bit. 'Urgh, here it is! *The dead climb on top of you.*'

Hal got to his feet. 'I can't do another night like that!'

'It's OK!' Josh watched as he paced up and down. 'We'll get to the bottom of it. Ask what the ghost wants. If she just wants to scare us off, we'll tell her we're leaving tomorrow anyway.'

That might work – they would be gone soon. Hal sat down on the edge of his bunk. But what if she was always here now? What if Noddfa was ruined?

Josh yawned again, and Hal's throat heaved in sympathy. His watch said 5.30. He lay back down, his eyelids heavy.

Hal was drifting off when Josh muttered, 'Why would Emilia climb on top of you?'

He snapped awake. How could he sleep now? It was six o'clock when he gave up trying. 'I might go for a walk…' he whispered, but he stood up to find Josh spark out, mouth gaping.

Would Dad be up for going? He'd perked up last night when they were laughing about lacers, as though the holiday had done him good. Hal felt cheerier himself and caught his eye when he was going up to bed. 'Night, Dad,' he said. But Dad's face fell as if he'd thought of something awful.

A strange sadness pressed on Hal. Maybe last day blues, like Grandma Lisa talked about. But this felt colder and heavier.

He pulled on jeans and a sweatshirt and opened the bedroom door to a drab early light. Mum and Dad's door was open a crack – was Dad up already? Maybe he was in the kitchen. Hal went downstairs, but there were no lights on. He stuck his head round the kitchen door and jumped.

Mum stood there in her nightie, hugging herself. She looked more shocked than Hal. 'Have you seen Dad?' she said.

'No. I thought you were him.'

Hal went in and put the light on, and she blinked. 'Oh. I woke up and… it doesn't matter.' Her hand fluttered and rested on her neck.

'Do you think he's gone for a walk?' Hal said. 'I might see if I can catch up with him. Last chance.'

Her cheeks hitched up in a smile and she glanced at the window. 'Which way will you go?'

'Down to the sea, I guess. Where we usually go.'

'OK. If you think… OK.' Even with the light on, she had a greyish look.

Hal couldn't look at her any more. 'I'm sure that's where he is Mum. I'm going to head off. See you later.'

'Have you got your phone?'

Hal felt its weight in his jeans pocket. 'Yeah. Why?'

'Oh just… Imogen should be back. She might call.'

'OK. See you.'

The day was dull and hazy: it might clear up later or turn to rain. Hal set off jogging along the track, then slowed to a walk, his legs heavy. He'd missed so much sleep.

Why would Emilia..? He cursed Josh for saying that, and the Chinese and Mexicans… He tramped on, seeing nothing of the hedgerows or the sea, just that flash of hair, rushing past the clock. A feeling like a rope tightening pulled at his insides.

There was the turn-off ahead. He ran, hope rising with the beat of his pulse. But there was no one in the shadowed lane.

'Dad?' he called, plunging into the shade. Maybe Dad was up ahead and would wait or come back to meet him. Hal's voice echoed back at him like a strangled cry. He hoped Mum hadn't heard it, waiting at the house.

What was she doing, frozen there, Carrie thought? Chris had seemed more relaxed last night – cheery almost. Perhaps he was looking forward to hearing from Imogen. Or to putting things right with her now he was feeling better. It made perfect sense, didn't it, that he'd go for an early walk?

But she had felt strung tight since she'd woken to find him gone. She saw the grim smiles he'd put on for her this holiday, right up until he broke down that day. *I had this feeling of dread that she'd never come back.*

Carrie's phone was charging on the work surface. No signal, of course. Still, she searched for a text or missed call. Was this for Imogen, this fizzle of nerves? Every passing thought set off a burst of fretfulness. She shuddered as though to shake it off.

Get a grip. The day would go on as the last day of the holiday always did. Chris and Hal would come back together for Grand's breakfast. Then there would be coffee at the Patio Café, and a final walk on the cliffs.

She should make tea, or go back to bed, but she stood there in the neon light, her gaze drawn to the hallway where the morning cast its shade.

Her parents would be up soon. It felt impossible to stay and talk. She could go and get petrol for the journey! She sprinted up to the bedroom and pulled on yesterday's clothes, then rummaged in her bag for car keys. Before she knew it, she was striding up the track, her arms clasped round her chest. She barely remembered leaving the house – had she even shut the front door?

In the car, she winced at the tyre noise on the stony ground. There was the turning into the lane where Hal would have gone. Chris too, if Hal was right. She craned her neck to look, but saw no one. What if Hal didn't find him? Her heart clenched – what if he did?

She drove on, chiding herself. She'd let the darkness seep inside her. The stupid panic over Imogen's trip. Telling Hal about Emilia. Chris.

Carrie reached the village road and turned right. She flicked on the side lights in the darkness under the trees. She found she was crouching over the steering wheel, so she pressed back her shoulders and pulled in a breath. They would go home and get everything sorted. It was always going to be hard this year, but there had been good times too: the evening walk, the dolphins. Hal and Josh's laughter. Last night the tea with lacers – Chris smiling, looking lighter. But his face when they mentioned that miner's girl…

You'd be better off without me. Carrie had come to the turn-off to the petrol station, but stamped on the accelerator instead of turning. The village passed in a blur.

She stopped at the first of the gates. It would take ages to get through them all, opening and shutting them herself. She pulled over, got out and locked the car, then scrambled over the gate and set off at a run. Sheep bleated and stumbled away as she crashed through their field.

Her breathing was panicky, stifling her fitness, but she dragged herself onwards. Be there, Chris, be there. She grazed her knuckles unbolting the next gate. *Those ghost stories of yours – they've made us all jumpy.*

There was their parking place, and looming above it, the hill. She'd skirt round and take a sheep track up through the bracken to the tin mine. She hadn't been up there for years, but recalled the weight of stones as you hurled them, the pause, then the clatter and crack deep down. What was she doing, dithering? He might be up there already. She might be too late.

It had been chilly and dim when Chris left Noddfa, the sun up in the east, he guessed, but not yet reaching over the mountains. Thinking through the geography of it helped to keep him calm. He trudged on through the gloom, focused and determined. A little sob escaped him. He shuddered, then sniffed and walked on.

Past dawn but no sunlight. Too far west, and the mountains in the way. He opened a gate and went through. It swung and crashed behind him. No going back now to the mess he'd left behind.

He thought of the drop into the depths, the darkness. No, don't let that weaken him. Reasons thudded with every footfall as sheep fled from him, crying. His work was impossible, on top of him. His wrongs were unforgivable. Imogen. Tyrone. Hal, their easygoing Hal, infected with all his darkness. Carrie – don't think of her. The final gate clunked shut.

It was the steep climb that was making him gasp, he was just trying to breathe. He clung on to bracken and hauled himself upwards. Not long now, not long. He remembered the gaps in the rusty barbed wire, the fenceposts sagging to the ground. It was a few years since he'd been up here. Last time he'd gone down the stream with Carrie instead. Carrie teased him for always remembering who did what and when these holidays. Don't now, though – don't remember.

With a last grunt of effort, he got to the top. The ruined building was infested with trees. He saw a rowan full of berries, but the red didn't shine in the shade. Before the sunlight reached it, he'd be gone. *Now, quick, while everything's clear*. He rushed for the mine as if he'd take it at a run.

He saw clean, fresh wood and rows of taut barbed wire. He pulled up and stood, panting. The rock dropped away into the gaping hole, saplings sprouting at odd angles from cracks. There was a tree over there that reached out over the fence. Perhaps he could use it to get over…

Then the memory. He'd been over here, poking round the ruined building. He'd looked up and seen Carrie near that tree, holding a rock with a shot-putter's stance. She let out a 'whooooo!' as she launched it, and he watched it rise and fall. The kids' eyes were wide as they heard it clack and boom: Hal not much more than a toddler, Imogen a lithe and wild-haired girl. Their scrabble to find their own rocks, their heady joy as she coached them. Her cries as crazy as theirs. Her childhood happiness reaching out through time.

He doubled over, racked by sobs.

Carrie ran round to the picnic place, gasping. Chris sat slumped on the bridge, legs dangling over the water, bathed in the amber morning light.

The world seemed to tilt and right itself.

'Chris!' She strode towards him, somehow gripped by a steely calm. He looked up. She had seen pictures of soldiers after battle with the same weary air. She crossed the wooden slats, grasped the hand he lifted and scrambled down beside him. His eyes were pink and brimming. They held each other hard.

'Sorry, Carrie,' he said.

'Did you..?'

A snort, of laughter or just release. 'It's fenced off.'

'Oh yes. Hal said…' Small talk – ridiculous. But what were you meant to say?

'I couldn't anyway.' He pressed at his eyelids.

'Of course not. Chris, it's all going to be fine.' Her head crowded with solutions and she babbled about the doctor, a counsellor, an email to the school. Some part of her detached and hovered, looking down on them, him slumped and her upright, falling quiet.

'I thought of you,' he said, 'teaching Imogen and Hal to throw rocks.' He gave a little chuckle that might have been a sob.

A buzz of headache pierced her temple and intensified to a gnat-like whine.

Wait, there really was a whining noise. Her pocket was vibrating. She pulled out her phone and they stared at it.

Hal was up on the left-hand clifftop, but there was no sign of Dad. He'd been so sure he'd find him there. He hadn't thought through what to do if he didn't. He stood staring at the shifting grey sea. A seabird gave a lonely cry.

The cliff path stretched into the distance. Dad wouldn't have gone that far, but Hal trudged on, kicking at stones. He didn't want to go back without him. A few paces on, his phone beeped. A signal.

Imogen was back in England! Hal stopped and began to scroll for her number. Maybe this was growing up, actually wanting to talk to your sister? At last he found her details and pressed the call button, hearing her usual breezy answer in his head. It always sounded fake to him, like the tone she used with her friends. Her number was engaged.

He let his breath out, then stood scanning the clifftop and the bay. Not a soul in sight. He might be the only person for miles. He tried Imogen's number again. Busy.

The rope tightened inside him. He had the urge to rush off somewhere, but he didn't know where. He started to head back the way he'd come, but that didn't feel right.

He'd scrambled down the steep rocky steps and was trying Imogen again when a voice from his phone said, 'Hal! Hi!'

'Imogen! I was just… How are you?'

'I'm good! What are you up to?'

'I'm on the cliff walk. I was looking for Dad.'

'I've just spoken to Mum! She's with him at the picnic place.'

'Oh.' With Mum. At the picnic place. He had a silly feeling that they'd tricked him and left him stranded.

'Hal? I had a chat with Mum. She said Dad's got anxiety. It's OK, he'll be all right. I know loads of people who've had it. It's just a bit shit for him and Mum at the moment. And for us too, really! Are you OK?'

'Yeah.' She hadn't said 'us' like that for ages. She liked to act like she was so much older. In fact she did sound more mature suddenly. Hal felt different too, as though two weeks apart had changed them both. 'Oh right,' he said. 'That's not like Dad, is it?'

'No, really, it isn't. He's usually the chilled one.' She was being nice – not making out he was some clueless kid. 'And he said weird things to me when he dropped me off for the trip, like he didn't want me to go. It freaked me out, to be honest. But Mum's got this plan, for counselling and stuff. She's really sure he'll be fine.'

'That's good, then. So – did you have a good time?'

'Oh, amazing! I'll tell you all about it when you're back. And I've got prezzies for you, from this cool market. So what about Wales this year, has it been brilliant?'

'Yeah. Josh thinks it's awesome. We had this great evening and saw loads of dolphins…' Hal tailed off. The sea was glossy near the horizon, but the rest of the bay was a muddy grey. 'Imogen,' he said, 'did you know all this about Emilia?'

He heard an intake of breath, then thought the line had gone dead. 'Imogen?'

There was a staticky noise that might have been a sigh. 'Ask Mum, Hal.'

'Mum's told me,' he said. 'She died last year. That's why we didn't come to Wales.'

'Oh… Right. Yes.'

'What??' A cold breeze wafted in Hal's face. 'Is there something else? Imogen?'

'You'll have to ask Mum.'

'Oh. OK, I will.'

'OK. See you soon, Hal. Take care.'

Sea sounds swooshed in over the sudden quiet. He'd go back, then. To Noddfa. He thought of breakfast in the kitchen and felt a longing so intense that it felt a bit like sadness.

CHAPTER THIRTY-THREE

Carrie came back to Noddfa while the others had a final walk in the village. She always made sandwiches for the return journey from fridge leftovers because of Grand's objection to service station prices.

She pulled the last loaves from the bread bin and stared into the fridge, both dazed and jittery. Breakfast had felt like a reunion after the relief of finding Chris and Imogen's call. The crisis is over, she'd thought, like someone wading through a dream. Chris will be OK now. Imogen is back and happy. Hal, thank goodness, is fine as always.

They had spent the morning in Llangrannog, where blue sky and towers of white cloud were reflected in the glistening sand. There were photographs to take and last sights to see – the usual drawn-out goodbye.

She took out cheese and leftover sausages: Grand had cooked up all that remained and complained when they didn't finish them. Ruth had turned down the offer of sandwiches: she and Toby would stop for 'proper ones' *en route*. They were already breaking up into their separate family units, ready for their ordinary lives. Carrie set aside bread for tomorrow morning's toast and began to butter the rest. She kept drifting from the task, her knife in mid-air.

Sunlight spotted the kitchen, filtering through a lacework of leaves. Dread hadn't quite left her after all. The house felt unstable, the air crackling with pressure. She remembered chocolate wrappers scattered, books hurled, the clock. Stupid – she was scaring herself. Ruth would be scathing if she knew.

She began to slice sausages.

A giggle sounded in her memory, or had she actually heard it? She tried to focus on the present moment: she should go soon to meet the others. But she was back at the wake. *She was so determined to move forwards. It was all going to change.*

Emilia had been planning for a future that never materialised. And it wasn't the first time, was it? She had been through that before.

Noddfa was dense with a melancholy quiet. Darkness could roll right over you if you didn't hold it back. Carrie tore off a sheet of foil with deliberate noise.

1998

'I'm up the duff, Carrie,' Emilia said in the kitchen at Mum and Dad's. She was living with them again. Carrie saw life in the flush of her skin, the shine of her hair and a feverish brightness in her eyes. She hugged her – in celebration or sympathy? Emilia had finally started doing well at college; there was talk of her applying to drama school.

'I'm freaking out, but it's brilliant,' she said. 'And don't ask who the father is.' She looked up with a quick smile. 'Not yet, anyway.'

So Carrie kept the pregnancy a secret until it couldn't be hidden any longer, then Emilia told Carrie's parents, but made them promise not to tell her own.

'They hate having to keep things from Uncle Rod and Auntie Jill,' Carrie told her, sliding into Emilia's room after the revelation and its aftermath.

'I'll tell everyone when I've got things sorted,' Emilia said, stuffing things in a duffel bag.

'Wait – where are you going?'

'To get things sorted!'

'How? Oh, with the father? Have you told *him*?' Em nodded and smiled, her eyes glossy. 'And – he's happy?'

'Yes! Oh look, it's not straightforward, like with you and Chris…'

'How was that straightforward? Imogen was a total mistake! The timing was terrible.' Emilia went still, doubt on her face. Carrie felt shaken by her own outburst; fury had come from nowhere and ambushed her. 'I mean, it felt like a massive complication,' she added more kindly, 'but in the end it was lovely, of course.'

Emilia started pushing clothes into the bag again. 'Well hopefully *this* will be lovely. And when people see us together… they'll get over it.'

'Your Mum and Dad, you mean?'

'No, *yours*!' Emilia laughed, the merriment not reaching her eyes. 'Mine will go ape-shit. It'll be another one of my disasters.'

She was away for days. When she came back, the flush and the brightness were gone.

233

2011

Carrie had wrapped the sandwiches in foil. She must go and meet the others. But memories were flowing as though a dam had broken. Sue in her slippers, that morning on the track. 'I saw her. She was right out here!' Drawing a big belly in the air.

Carrie leaned on the table. A chattering rose from the quiet – the house was fraught with voices, fractured, rising. She made herself stand upright and wiped her hands on a tea towel. Sue had been right about Dad's Mum, hadn't she? Her strange, unlikely story had turned out to be true.

She stooped to put the sandwiches in the fridge and stood up to shut the door. Shadows whipped round the kitchen – the wind must be tossing the leaves. But outside it looked still. Alarm sprang in her chest. She snatched up her bag. It was just panic ringing in her ears – not voices rising to screaming pitch as she ran out of the door.

Away from the house, before she even reached the car, the frantic feeling lifted. There were just the usual country sounds, wafting on the breath of the sea.

'Oh, dew, yes I remember...' Sue had insisted on making tea, though Carrie said she only had a minute. Her rheumy eyes focused far beyond the picture window as they sipped from her best china. 'Whatever they say, the doctor and whatnot. Well, you can't be a schoolteacher if your memory's no good!'

'No of course not... So, what happened?' Carrie was perched on the edge of a hard chair.

Sue narrowed her eyes. 'Roslyn said she'd heard there was someone at Noddfa. I said they're not due, Roslyn. Not in winter. But I walked along to see for myself... And there she was, walking down the track. She smiled at me and went *Shhh*.'

'Who, Sue? Who was it?'

Sue frowned, uncertain. 'You know, I told you, the girl. There's an M in it… Or M was actually her name.'

Carrie's insides shivered. Her teacup rattled. 'You mean Em? Emilia, who used to come with us?'

'Yes, that's it. She came without you that time. I wondered if I should ring your father, but she looked so happy and sure of herself, I thought he must know all about it. And I didn't want to pry, Carrie, when I saw her bump. I didn't want David thinking I was a nosey old fool.' She looked troubled, clenching her tiny, age-spotted hand. 'Roslyn, well, you know what a busybody she is! She said I'd better go back and check it was all above board. So I went the morning after. That's when I saw her so upset. Driving away.'

The others would be waiting. They didn't need any more dramas. 'Thank you, Sue,' Carrie said, standing up to go. 'We'll all stop by later to say goodbye.'

'Goodbye? Oh. All right, then.' Sue's eyes were still focused elsewhere. Carrie was halfway down the path when she heard a hushed call. 'What happened to it, Carrie?'

'Happened to what?' She was struggling to think straight.

'The baby. What happened to her baby?'

1998

This was it. Her future was racing towards her. Emilia stood under the sloping roof of the brand-new attic room at Noddfa. Uncle David had had it built, saying the family was growing. More than he knew, Emilia thought, a soft shifting inside her. Would her baby sleep here one day?

The room had an amazing view down the track, with a splinter of sea shining to the West even in the winter grey. *We are the first ones in here*, she said, breathing in the fresh wood smell. What a brilliant place for a new beginning!

He'd come down the track any minute. He'd have put his foot down all the way from Tunbridge Wells, and he'd pull his red Golf in next to the battered Fiat Panda that Carla from college had lent her, not realising how far away she would drive it.

Emilia had seen Sue earlier. She had half wanted to invite her in or go to the bungalow for tea as they did on their summer holidays. She needn't know that Emilia had nicked the keys to Noddfa from Uncle David.

But this had to be just Emilia and Nick. It wasn't a holiday, it was real life. The beginning of their life together.

Her heart thrilled. They could do this. Carrie and Chris had done it – they'd gone from muddling through life like most people their age, to focused, immersed, besotted with Imogen. Even Ruth and Toby, for all their bickering, were kinder and calmer for little Dan. And Uncle David and Auntie Lisa, who had been fading into tired old age, had transformed for these little ones into Grand and Grandma Lisa, fond and silly and full of joy.

Emilia saw things like this and stored them away. It was what actors did, spotting the essence of people, noting their character arcs. Nick had pointed out her powers of observation to the others on the drama course. She had tingled with his praise. Onstage at college productions, she sought his shape in the darkness beyond the lights. With him watching, she was gifted, talented, good at something at last.

After that first time in his car, he'd stopped singling her out in class. He wouldn't even catch her eye. She told herself it was for discretion's sake, but his harrowed look made her heart shrink. She still needed his admiration as a teacher, even though a lift home after a rehearsal had turned into kissing and touching and the sudden revelation of his anguished passion, which he said he had tried and tried to control. They'd had full sex – or as full as you could, wrenching clothes aside in the cramped back seat of a Golf, parked in a layby in a country lane.

In the aftermath it was as if the sun had gone out. He looked as desolate as she felt – the other students noticed it. Carla thought maybe there was something up with his wife. Then his note in Emilia's exercise book a few days later. There was light again.

She kept thinking she'd heard an engine. It would put everything right when he got here. The murky worry about what her Auntie Lisa and Uncle David would say if they knew the truth. The worse thought of her and the baby in some miserable flat, alone. She wouldn't cope like Carrie or Ruth – she'd be a disaster.

Wait, was that him? Yes, it was an engine, its roar was getting louder! She pushed open the dormer window, heart bounding, almost certain. Her eyes strained into the distance where the muddy ruts led, but the track was empty. The car noise reached a peak and subsided. It wasn't coming here.

This was the first place she'd thought of when she decided to ask Nick to come to her. Not for an hour or a day as usual, not a weekend tangled in lies. But once and for all, like they'd talked about. A new home while they got things sorted. A family of their own.

His voice on the phone had been strangled. 'Yes. All right. I'll come.' His laugh had sounded crazy with freedom. And love. That's what she'd heard with her talent for observation.

She shut the window with a bump. How long had she stood here? Her belly and hips were a dragging ache. There was nowhere to sit – she should bring up a chair. Cold was creeping inside her.

She thought back over all those holidays, trying to remember if anyone had ever put the heating on, perhaps to dry clothes after rain. Could she work out how to use it? She stared into the shadows, wandering through time. She used to miss Carrie and the others so much when she went home, full of stories. Mum had snapped at her once to stop going on about it.

When she turned to look down the track again, the horizon was leaking pink.

Nick had planned to leave before Elsa got up, as if he were just going out for his run. Emilia had been expecting him since late morning. She had made allowances for traffic when he wasn't there for the lunch she'd bought at the motorway services. She'd thought, well, a late lunch. And then, an early tea.

Crimson was bleeding into the sea now, the sky a deepening bruise. She'd had nothing to eat; she had been waiting for him. If he came now, he'd find her crashed and spent, her bright mood from earlier in ruins.

But he wasn't coming. The darkening landscape swelled and distorted. This wasn't a beginning at all.

CHAPTER THIRTY-FOUR

2011 Day 14: Friday

Hal was with the others, waiting for Mum at the end of a lane. They didn't usually walk that end of the village, but Dad wasn't keen on the picnic place because he'd been there earlier. Grand had said, 'I know, I'll show you the dark place with the waterfall. I was terrified of it as a boy.' Which got Josh all excited, of course.

Hal saw Mum coming. She was looking down, her arms crossed, but when she saw them, she smiled. 'Sorry, I've been ages. I popped in to see Sue. What about this!' She gestured at the sky, full blue now, the fields and woods around them glowing gold and green.

'A heartbreaker!' said Grandma Lisa. It was Grand's word for when the last day of the holiday was brilliant weather.

'All right?' Mum said to Hal as they set off down the lane. He must ask her about Emilia, like Imogen said. He hadn't had a chance until now.

The lane wound down into deepening shade, the stream rushing below it, edged with thick, black mud. They followed a sharp bend and continued downwards, the trees arching over them. The ground was lush with moss, the trees blackened as though they had soaked up the darkness.

'It's beautiful!' said Grandma Lisa.

Auntie Ruth made a face. 'In a grim way… It's like a cave.'

'So why were you scared of it? Were there stories about it?' Josh peered around him, hopping from stone to stone on the mushy waterside.

'Oh all the children were scared. Hugh used to tease me about eels eating sheep's brains.'

'Eels?!' Josh leaped back from the edge as though one might shoot out and bite him. He crashed into Hal, making him stumble. Hal shouted as his foot sank into soggy ground and cold water soaked through his trainer. Everyone chuckled, but he felt like shoving Josh away.

Grand led them further along the stream, the water rushing ever louder until they came to a foaming torrent crashing into a pool.

'And there were *dŵrgi* here,' Grand said. 'Everyone said so.'

'What's der-gee?' said Josh.

'Well that's it, I didn't know. I imagined something horribly ghoulish. Years later I found it in a Welsh dictionary. *Dŵrgi*: from *dŵr*, meaning water, and *ci* meaning dog. Water-dogs.' They all looked at him. 'Otters!'

The adults made delighted noises, but Josh looked unimpressed. 'I think there is something ghoulish here, though. I reckon someone drowned. Or maybe a murdered body was dumped here? It'd be the perfect place.'

'You've really thought this through,' said Dan, taking a big step away from Josh, which made Uncle Toby laugh.

Hal thought of saying something about Britain's Most Haunted Stream but found he couldn't be bothered to shout over the water. Wasn't the nightmare at Noddfa enough for Josh? Was the whole thing a lark to him?

'Who's for a walk up the hillside?' said Grand, turning back upstream. 'We go up here I think. There's a fantastic view from the top.'

'I might stay here,' Josh said to Hal. 'Do a bit of investigating. Or we could dam the stream?'

The others were all following Grand. Hal liked the idea of a new walk. He saw Mum hanging back, waiting for him as if she fancied a chat. 'Coming, Hal?'

'Actually,' he said, 'I think I'll stay here with Josh.'

Carrie followed her father up through a steep field of scrubby grass. Grandma Lisa stopped frequently to have a breather and ask him questions. He answered with gusto: that dark crop in a sloping field was for nitrogen fixing. They looked down onto a big Victorian house with horses in the surrounding fields.

'Cefyn Gwyn,' Grand said. 'Do you remember, girls? We went pony trekking there when you were little.'

Carrie did remember: Ruth had the tallest horse and looked down on the younger girls as if she were a proper rider. Carrie's pony walked the route placidly like an old sofa on legs, but Emilia's was frisky and made her scream. Then a fly gave her a nasty bite. They had never gone again.

'Yes, I remember. It was brilliant.'

Did her parents know that Emilia had come to Noddfa when she was pregnant? Of course they had guessed at a failed love affair, but Emilia would not talk about it. She must have wanted to be here with the baby's father. She had come home heartbroken.

They walked on past old stone dwellings, now collapsed and used for farm equipment. Carrie saw the spindly ribcage of a sheep with wool clinging to its bones. Why hadn't Hal come with them? He usually loved a walk. Grand nudged Chris and pointed out two sheep skulls, nose to nose in the long grass, grinning at each other.

The path rose further, shaded by moss-covered trees. Bushes here had died away into bleached wooden sculptures, twisted into knots. Grand pointed out a rowan tree with orange berries shining against the blue. On they climbed.

'There.' Grand paused. 'Bont Goch.'

Through a gap in the hedge they saw the village nestling under summer trees: grey stone here and there poking through the green.

'Beautiful!' said Grandma Lisa, panting. 'Is it much further, David?'

'It is up a bit, for the best view. I hope it's not ruined by those awful fucking windmills.'

'*Said Father*,' chirped Ruth in her Enid Blyton voice. 'I'm staying here, I'm knackered. Toby?'

'You know I never like to leave your side.' Toby sat beside her on the wall, his face all mock sincerity. Ruth poked him with her elbow and he grunted, then laughed.

'You go on up,' Grandma Lisa said. 'We'll wait for you here. Chris? Dan? Are you going for the peak?'

Dan said, 'Nah, I'm good.'

Chris shook his head and sat on the wall, looking more tired than anyone. Weakened by it all, Carrie thought. But there'd be help for him at home.

'Just you and me then!' said Grand, beaming at Carrie, and they headed onwards.

Later they turned off the path and climbed through fields. The air had the wild feel of high places. Thistles clawed Carrie's ankles as they crossed rutted, sloping ground. I'll ask him if they knew about Em at the top, she thought, gathering her courage. Why did it feel as if she'd be breaking a vow of silence? But then he had kept them in the dark all those years, about his mother abandoning him.

They trekked on towards a stile in a thorny hedge. On the other side was a bizarrely well-tended field, its grass as tidy as a bowling green. 'There they are, bastard things,' said Grand. The wind turbines stood sentinel over the stunted grass, a dystopic vision amid the wider beauty. A moan filled the air around them, a sinister undercurrent to the waft and hush of the breeze.

Carrie braced herself for a rant, but with a shake of his head, he just led the way past them. There was a raised ridge with a fence on it at the far edge of this field. He hoisted himself up and called out, 'Here we go!'

She pulled herself up beside him. The valley was an undulating patchwork flowing up and out from the hidden village. At the edge of the world were wild, bluish mountains and a sparkling ribbon of sea.

Here was the backdrop to her father's childhood. She didn't have the heart to disturb it with her questions. Was he upset already that the turbines had ruined the place? She looked over – no, he had simply turned his back on them. He saw what he wanted to see and kept the rest behind him.

Dazed, Chris thought, that's what this feeling was while others chattered and laughed and kept getting up off the wall to photograph the family group. Not terrible, like earlier. There was a fuzz of exhaustion over everything, but that oddly made it more bearable. He pictured himself describing it to the counsellor that Carrie had suggested. Huh – he was thinking of going then. Perhaps just for her sake – if he could find the energy.

'Will you take one, Chris?' asked Grandma Lisa. He searched her face for her meaning. She smiled, with a little knit in her brow, and put a hand on his arm, 'Oh, I expect you want to wait until we're all together.' Photographs. She meant he'd wait to take a photograph. He nodded. He didn't have his phone with him anyway. Then he felt a weight in his hand. Carrie's phone..? Oh that's right, she had handed it to him when she was putting her hair up in a ponytail. He was gazing at it when it rang.

Imogen. He hadn't spoken to her yet. Carrie had got up and walked away, off the bridge, when she rang before.

His reactions were slow, his fingers heavy, but he pushed the button, stood up and stepped away from the family. 'Hello,' he said, 'it's Dad.'

'Oh! Hello, Dad! All right?'

'Yes, I… we're on a walk. Mum's gone up a mountain with Grand.' So mundane, like news from any other holiday! Was it real, what he'd been going to do? To Imogen, to all of them? If the fence hadn't been new… He let his breathing settle. 'How are you, love?'

'I'm good, Dad. I just wanted to let you know… I went out to get some bits, and I bumped into Kyle's mum outside nursery. She says Tyrone's turned up.'

'Really?' His heart managed a weary leap. Her tone said, *turned up alive.*

'Yeah, he's in London. He'd gone to find a cousin of his, but he was away. Tyrone must have hung around or something until he came back. His mum doesn't really know. But anyway, she's in touch with him and apparently he's OK.'

'Oh,' he said. 'That's good. Thanks.' There was a slow-motion shifting in his head as things reordered themselves.

Imogen started to say, 'Mum said you were worried, so…'

'I'm really sorry,' he said, 'about when I dropped you off.'

'It's fine, Dad.' There was a pause as he took this in. 'I'm sorry I freaked out.'

'No, it's my fault, I must have ruined…'

'You didn't. I had a great time. I'll tell you all about it when you get home.'

'Oh. That's good. I'll look forward to it. We'll see you tomorrow, won't we?' A thorny tree rose out of a hedge against an impossibly deep blue sky. The sun was warm on his face as Imogen said goodbye.

Ruth had helped Carrie to organize a last meal of pizza and garlic bread, the boys rejoicing that there was no salad left. 'Although you could have this!' Ruth threatened, waving a cucumber that had collapsed in on itself and begun to ooze. They were all finishing their packing now, with a plan to regroup in the living room for a final drink and a game.

When Chris told her about Imogen's call, Carrie hoped she had seen a glimmer of his old self in his eyes, although mainly he looked tired. They had packed up their room in wordless but peaceful cooperation, and he had gone to put some bags in the car.

It seemed chilly in the bedroom, and Carrie looked up from her suitcase with the sense of being watched. But there was no one in the doorway. She was like Josh in Grand's scary place, she thought, looking to be spooked. It had seemed quite normal there to her. Although Noddfa this morning had felt strange...

The suitcase was ready: she took hold of the handle, oddly reluctant to turn her back on the doorway. Shadows darkened her vision's edge and a shiver touched her shoulders. She dragged the suitcase onto the floor with a slither and a bump.

A movement at her back made her spin round and gasp.

It was Hal. She gave a shrill laugh. 'Oh! You made me jump. All right, darling?' He came in without answering, chewing at the edge of a fingernail. Her heart tightened. 'Well, I think I'm done. How are you and Josh doing?'

He sat down on the edge of the bed without looking at her. 'Imogen said I should ask you. About Emilia.'

'Oh!' She pushed at the suitcase with her foot, but seemed to have no strength. Hal had shifted to face her. She was trying to look at ease, but her face felt stiff and strange. 'She must have meant about her dying, darling.'

Shock, then suspicion, flashed in his eyes. 'It's not just that, is it? Mum?'

There was a shuffle in the doorway, and Chris was there, staring. 'Come in,' she mouthed, motioning to him. He came in and shut the door.

So then they were sitting on either side of their son.

'Hal,' said Carrie, 'we were always going to tell you…' The life drained from his face. Carrie found his hand and clutched it. 'Emilia was your mother. She really loved you but… she had problems. It hadn't worked out with the – with your father. We don't know who he was, I'm afraid. Emilia couldn't look after you. And we loved you so much, as if you were already ours. We'd often looked after you, so when she couldn't cope any more, we adopted you.'

Silence shrouded the room. He took his hand from hers. She had forgotten to breathe.

'You're not my Mum?' He was bone-pale, his pupils huge. 'You're not my Dad?'

'We are… Just not…'

Hal's features distorted. He hunched over with a moan like an injured animal.

His whole life, she had done everything to avoid him being hurt.

CHAPTER THIRTY-FIVE

2011 Day 14: Friday

'They *act* like you're theirs,' Josh said. He had begged Hal to let him in the bedroom.

'But that's it, it's an act. Imogen's theirs but I'm not. I'm some *cousin's kid*. And they never even told me. I mean, what the hell?' Hal kicked his holdall and felt a hot spurt of pain in his toes.

'They are cool though. Your family.'

'They're *not* my family.' A sick wave went through Hal like when Mum first told him. Except she wasn't Mum. He sat down on his bunk. Downstairs, worried voices murmured, hers cutting through them at a tearful pitch.

'I know. Shit. Sorry.' Josh sank down the wall opposite. A bit later, he whispered, 'Do you think that's why all this stuff has been happening, Hal? Because the ghost is... well, 'cos you're being haunted by your Mum!'

Hal looked up and the room swam. His head was throbbing like his foot. 'Just leave me alone.'

'I didn't mean...'

'Just go!'

After he'd gone, Hal lay down on his side and curled his legs up. The holiday was playing back to him in sickly bursts. Their faces in Sylvia's when he asked about Emilia. Then Mum on that walk. *Terrible news... found in a hotel room... so sorry we didn't tell you.*

He remembered being glad she'd told him, as if she trusted him like a grownup. Now he felt like he was falling. And a stupid part of him wanted to run to her for comfort.

It was getting dark. He got under the duvet and pulled it over his head. Grand's voice came from far away, a bassy mumble.

Later he heard them call 'night night' to Josh and had a stab of jealousy for his simple boyish life. There was muttering and creaks, and then a whisper, 'You all right?'

He lay still and silent. Josh crashed and shuffled for a bit. The sounds washed over Hal, muffled by the duvet. It was actually OK Josh being there, as long as they didn't have to talk. Better than being alone. A landslide of tiredness was dragging him down.

Hal woke, heart pounding, from a dream about snow. He must have pushed the duvet off – it was freezing. There was a sound like the tail end of a whisper. He strained to listen. Nothing – just Josh snoring above.

It all rushed back. Their announcement. Him not believing it at first, then shouting and pushing them away. Mum crying. Dad just standing there. Them going on with their evening without him. The last night of Wales.

A pressure touched his fingertips. For a second, it was comforting, but then he snatched back his hand. He could see the grey oblong of the window. Oh God, was that something moving towards him? He tried to shout but something closed over his mouth. He was pulled to a sitting position, a tightness round his waist. There was a whispering, chattering, rushing in his ears.

He gave a stifled cry and heard hushing. He was held – like in a hug – except an earthy chill seeped through him. He thought of the others, warm in their beds, then heard a whimper and realised it was him.

He was squeezed, then swayed, side to side, side to side. There was a soft touch on his face, then his hand. He felt quieter – almost dreamy – if he hadn't been so cold.

Then he was pulled upwards, he was on his feet. He tried to shout again. There was a shushing, a breath on his cheek. He turned towards it and breathed a putrid smell. He was gagging, he had to wake Mum and Dad! They'd come running, put the light on, grab him… All this would be gone. They could pack up and go without waiting for morning… he pictured the whole family, running in the dark to the cars.

But why should Hal go with them? They'd lied. He couldn't carry on as if nothing had happened. And now his foot was moving. It took his body forward, and then the other one followed: a lumbering step, like a monster in a film. Could he stop it? Could he break away? The pressure clasped tighter. Someone breathed near his ear, and then that smell again, of rotting.

You could fight it, Hal told himself. *It isn't all that strong!* But he was watching himself like a separate person. And he was walking towards the door.

Carrie snapped awake. Hal. She could feel his alertness, electrifying the air. The house was thick with fear and misery – the lingering echo of a nightmare.

Then it engulfed her: his face last night. The fear she'd always pushed under. She had only ever meant to find a way out of the mess. A way that was bearable. *But not for Emilia.*

There was a creak in the corridor. She got up and opened the door to a waft of cold.

Josh stood there in his too-small t-shirt. Alarm hitched higher at the look on his face. 'Something woke me up,' he said, 'and now Hal's not there.'

'I'm coming!' She pulled a jumper over her pyjamas and sprinted out of the room. She almost crashed into him, standing in the darkness, staring downstairs.

'Can you hear that?' he whispered.

She heard a rush like a sigh, then another and another. A creaking, a whispering. *Thud.*

'Carrie? What's going on?' Chris was half-sitting up in bed, leaning on his elbow.

'Hal's up… It's OK, I'm going.'

Her eyes were adjusting to the darkness as she stumbled downstairs, Josh following. She felt wrenched from sleep and time spasmed – she might be looking for a toddler, not a twelve-year-old. She snapped on the hall light and the dark outside looked blacker.

Hal wasn't in the kitchen. The air was fraught as if the house were under pressure. At the living room door, she turned the light on – just as the bookcase pitched forwards, hurling books to the floor. The door to her parents' room banged open.

'What on earth is all that noise?' said Grand from his bed.

She couldn't answer, and now Chris asked behind her, 'Is he here?'

'No. Have you looked upstairs?'

'Of course!'

'S'happening?' said a sleepy male voice. She spun round, but it was Dan, blinking. She heard his parents muttering, coming down the stairs.

'Hal!' Chris called, his voice raw and loud. 'Hal!'

No answer. Just wind noise like a groaning wail. She ran to the front door and stuffed her bare feet in trainers.

'David! What is it?' Her mother was calling.

'I don't know any more than you do!' came his gruff reply.

'I just want to know what's happening!' Her voice was anguished. But Carrie couldn't deal with them now – she had to get to Hal.

Chris grabbed her elbow. 'I'm coming too!'

The wind rushed and gasped; cold shuddered up Carrie's back. She got the front door open while Chris fumbled with shoes. Did he have to come? She'd only worry about him too. Outside it was windless – the air felt thick and warm.

Chris brushed past her. 'Let *me* go! I'll get a torch from the car. You stay with the others,' he said, running into the darkness.

Carrie stood on the threshold and everything went still, like the quiet before an explosion. And then she knew. That old instinct. Hal was in the house.

She gazed up the stairs. There was a shriek and something flew out of the living room. The others were in there – she heard cries of alarm, then thuds and crashes.

A great gust rushed downstairs at Carrie, almost hurling her to the floor. A football flew at her, thumped her temple and ricocheted off. She reeled, punch-drunk, then grabbed the banister rail as the ball bounced wildly about.

'It's the ghost!' Josh shouted from the living room door. 'Don't go up there, Carrie!' He looked so young in his t-shirt and boxers, his face a sickly white.

There was a roaring in her ears. 'I have to. Hal's up there.' His fists were clenched against his chin. 'Josh, you're the expert. You'll know what to do. Look after the others.' His gazed at her, then his mouth set in a line. He nodded.

Carrie dragged herself upstairs like someone walking into a gale. Josh's thin voice sounded from the living room, 'We should stay together, in here! No one should be alone.'

'What?! Oh for goodness sake!' Ruth's voice sounded as Carrie struggled upwards.

At the top of the stairs, the downward force abruptly stopped and she pitched forwards, her head hitting the wall.

'Hal?!' Pain waved through her, then quickened to a throb. She struggled to her feet. There was a wetness in her hairline; the skin felt split. She turned to the attic stairs and gripped the handrail.

It was cold at the door to the attic room, with a dank, rotten smell. She heard a commotion inside, but then everything went quiet. Wait, was that breathing? Her hand trembled over the door handle. She heard a soothing murmur. 'Hal?'

There was a low, angry growl. Her vision wavered, dissolving.

A crashing and dragging noise came from inside. The growl rose to a snarl, and then subsided into panting. A gasp of fear, then the murmur again. Carrie banged on the door. 'Open up! Please! It's me!'

She went to bang again, but the door swung wide – to no one, to darkness. The light came on, went off and on – Hal! Hal was there, crouched on the edge of the bed.

'I'm here, Hal, it's OK!' The flashes got faster, piercing her headache. Hal was staring ahead, his eyes sleepwalker blank. 'It's Mum,' she said, and stepped towards him in the light, sure now that she could help him.

Pain crossed his face and his jaw set hard. 'But you're *not*.'

The light went off and the room filled with snarling. Her throat closed, then a crash made her shriek. In the next flash, she saw the mirror from the chest of drawers in shards all over the floor. 'Hal, we have to get out!' She reached out and grabbed his arm.

A spasm threw him on his back, jolting his arm from her hand. He was dragging backwards across the bed... You would swear something was pulling him! His eyes were wide but blank again, and then the room went black.

There was a roar, then a rumbling: the furniture was juddering and the door slammed shut.

Light again. The curtains flapped wildly, then settled and hung still. Her ears rang in the sudden silence. Hal was slumped, limp, in the middle of the bed, eyes closed.

She sat down, her voice shaking. 'It's over. Come downstairs, darling. The whole family is there.' Slowly, his eyes opened. 'That's better!' she said. 'It's OK now. Come on…'

There was a rushing outside the door – then inside, then whooshing through her, cold as a wave of dread.

She clutched Hal's hands. His lips parted and he bellowed, eyeballs bulging, bloodshot, his fingernails gouging her palm. She leaped up and staggered backwards, her back hitting the door. She scrambled blindly for the handle. It was stuck.

Lisa was huddled on the sofa, hugging her dressing gown around her. She seemed to have woken up in a nightmare, in which Hal was gone, and things were flying. A big black book had knocked over the lamp. It had gone quieter in here now, but the noise had gone upstairs.

Toby stood up, retying his burgundy bathrobe. 'I'm going out,' he said.

'Going where, for goodness sake?' Ruth said, sitting beside her mother in silk pyjamas, her legs drawn up.

'To help Chris look for Hal of course.'

'I told you!' Josh said, 'He's upstairs. Carrie's gone to find him.'

'I'll come too, Dad,' said Dan.

'What good will that do?' said Ruth.

'Oh, thanks!' Dan looked furious.

David gripped his chair's arms – surely he wasn't thinking of going too? 'You're not going to walk out and leave us?' she said.

'With all this going on?'

'All that's *going on* is that Hal's not in his room! Wherever he is, we'll find him.'

'But it's all gone mad... Look around you for goodness sake! Listen!'

There was a rumbling far above them, and a rushing on the stairs.

'It's just a windy night,' said David. Lisa looked round at them all. They knew it wasn't outside. Did they think she was a stupid old lady they could lie to?

Toby said, 'Right,' and moved towards the door.

Josh stepped into his path. 'No! I told you, we should stay in here!'

There was a crack like a gunshot as the door slammed shut. Josh sprang away, his eyes like black holes.

Toby strode over and tried the handle. 'Oh that's brilliant, it's locked.'

'It can't be!' said Ruth. 'It won't ever shut properly.' And she was right, it was warped – David always complained about the draught.

Toby rattled away. 'Great idea, Josh, staying in here. Now we're all bloody stuck.'

'S'not *his* fault,' said Dan.

Look at them, snarling! Some miserable, angry mood had got hold of them all. Lisa could have joined in and told them all what she thought of them – but no, she had to pull herself together. 'No it's not his fault. Come and sit down, Josh.' She had tried for kindness, but it came out sounding irritable.

Josh plonked himself down between her and Ruth. He gnawed on his thumbnail and tore a strip off. Blood beaded on the pink beneath. She put an arm round his shoulders and found them tensed hard.

'It's not the wind,' he said. 'It's Emilia. She's come for Hal.'

Ruth tutted, but without conviction.

Emilia. Lisa let the thought seep through her. It made a nightmarish, impossible sense: all that old anger and heartache, hurling things round the house. No, she was just overwrought. It was the hour of the night, the awakening. But when David rolled his eyes, she wanted to scream at him for being blind – to the weird goings on all week. And now this awful night...

Toby straightened up the lampstand and picked up the book that had knocked it over, as if that made things better. 'Hey... she kept throwing that book!' Josh said. 'Maybe she wanted us to see it. Here!'

There were bouncing noises – the football? Something crashed against the wall outside the room.

'Carrie?' Lisa called, her heart racing. Silence. 'Maybe she's gone out after Chris,' she said, perhaps to convince herself.

Toby handed the book to Josh and slumped into an armchair as Josh turned the pages. Lisa recognised the Wales photo album. She hadn't looked in it for years. They used to get prints done and stick them in the following year. She found herself staring at Nick and Elsa, sitting on the back steps at Noddfa. Carrie was there by David's side; and Emilia was next to Nick, her smile tight, eyes bright.

A jack-in-the-box memory burst out on Lisa: that note in the jewellery box! Emilia was pregnant and heartbroken and wouldn't tell them a thing. She'd slammed out of the house, accusing them of interrogating her. In the silent aftermath, Lisa searched her room for clues. Under the tangle of earrings and necklaces, she found this square of lined paper, blotched and worn almost through at the folds: MY FLAT AFTER COLLEGE? ELSA AWAY X.

She gazed now at Nick's brown eyes, the shape of his forehead and jaw. The secret was staring out at you if you knew what you were looking at.

David had searched his fretful soul when his friend left so suddenly, worrying away at the mystery as if poking a sore tooth. 'I know he was sick of the management at college, but why couldn't he tell *me*?' Then as time passed, and no news came, he stopped mentioning Nick at all. Lisa never told him, or anyone. She was half afraid they'd look now and see: Nick's face in the picture – the very model for Hal's.

There was a crash way above, like glass breaking. 'Emilia! Going mental!' Josh said.

'For goodness sake, Josh, it's nothing,' David said. 'That book of yours has addled your brain.'

But now there was a rumbling – she could feel it, like an earthquake! They stared at each other. A door slammed up above.

'Don't tell me that's nothing!' she shouted. 'David! Are Carrie and Hal up there?'

David got up, went to the door and tried the handle, but it wouldn't move. The room shook and knick-knacks wobbled. Something fell off a shelf – that red dragon of Emilia's. Ruth shivered in revulsion and batted it from her lap. It made a strangled noise that ended in a wail.

The air rushed about as if a wind had got in – it passed through Lisa in a nasty wave of cold. What a hateful night – how infuriating they all were. Things had gone so horribly wrong, and she could never put them right. Nothing would be the same again – everything good was lost. Tears swam in her eyes at the dreadful, deadly truth. Then with a lurch in her chest, the feeling left her. The lamp fell against the wall again and the doorknob rattled.

David staggered, knocked sideways, and Toby leapt up to help, but David fended him off irritably and went to sit down. There was a roaring in the hallway, and on the floor above, more slams.

She was so spent – she might faint, but then something grabbed her arm. She opened her eyes to Josh's frantic stare.

'It's OK,' she said, putting an arm around him, 'it's gone quiet now. Listen.' And it had. They heard the football bounce on every stair, then tap and patter to a stop.

'Is everyone OK?' said Ruth, her voice shaking. 'Dan, darling, are you all right?'

Her poor family, all white as ghosts! Lisa reached behind Josh to take Ruth's hand, and Ruth actually let her hold it – her oldest girl and this dear, frightened boy, both in her embrace. She felt stronger now, she could help them all. But where were Carrie and Chris, where was Hal?

At the top of the house they heard bellowing.

CHAPTER THIRTY-SIX

Carrie whirled round to try the handle again. Still stuck. The light flashed and puttered out. She turned in near-darkness: only Hal was visible in a shifting glow. His eyes looked trance-like, but not bulging – had she imagined before..? But his hair was on end, bristling with a life of its own. *Josh thinks I'm possessed...*

'Hal!' she said, as if to wake him or call him back. Was that a strange light rippling down his face and arms, or was his skin moving? No! Maggots were pouring from his hair... writhing and cascading onto the bed. Her throat filled with a sickening stench. She retched, and darkness rose from the floor; the doorknob bumped her back.

A flash revealed Hal, his skin clean. No maggots, nothing. Concussion, that must be it. She'd banged her head. She sank to her knees.

Everything was bleak and wrong. It had been building all holiday – half-glimpsed at the edge of vision; crouching in corners ready to pounce. All those cheery breakfasts, tea and scones – they couldn't hold it back.

Hal's eyes were empty in the weird light. She had to save him, she had to get him back. 'Hal! Hal, can you hear me?' She gulped rank air. 'It's Mum. I'm sorry. I know you're angry. I shouldn't have kept it from you. But I'm telling you the truth now. Emilia couldn't look after you. We had to step in, for your sake. I... I suppose I always thought that one day she'd get herself together. And then we'd tell you. And she'd be back in your life. But it never happened.'

Wait, was this the truth, even now? She thought of the talk with Paul at the funeral.

Hal blinked. His eyes rolled back, gaping white. A twitching motion was coursing through his hair. A force out of nowhere crushed Carrie against the door.

Light fizzled on and off. Hal thrashed on the bed, let out an unearthly roar and went limp and still. But now he seemed to come to. He opened his eyes. There he was, looking at her! 'Mum!' he croaked, desperate. 'It's Emilia!'

The light bulb swung back and forth and shadows lurched. Thoughts shattered into pieces. Could this be Emilia? This rage, this chaos? Hal's body lifted inches off the bed, then all four limbs thwacked down. It was ugly. Impossible. It couldn't be Hal.

Had this been here all holiday? Here at Noddfa; in all their favourite places?

'Emilia!' The bulb stopped swinging and trembled on its wire. 'I just wanted to help him!' Carrie bellowed, surely to herself. Was there a pause, though, a sense of listening? 'We tried to help you with him. But that day of the cliff edge, and afterwards – what was I supposed to *do*?'

A pause full of dread. Then Hal was lifted like a puppet, his arms hanging, his stare lifeless, like those dead people in old photographs, propped up for the camera. A shudder wracked Carrie and when the window banged, she shrieked. Hal turned his head.

The catch was broken, the window gaping too wide. Carrie had a burst of concern – a Mum-fuss, Hal would call it. When she turned, he was standing with his back to her. He began to shuffle towards the window.

Chris plunged through the night in the cold ellipse of torchlight, running, sweating, bargaining with God. *I'll do anything. I'll believe in you...* Panic-fuelled energy overruled his struggling lungs. *I'll get better, I'll be a brilliant Dad. Just please let him be there.* He'd been everywhere he could think of, the torch raking the darkness of the lanes, the beach, the cliff. All those heart-stopping, hopeful movements had turned out to be sheep or birds. But Hal could have gone the other way. He could be back at the house now. Someone would appear soon, coming out to tell him, 'It's OK, Chris! He's here!'

He turned the bend. The windows of Noddfa were two rows of squares and a flickering above. What was that in the attic room? He slowed down, panting, all power deserting him. A silhouette moved in the dirty light from the dormer window. Chris jogged to a stop and slanted up the torch.

Hal! It was Hal! Relief washed through him – but was abruptly choked.

'Hal! What are you doing?' He lurched forwards, staring. Hal had climbed out of the window onto the flat roof. 'Hal get back inside! You'll fall!'

Hal turned stiffly to face him, his face like a sleepwalker's, arms lifted from his sides. A panicked cry – Carrie's – ripped the night from inside. Hal shuffled forwards, heading for the edge.

'Hal NO!'

No flicker of response. Should he stay and try to break his fall, or go in and scream for help? He couldn't move anyway, couldn't tear his eyes from his son.

'STOP, Hal, it's DAD!' The yell tore from his chest with all the strength he had.

Carrie clung to the dormer window frame. Hal had stopped – thank God. He stood at the edge of the roof with his back to her in bluish torchlight, his fingers quivering. Heat-of-battle clarity lit up her head. She couldn't snatch him back now like the baby on the cliff edge.

'Hal! Can I come out there with you?'

'No!' A snarl – nothing like him – but then a trembling breath. Think. Think Emilia, chaotic and furious. Selfish, reckless, impossible to trust. She'd abandoned Hal and left Carrie forever in the wrong, forever braced against the threat of her.

But that day with the rabbits; her curls in the sunlight when they were damming the stream... When she was little, Carrie had ached to cuddle her. She had loved coming here with them, and had always gone quiet, then tearful, as the time approached to leave. On the last night, Carrie would comfort her, and they would cling together in the car before Dad dropped her off at home.

A soft moan sounded – perhaps she had sighed out loud. 'Em,' she whispered. Stillness seemed to fall. 'Did you want to be with us this holiday? Is that why you're here?'

Hal was looking out over the track, but he turned his head

towards her. It wasn't the child she saw in him now, but Em's adult face against a halo of torchlight. Her gaze connected with Carrie's, then swept back towards the track.

And then Carrie knew. Sue's full-bellied gesture. *Out here.* In daylight, you could see right down the track from here. This is where you would come to wait and hope.

'Did you come here to meet Hal's father?' The torch beam slipped; Hal turned to her, his face crumpled. There was a keening sound in the attic room – or a ringing in Carrie's ears. Sorrow flooded through her. 'This is where you came to sort things out with him… Oh, Em, I could see you were broken when you came back, I just didn't know what to do.' Had her words brought calm in the madness – was Hal coming back to her? 'I'm sorry,' she whispered, 'I really am… that you couldn't keep your baby…'

Hal swayed. 'Hal! Be careful! Hal!' She had to focus – it was him she was here for. There was a crushing force, an ache in her ribs. 'Please don't take him, Emilia! I *love* him! He's so lovely.' Hal tottered and his arms flew out like a tightrope walker. Carrie whispered crazy words to an impossible presence. 'I'm so sorry you had to leave us, Em. I'm sorry that you died.' Then she cried out, full volume, 'But he's got everything to live for. He deserves to grow up!'

Hal turned back towards the night, his hands clenched, looking down.

Pain shot through her fingers from her nails digging into the window frame. 'Please don't hurt him. Please let us have him back.'

A gust from the window swept over her, chilling the wetness on her cheeks. And then it blew again from inside the room, lifting a strand of her hair. Then stillness. Silence.

'Mum!' Hal stepped away from the edge. He was coming towards her, she was helping him through the window, grabbing his hand and pulling. His looked dazed in the attic light, teeth chattering, weary.

They held each other. Was the trembling him or her? There was a click and a creak and the door swung ajar.

Hal slumped against Carrie, his face cold on hers. He slurred as if sleepy, 'I think she's gone, Mum,' he said.

CHAPTER THIRTY-SEVEN

2011 Day 15: Saturday

Hal followed Mum down the attic stairs on legs like cotton wool. He could almost believe he'd had a strange and terrible dream… if it weren't for his wobbliness now and the rotten aftertaste at the back of his throat.

'He's here!' Mum called.

He turned on the landing and saw Dad leap up the stairs. He grabbed Hal, crushed him against his chest and muttered, 'Thank God' into his neck.

Hal could hardly breathe. 'Dad, I need to sit down.'

The three of them clambered down to the ground floor. The living room door was rattling. There was a bang and it swung open. Exclamations, then quick footsteps came from inside.

Josh appeared. 'It's open!' he shouted. 'Let's get out, quick!' Then he turned. 'Hal!'

Dad bundled Hal over to an armchair, where they all gathered round and fussed, apparently forgetting the need to get out.

'What the hell *happened*?' Uncle Toby said.

'He was in the attic room…' Mum said from the sofa. She looked round at them, then caught Hal's eye and came to a stop. And no wonder – what could you say? 'It's – hard to explain… but he's OK now, aren't you, love?'

'Oh, that's all that matters! You're all that matters, Hal,' Auntie Ruth said in a strange voice. She made a sniffing noise, almost tearful. Hal had never seen her like this before.

'Who are you – and what have you done with Mum?' Dan said. Something rose up in Hal's throat and he wasn't sure what it was. But it was a laugh that came out. And then everyone seemed to relax.

'Your mum's right, Dan,' said Grandma Lisa. 'We're OK if Hal's here.'

'Was it the ghost? Did she get you?' said Josh.

'Oh Josh, not now…' Mum said, her hands to her head. She flinched and brought her hands down, and there was a smear of blood on her fingers.

'Carrie!' said Dad. 'Are you sure you're all right?'

'It's fine,' she said, taking a tissue from him and dabbing it under her fringe. It came away with a small reddish patch. 'It's just a graze. I'd forgotten, I tripped and banged my head going upstairs. Maybe that's why it was all so strange up there... And Hal... well, Hal had had such a shock.' *Is that how we're playing it?* Hal thought. But he didn't know what else to say.

'Exactly,' said Grand. 'And we were woken up in the dead of night. We all got overwrought.'

'There is a little graze,' Dad said riffling through Mum's hair. 'Let me know if you don't feel right, though. We'll get you checked out.' He sat back, taking her hand.

Hal felt his eyes closing. Could he calm down enough to sleep?

'Was it Emilia?' Josh said.

'Don't be ridiculous!' said Grand.

'Josh does know about these things,' Mum said. Grand gave her a look and she shrugged. They all started talking, mainly asking Mum if she was feeling OK.

'So *was* it?' Josh hissed, leaning closer.

Hal felt too tired for Josh right now, but it wasn't fair that Grand had snapped at him. He leaned closer. 'I thought I was asleep, and I was dreaming that I was upset and this woman was there, like, being nice... but it kept turning into a nightmare.'

'So, what, *was* it just a dream?' Josh said.

'No... No, I don't think so. Because then Mum was there and she was definitely real, so I knew I was awake. Then it's like I was out of it again, but then I heard Dad shouting at me. And I was right on the edge of the roof outside the attic room. I was about to walk off the edge. Feeling like I *had* to.' His gut lurched recalling the drop, the thought of hitting the ground.

'*Shit?!* Are you OK?'

Everyone was around them in the living room, like a normal day in Wales. Except at night. Hal said, 'Yeah.' Josh sat back in his chair, white and confused. 'You were right, Josh,' Hal whispered. 'It was Emilia. It's like she'd got hold of me. But Mum sort of – talked her down. I felt her go.'

There was a noise in the hallway. They all spun round. Something flew at the walls and thudded to the floor – their shoes from by the front door.

Dad said, 'Oh, I left the front door open…' As if this explained it. He stood up and edged out into the hall.

'Prop this door open!' said Grand. 'We don't want to get shut in again!'

Auntie Ruth stood the lampstand against the open door. 'I'm sure it'll be fine,' she said. But she didn't look sure. Nothing was moving now but there was a tight feeling in the air. Hal thought he heard a sigh.

It was quiet for a bit. Everyone had plonked down now in chairs and on the sofa, heads lolling.

'God,' said Dan. 'Cheer *up* everyone.'

They all talked then, in a tired way, as if trying to keep their spirits up.

'We need a cup of tea,' said Grand. He got up and shuffled out.

'Are you sure she's completely gone, then?' whispered Josh.

There was a cry, like a bird-call, carried by the wind. Or like the saddest sound you ever heard. Hal didn't want to admit it – he so needed to sleep. But he couldn't lie to Josh. 'No,' he said. 'She's still around.'

Grand knew he shouldn't have snapped at Josh, but it had all been so unnerving. After a night of uproar, he had just wanted order to reign again – after all, Hal was back, and with his parents, not locked away furious and alone. It was bad enough that there had been such ructions. The last thing they needed was the thought of Emilia back from the dead. Josh's words had made him shudder; his words had flown out.

He leaned on the worktop in the shadowy kitchen, lit only by the glow from the lights under the cupboards. He was too befuddled even to gather the tea things.

He'd always had time for Emilia. Funny, because most people got on his nerves – even the ones closest to him. Especially them, if he was honest! But he'd had a soft spot for that little girl, and for the troubled youngster she became. Perhaps he'd just wanted to make things right for her, after the rotten start she'd had.

He hadn't managed it, though, had me? She'd never even got to know her boy. And now she never would. He bowed his head over the worktop, feeling empty and cold.

'Grand?'

'*Jesus!*' He thought his heart would explode.

'Sorry!' said Josh, backing away.

'Oh! Josh, come in... Sorry. I'm jumpy. Did you want a hot chocolate?'

'No. Well yes. But I had an idea.'

Grand filled the kettle, clutching at the pantomime of a routine task. There was the teapot. Good. And teabags in the tin. 'What's that then?'

'Promise you won't freak out.' Grand raised an eyebrow and Josh flushed. 'Or laugh.'

'Of course not.'

Josh pushed the door to behind him. 'You said Will and Hilda might be here, and that they always looked after people.'

Had he said that? He didn't think so. He frowned, but nodded. Josh crept closer, glancing all round. 'Hal thinks Emilia's still here, and that she's sad. And it does feel like that, doesn't it?'

Grand tried to arrange his features to suggest polite amusement, but he was too bloody tired, his face drooped. God, it did feel miserable, and he'd never felt that on holiday here. Or not until last night. He raised an eyebrow, not quite in disagreement.

'Well, you could ask Will and Hilda to look after Emilia. I know they're not from the same era, but maybe that doesn't matter with spirits...'

Grand looked at his peaky face, full of urgent hope. And ridiculous logic. 'Maybe not,' he said, pouring boiling water in the pot.

'So will you give it a go?'

He tried for a chuckle, but only managed a sigh. 'Well... I can but try.'

'Right! I'll leave you to it then!' Josh turned at the door with a go-for-it face and a thumbs-up.

The boy was priceless. Grand sank into a chair, just for a minute, while the tea brewed. He hadn't made hot chocolate, but Josh seemed to have forgotten it with all his ghostly nonsense. Grand's eyelids were heavy. Perhaps they could all get some sleep now? But his skin prickled with alertness as if something were unfinished.

Imagine if Emilia could be at peace at last. He had a sudden, vivid memory of the comfort of Hilda's lap. Are you a child again in your dotage, he thought? He sighed and breathed in, and could have sworn the air was warm and spicy, with the buttery promise of baking day – wait, hadn't he felt chilly only moments before? He tried again to dismiss the illusion, but there was the fragrant sizzle of dough pressed on the pan. He couldn't rationalise it or fight it, not after the night they'd had. So he let it bathe his nerves. At the edge of vision, within touching distance, maybe – maybe – someone was moving, and a tune wavered in the drone of the fridge, then broke into a rich and sibilant murmur. There behind him came a deeper response, the words just out of hearing or beyond understanding, almost as if they could really be there.

'Will you look after her?' he whispered, talking to no one – to memories. 'I tried, but I didn't manage it ...' His voice cracked. 'Could you have her with you?'

The fridge gave a violent shudder and returned to its usual hum. His chest heaved and he let out a sob, his chin on his chest, head weighed down with it all. Jesus, don't let anyone walk in on him now!

The taste of putrefaction still coated Carrie's throat. She was cold right through, and so tired she was trembling. Chris had pulled his chair close and grasped her hand; they were both gazing at Hal as if to make sure he was still there. She heard Josh hiss his name from the doorway, and Hal hauled himself up.

'It's OK,' Chris reassured her, as whispering came from the hall. 'They're sitting on the stairs with that book of Josh's.'

Carrie let herself sink back into her armchair as if she might rest at last. But time shivered and flowed backwards, tugging her in its wake.

2003

It was dark and silent, in the dead of night, but Carrie was awake. Emilia had gone out and missed Hal's bedtime. He had been with them, in the small bedroom, since that summer of the cliff edge drama. They'd still called it the spare room for a while, but then Imogen started saying 'Hal's room' and that's what they all called it now. He was an enthusiastic three-year-old and needed his bedtime routine so that he could sleep: a bath and a towel-wrapped snuggle, songs and rhymes and their silly sayings, then a story in bed.

Emilia was staying with them again. She came periodically, making a new start, 'leaving all that behind.' Carrie learned snippets of what 'all that' meant from Em's old college friend, Carla. Drink and drugs, reckless friendships and relationships. She didn't share all of it with her parents, but told Ruth. 'Why are you even surprised?' Ruth said. 'It's what she does! It has been going on for two years. Longer!'

Emilia had a bed on their sofa at the moment, so she could regroup and connect with Hal. She'd done well for a few days, coming with them to the park and to nursery, where everyone assumed she was Hal's auntie. Tonight she was going to do bathtime and bedtime on her own. But she'd been irritable all afternoon, then picked a fight when Carrie asked her to shut the stairgate. 'Well, clearly I'm not good enough,' she'd said, 'I might as well go to the pub.'

Carrie had heard her come in around midnight, and had come down to find her bright-eyed and upbeat, slurring a greeting, their argument apparently forgotten. She'd met Carla at the pub and they'd bumped into Johnny, another friend from college. He'd said how he'd always admired her in drama classes. He thought she had real talent. He'd had a messy break-up with his girlfriend and she'd gone back to her parents, leaving him alone in their campervan. Emilia never even apologized for missing Hal's bedtime. Carrie didn't bring it up; she couldn't face another row.

But she lay in bed now, her pulse racing, muscles tense. Emilia's excitement at Johnny's ego-boosting flashed in front of her, then Hal's confusion when she explained that she'd be doing bathtime instead of Emilia, who had made him giggle so much the night before. He'd been looking forward to more 'mad splashes', but she was too busy getting pissed like a teenager.

Carrie was so tired – she tried to relax, from her toes upwards, one body part at a time. But when she got to her head, she was off again, going over it all. She couldn't find a comfortable position in which to try to sleep. Then she thought she heard a noise downstairs, and strained taut, listening. Later, when she'd dropped her guard, there was a noise like a creak on the stairs. She sat up, gripped with dread, until certainty faded and she tried again to sleep. It went on and on like this, until she didn't know if she was hearing sounds, or imagining them. She lay core-tight, picturing worst case scenarios.

She thought she hadn't slept at all but woke with a gasp from a terrible dream of an empty toddler bed. Ten to six. She got up and ran into Hal's room. What a sweet rush of relief when she saw him, lying on his front with his knees pulled up, his bottom in the air, asleep. Thank God. Her boy, her baby, not stolen away, not gone.

It was the sofa that was empty, and Emilia and all her things were missing. Relief still surged like spite in Carrie's veins. She relaxed for the first time in days.

It was five months later, after Johnny went back to his girlfriend, that Emilia made what might have been a suicide attempt. They started proceedings for Hal's adoption a month or so later.

~⇌

2011

'All right, Carrie, love?' said her mother now in the Noddfa lamplight.

'Yes, fine,' she said, and burst into tears. She covered her mouth so the boys wouldn't hear. There were sounds around her of concern and embarrassment, but Carrie couldn't begin to explain. She'd had her heart set hard against Emilia for all these years. She'd been so utterly focused on Hal. But up there in the attic, she'd remembered. Hal was sweet because Emilia was sweet. They'd both melted their way into her inner soul, where she could hold them close and keep them from any pain. 'This is all my fault,' she said, 'for taking him from her and not telling him about her.'

'Oh no, Carrie. You had your reasons for not telling him!' her mother said.

'I felt guilty. That was the reason. And I was afraid he'd want to know her and she'd take him back… What did I do to her?'

Chris gave her hand a shake. 'It was an impossible situation… we couldn't do right by both of them. We had to choose Hal.'

'Oh, for goodness sake, Carrie!' said Ruth. Carrie braced herself for a scornful tirade. Why had she started this now? Ruth's voice was raw. 'You were the one who took responsibility while we all stood by. I was too busy with my precious career. Oh, I know I had Dan, but you had Imogen, didn't you? We were all watching this car crash happening in front of us, and you were the one who stepped up. You rescued Hal, Carrie! You did! And you were only ever in it for him. I could see that. We all could. And you did such a brilliant job.' She ripped a tissue out of a box and dabbed her eyes. 'Oh it's *true!*' she said to the others, as though they'd argued. 'We just don't *say* it!'

There was a shocked pause.

'Well. That told you, Carrie!' Toby said.

'Oh. I'd better pull myself together, then.' Tired as she was, Carrie laughed in surprise. She accepted a tissue from Ruth and wiped her nose. Knots loosened in her head. She shivered, but then felt lighter, a blush of warmth rising within. She and her sister looked at each other with sheepish sniffs and smiles.

'Yes, you mustn't blame yourself,' Grandma Lisa said. 'It doesn't always do to have everything out in the open. And it will all be fine now. We're all right, aren't we?' She looked around her with a rallying smile.

They did all look brighter. Had something changed in the house?

'Of course we are,' said Grand, coming in with Hal and Josh. 'It'll be light soon.'

'We could go out and watch the sunrise,' Hal said. He plonked himself down on the arm of Carrie's chair.

'I don't know, love, you look exhausted.' He yawned and shrugged but didn't protest. 'There'll be other sunrises,' she said.

'Yes! Next year,' said Grand. 'Right, I'm off to get some kip before the journey. Night night, everyone.'

'Night night, Grand,' they said.

Sophie Kersey

Sophie Kersey worked in publishing for almost thirty years before going freelance to pursue her lifelong writing ambitions. She is now a freelance writer and editor. Her first novel, *Unspeakable Things* was published in 2018. Her articles have appeared in counselling and parenting magazines and in the US collection *Enduring Love*. She lives in Kent with her husband, Jon, and has two grown-up sons.

Look out for news on Sophie's website: sophiekerseyauthor.com and Facebook page: Sophie Kersey, Author.

SOURCES

Ein Canrif/Our Century, National Library of Wales, 2002

O'r Gwaith i'r Gwely/A Woman's Work: Housework 1890–1960, Tibbot, S. M. and Thomas, B., National Museum of Wales, 1994

Salem Soldier: A journey from North Cardiganshire to the ravages of war in North Africa and Italy, Davies, E. & B., 2012

The Home Front: Civilian Life in World War Two, Cooksley, P., The History Press, 2007

I am also indebted to the many true stories available online of children evacuated during the Second World War.

UNSPEAKABLE
THINGS

You're pregnant.

You find out there's madness in the family.

What are you going to do now?

Sarah moves back into her abandoned childhood home, hoping to connect with what's left of her family. She is thrilled to learn about her long-dead mother from Uncle John, who runs the Woodlands Clinic nearby.

Then he tells her that her mother tried to kill her and died a mental patient at Woodlands. But is the truth even more shocking than that?

Sarah's desperate search for what really happened to her mother rocks her marriage, career and friendships. Can she discover the family's bitter secret before her baby is born?

Or will she go mad trying?

Unspeakable Things by Sophie Kersey is available on Amazon in Kindle and paperback versions.

The Shop, Bontgoch.

The one real person who features in this fictional story is Jim Siop, who runs the Bont Goch shop where David hears a ghost story. Jim was my great-grandfather, James Pierce Evans. If you are curious about him or any of the real inhabitants of Bont Goch over the years, see Richard Huws' 2020 book *Pobol y Topie/Bont Goch Lives*.